THE SLIPPED KNOT

IAN MEACHEAM and MARK PECKETT

APS BOOKS
YORKSHIRE

APS Books
The Stables,
Field Lane,
Aberford
West Yorkshire,
LE25 3AE
www.andrewsparke.com

APS Books is a subsidiary of the APS Publications imprint

First published worldwide by APS Books in 2024

A catalogue record for this book is available from the British Library

To Cathy and Ann
and, of course, the good people of Lichfield

PROLOGUE

Tears fill my eyes. Water blurs my sight. Merging the dark and the light.

I can't speak. I'm choking. I can't breathe.

A big mistake?

A mis-judgement? Thoughtless?

Perhaps it wasn't. Perhaps it was deliberate. Intentional.

I can just about hear them. Are they shouting, screaming or laughing at me?

Is it fear that they're feeling? The same fear that I'm feeling now?

So close to them and yet they're so far away.

I can't trust my instincts. I shouldn't have trusted them or theirs.

I tried to fit in, but look where it got me.

It's all for nothing now, because I'm nothing now.

It wasn't always like this …

Looking back, there were times in my life when I was comfortable and respectable. There were actual moments when I was happy and pleased with myself. Like when I won a prize for my Art work in primary school; when I kissed Beth for the first time after I walked her home and when Secreto won the Epsom Derby at 14/1.

But there were many low points as well. So, what did I do in those dark times? I hoped and prayed. I hoped for better and in desperation sometimes I prayed that, somehow, I could be a better person. A person that others could like and maybe admire. But it never happened. In time, no-one seemed to like me or, for that matter, hate me. They just didn't care, one way or the other. I was invisible. Invisible on Earth.

But I carried on praying and hoping that if no-one could see me here at ground level, then maybe someone or something who was looking down on us all, would actually see me from on high. So, as darkness fell, I would look up into the night sky and watch and wait for a sign. But there were none. Each day I'd wander aimlessly about or sit still, frozen to the spot, while others moved purposely with goals to achieve, targets to meet, lists to tick off, hurdles to jump, personal bests to better. Chasing down the end of their own rainbows. But there was nothing for me to strive for. But it didn't stop me competing in the race. I carried on, blinkered and blinded by something that I thought would lead me towards something bigger and brighter in the distance. But every time I moved slowly forward, it would vanish in front of my sight-for-sore eyes.

There'd always be a bump in the road, a diversion, a twist of fate that took me down the wrong path. Why was that? Why couldn't I play it safe? Cash in my chips. Quit while I was not behind. It was just not who I was. Just not my luck.

Some rock band from the 60s or 70s, it may have been Cream, I can't really remember now, sang about "If it wasn't for bad luck, I wouldn't have any luck at all." Well, that's definitely me and not those mega-rich, good-for-nothings who are adored by fans and noticed everywhere they go.

Now, I'm just the sad guy that people try to ignore or avoid. Particularly in recent years. These last few years, I've begun to hate myself. I hate what I've become – suspicious of everyone and cynical about everything. I trust no-one but myself and I'm not even sure about myself. I'm always on my guard.

I'm totally alone. No-one's looking out for me. No one's looking over me. A no-one. Invisible to the naked eye. If I was naked no-one would notice. No one would stop and admire or even enquire. For so long I've just felt like a ghost that exists in the land of the living. Someone that doesn't leave footprints in the sand or impressions on people's hearts or minds. I'm empty. Void. To be avoided at all costs.

That was until a few hours ago when I foolishly let my guard down ...

I was caught, hook, line and sinker ...

Caught out in the cold ...

No warm blanket ...

No hot drink ...

Is that a hand?

A helping hand?

Is it God?

God help me...

Please ...

Someone...anyone...tell my story

PART ONE

CHAPTER ONE

Darren, Willow - Monday

"All present and correct, Sergeant?"

Darren Mitchell snapped to attention. "Yes, sir," he barked, and threw a salute, longest way up, shortest way down. He knew people were staring, but he didn't care. This man had saved his life.

"At ease, Sergeant." At the command, he relaxed and turned round.

There was something about the man in front of him that said soldier. Not the smart casual dress or the fashionable haircut. It was something else – maybe the way he carried himself, or the extra attention to detail in the sharpness of his parting or the shine on his shoes.

Daz always felt self-conscious around Shaun Wilde. He was exactly the opposite of the man: a man who had served two tours with the Staffs in Iraq, was mentioned in dispatches, left the army with the rank of captain and then set up a charity, Home and Heart.

Daz had dropped out of the army after the Battle of Garmsir, lost himself in a fog of drink, drugs and petty crime, and lost his wife and daughter somewhere along the way as well. There were arrests for possession and assault and he ended up sofa-surfing and then homeless in hand-me-down clothes that needed a wash just like he did. He knew his clothes smelled stale and he smelled stale too. That smell of staleness was his whole life.

It was Shaun who had found him on the streets, got him on the 'vulnerable housing' list, got him selling *The Big Issue*, and finally an assisted housing flat in the Dimbles. It was Shaun who had helped get his life back on track.

But today, Shaun didn't have his usual brisk look. He seemed distracted, not as committed to their game of soldiers as usual.

"Everything alright, sir?" asked Daz.

Shaun straightened up and squared his shoulders. "I'm fine," he said. "I should be asking how you are."

"Can't complain, sir," said Daz. "Just got this Big Issue to sell, the girl from the library café usually brings me a coffee in about half an hour and next week, hopefully, I'm seeing my daughter."

That wasn't true. He hadn't seen his daughter in four years, but he didn't want to let Shaun down.

Shaun clapped him on the shoulder. "That's great news, Darren. I knew you'd turn things around."

"Couldn't have done it without you, sir."

"Rubbish. I just gave you a helping hand when you needed it. That's what comrades in arms do - " his face darkened. " – or at least, it's what they're supposed to do."

"Are you sure everything's OK, sir? Anything I can help with?" Daz had no idea how he could help a man like Shaun, but it made him feel good about himself to make the offer.

"No," said Shaun, sticking his hands in his pockets and staring off into the distance. "Just someone I have to speak to. Should have done it ages ago, but once I've got it off my chest, everything will be fine."

The way he said it made Daz think that maybe it wouldn't be fine, but Shaun shook himself, took a handful of change out of his pocket and said, "Well, I'll take that last Big Issue off your hands. Maybe it'll bring us both luck."

Daz handed him the magazine and pocketed the money. "If you're sure, sir," he said doubtfully.

Shaun rolled *The Big Issue* up and tapped him on the chest. "Stand Firm, Strike Hard, Darren," he said. It was the motto of the Staffordshire Regiment. He pushed back the sleeve on his left arm and there was a tattoo of a knot topped with the three feathers of the Prince of Wales. It was blurred with age and looked like he had done it himself. The knot was crooked, the feathers looked like fat fingers and it faded away into lines and splotches as if he had run out of ink or interest.

Daz slid his sleeve up too and there on his forearm was the same tattoo, professionally inked. It was as sharp as the day it had been done almost twenty years ago, no crooked knots, fat finger feathers, or dashes and splotches. "Stand Firm, Strike Hard, sir," he repeated.

"Call me Shaun."

"Yes, s – Shaun."

Shaun nodded. "See you tomorrow, Darren."

Daz watched him go, back straight, shoulders back, chest out, heading down Dam Street towards the cathedral. He'd walked like that himself when he was being marched between two MPs to his court martial.

It was turning out to be a very good day for Daz. It was mid-March, but the sun was shining and he'd already sold half of *The Big Issues* that he bought from the local co-ordinator in Lichfield and it was only ten-thirty. At eleven the girl from the library café would come out and bring him a coffee, and he'd make it just in time for the NA meeting in the church on Wade Street at twelve.

He went and sat on the pedestal of the big white statue in the marketplace and turned his face to the sun.

He must have nodded off, because a touch on his shoulder shocked him awake. He lashed out with his left hand and leaped to his feet, balling his right hand into a fist, even before he had opened his eyes.

He heard the stutter of an SA80 assault rifle. Somewhere a long-range sniper rifle coughed. Above him a Black Hawk roared, somewhere an 81mm mortar shook the ground, a Sea King clattered overhead, deafening him. Shouted commands he couldn't make out and screams of men injured, dying and afraid, pierced him. He could feel warm blood on his chest –

- and he opened his eyes. And it was a warm day in early spring in Lichfield, he was in the marketplace and the girl who brought him his coffee was the one who had screamed. Her face was white under her shock of dyed purple hair. Her eyes, ringed with heavy mascara, were fixed on his raised fist and her mouth, slashed with black lipstick, looked like old bullet wounds.

Daz looked up at his fist and down at his chest. There was coffee spilled on his clothes. Slowly and painfully he unclenched his fingers and he started wiping at his stained sweatshirt. He kept his eyes down because he could feel the eyes of the people gathered round burning into him. "Are you alright, miss?" he heard an elderly voice quaver, and another, sharper, added, "Shouldn't be allowed out."

Although he had terrified her, she wasn't going to give *these* people, who already looked down their noses at him, the satisfaction of seeing her cry. She blinked back her tears, swallowed and said firmly, "It's alright. I know him. It was my fault. He was sleeping. I shouldn't have woken him."

It was a voice he recognised. Usually, it said, "Morning – I brought you a cup of coffee," or "How's it going today?"

He looked up. The crowd were drifting away, casting grim looks over their shoulders and muttering to each other, but the girl was smiling at him. It was a nervous smile. "I'm sorry," he said. "You startled me."

"It's alright," she said again. "It was my fault." She hesitated, and then stuck out her hand. "I'm Willow. I'm afraid my mom was in her late hippie phase when she named me." A joke to lighten the mood.

He looked at her hand. He couldn't recall the last time he had touched someone of the opposite sex. Self-consciously, he wiped his hand on his trousers and touched her hand briefly. "Daz," he said.

"It's funny. I've been bringing you coffee for six months now, and I know you like it white with three sugars, but I didn't even know your name." She rattled on, filling the awkward silence. "I left school last year. I work at the café in the library, and I help out in a care home - " She realised she was babbling , and she cast about for something else to say and noticed the coffee stain spilling down his front. "Oh! Your coffee. Let me get you another one."

He started to protest, but she'd darted back inside the church that had been turned into a library and a café, so he stood there awkwardly, aware that there were still people watching him warily. He didn't want to stay, he wanted to walk away as fast as he could and never come back. How many people would buy *The Big Issue* off him now that they thought he assaulted young girls? He'd have to find a new pitch – if the local co-ordinator didn't find out what had happened and de-badge him.

But the girl had always been nice to him and she didn't know how he'd react when she woke him up. She wasn't rude, but if he slunk away now, *that* would be rude. *Worse than almost hitting her?* His thoughts just whirled round in his head and the next thing he knew, she was back with another cup of coffee, and *a pain au chocolat* in a napkin.

"Here you are," she said. "And I brought you this too. It's a bit dry because it's yesterday's so they were going to throw it out."

He took it and mumbled an awkward "thank you." She sat down on the statue's pedestal and he had to sit beside her. "I'm really sorry about that, Daz," she said. "I hope it won't make trouble for you. I'll go to the police if anyone says anything and explain."

He shrugged. "It's alright. I get a bit jumpy sometimes. I should learn to behave better."

"It's not your fault. Things can't have been easy for you."

"That's where you're wrong. It *is* my fault. It's *all* my fault."

I don't know about that," said Willow. "We all make mistakes. Look at me. I threw coffee all over you and then I gave you a stale cake."

Daz dunked the end of the *pain* in his coffee. "I prefer it like this, honestly," he said, sucking the soggy pastry into his mouth.

Willow lit up. "See, you're a nice guy." And against his will, Daz smiled.

"I'd be nicer if I hadn't nearly knocked your head off your shoulders."

"Well, I'll forgive you, but only if you forgive yourself first. My favourite poet at school was Maya Angelou and she says you have to forgive yourself for your failures."

"So I'm told." Daz wiped his mouth with the napkin and crumpled the cup. He stood up and put his rubbish in a bin. "I've got to go." And he shouldered his bag.

"See you tomorrow?"

Because he didn't have an answer, he gave a non-committal duck of his head and turned away.

Forgiveness? That was Step 9. *See you tomorrow?* One day at a time. Maybe *she* should be his sponsor.

The meeting was held in the old Methodist Chapel on Wade Street. He was late so he slipped quietly into a chair in the circle. Churches always had the same smell, he had noticed. He had been to meetings in enough of them. They smelled of polish and candle wax, which he could understand, and damp plaster, but why did they always smell of sawdust?

They had just finished reciting the Serenity Prayer and Daz thought God hadn't granted him much serenity or wisdom today. Perhaps just enough courage not to run away from Willow and to come to this meeting.

Eugene, the meeting leader and his sponsor, caught his eye and looked a question at him. Daz gave him the same head bob he had used with Willow, that didn't mean yes or no, but was a bit more positive than a shrug. He knew Eugene would try to speak to him after the meeting, and, no matter what he said, would see clear through him. Eugene was twenty years clean and had seen and heard everything and was one of the few black people in Lichfield. He liked to joke that he had to make a clean break and where better than in "a white ghetto."

There were only a handful of people at the meeting. A new face stood up and introduced himself as an addict and they all welcomed him. He told his story and it sounded depressingly familiar – or was it reassuring, Daz wondered. Other people were going through the same struggles as he was, having good days and bad days, and still getting up in the morning. When he had finished they told him to "keep coming back" and Eugene gave him a '24 hours clean' coin.

Then they went round the circle and someone read something from somewhere and someone talked about how good their life was at the moment and someone else said how difficult theirs was and everyone thanked them for sharing.Some people, like Daz, just passed. He wasn't really listening and then Eugene brought the meeting to a close. They all joined hands and recited the Lord's Prayer and then headed to the table at the back where there was a kettle, a jar of instant coffee, tea bags and a plate of chocolate Hob Nobs.

"I'd ask you if you wanted a coffee, but it looks like you've already had one." Eugene was at his elbow.

"I had an accident," Daz muttered, avoiding his eyes.

"Want to tell me about it?"

"It was nothing."

"Want to tell me about it?"

And like a tap, the story started pouring out of Daz. Eugene led him to a chair and sat and listened quietly until Daz ran dry. "She brings me coffee every day," said Daz, aware that his eyes were leaking, and he scrubbed them fiercely with his hands. "I could have killed her and she got me another drink and cake. I shouldn't be around people. How can I go and see my daughter if I don't know what I'm going to do next?"

"It's PTSD, Darren," said Eugene. "Do you have a counsellor?"

"I used to. I lost contact when I ended up on the streets. And then I got into drugs."

"But you're not on the streets now. And you're not into drugs any more, are you? Do you feel like using now?"

Daz shook his head. "No, I'm alright," he said, and he was surprised to find he was. "I just feel so angry with myself."

"What are you angry about?"

"I don't know...everything. I'm angry about being angry."

"Have you heard of something called *Kintsugi*?" Eugene asked, after a pause.

Daz shook his head.

"It's the Japanese art of repairing broken pottery by mending the broken parts with lacquer mixed with powdered gold. Instead of throwing away something damaged, they repair it and make it beautiful. They look at breakage and repair as part of the object's history, rather than something to hide. They call it 'The Art of Precious Scars.' It's not a bad philosophy for life."

"What's this got to do with Willow?"

"She sounds like some of the gold you might need in your life to help repair yourself. Are you going to see her tomorrow?"

"If she'll see *me*."

Eugene clapped him on the shoulder. "One day at a time, Darren. One day at a time."

The meeting drifted to an end, the way these meetings usually did. Daz felt better, better than he had when he spoke to a counsellor. Perhaps it was because counsellors hadn't loaded the bodies of their friends on a wagon, because they hadn't been at the dirty end of a needle. They said they understood, but they didn't *know*. At least Eugene had been there, at the bottom of the hole, and he knew what it took to climb out again.

Daz didn't embarrass either of them by thanking him, just gave him the head bob, shouldered his pack and headed out to sell to the afternoon rush.

Back on his pitch, he sold all of his remaining magazines in a couple of hours. He thought he got a couple of odd looks, but mostly people either ignored him completely, speeding up their walk and turning their head away, or they smiled as they drifted by, or they stopped and bought a copy and stayed to chat.

Nothing he was worried about had happened. Just talking to Eugene made things seem not so bad after all. The sun was still shining, he'd sold all his magazines, he'd learned the girl's name and she'd given him a *pain au chocolat.* He could go home early, and have something to eat and spend the evening in front of the telly. It had turned out not to be such a bad day after all.

CHAPTER TWO

Willow - Monday

At 4.00 pm each weekday Lichfield Library closed its doors. That meant that the library café had to stop serving at 3.30 pm. The café staff had half an hour to clean down the coffee making machine, load up and start the two dishwashers, wipe over the tables and chairs and set up the counter for a 10.00am start the next day.

There had been a steady stream of customers during the day. There were the elderly regulars who had developed a routine of exchanging their books in the library after which they popped into the café for a cup of tea, a slice of cake and a friendly chat with a member of staff. Then there were small groups of students who used the IT suite for research before rewarding themselves with sugary drinks, chocolate bars and the chance to talk about things on their minds, like their study assignments, friendships and sex. The topic of conversation usually moved quickly off items 1 and 2 and on to item 3. Then there were the office workers who wanted somewhere peaceful to have lunch. It wasn't silent but it was close enough.

The noisiest part of the day was when all the eaters and drinkers had gone and the staff were left to clean up. There were usually three café staff working at high speed to mop up any spillages, crumbs and detritus from the day, systematically recreating order from the customers' previous five and a half hours of chaos. The manageress would orchestrate the clear-up by giving instructions to her juniors.

"Willow...Willow, can you check the sauces and sugar sachets next, after you've wiped down the trays?"

"Sorry, Susan, I was miles away...what did you say?"

"I said, can you see if we've enough sachets of sauces and sugar at the end of the counter...once you've cleaned the trays," repeated Susan. "Willow, are you sure you're OK after that incident with that bloke earlier?"

"Yeah, I'm fine, honestly. I'll sort out the trays and stuff," replied Willow.

Willow had no problem at all with systematically and mindlessly disinfecting the trays and counting packs of sugar. In fact working at the café wasn't difficult or taxing at all. She liked working here because it didn't stretch her. Willow had had enough of being stretched at Lichfield Cathedral School. She was glad to leave after finishing Year 11 with a suitcase full of A* grades. After all, she'd been there since Year 1.

Willow's father wanted his daughter to study A levels at the school, specialising in Law and Politics. He had hoped that one day she would follow in his footsteps and join the practice. Willow's mother, however, knew that her daughter was not interested or cut out for a career in law, but she was disappointed that her very bright daughter wanted to leave the school after her GCSEs. Following two months of debate, argument and tears, her parents had compromised and agreed that Willow could take a year out of education and then go to a different Sixth Form College and take the A levels she wanted to specialise in. The bargain with her parents was that she would spend a day a week in her father's office on Dam Street observing him working, doing some clerical work and making the partners in the firm cups of tea or coffee. She would do some voluntary work that her mother would organise that would look good on future application forms and CVs and for three or four days a week Willow would secure a job, even if it was for pin money.

Within two days Willow had found the part-time vacancy at the Library Café inside St Mary's Church.

At the end of August when the pupils at the Cathedral School were trying on their newly-bought school uniform and having the most fashionable hairstyles they could get away with before returning for the Autumn Term, Willow bought some ripped jeans and a couple of colourful tops. She also had purple streaks applied to her long blonde hair, much to the surprise and horror of her father and quiet admiration of her mother. So, at the beginning of September, Willow stopped being a school pupil, turned her back on formal education, for a year at least, and the recently seventeen-year-old became a young, working woman.

The truth was that Willow had hated her last few years at school. She began to resent the religious teachings, the strict uniform and the random rules. She disliked the privilege, wealth and arrogance of the pupils and their parents. She found it hard to tolerate the 'Never Good Enough' and 'Could Do Better' attitude of the staff and, more than anything else, she hated the bitchiness of the girls in her year group. Unlike most of the precious girls in her class she was not interested in taking filtered selfies, dating boys or being an influencer on Tik-Tok or Insta. She knew what she wanted – and it wasn't any of that. She was quite happy to distance herself from the in-crowd and smile at them from the outside. She had moved on greatly from the Year 7 Willow Cartwright who was given the nickname 'WC' based on her initials. She spent a few months or so worrying if some of the other girls in her class would try to stick her head down the girls' toilet, but it never happened. Willow kept her head up, well above toilet level and the level of most of the other girls in her class. She finished Year 11 with impressive GCSE grades but vowed never to set foot in that school ever again.

Now, six months into Willow's gap year, her mother was beginning to see her daughter developing into a young woman. Headstrong, caring and, at times, care-free. Willow's mother, in particular, loved her engaging personality and sense of humour and respected her deeply held views and convictions. Willow would argue tirelessly on climate change issues and animal welfare, and staunchly defend the down-trodden and disenfranchised. Willow and her father would often go ten rounds in the evenings playfully arguing about politics, meritocracy and charity. Her father was a tough opponent in a debate but she always gave as good as she got from him. He drove her mad at times but she did love him even though it was hard to say it, especially when he kept moaning at her about the clothes she wore, her make-up and the colour of her hair. Gradually since last September her appearance was getting more "colourful" (as her dad would say).

"Willow, how are you doing? It's almost 4 o'clock. Time to go," announced Susan.

Willow was keen to leave and get some more fresh air, but she was still worrying about the incident she had had with *The Big Issue* man earlier on today.

As Willow left the cafe and said her goodbyes, she looked out on the town square. It was fairly quiet as today was not a market day. If she turned right, there was a slight possibility that she would bump into the man again, but she'd had enough of him for one day. So, she turned left and decided to walk the long way home. Her plan was to keep her head down at first, walk along Market Street and then turn right on to Bird Street, before heading towards the Cathedral. From there Willow would be able to cut through to Stowe Pool, sit on a bench to gather her thoughts for a while and still arrive home a good hour before either of her parents.

As Willow relaxed into her walk and looked at a few shop windows, she wondered what was behind the man's strange reaction and behaviour. She was shaken by it. Over the months she had thought they had got on quite well, trusted one another, all things considered, and yet there were clearly things that she didn't understand about him. Perhaps she would never know certain things and that was OK, she didn't want to pry. If he didn't want to tell her about his past or how he ended up selling *The Big Issue*, that was fine. Willow just wanted him to know that she was not judging him and she was definitely not trying to gain Brownie points by handing him a free coffee on the days when she worked at the café.

On the way up to the Cathedral she passed the entrance to her old and only school. She quickened her pace and looked down in case she saw any reminders of her past. The pupils would have all gone home by now, unless the odd pupil had been given a detention for breaking one of the school's ten commandments such as "thou shalt not smile" or "thou shalt not think for thyself." The teachers, or Voldemorts, as Willow called them, would not recognise Willow now as her appearance broke every single rule in the uniform code. Anyway, thought Willow, the staff would all have flown off home on their broomsticks by now.

As she turned right on to The Close, a small street that wrapped itself around the Cathedral, Willow became aware of a few emergency vehicles parked up by the front entrance of the massive building. The lights on an ambulance and three police cars were flashing. Several police officers were cordoning off the area around the building.

Willow slowed to a stop to have a look at what was going on. She could have turned round and found another route home but she had time on her hands and decided to wait around to see what was going on. Her irreverent imagination ran away with her. *Had someone stolen the donations' box? Had someone been caught eating a Big Mac in the pulpit? Had a pensioner dropped their dentures in the font? Had someone actually gone into the building to worship as opposed to just taking photos of the place?*

Willow moved as close as she could get to the blue and white Do Not Enter Police tape that divided the emergency service personnel off from the Looky-loos. She tried to earwig other nosey people but no-one seemed to know what had happened.

Just then another car pulled up and a couple of people not in uniform got out, showed their badges and were allowed to enter the exclusion zone as the tape was held up for them to pass underneath. The old bloke seemed to be Mr Fairly Big in the Lichfield Police Force and following him in his wake was a younger woman talking on her mobile.

Willow was becoming more and more intrigued. She had seen enough TV crime shows to know that this looked fairly serious. She was quite excited at the prospect that Line of Duty was coming to Lichfield. This was a real-life TV show happening in boring old Lichfield where nothing interesting ever seems to happen.

More and more people were congregating at the police tape. Two young officers were guarding the taped off area as if someone had planted landmines on the other side.

"Folks, there's nothing to see here!" shouted one of the officers.

"Please go. Make your way home. If you usually use The Close as a cut-through you will have to go back down Bird Street and walk by Minster Pool," said the other.

No-one in the crowd moved.

Willow smiled as she realised that this was potentially the most excitement the residents of Lichfield had had for years, so they were going to stay put no matter what these officers advised. She also smiled when she thought that other than the Christmas Eve service this was the biggest crowd the Cathedral had seen for months.

Willow edged her way towards the tape and stood by a man asking questions to one of the officers.

"Sorry, sir, I can't comment on an ongoing investigation," said the young police officer using a stock phrase from the Police Officers' Training Manual. "I'm sure a statement will be issued later."

"But I heard on one of your intercom things that someone had died in suspicious circumstances," said the man.

"Sir, I can't tell you anything. I just need you to leave the scene. Please move back."

An elderly woman on the other side of the man then got involved. "Was someone killed? Oh my God, my friend works in the gift shop in the Cathedral. Oh my God!"

"I'm sorry I can't give you any information for now. Please don't upset yourself. The details will be released as soon as possible. Now if you don't mind can I ask you to slowly walk back up The Close. There are emergency vehicles that need to come and go and we don't want any other...we just want everyone to be safe."

People reluctantly started to move away. Willow followed closely behind the man and woman as they chatted. The man was consoling the woman, Willow heard him say to her …" I think it was a man who died...I overheard someone say he fell...the viewing gallery...tragic accident...suicide maybe...I'm sure it won't have been your friend...why don't you give her a ring when you get home …"

They parted and went in different directions and Willow re-traced her steps down into Lichfield walking by the side of Minster Pool. She started to feel guilty. She had been playfully imagining in her head that this was all a daft scene from the cop shows her parents liked to watch, but now, it appeared that someone had died. Just occasionally Willow was aware that her bizarre sense of humour was not to everyone's taste. Maybe she ought to keep it in check. God, she hated herself at times. And why did she just use the word God in her thoughts when she wasn't religious. God help me, she thought and tried to suppress a slight smile under her black lipstick.

She found an empty bench on the footpath overlooking Stowe Pool. Her house, or rather her mother and father's house, was just behind her. From Willow's bedroom she could see the water and she could also see the envious people on their constitutional walks looking towards their big house guessing how much it was worth. At least by sitting on the bench she was distanced from her parents' privilege. She sat watching the ducks, geese and swans at the edge of the water making a noise to attract any generous human beings with bags or pockets full of bread. Willow's thoughts went back to Daz who spent a good deal of each day shouting out to passers-by for them to dip into their bags or pockets so that they could buy a copy of *The Big Issue* which would probably never be read. Her mind started to join dots between Daz and the birds on the water. Wild life! Daz was normally pleasant to Willow, but she had got too close to him today and he had reacted badly. Or was he just being defensive or protective like most animals are when you get too close to them or their young. Clearly, she had overstepped the mark earlier today. She would try to make things right tomorrow.

CHAPTER THREE

Willow, Darren - Tuesday

It was that time in the morning when Willow made a drink for Daz. Coffee, three sachets of white sugar and a sippy lid pressed carefully on to the disposable cup. Susan, the manageress of the Library Café, was fine about Willow popping out for five minutes or so each morning to give *The Big Issue* guy a free drink. Susan liked and trusted Willow – even if her appearance was odd to say the least – the manageress saw a girl who was a hard worker, reliable, with a heart of gold and really good with the customers, whether they be young or old.

Willow would always choose a quiet time in the cafe to ask Susan if she could take *The Big Issue* guy a drink. Now she knew his first name, but to save any explanation of yesterday's events she continued to refer to him by the nickname that had come into common parlance between the staff at the café.

Possibly, since the very first time Willow offered him a coffee last September, she was apprehensive about saying hello to "Big Daz" this morning. This was her new secret name for him. He was a big guy who looked as if he could take care of himself in a fight, if needed. He could probably lift Willow above his head with one hand so she was not going to make the mistake again of catching him off guard.

It was not as warm as yesterday so Willow decided to go into the stockroom to get her coat. She loved her greatcoat that she had bought from the Oxfam shop round the corner a few weeks ago. She checked in her pocket to make sure her mobile was still there. Out of interest, Willow quickly looked at the local news feeds to see if there were any updates on the incident at the cathedral. There were. She would look at the reports properly later but it appeared, at first glance, to be an accident or some sort of tragic event. She popped her phone back in her pocket and made her way across Market Square to "Big Daz."

Daz was there in his normal spot, shouting "Big Issue" at anyone and everyone who walked within ten metres of him. Willow was slowly approaching him from behind, armed with a hot coffee. She changed tack and tactics and circled around him before facing him at a safe distance.

"Hi...Daz...I come bearing a gift as a way of an apology for yesterday," said Willow, smiling at him and offering the coffee at arm's length.

Daz moved forward and held out his hand. Willow tried not to flinch.

"About yesterday...it's me who should be apologising to you. I scared the shit out of you. I'm sorry," said Daz, looking down at the cold hard floor.

"Let's forget about it now. No more apologies. It was just one of those things. OK?"

"OK," Daz said and took the coffee off Willow. "Thank you …" He still looked a little uncomfortable talking to Willow even though they had been sharing brief small talks for six months now.

Willow was not to be put off. "Daz, listen, I'm going to reach into my left-hand pocket very slowly and pull out something and point it at you. Please don't over-react, I promise you it's not loaded, but I want you to have it and I won't take no for an answer ... it's a chocolate bar!" Willow, true to her word, pointed a Dairy Milk at Daz. They both looked at each other, then at the chocolate bar and back at each other again before smiling and laughing.

"Thanks. You didn't do nothing wrong yesterday. I was a wan… – soz...I ought to give you something."

"It's only a chocolate bar. We've always got some in the kitchen," said Willow looking down at the hard-standing.

"D'you want half? I can't eat it all," Daz lied and pointed it back at Willow.

"No, you're OK. I'll have something at lunchtime in the café," lied Willow. There was a short pause before she said "S'pose I ought to get back...but I just want to have a quick look on my phone to read about what went on yesterday at the Cathedral."

"What incident?"

"Did you not hear anything about it? Apparently, someone died inside the Cathedral. I was on my way home yesterday and there were loads of police outside stopping people getting near the place. They'd taped off the area. Nobody would say anything, but clearly something serious had happened. There was nothing on the local TV news last night, but I just noticed on my phone, on the way to see you, that the police have made a statement."

Willow took her phone out of her other coat pocket and scrolling her way to the story, skimmed through the statement.

"It says that at 3.30 pm yesterday afternoon a man fell from the upper gallery inside the Cathedral and was pronounced dead at the scene. The police are continuing to look into the incident, but from the initial findings of the investigation, it looks like it was an unfortunate accident or possibly suicide. The police are attempting to contact the man's family but haven't been successful so far."

"Blimey, that's sad. I didn't hear anything. That's bloody awful. Poor bloke," said Daz.

Willow was continuing to read from her phone. "The latest update from the police is saying that 'the gallery was not open to the general public and the incident is not being regarded as suspicious.' Could be suicide, then?" said Willow bleakly.

"Yeah, poor fella. Won't know anymore 'til the police have got hold of his family," replied Daz.

"Is that how things work?" asked Willow.

"Yeah..."

"Oh, hold on!" Willow interrupted Daz. "There's a name. Shaun Wilde, local man, head of a charity …"

The demeanour of the man standing in front of Willow suddenly changed.

"What...did you...say? What...was...his name?"

Willow looked down at her phone again and checked," Yeah, the suicide guy's name is, or should I say was, Shaun Wilde."

"No! It can't be!" shouted Daz. Willow flinched and stepped backwards involuntarily. "I saw him yesterday. This isn't right. He wouldn't have fallen. He wouldn't have killed himself. It's not suicide ... it's murder!"

"But …" Willow tried to say something calming, but it was too late. Daz's emotions had got the better of him; he was cursing and his body went into a spasm before he threw the chocolate bar on the floor, kicked a small pile of *The Big Issue* across the market square and ran off along Dam Street.

Willow was frozen to the spot and, for a few moments, stunned into silence before shouting after him. "Wait! Where are you going? Daz! Hold on! Daz!"

But Daz was not listening or responding to Willow's cries. The blood was pounding in his ears as he ran and the innocent bystanders and pedestrians took cover as he barged through them shouting, "Get out my way!"

Willow should have been heading back to the café by now. She had been gone for over ten minutes and Susan would not be impressed if she was any longer. But as her head turned from the disappearing Daz towards the café and then back at Daz running like a thing possessed, she knew what she had to do.

She pocketed her mobile phone and chased after Big Daz. Willow was no athlete but she could run relatively quickly, even wearing a bulky greatcoat and as she was running in Daz's wake her path had been cleared of casual shoppers and sight-seers seconds earlier by Daz resembling an out-of-control snowplough.

As Willow ran past Minster Pool she realised where Daz was heading. The Cathedral loomed large ahead. She might know where he was going but not why. Why had he reacted like that? Why was he behaving like this? She didn't know why, but she cared. She stopped shouting after him. Willow could tell that this man was not for turning or listening to reason. The switch in his head had been flicked again. The second time in two days. And on both occasions, Willow had been responsible for flicking it.

She could see Daz about a hundred metres ahead of her. As he approached the grounds of Lichfield Cathedral, he turned left onto The Drive that circled the building. Willow was certain that Daz was heading for the front entrance. Sure enough, he was slowing down as he turned right towards the entrance. Ten seconds later Willow could see Daz at the front of the cathedral and she performed an emergency stop. There was Big Daz, shouting at a couple of police officers who were stationed at the entrance. In the next five minutes or so Willow, from a safe distance, witnessed what could only be described as an unhealthy disagreement that progressed from a difference of opinion to a heated discussion to a physical altercation. There was swearing and shouting, fingers pointing, fists being raised, *Do Not Enter* tape being torn, and pushing and shoving – all by Daz aimed at the two unsuspecting young police officers. Willow found it difficult to hear the exact words that were coming out of Daz's mouth, but it was obvious that he wanted to set foot inside the cathedral. It was also clear that the two officers had been assigned the specific duty of preventing any member of the public from stepping inside the place of worship that was doubling up as a crime scene.

Willow looked on in horror as the man she was laughing and joking with a few minutes ago was restrained by a total of four police officers who just about managed to get the better of him. He was handcuffed and unceremoniously dumped in the back of a police car and driven off. The two officers returned to their sentry duty. Apart from the odd length of torn police tape drifting along the ground in the slight wind it appeared that nothing unusual had happened in the last few minutes. Peace and harmony had returned. Willow looked around the area in front of the cathedral. The place was deserted; no-one else had been witness to this drama.

Willow stood still for a minute or two and wondered if she should go up to the police officers and ask a few questions. What good would it do? They wouldn't tell her anything. After all, she was a girl with brightly coloured hair. Would they take her seriously? No chance.

Willow slowly walked back down Bird Street and made her way to the café. On the walk back she was consumed by what she had seen and then shocked back into reality by having to quickly devise a plausible reason why she had been away from the café for almost half an hour. It meant a mixture of grovelling to Susan and lying about a visit to Boots the Chemists to urgently buy some sanitary pads. 'That would do the trick,' thought Willow.

She managed to pacify Susan by not bothering with a lunch break and she tried to put the Daz episode out of her mind until she finished work. She took the short route home at 4.00 pm. She was hoping and praying that Daz would be at his post when she walked across the square, but he wasn't. No surprise there. But there were three or four copies of *The Big Issue* scattered and flapping around the monument. Willow picked them up. Any other magazines and people would have pocketed them, but not *The Big Issue*. 'No-one reads it. They just pay Daz to shut him up.' But no amount of money was going to silence Daz today. Something had lit the fuse and made him explode.

She walked home with the discarded copies. She was tempted to shout "Big Issue" when people passed her to see if she could make a few quid for Daz, but she didn't have the energy or courage to get into a dispute with anyone for the rest of the day. She just wanted to find an empty bench overlooking Stowe Pool, sit and look at the ducks, geese and swans and think about her second weird and scary day involving Big Daz.

She found a bench, sat down and stared across the water. Life was continuing and moving around her. There were pairs of joggers, dressed in their Lycra, padding around the footpath, occasionally looking at their watches or Fitbits. Couples and family groups were strolling and chatting. Small huddles of school pupils were making their way home from after-school clubs or detentions. A gang of ducks were bunching up on the water to protect themselves from potential bullies. It seemed to Willow that at this moment in time she was the only living creature who was on her own. The only one not moving. Still life.

Willow was half way through her 'gap year' which seemed more like a void or a black hole rather than a breathing space to 'find herself.' She had made a few casual acquaintances at the places where she worked, but no real friends. Her one or two good friends from school had moved on and away from her as they were now consumed with studying 'A' levels. And the one person that she related to, a seller of *The Big Issue*, was, to say the least, erratic and odd. So why was she fascinated by him? He was old enough to be her dad. He wasn't good looking. He clearly had some strange hang-ups. So why was it that she couldn't stop thinking about him? Was it that Willow saw Daz as one of life's underdogs? Was it that she saw something good in him that was worth saving, or was it that she saw herself in him?

"Oh God!" Willow said aloud to her audience, who were a crowd of ducks poised ready to mug her if she started to unwrap a sandwich, little knowing that they were going to be bitterly disappointed. She stood up and decided to walk once around Stowe Pool before going home.

On her lap of the pool, she decided she would not mention today's incident with *The Big Issue* seller to her parents. Willow's mother would be worried for her daughter's safety and tell her to stay away from Daz as nothing good would come of befriending a man of that age and type, while her father would literally make a big issue of it. He would go off on one about how most homeless people secretly live in their own houses and drive posh cars. Willow would hide the copies of *The Big Issue* in her bedroom and give them back to Daz when she saw him next.

And when would she see him next? The last time she saw him he was being driven off in the back of a police car. Willow didn't know that much about the law, but she assumed that he would be charged with assaulting one or both of the police officers and causing affray. Would he be locked up? Could he get bail? Could he afford bail or a solicitor? Maybe she could ask her dad a few hypothetical questions at the dinner table tonight. If not, she would have to sit down with her laptop in her bedroom later and try to work out what might happen to Big Daz.

Willow checked herself again. "What am I thinking? Worrying about a man I don't really know!" she said too loudly as a jogger breezed past her giving her a wide berth, thinking that this purple-haired, greatcoat-wearing weirdo was as high as a kite. She kept the argument with herself internalised for the rest of her journey home and eventually agreed with herself that she was not going to ask her father anything, she was not going to Google anything about criminal offences and she was going to forget about these two bizarre incidents that she had experienced with Big Daz. He was not her responsibility. She would keep her distance and try to get on with her life, even if she was not sure what her life was or should be.

CHAPTER FOUR

Daz, Krys - Wednesday

Darren was sitting in the interview room. A police constable with a blank look on his face was standing by the door. It wasn't the first time he'd spent a night in the cells. When you're on the streets, sometimes you'll do anything for a warm bed and something to eat and there were so many petty rules to be broken it was easy to get arrested.

But it didn't matter what you smelled like when you went in, you always came out smelling the same. Stale. Your clothes and your life.

The door banged open and a man who looked about fifty, but dressed twenty years younger came in. His fashionable sports jacket hid the bulge of his stomach over his skinny trousers, but his expensively tousled hair and neatly trimmed short beard couldn't hide the bags under his eyes and the sagging chin. He looked like a bulldog standing up on its hind legs, wearing a pair of shiny brown wingtip brogues.

He let the door slam back in the face of the young woman following him, and she just got her hand up in time to stop it hitting her. Daz caught the look of irritation that crossed her face before she hid it behind standard issue police blankness. She had the pale face, blue eyes, high cheekbones and sharp nose that made him think of Eastern Europe.

"You can go," the man snapped to the police constable, scraping a chair out, collapsing into it and banging a buff folder on the table. After the quiet, it was an assault of noise. Daz recognised it. They'd used it questioning prisoners in Afghanistan.

"Right. I'm DI Potter and this is DS Kendrick."

Kendrick pulled her chair out quietly and sat down. Potter flipped open the folder.

"You are Darren Kenneth Mitchell." It wasn't a question. "Yesterday you assaulted a police officer at Lichfield Cathedral."

Daz had learned from bitter experience not to make eye contact and not to say anything.

"You claim that the death in the cathedral was not, in fact, accidental or a suicide, but a murder. Is that correct?"

Daz nodded.

"Did you know the victim?"

Now was the time to speak. "Yeah. He helped me get a flat."

"Ah, yes." Potter looked down and flicked through some of the papers in the folder. "You live at Flat 3a, 67 Dimbles Court. Is that correct?"

Another guarded nod.

"Assisted housing which you claim Shaun Wilde helped you find through his charity, Home and Heart. Is that correct?"

This time, Daz didn't even bother to nod. Potter wasn't asking questions to get answers.

"And you have been resident there for – " A flick backwards and forwards of some papers. " – eighteen months?" Nod. "And during that time you have supported yourself by selling *The Big Issue*." Pause, nod. "Prior to that you were sleeping rough in Birmingham. Is that correct?"

Daz knew what was coming. He waited. It was like hunkering down in the compound, waiting for the missile attack everyone knew was coming. "And while you were there you were issued with a total of ten fixed penalty notices for rough sleeping, begging, and loitering and you were issued with a PSPO for Birmingham city centre. You also have five convictions for possession and two for ABH, one of which led to a Community Service Order and the other to a custodial sentence of six months. Is all that correct?"

Daz sat forward in his chair. "I've had problems," he said, "but Shaun was helping me. I'm getting my life back together again."

"Until you assaulted a police officer."

"I was trying to see someone in charge. I know Shaun didn't kill himself. I have information."

"And you thought the best way give me that information was to attack one of my officers."

"He wouldn't listen to me. He told me to piss off back to my cardboard box."

"So you hit him in the face."

When Daz was at school, there had been a teacher just like this detective inspector. He would catch Daz doing something and then pick at him and pick at him until Daz flipped out and then get him excluded from school for five days. Daz could feel himself getting worked up. It was like being fifteen again. He clenched his fists and dug his nails into his palms. "I had information," he repeated sullenly, "about Shaun Wilde's murder."

"It took four officers to restrain you," Potter went on in the same tone of voice, not looking up from his papers. "You trashed the cell we put you in."

"I was angry."

"Mmm, you seem to have a problem with that. You were - " flicking papers backwards and forwards. " – in the army. Court-martialled twice, demoted, and discharged in - " Flick. " – 2010."

"I've got PTSD."

"And a heroin addict."

"Recovering. I haven't touched anything for nearly two years now."

Potter shut the folder with a slap and finally looked Daz in the eye. "So why should I listen to anything you have to say?"

Daz glared back. He could feel the muscles in his jaw working and the roaring was building up in his head. Any second now, the room would go red, his chair was going to go flying back and he would be across the table and have that bastard by the throat. Then half a dozen police would burst in and wrestle him to the floor. He'd get a good kicking in the cells and go down for five years.

Then a woman's voice dropped into the room like cool, clear water. Daz didn't hear what it said, but the tension was washed from his body and he sat back in his chair. The colours came back, the dull browns and greys of the room, the hard, dark shape of Potter and the subtle shades of the Detective Sergeant and her very blonde hair and very blue eyes.

"What?" said Daz, shaking his head clear.

Her voice had the faintest hint of something foreign. Perhaps it was the precise way of speaking Daz had noticed used by people whose native language wasn't English. "I said, what information do you have to give us, Mr. Mitchell?"

Daz took a deep breath. "Yesterday morning - "

"When you were selling *The Big Issue*," interrupted Potter.

Another breath. "Yes, when I was selling *The Big Issue*, I met Shaun and he looked a bit off. I asked him if he was OK and he told me he had to see someone, to get something off his chest." Daz sat back.

Potter snorted. "That's it? You thought he looked a bit off, and because of that you think he was murdered?" He stood up and picked up the file. "Come on, Sergeant, we're needed back in the real world. And you - " he jabbed the file at Daz. "Just be grateful you're being let off with a caution, because I ought to have you locked up and throw away the key."

The Detective Sergeant didn't move. She was studying Daz closely. "You go on, sir," she said casually. "I just want to check a couple of things with Mr. Mitchell."

Potter glared at her and she met his gaze coolly. "Five minutes, Kendrick," he snarled and banged out.

She turned back to Daz as if nothing had happened, flipped her notebook open in front of her and said, "Now then, you say he seemed off. What did you mean by that?"

Daz explained about him not being his usual self, preoccupied and complaining and not looking like he was in charge. It was nothing he could put his finger on, but …

"...but he wasn't behaving normally?"

Daz nodded enthusiastically. That was it exactly.

"And he said - " This time it was Kendrick's turn to do some flicking. " – 'comrades are supposed to help each other.' What do you think he meant by that?"

Daz shrugged. "I don't know. It's like when you're fighting, the most important thing is watching out for your buddies. Shaun found me on the streets in Birmingham, and when he found out I'd been in the Staffs, he moved heaven and earth to help me. He got me on the vulnerable housing list and into a drug dependency unit. I wouldn't even be here without him. He was behaving like he'd been let down. He was..." Daz groped for a word. "...sad." He clicked his fingers. "That's it! He seemed sad."

"Do you have any idea who he thought might have let him down?"

"Not really. I only see him once a week when he buys a copy of the Issue. He's come to my flat a few times and helped me with things like paying my bills. And then sometimes at the charity office if I had a problem."

Kendrick bit on her lower lip. "You see, Mr. Mitchell, the thing is, no one should have been up in the..." She glanced at the notes in the folder. "...triforium. It's strictly no entry. If anyone got up there, it wasn't an accident."

Daz banged the table with his fist and Kendrick jumped. "So it's got to be murder."

"I'm not saying you're wrong," she said, holding up a hand, "but do you have any more than 'he seemed sad?'"

"He had no reason to kill himself. He had everything to live for."

"Isn't that the point, Mr. Mitchell? If we knew why people committed suicide, we could save them. People kill themselves and we have to keep on living and try not to blame ourselves."

"I've got more reason for killing myself than him," he said angrily.

She reached out and almost touched his arm. He pulled it away.

"But you're still here," she said.

"Did he leave a note?"

"Many people don't. They don't think about it. If they did, they wouldn't kill themselves." Daz slumped in his chair. "Are you alright?" she asked.

He shrugged. "I'm fine. Can I go now?"

"Of course. You're not being arrested, this time, but we will be issuing you with a caution, conditional on you staying away from the cathedral until we finish our investigations. Will you accept a caution?"

"Suppose so."

She stood up, but before she called for the constable to escort him to the desk, she hesitated. "Mr. Mitchell," she said. "I know you had PTSD. Do you think this might have brought it back? Is there someone I can call for you?"

"I told you, I'm fine." He squared his shoulders and stood up and she fetched the constable in.

Twenty minutes later, he was standing on the pavement outside, squinting in the daylight after the artificial lighting in the police station and thinking about the walk home. It was about the same distance as from his patch by the cathedral, but without the comforting jingle of a day's sales in his pocket.

What to do next? He needed breakfast, and he needed to talk to Eugene and he needed a new supply of *The Big Issue*. And he needed to find out who had killed Shaun.

The first one was easy. A walk back to his flat, and a bowl of Lidl Honey Nut Flakes. And so was the second – he just had to pick up his phone. The third one – not so easy. He probably ought to avoid the local co-ordinator for the next few days, in case she'd heard about the trouble at the cathedral and de-badged him. That would mean things would be tight for a while. He had just enough money to keep the gas and electric meters topped up for cooking and lighting, but not much else. No telly, no video games and no trips to the laundrette. And no cigarettes. Just as well it was Spring and he could live without the heating, but it might mean Honey Nut Flakes for dinner and tea as well.

The last one was hardest of all, but the one he had to do. And now he had time.

CHAPTER FIVE

Daz - Thursday

The offices of Home and Heart were in Whittington. Daz was going to take the bus, but when he found out it was £4 he decided to walk. Fifteen minutes on a bus – how long could it be?

It turned out to be about an hour and a half. In the old days, when he'd been stationed at Whittington Barracks with the 2nd Mercian, getting a lift was easy. Everyone stopped for a soldier and thanked him for his service. He wasn't going to get a lift now – he had no illusions. Maybe he didn't look down and out any more, but he didn't look like the sort of person you'd give a lift to – more like the kind you'd cross the street to avoid. And back then, if he had to walk, he was younger and fitter and it was usually with mates to make the time pass quickly with jokes and horseplay. He didn't have any mates now.

So he jammed his hands in the pockets of his hoodie, flicked the hood up and walked along with his head down trying to be invisible. But when he turned off the main road to Tamworth and left behind the stink of diesel and thunder of lorries and the roar of cars going too fast, he looked up and his spirits lifted.

He was in the country. Over the hedge, there were green fields with cows in and ploughed fields the colour of flowerpots. There were birds twittering in the hedgerows, and soaring high above in a sky that was far away and very blue. When was the last time he had been in the country? Back when he'd been in the army. Those were the best of times...and the worst.

Born and raised in Chelmsley Wood in Birmingham, straight to AFC Harrogate at sixteen and then to ITC Catterick. Married at eighteen, on to the Staffs and father to a baby girl six months later. He had left home and found a new home. Those had been the best times. And then there'd been Afghanistan and the worst of times, and he'd lost everything.

He carried on walking, and soon low houses built of old red brick started appearing, and then a church with a graveyard of leaning slate gravestones, and then newer houses with expensive cars on the drives.

When he got to the centre of the village, he bought a meal deal in the Co-op and ate it at a table outside the pub next door.

At the end of the last century, he had been stationed a mile up the road, and he had never come here. What teenager wanted to sit in a quiet English village? They wanted to see the world, and they wanted excitement. Fast forward twenty years, and if he could, he would have sat there all day. Nobody asked him to move on, but he could feel the eyes on him and he kept his hood pulled up and his head down.

It was another twenty minutes before he got to the barn conversion by a canal that housed the offices of Home and Heart. It was all reclaimed brick, oak beams and floor to ceiling windows. Daz crunched across the gravel and pushed open a glass door with *Home and Heart* engraved at eye level. It opened with a whisper.

The office was very modern too. Bare brick walls with pictures of mostly men and a few women, posing outside doors, holding keys and shaking hands with Shaun, smiling awkwardly at the camera. His picture was up there. He hadn't thought this through any further than getting to the office, but that might help.

The floors were carefully polished, sealed flagstones and a lot of the room was taken up with a large table that looked like it had been made from recycled pallets. It held up a slim keyboard, a large flat screen and a young woman with puffy eyes and a red nose, clutching a bunched-up handkerchief.

She looked up and pulled herself together as the door hissed closed. "Can I help you?"

Here goes nothing, he thought. "Yes, my name's Daz – Darren Mitchell. Mr. Wilde got me a flat."

She nodded. He went to the wall and pointed at his picture. "That's me there." She nodded again. Either she didn't trust herself to speak, or she didn't trust him. "Thing is – when I was homeless, Shaun looked after my medals..." This time no nod, just a blank look. "He said he'd keep them in his office for me, and I was wondering if, now that he's...you know...I was wondering if I could get them back?" She looked as if she was waiting for someone to tell her what to do, so he carried on. "There's my OSM and MiD -" He'd lost those God knows where years ago, but since he wasn't looking for them, it didn't matter so he gave himself a couple more. " – and the CGC and the MC."

"The OS...MD GCM?" she repeated, stumbling over the letters.

"The Operational Service Medal, Mentioned in Despatches, the Conspicuous Gallantry Cross and the Military Cross."

She pressed her lips together and stood up, trying to look like an efficient secretary and not someone who was falling to bits. "I'll get them for you," she said firmly.

"Wait!" Daz said, louder than he intended and she jumped. "You...uh, you don't know what they look like. The OSM looks a bit like a ten pence piece with a Union Jack and a compass and four crowns on it. My MiD looks like a leaf, and the CSG is a cross with a crown in the medal and leaves around it and the MC is a cross as well with four crowns on it, no leaves. They're all silver - " She was looking confused, so he piled it on. "They've all got ribbons – the CSG's is red, white and blue, but the OSM is gold, blue, black and red, but it's a different blue than the CSG and the MC is white and purple and the MiD hasn't got any ribbons at all."

She tried to get it straight. "A blue ribbon with...white and, gold - " And Daz tried to add to her confusion by correcting her, and in the end the girl suddenly burst into tears and collapsed into her chair, covering her face with her handkerchief.

And Daz didn't know what to do next. In the end, he held one hand with the other to stop them flapping about, and said, hesitantly, "Look, why don't I just go and look for the medals myself?"

The girl sniffled into her handkerchief and nodded and Daz quickly ducked into Shaun's office.

Shaun had once told him, "It's not what you are, it's what people think you are." And he added, "You can't sell *The Big Issue* looking like a drug addict, and you can't do it in a suit and tie either. You have to be what people expect you to be."

The office was exactly what Daz would have expected from a charity. The walls were covered with photographs of Shaun with important people like Tony Blair, David Cameron and Paddy Ashdown and actors, sportsmen and celebrities committed to the cause. There were framed testimonials and awards and in the middle of it all a faded black and white picture of four young squaddies, smartly dressed in their fatigues and three looking seriously at the camera, and one looking at the person standing next to him, all with their right sleeves pushed up, displaying their tattoos. Daz looked closer. Much younger, but already with a shadow of future pain and worry etched onto his face, there was Shaun, his tattoo still as sharp as the creases on his uniform – not yet faded and blotched by time. Daz was surprised how grim they looked – he recalled displaying his tattoo with pride at the pub the first time he went home on leave.

Daz glanced back through the glass wall at the girl. She still had her face buried in her handkerchief. He slipped his cheap Nokia mobile out of his pocket and snapped a picture.

On to the desk. Even though it was as modern as the secretary's, it was as organised as a soldier's. Neat piles of papers, a full out-tray and an empty in-tray, a phone and a computer set at right angles. Nothing personal, just business.

A pile of bank accounts from a bank Daz had never heard of were covered in Post-It notes and highlighter and front and centre was a letter headed "The Charity Commission" with the crown logo that Daz had seen more times than he cared to count on rules and regulations.

He sat down and read it.

Dear Mr. Wilde

You are hereby given notice of the Commission's intention to launch a statutory inquiry into serious concerns about the governance and financial management of the charity, Home and Heart, relating to potential misuse of the charity's funds.

This investigation is not an indication of wrongdoing, but equally it is not undertaken lightly. The Commission's interest will focus on concerns over the management of related-party transactions and false accounting, by yourself and the Trustees, particularly in relation to…

There were a series of bullet points underneath, but at that moment Daz heard the scrape of a chair on the floor in the outer office. He started miming going through a desk drawer and glanced up, but the girl wasn't interested in him. She had got up and was staring out of the door. Daz swept up the letter and the accounts and tucked them inside his hoodie and stood up.

He went out and the girl turned around as the door clicked shut. He tapped his pocket. "Got 'em," he said. She just nodded and went back to staring hopelessly through the glass wall at the canal. Daz felt he had to say something. "Are you alright?"

She shrugged. "I don't know," she mumbled. "Mr. Wilde was so lovely and caring, and now..." She shrugged again. "I suppose Mr. Russell will come and take over, but..." Another hopeless shrug and a sigh.

"Who's he then?" Daz wanted to know.

"He's one of the trustees. He's out of the country at the moment and I can't get hold of him."

"Can I help?" Daz had no idea why he said it, and when the girl turned round and looked at him, he could tell by the look in her eye that she had no idea why he'd said it either. "Well," he said awkwardly, "I suppose I'd better go."

He edged past her and trudged across the gravel, his arms pressed close to his sides, holding the papers in place. He kept them there all the way back to his flat.

CHAPTER SIX

Willow, Daz - Friday

There was no sign of Big Daz again this morning as Willow made her way to work. She was hoping to see him or even hear him shouting "Big Issue" at the top of his voice. Their last encounter was still haunting her and she couldn't stop asking herself questions – what made him freak out like that? Why did he run straight to the cathedral? Why was he aggressive with the cops? Where had he been since he was bundled into the police car? Was he OK? Was he still alive?

Willow had to stop herself asking these questions. It wasn't doing her any good. She was getting involved in something that was none of her business. Daz was clearly unpredictable and odd. He was also from a different generation altogether – they could never be friends – that would be weird. She would try her best to forget about him and get on with her life.

Willow opened the doors to the library, said hello to a couple of librarians and made her way to the café.

"Morning Willow," shouted Susan from the other side of the café.

"Morning Susan, did you have a nice time last night?"

"Yeah, Ben took me to The Indian Spice on Bird Street and the waiters sang Happy Birthday to me. Don't get too close to me today though after all of that spicy food I ate."

"I'll keep my distance...in front and behind you!" said Willow with a smile on her face.

"You cheeky young devil. I'll have you know that real ladies from Lichfield are not in the habit of botty burping," replied Susan with an even bigger smile on her face.

"Well, my mom must be from Tamworth then, 'cause she can fart for Great Britain!"

Both the teenager and the Lichfield lady were laughing so much that Susan was having to clench her cheeks together in case she was banished to Tamworth.

The first customers of the day arrived ten minutes later and Willow took their orders while Susan took charge of the till and the coffee machine. There were only the two of them working until half way through the morning when Patti joined them. Patti was assigned to cleaning the tables, loading and emptying the dishwasher and making sure the customers had everything they needed. After a few hours Patti and Willow would swap roles or sub for one another when it was their break. As manageress, Susan didn't like to leave the café; she'd often grab a drink and a bite to eat and sit at a spare table scrolling through her phone. It wasn't that she didn't trust her workforce, but she liked to be on hand if there were any issues.

Willow had not even thought about making a coffee for Daz this morning. She just knew that he wouldn't be around. As it approached midday, Willow was due to have her lunch break. Unlike Susan, she was keen to get some fresh air and walk about the busy streets for half an hour. Patti and Susan would be behind the counter and the tables would go unwiped for thirty minutes.

With her coat in her hand Willow walked towards the thick glass café doors. She noticed Big Daz on the other side of the doors staring in. Willow was partly relieved to see him and partly scared of the expression on his face.

She braced herself as she opened the door.

"Hi," said Willow, trying to keep things cool and calm.

"I need to speak to you," Daz replied, without any exchanging any traditional pleasantries.

"Sure," said Willow. "When?"

"I need to show you something...now."

"OK. Do you want to sit with me in the café and have a coffee? I sort of owe you one from this morning. I didn't think you were selling *The Big Issue* today."

"Long story. Are you OK with me coming into the café?"

"Yeah. Course. Why wouldn't I want you to come in?"

"Because...because I look a bit...you know?"

"You're fine. Come with me. Find a table and I'll get us some drinks."

Daz found a table as far away from the counter as possible and Willow went up to Susan at the counter.

"That was a quick break," said Susan.

"I didn't leave the building. *The Big Issue* guy, Daz, wants to talk to me. Are you OK if we sit in the corner and talk?"

"Yes, that's fine. But let me know if it gets uncomfortable...I'll be straight over, OK?"

"Thanks, Susan. Can I have two coffees when you have a minute?"

"Sure. They're on the house."

"You're the best."

"I know," replied Susan with a grin on her face.

Willow joined Daz at the table. Willow felt that this big unkempt man looked really out of place in the library café. His body language gave the same impression. He was scanning the room suspiciously while fiddling about with a small sachet of sugar.

"I've ordered you your usual coffee, but it will probably come in a cup and saucer this time. Is that OK?"

"Thanks," whispered Daz with a nod.

There was nothing else coming out of Daz's mouth yet, so Willow tried again.

"I haven't seen you about in the last couple of days. Is everything alright?" Willow asked casually and innocently.

"Yeah...well no, not really. I need someone to talk to about some stuff and..." Daz stopped as a cup or saucer smashed to smithereens behind the counter. Willow smiled for a second as she knew it would be Patti's butter fingers that would be the cause of the accident. Those very same fingers would be quickly using a pan and brush while Susan rolled her eyes at her. The noise was no laughing matter for Daz. He seemed shocked and lost the thread of what he was trying to say.

"It's OK. Patti dropped a cup or something. She works at the café with me. She's always doing that. It drives Susan mad. Susan's my boss...the older woman behind the counter. By the way, you don't have to whisper in here. It's a café not the actual library. You can talk normally. As long as you don't shout "Big Issue" at the top of your voice. Susan may ask you to leave then," said Willow trying to lighten the mood.

There was a glimmer of a faint smile on Daz's face as he said, "Thanks for giving me the heads up."

"So, you were saying you needed to talk to me about something." It was Willow's turn to go quiet. She couldn't carry on prompting him. What was the expression her dad used sometimes, 'It's like pulling teeth' or something like that. She would just sit here and wait for Daz to explain.

Daz looked at Willow and around the café and was about to open his mouth when they were interrupted again.

"Two coffees and a few biscuits that were going spare," announced Susan as she placed the tray on the table. "I've put your drinks in mugs as we'll be running out of cups soon, the way Patti is dropping them. Enjoy."

"Thanks, Susan," said Willow.

"Thanks," said Daz at normal volume.

"You're welcome," replied Susan, turning on her heels and leaving this unlikely couple to their drinks.

"She's nice," observed Daz.

"Yes she is, but I've only got twenty minutes left of my lunch break and after that Susan will turn from nice to nasty if I'm not behind the counter. Talk to me. Tell me what's wrong."

"You know the other day when you showed me that article about the suicide at the cathedral…"

"Yes…"

"Well, I knew the guy who died. This is a picture of him."

Daz showed her the photo he had taken on his phone yesterday and pointed Shaun out.

"Who are these other people?"

"I dunno. They look like squaddies to me. Maybe he did his basic training with them."

"So how did you know him?"

Daz spent the next five minutes painfully explaining his friendship and special bond with Shaun Wilde, how his friend helped him get a flat and his firm belief that Shaun would never commit suicide.

"You told the police all of this?" asked Willow.

"Yeah, but they didn't believe me...particularly the bloke."

"I'm sorry. That's terrible. I hate it when people won't listen to you. I thought the police were supposed to help members of the public. But...I'm not sure what I can do to help? I'm seventeen. I'm just a child in the eyes of the law. I can't persuade the police that they're wrong. I don't even know Shaun. I wasn't there when he died," said Willow, feeling out of her depth. "Look, send me a copy of that picture and I'll print a copy off for you. At least that way you've got something to remember him by."

"It's OK. I'm not expecting you to fight my battles or anything. It's what happened when I went to Shaun's office in Whittington yesterday that I want to talk about."

"Go on."

"I...erm...found some interesting stuff at the office."

"What do you mean – interesting to the police? And how did you find these documents? How was the office open just a couple of days after Shaun had died?"

"There was a receptionist who was there."

"And she just gave you some documents?"

"Not exactly."

"Don't tell me you took them without her permission...you stole them! Daz, you idiot, you'd just been released by the police and then you go and steal some stuff from an office. What if she reports you?"

"She won't."

"Well, what are these documents?"

Daz looked around the café and slowly pulled out from underneath his hoodie the letter and accounts. As he slid them across the table it was Willow's turn to look around the café. It felt like a scene from an old spy movie, but with very bad actors in the lead roles. Willow read the letter from the "The Charity Commission" and flicked her eyes over the accounts.

"So, 'Home and Heart' may be in financial trouble, but I guess a lot of charities are struggling for cash. This letter could support the fact that Shaun took his own life if the charity was being financially mismanaged. You'll have to give the letter and the other stuff to the police," said Willow, pushing the documents across the table towards Daz and away from her.

"No!" shouted Daz.

Most heads in the café turned in the direction of Daz. Susan made her way over to Willow.

"Is everything OK, Willow? Five minutes and then I need you back behind the counter," said Susan assertively.

"We're almost done here. Thanks, Susan," replied Willow.

Willow looked at Daz.

"You need to take them to the police. You'll be in even more trouble if anyone finds out you stole those papers."

"I can't, yet. Not until someone can explain these documents to me. I don't understand money, but what I do know is that Shaun was an honest guy. He wouldn't cheat anyone. But if the police see these documents, they'll just say he killed himself. Full stop."

"What about his death being an accident instead? He could've slipped over on the floor of the cathedral and banged his head on the stone floor, although I still think that suicide will be the obvious conclusion.

Just because he was your friend, a nice guy who helped people, doesn't mean that he didn't kill himself when he was found out fiddling the books." Willow's eyes widened as it dawned on her that Daz had a different theory. "You're not seriously thinking that Shaun was murdered, are you?"

"Yeah, I am. He didn't accidently slip and fall from the gallery or kill himself. It just doesn't make sense. and if you can't or won't help me, then I'llhave to find someone else who can. I won't let this go."

Willow stared at Daz. It was a similar look she gave him as when she saw abandoned cats and dogs on the TV in those RSPCA adverts. She couldn't let this go either.

"Fine," sighed Willow, "I'll help if I can but we'll need help on this. Professional help. My dad's a solicitor, but I'm not involving him. He would go berserk if he knew what I was doing. We need proper advice about finances and accounting, but the two of us can't afford to pay anyone." Willow paused for a moment as a dark suspicion entered her mind.

"I need to ask you something now, Daz. Why are you asking me for help? Did you know my dad was a solicitor already? Or was it that you thought my family were well-off and could bail you out of trouble?"

"No...I swear...I didn't know that your dad was a solicitor and compared to me everyone's wealthy. But that wasn't the reason...you're different to most people I come across. You're kind and I trust you. Nothing more. I promise."

Willow looked down at her cold coffee for a moment, feeling a little awkward and ashamed.

"I've got to go back to work now. You can stay here if you want and finish off the biscuits. I'll see you at your usual place at 11.00 tomorrow – that's if you're selling *The Big Issue* tomorrow. We can talk some more then. Is that OK?"

"Thanks...Willow."

"Don't forget to send me that photo." She stood up and smiled. "And don't do anything else that's stupid or illegal in the meantime!" She left him to his biscuits.

CHAPTER SEVEN

Sam, Willow, Daz - Monday

Sameena slumped in her chair, took off her trainers and replaced them with the habitual heels she wore behind a desk. She bent down and took out of her briefcase a notepad, pens, a calculator, mobile phone and a sandwich she'd grabbed at Greggs' when between workplaces.

At 1.30 pm each Monday she left Allcocks Solicitors on Lombard Street to dash across the city to the Citizens' Advice Office to do her voluntary duty for three hours. She didn't mind volunteering; in fact, she loved it. There was a freedom attached to giving free advice to people who needed help on anything from debt, welfare benefits, housing, consumer and employment rights, to legal and family advice. But it was also helpful for Sameena. She was nearing the end of her training. After achieving a first degree in Law and having completed the Legal Practice Course, she was half-way through the two-year period of in-house training before being fully qualified as a solicitor. Giving up one afternoon's pay a week to help out at the CAB would look good on her CV in the future.

Sameena could afford to lose a tenth of her weekly pay as she was not spending that much presently. For the last two years she had been living with her mother at her parents' house. Although this saved her money, it was not an intentional cost cutting exercise. It was out of emotional necessity. Her father had disappeared when on Hajj and it had become increasingly clear that he would not be returning to Lichfield. Everybody now presumed he was dead. Her mother, understandably, had found it very difficult to cope with this sudden and then prolonged stressful situation. Sameena's older brother and his wife, along with their two teenage children, took the responsibility to manage and oversee the chain of mini-supermarkets that their parents had built up in Birmingham. Sameena gave up her flat in Moseley – a suburb of mixed poverty and wealth - and moved in with her mother. This was not part of Sameena's action plan for her life or career, but the whole Akhtar family had had to re-think and change lanes when the head of the household vanished without trace.

In those two years, Sameena had fallen victim to her mother's home cooking. She had put on a few pounds and one or two of her work suits were straining at the waist. Sameena still turned heads whatever she was wearing, but the days of parties and dates were on hold until she was fully qualified. She rarely had an opportunity to wear her glad rags in the evening. After eating her mother's evening meal, Sameena was either writing reports generated from her day at the office or researching and prepping for the next day. When she gave herself some free time away from her laptop, she was too tired to drag herself away from the settee and the television. Most evenings after watching the news headlines at 10.00 pm, Sameena would excuse herself from her mother's company and escape to her bedroom where she put on her pyjamas, lay on the bed and read a murder mystery on her iPad. She loved her mother, but she needed some quiet time on her own because if she sat through the whole of the thirty-minute news with her, she knew that her mother would want to talk about the end of the civilised world and how things were much better when she was her daughter's age. Her diatribes occasionally became even more depressing when her mother would ask Sameena about eligible men at work and the prospects of her having more grandchildren. Sameena was always quick to feign a headache when this topic surfaced and would hurry off to her room for painkillers. Sameena's main focus was her career. A love life of any description was low down on her list of priorities. She would look for the man - or woman - of her dreams once she was fully qualified and had decided what and who she wanted.

There was a knock on the office door, which shocked Sameena back to her current reality, and in walked one of the many ineligible men that she worked with at her two offices.

"Hi Sam, good to see you. Are you set up and ready to start? Your two o'clock is here," said Thomas who was front-of-house at the office. His job was to triage drop-ins and point people who had made appointments to the right office.

"Hello, Thomas. I'm just logging on to the system. Give me thirty seconds and then I'll be all set."

"Thanks, Sam. We really appreciate you doing this each week."

"It's really not a problem. I like coming here and helping out. I wish I could do more, but..."

"You have enough on your plate without being a volunteer case worker here at the Bureau."

Sameena smiled. If only Thomas knew that she always had too much on her plate, particularly when she sat down in the evening for a home-cooked meal prepared by her mother.

"OK then ... I'll show Mr Gibbs in," said Thomas and he disappeared into the foyer.

Sameena looked down at her screen. She had five 30-minute appointments which would take her up to 4.30, but that would not be the end of her day. Thomas would more than likely send her a drop-in after that.

Sure enough, just after Sameena's last scheduled client left the office, Thomas poked his head around the door and informed her that there was a couple waiting to see someone. She smiled at him.

"Yes, that's fine. What are their names?"

Thomas looked down at his notebook. "A Mr Mitchell and a Miss Cartwright...I'm sure they're not a 'couple' couple, if you know what I mean?"

"Thanks, Thomas, show them in," instructed Sameena.

Sameena was aware of raised voices walking towards her open door. 'Family Problems,' thought Sameena as a teenage girl followed by a man (possibly her father) entered the room. The young woman, who had recently changed her purple hair to bright pink was half-smiling but the older man was scowling.

"Hello. My name is Sam. Please take a seat. How can I help you?"

"Um...I found out about the Citizens' Advice office over the weekend...my...friend here needs some help and advice and we...I thought you might be able to suggest something," said Willow, looking first at Sameena across the table and then glancing at Daz.

"Friend? You're not related?" asked Sameena gently.

"No. Does that matter?" snapped Daz, looking directly at Sameena for the first time since sitting down.

"No, of course not," said Sameena defensively and smiling pleasantly at both of them, "I'm just trying to get a general picture in my head of your situation before I try to help."

"Perhaps, I ought to explain rather than you," said Willow glaring at Daz.

"Yeah, OK," mumbled Daz and reverted to staring at the floor.

"That's fine," Sameena said, knowing that this was going to take longer than 30 minutes. "Take your time. You don't have to tell me anything personal. Just focus on the problem if you like. I'm not here to judge you."

It then dawned on Willow that this woman across the desk had perhaps jumped to some conclusions that were way off the mark. Willow didn't want to raise anything with her that would make Daz feel any more uncomfortable than he was, but she needed to set the record straight. So Willow thought the best tactic was to give some context to their "friendship." She explained to the woman about her friend selling *The Big Issue* and how she brought him a coffee most days from the café where she worked and that he needed some advice about a recent problem.

"Fine, let's see what I can do for you...Mr Mitchell," said Sameena who realised that she had seen and heard him shouting in the market square. She didn't acknowledge this to either client as that would make her feel guilty for not once buying one of his magazines.

"Daz...call me Daz," murmured *The Big Issue* guy.

Willow continued trying not to look at or listen to Daz. "I don't know how much you heard about the...death at Lichfield Cathedral a few days ago, but Daz knows the chap who...died. It's been reported in the press and on local TV as a suicide. The police are saying the same. Daz is certain that it isn't. He believes that this man, Shaun Wilde, was pushed from the viewing gallery. Not accidentally. Daz believes that Shaun was murdered."

"Mr Wilde was murdered. Is that what you believe to be the case, Mr...Daz?" asked Sameena.

"Yeah," Daz replied.

"And you have proof of this?"

"Well, he's got some information that might help prove it," Willow jumped in quickly. "There are some documents that Daz has. They show that Shaun had a problem with money and he was going to be investigated."

Sameena paused for a few seconds before replying, "Wouldn't that back up the story that this Mr Wilde killed himself. Money problems will often lead people to have suicidal thoughts."

"Look, lady," shouted Daz. His chair tipped backwards as he stood up. "Shaun didn't kill himself. There's more to this. But you're like everybody else – making assumptions. I thought someone like you would know something about prejudice." Daz turned his furious eyes at Willow. "I should never have let you talk me into this!" he said and stormed out of the office.

Willow and Sameena sat in silence for a while before Thomas knocked on the door.

"Is everything OK in here, Sam? I heard some shouting. Are you alright?" Thomas asked.

"Err...yes...we're fine. Thomas...do me a favour. Would you make us both a cup of tea? Willow, how do you like your tea?" asked Sameena.

"Um...Oh...milk with one sugar, please...thanks," said Willow, picking up Daz's chair and regretting bringing him to The Citizens' Advice Office.

Thomas disappeared and closed the door.

"Miss Cartwright. What's going on here?" said Sameena quietly.

"I honestly don't know. He just has these outbursts every so often. It's difficult to predict. I'm sure he doesn't mean any offence, but it's still unpleasant. I'm so sorry he shouted at you and said what he said. I shouldn't have suggested this. I think I had better leave." Willow got to her feet.

"Please, Miss Cartwright, sit down and have a drink with me before you go."

"It's Willow. Willow Cartwright."

"Please, Willow, stay, just for a few minutes. Let Daz cool down for a bit."

"OK," said Willow sitting down.

"First, before we try to get to the bottom of this, I am not offended or hurt by what Mr Mitchell said. I've heard a lot worse. Secondly, what we say in here is in the strictest confidence, so you don't have to worry about what you say. Is that OK?"

"Yes, thank you …"

Thomas knocked, brought in two mugs of tea and then retreated again.

"Willow, can I ask you something before we begin. Is Daz really a friend? He's not making you do or say anything, is he? I need to know that you are not being forced into anything. Please tell me the truth."

"I promise you, Sam, there is nothing weird going on between us. He's just a mixed-up guy and I feel sorry for him. But he is weird. Definitely weird."

"I just don't want you to get involved with someone who has anger issues or is delusional. He may do something...you know?"

"Sam, I'm seventeen. I can handle myself and if this all gets too much, I'llwalk away."

"Do your parents know that you are helping Daz?"

"Yeah...I told them last night what I was going to do," lied Willow.

"So what are you trying to do? Are you just humouring a troubled soul, or do you think he really believes that this Shaun Wilde was murdered? You know deep down, Willow, that whatever the reason you are helping him, it has to be a matter for the police...not Daz, not you and not me."

"I know, but I don't think he'll give up until he is a hundred percent certain that his friend's death was an accident. And he's nowhere near that yet. He thinks these documents prove that he was murdered."

"What are these documents, anyway?

"There's a letter and some statements from the bank."

"I don't understand."

Willow explained about the letter from the Charity Commission. She told Sameena about the friendship between Shaun and Daz, their connection with Home and Heart and how they met just before Shaun died. She added that Daz is convinced that his friend was acting strangely.

"Maybe he was a good actor?"

"Could be, I'm not sure. To be honest I don't know much about him but the letter suggests that Shaun's charity was financially in trouble and it wasn't well-managed, so the Commission was investigating the charity and, of course, its boss, Shaun."

"How did Daz get hold of these documents?"

"Don't ask."

"Oh God! Pretend I didn't ask that. I don't want to know. But he should still show it to the police; you never know it may be significant evidence."

"What I haven't told you yet is that Daz did actually try to speak to the police, but his temper got the better of him and he ended up spending the night in police cells."

"This just gets worse and worse!"

"Tell me about it! That's why we came here today. For some advice on what to do next."

"Willow, as much as I'd like to help you, all I can do is give advice and my advice would be for you to take the letter to the police station, drop it off and don't look back. You shouldn't be getting involved in this. It's not your fight. I know you want to help Daz, but from the little I've seen of him today, I would steer well clear of him, if I were you. I'm sorry, that's not the advice you wanted to hear, but I don't want you getting hurt."

Willow stood up and Sameena followed her to the door. She shook Sameena's hand and thanked her. As she watched the girl with the pink hair leave, Sameena knew that she had given her the best advice she could, and she knew that Willow wouldn't take it.

Sameena had never been a rebel. Her family had worked hard to send her to university – her father held down two jobs before he opened his first corner shop – and she would never have dreamed of going against their wishes. She thought about Willow – probably a nice middle-class girl from a nice middle-class family with no idea how lucky she was, and parents who had no idea how to handle her.

But she was young, and she could get herself into trouble if someone didn't look out for her. Maybe there was more she could do to help her. She turned back to her desk and saw the papers the man Darren had brought in. Thoughtfully, she picked them up and put them in her briefcase.

CHAPTER EIGHT

Daz - Monday

Well, that was a complete waste of time.

He had spent an hour storming round Lichfield with a face as black as thunder, not even noticing that people moved to one side or even crossed the road to let him pass. By the time he got back home he was no calmer, and after a difficult few days there was only cereal and bread in the cupboard. But he didn't feel like eating anyway.

He prowled the flat, flung himself down on the sofa hard enough to make it creak, and flicked the television on, scrolling restlessly up and down the channels. 57 Channels (And Nothin' On) – the old Bruce Springsteen song. Back in Helmand, there had been men who loved The Boss. They played him to get psyched up before they went out on patrol. Some of them hadn't come back.

Daz's music was more house – The Chemical Brothers, Goldie and the Prodigy carried him back to a happier time, nights out stomping until dawn, high on E, at The Sanctuary in Digbeth and Subway City under the railway arches. And then there were the illegal raves in tunnels under the M42, and the glorious summer in Ibiza, the year he joined up. Once the drugs wore off he had to get a grip and start dealing with reality, but if he hunted up and down the dial on his DAB radio he could still find pirate radio stations with shouty DJs playing his kind of music.

He realised with a start that he had been staring at the television thinking about music while the news scrolled on, with an earthquake somewhere, one man at a desk droning on to another man while a graph flashed up behind them, a woman in a street somewhere talking into a fluffy microphone, and soldiers some place grinning into the camera and waving guns. He usually tried to avoid the news, and he quickly flicked it off.

A trip to the kitchen, a bowl of Honey Nut Flakes and a slice of toast and jam. Stare out of the window at the world going by slurping a cup of tea as the night closed in, restlessly back to the living room, leaving the lights off and playing a computer game in the dark on the second-hand Xbox he'd picked up in a charity shop. It was Formula 1 2013 – he only played sports games, FIFA 07, NBA 05 and he'd even found the London Olympics, trawling through bargain bins – but he kept crashing and in the end he threw the handset aside in disgust.

Nothing was working, but he couldn't go to bed yet. He wouldn't be able to sleep. Thoughts would just go round and round in his head, starting with Shaun, going back down the rabbit hole to the streets, and his family and Helmand. And when he finally closed his eyes, there would be nightmares, and by the time the grey light of dawn came, he would have been wide awake for hours and useless for the rest of the day.

He clicked on the dim lamp and his eyes roved round the room. The sagging sofa, the dingy curtains and the garish carpet had come with the flat. Shaun had got him the television and he had found the coffee table by the side of the road. On it was something else Shaun had given him. A paperback, as battered and worn as everything else in the room. It was called 'Man's Search for Meaning' and Shaun had told him he should read it, that it would help. On the cover was a picture of a bird perched on barbed wire.

Daz had never read it. He'd opened it a few times, but the print was so small that he hadn't bothered. He picked it up now and flicked it open and came across a passage that was underlined in pencil. He supposed Shaun had done it. He read it and when he was done, he wasn't sure he understood it, but it seemed to be saying that you can survive anything, even a concentration camp if you realise the one thing they can never take away from you is the freedom to choose how you react to what they do to you. It felt like Shaun was speaking to him from beyond the grave, saying, "It doesn't matter what the cops think, it doesn't matter what Willow does or what that bitch at CAB says, you know I was murdered, and it's up to you to find out who did it."

He put the book down carefully on the table and fetched his bag that he had thrown down in the doorway when he came in. He opened it and reached inside for the papers he had stuffed back in when he stormed from the Citizens Advice Bureau. He groped around, but the bag felt almost empty. Desperately, he started pulling things out frantically and scattering them on the floor. A few old Big Issues he hadn't sold , a flier for the NA meetings at the Methodist Chapel and some leaflets about the Citizen's Advice Bureau. Where were the accounts? Still on her desk! He turned the bag upside down and shook it and, in a shower of crumbs, out fluttered the letter from the Charity Commission.

He snatched it up angrily from the floor and stalked back to the sofa. What was it that the book had said? You can only control the way you react. He hadn't and look where it had got him. He had to calm down and tomorrow or the next day he would ask Willow to go back to the Advice Bureau and get those accounts back. He couldn't go there, after what he'd said. But still, he could read the letter again, more carefully. It looked a lot easier to understand than the accounts, anyhow.

The name the girl at the Home and Heart office had used came up again and again – Russell, Andrew Russell, the man who was out of the country at the moment. The letter said the last set of accounts showed a manor house in Normandy, owned by the charity, was rented to him for £2,500 a month. That was more than Daz paid in rent for a whole year, but he supposed that it was chicken feed to them. And Russell's wife, Phoebe, had been paid £12,500 by the charity for interior design services, on top of £50,000 for the year before. And the accounts had been handled by an accounting service called Surety. One of the directors was Russell's brother-in-law.

What the hell had Shaun been thinking? Everybody knew you couldn't trust that sort of person. You don't find them on the front line ever. They were always back in Blighty making a fat profit, staying safe and getting honours. Russell even had an OBE.

Maybe Shaun had committed suicide, but Russell had killed him, just the same as if he had put a gun to his head and pulled the trigger. Or maybe Russell had really killed him – faked the suicide and was going to put all the blame on Shaun. Dead men tell no tales. And if you were rich and you were going to have someone killed, you'd make sure you were out of the country when it happened, wouldn't you?

Shaun deserved justice, but he wouldn't get it. Daz knew the way the world worked. What could he do? The only thing he knew how to do was kill.

He leapt to his feet. And what the hell was he thinking? His mind was racing down a very deep, dark rabbit hole. He threw the letter down as if it had burnt him.

He got himself a drink of water and stood looking at the letter, lying on the table next to the book with the picture of the bird on the barbed wire. Anger was his usual reaction – he had been angry for most of his life. Angry at his parents, his school, his officers in the Army and the enemy in Afghanistan. He had been taught to channel that hot-uncontrolled-lash-out-and-hurt-everyone anger into an ice-cold anger that killed the enemy.

But when he came home, look where that anger had got him – alone, on the streets and in prison. No one had taught him how to tell an enemy from a friend. Maybe now was the time to choose to put the broken parts of his life back together and make something else – not new, but different. Like one of Eugene's pots.

He needed to find another way to avenge Shaun, but what was it? Back in Afghanistan, Daz's commanding officer was fond of saying, "Know thy enemy." Of course, he was one of the dead bodies Daz had loaded into the back of a truck, so that hadn't worked out well for him, but Daz didn't have any other ideas. One way or another, he would track Russell down and prove that he was responsible for Shaun's death.

Tomorrow he would start getting to know Andrew Russell a bit better

Daz was back at the library, hunched over a computer. He'd spent the morning selling the Issue, but at a different spot so he didn't have to run into Willow. Luckily, there weren't many sellers in Lichfield, so he didn't have to compete for spots. If he spent a couple of hours in the library, he could make the lunchtime meeting at the chapel and scavenge a few biscuits and a cup of coffee. He could catch the rush hour crowd later, and then he'd have enough money for tea and breakfast and a few more Big Issues tomorrow.

He scrolled through Google and it didn't take long to find Andrew Russell.

Born: Andrew William Ellis Russell
24 March 1964
Cheltenham, UK
Nationality: British
Education: Whatmore Comprehensive School
Solihull College, BTEC Extended Diploma in Construction and The Built Environment Level 3
Occupation: Entrepreneur
Businessman
Charitable trustee
Net Worth: £75 million

As far as he could tell, reading between the lines, Russell was a dodgy builder with a good line in patter. At least, he'd started out as a builder, got into property and never looked back. There were links to newspaper articles which he followed about the young working-class lad from the back streets of Birmingham who had made his first million by the time he was thirty. Then there were night clubs, and casinos and more newspaper articles, and photographs. Now Daz knew what Russell looked like, with his arm around the shoulders of darts players and boxers, and DJs and rappers. Daz realised with a start that he must have gone to some of Russell's clubs back in the day.

Then he found a shot of Russell and Shaun shaking hands and smiling at the camera. He read the article underneath.

A former captain in the Staffordshire Regiment has joined forces with Birmingham's King of Clubland to set up a charity for homeless veterans in the West Midlands.

Shaun Wilde, a veteran of the Iraq conflict, says he wants to help soldiers who struggle in civilian life, and he has found an ally in Andrew Russell, the well-known owner of a number of nightclubs in Birmingham, including Zoom, Statik and The Zoo. Together they have set up the charity 'Home and Heart', and their aim is to provide accommodation for ex-servicemen who find themselves on the streets.

"I was one of the lucky ones," says Shaun. "Leaving the army wasn't hard for me, I coped with civilian life pretty well. Others aren't so lucky – because of what they've seen, and done, they struggle to settle down, and end up on the streets. Because I was lucky, I wanted to pay something back."

"We met in one of my clubs and got talking," explains Andrew. "I've been lucky too, and when Shaun told me what he wanted to do, I decided I wanted to get involved."

From small beginnings they set up a national network operating out of every major city in the UK, working with other charities to help homeless ex-servicemen off the street and back into training and work. So far they estimate they have helped over 5,000 servicemen and their families.

It went on to report a conversation with an ex-soldier who had been helped. Daz didn't read that bit. It was too close to home, but at the bottom he found what he wanted. It talked about Russell, the working-class boy who built a business empire up from nothing, and mentioned his cars, and his villa in Spain, and his ten-bedroom mansion with a swimming pool in Solihull.

He sat up with a jolt. How hard could it be to find a fucking great big house in Solihull?

CHAPTER NINE

Willow, Mary - Wednesday

Willow thought the path around Stowe Pool was a road to nowhere. A gritty track around dull grey water flocked with ducks, geese and seagulls, honking, quacking and screaming and leaving shit to be trodden in. And elderly couples sitting on the benches staring at nothing, or young mothers with a phone in one hand, a Costa in the other and managing to push a pram as well. And dog walkers.

Not enough room to push a wheelchair. A wheelchair with an old woman in it who was quite happy to comment in a loud voice about elderly couples sitting on the benches staring at nothing, and dog walkers and young mothers with a phone in one hand, a Costa in the other, pushing prams.

"Honestly, call that a dog? It looks more like a drowned rat on a string. When I was in Korea they wouldn't even have served that as an appetiser!"

"Mary!"

Mary was about a hundred years old and Willow was pushing her round and around Stowe Pool.

"What's the matter?"

"You can't say things like – at least not that loud."

"Why not?"

"Because it's not polite."

Willow had been doing this almost as long as she had been working at the library café, another concession to her dad that she "shouldn't waste her time hanging around in her room on Facebook." He really didn't know her at all. He didn't know teenagers at all. Facebook? Really? Her mum had got her volunteering every Wednesday at an expensive care home called Abbeyfield Residential and Nursing Home. "It's very good," her mother had said. "It doesn't smell of wee at all."

They broke her in slowly, helping with the social activities. That was when they got all the residents into the lounge and did a quiz, or the karaoke man came in and sang songs from the fifties and sixties. Then there was painting and indoor bowls. Everybody came, walking or shuffling, leaning on their sticks and their walkers or even in their wheelchairs. They were going to have fun – whether they wanted to or not.

Willow soon noticed Mary, sitting slightly to one side, watching the proceedings with a sour expression on her face. "George wouldn't have liked it," she commented when the karaoke man did "Here Comes the Sun."

"Was George your husband?" Willow asked.

Mary gave her a straight look. "George Harrison. One of the Beatles."

"Oh, I've heard of them."

"I helped him write it."

"Really?" Willow was learning how to handle these old people. Don't disagree with them, but don't agree with them either. Especially the crazy ones. Ones with dementia, she corrected herself.

"Well, not exactly, but I bumped into him one day in – let me see, I think it was 1969 and I told him he looked sad. He'd just had a terrible row with Yoko over a biscuit. He said it had been a long winter, and I told him, never mind, the sun will be here soon. Next thing I knew, it was on their next album!" She cackled with delight.

Like a moth to a flame, Willow was drawn to Mary - Mary who had gone to Oxford when she was fifteen, worked at Bletchley Park as a codebreaker by the time she was nineteen, had compiled crosswords for the Daily Telegraph, been a hippie in the 1960s, lived on a commune in Wales and gone to Kathmandu. Or so she said. Mary who had a family who only visited her with a solicitor, and then there was a lot of shouting. After those visits, Mary always wanted to go out, and finally Willow was allowed to take her.

And so they had got into the habit of a trip around Stowe Pool, a stop at a coffee shop and back to the home. Of course, the coffee was never as good as the coffee Mary had had in America, or France, or Italy or Vienna. Slowly the story of Mary's life had unfolded and

Willow didn't believe a word of it. How she married almost immediately after the war ended and raised a family, but after the excitement of Bletchley, she always felt something was missing. She kept her brain sharp compiling crosswords for the Telegraph under the name Oppia - "It was an old Roman law that controlled how much money women could have, where they could live, even what they could wear. I thought it was funny since the crosswords gave me some financial independence."

But in the sixties, something snapped, she said. The children were grown and didn't need her, her husband had never needed her - "Except for his meals and you-know-what!" - so at the age of forty-six she upped and left home and became a hippie. "Oh, my dear, I travelled all over the world and met everyone. Bob Dylan in Crete, the Beatles in India, Allen Ginsberg in California." Although most of the names she dropped, Willow hadn't heard of, she was perfectly happy to let Mary ramble on, but one day, trying to let a little reality into her world, she asked her how she could afford to live in Abbeyfield.

Mary glanced round suspiciously and beckoned her closer. "You've heard of Morse Code?"

"No," said Willow.

Mary tutted. "Well, we didn't have mobile phones in the war, you know. We transmitted long and short electric pulses to each other called dots and dashes. Does that ring a bell?"

Willow shook her head. Carefully looking around again, Mary rooted round in her handbag and pulled out a bar of chocolate. "What's that?" she said, tapping the wrapper.

"A barcode?"

Mary cackled delightedly. "Dots and dashes, is what it is! I invented it in 1945, just after they bombed Hiroshima. Alan Turing was a clever man – he knew how the world would treat women and poufs now the war was over." Willow winced at the word. "He told me to patent it. So that's what I did. Well, it was totally useless until someone came up with a way to read it, and other people came up with different versions, but mine was still the first, and it still makes me a lot of money. That's why my blessed children turn up once in a blue moon with that awful solicitor. They want to get me declared barmy and get their hands on my money." She guffawed again. "But they won't! You don't think I'm crackers, do you?"

Willow shook her head, but she thought Mary lived in Crazy Town and tried to navigate her way out. "Mary," she asked, "if you've got so much money, why don't you live in your own house with a helper?"

"Oh, my dear, I've never owned a house. And anyway, I've always preferred company, even if it's the company of a lot of old fogies!"

So here they were, going back round Stowe Pool and to stop Mary embarrassing her commenting on the world at large, she started talking herself.

"That's my house there," she said, pointing out one of the 1960s houses that pressed up to the edge of the pool.

"I expect that cost a pretty penny," Mary remarked.

"I don't know. I expect so."

"What does your father do?"

The last thing Willow wanted to do was say 'solicitor' so she said, "He's a doctor."

"That would explain why you're such a good listener."

Embarrassed by the praise her lie had brought her, Willow went on, "They fished a dead body out of the pool, just here, right by my house."

"Really? I didn't see that on the news."

"Oh, ages ago before my parents bought the house. I wasn't even born then. Sometime in the 1980s, I think."

"Ah, the 1980s – I was in the Peace Camp at Greenham Common then. I shared a tent with that nice girl off the TV, Fiona Bruce."

Willow pressed on. She didn't want Mary to move further out into Crazy Town. "I've got a friend I'm worried about. He's called Daz."

"Oh no, he doesn't sound your sort at all."

"What do you mean?" Willow bristled.

“Well, you’re Willow which is awfully middle class, and Daz sounds so common.”

Willow couldn’t see her face and didn’t know if she was joking. “Well, he is my friend, anyway,” Willow insisted petulantly, “and I think he’s in trouble.”

“Trouble?” Mary’s head swivelled round and her eyes glittered with interest. She looked like a hawk that had spotted a mouse.

And it all came pouring out, from the time when she had first given him a coffee to the moment when she thought he would hit her, the suicide at the Cathedral and Daz getting arrested, his stealing the accounts from the charity and then swearing at Sameena, and how she hadn’t seen him since. By that time they had got as far as the nice little coffee shop on Dam Street. It wasn’t big enough to take a wheelchair, but she pushed Mary up to a table outside and went in to get coffees – a latte for herself and a double espresso for Mary. She always felt guilty buying coffee so close to the coffee shop in the library.

“Ah, lovely,” said Mary. “Espresso doppio.” And she took one sip and then downed it in one. “Now, my dear, shall I tell you what the Dalai Lama once said to me when I was staying in Dharamsala?” Willow nodded doubtfully, so she went on, “I asked him why as a Buddhist he let Tibetans be trained by the CIA to fight and kill Chinese in Tibet when he could order them to stop. Do you know what he said?”

A shake of the head and a sip of the latte.

“He said, he could tell them to stop, but that wouldn’t stop their hearts. In their hearts they still wanted to fight the Chinese. He said, when they didn’t want to kill in their hearts, then he could tell them to stop.”

“I don’t understand.”

Mary settled her blanket around her. “Push me back to the home, and I’ll tell you,” she said. Willow juggled her sippy cup and the wheelchair through the crowds. “Your friend Daz is still fighting in his heart. He’s fighting his demons, the police, life in general...and you. You’ve just got to wait until he stops fighting.”

“What if he never stops?”

"That's his karma," said Mary.

"But I want to help him."

"And that's yours."

CHAPTER TEN

Willow, Daz – Wednesday/Thursday

"For God's sake Willow, listen to what this woman from Citizens' Advice is telling you..."

"But I can't."

"Willow, the clue is in the title – Citizens' Advice. You, as a citizen, went to her with this mad man and for the second time he's acted like a lunatic. Take her advice. Ditch him."

"But…"

"But nothing...he's trouble, stay clear. You have enough issues in your life without this Daz character playing a part."

"That's not fair."

"You have no idea what you want to do next year, you have very few friends and …"

"And what?"

"And you're weird. Sorry, perhaps that's a bit harsh but you are a little...unusual."

"I'm different, that's all. I don't want to be like the other girls at my age, tarting themselves up for boys, showing their tits and legs off, trying to get into nightclubs so that they can get stoned and jump up and down for three hours."

"So, you're better than everybody else...Little Miss Too Goody Two Shoes."

"No, I'm not saying that. I'm not good at all. I'm a mess. I admit it. I don't know what I want, but I do know what I don't want. I don't want to conform and do what my parents want me to do or join a flock of teenage sheep."

"So, you'd rather hang about with a guy three times your age who's clearly three times more crazy than you are ?"

"I'm not 'hanging about' with him. I'm trying to help him because he believes that his friend was murdered. Nothing more."

"Yeah. He 'believes' his friend was murdered. No-one else does; not the police, not the local news, not even you!"

"He may be right."

"And he may be wrong. You have no proof that he was killed. You just feel sorry for him; admit it, Miss Too Goody Two Shoes."

"I hate you...I bloody hate you."

There was a knock on Willow's bedroom door.

"Willow...are you OK?" asked her mother as she entered and saw her daughter sitting cross-legged on her bed staring at her laptop.

"I'm fine, mom, thanks," replied Willow, quickly closing the laptop lid.

"You were arguing quite loudly. Were you Facetiming a friend? Has someone upset you?"

"No...it was just a silly discussion that got out of hand. It was just a boy thing ..."

"Well, don't let a boy come between you and your friends. I'm sure by tomorrow, after you've both slept on it, things will be fine between you. Anyway, your dad and I are off to bed. Don't stay up too late. Love you, sweetheart."

"Love you too, mom."

Willow's bedroom door closed. She would get ready for bed in half an hour or so but first she wanted to see if the local news had any more updates on Shaun's death.

She flipped up the lid again but this time she would turn the machine on and not just talk to a blank screen.

The next morning Willow sat with her mother and father while they had their breakfast. Her mother offered to make her something, but as usual she said that she would have a bite later on when she clocked in at the library café.

Her father sat scrolling through the day's news on his iPhone, eating toast and jam and sipping tea from a mug that said "This Is What The World's Greatest Solicitor Looks Like" with a little arrow pointing upwards. Willow's mother engaged her daughter with talk of a possible holiday adventure in the summer before she went to college and also a mother and daughter shopping trip on the train in Birmingham. They talked about the prospect of new clothes, new nail colours and new hairstyles. It was only when Willow mentioned that she fancied another change of hair colour from pink to blue that her father looked up and rolled his eyes despairingly. Willow did not react or engage; she merely smiled at him in an exaggerated way and continued her conversation with her mother.

"Don't forget you're last out today," said her father, "so you have to set the alarm. There's plenty of dodgy customers about in the town centre. Thank God we've got CCTV at the office is all I can say."

An hour or so later she set the burglar alarm for the house, locked the front door and walked towards the centre of Lichfield.

Would Daz be in his usual spot? The answer was no. She walked around the shops to pass the time for a few minutes to see if he was just late but clearly he was not selling *The Big Issue* today.

In her head Willow aimed an angry diatribe at the invisible Daz. 'Well, fuck you then. You can sodding well sod off. No more help from me. Find another gullible person to take pity on you. And forget free fucking coffees from now on.'

Willow was not sure that venting like that made her feel better, but it did make her blush. She was normally not one to swear, even in her head!

"Hi, Willow," greeted Susan as she walked into the café. "Are you OK? You look a little flushed. Have you been running?"

"No, just swearing!" said Willow with a smile on her face.

"It's not that Big Issue guy, is it? Has he said something or done something?" asked Willow's manager.

"No. I haven't seen him for a couple of days now. Maybe he's left Lichfield. He's a bit unpredictable to say the least."

"That's one word to describe him, I suppose. So, who were you swearing at?"

"Oh...no-one in particular. Just the people who drop litter in the streets...it just annoys me, that's all," explained Willow quite convincingly.

"It's not just in the streets. Some of our customers are bad enough. They just expect the fairies to clean up all of their mess. Fairies like Patti, you and me," responded Susan.

"I think we're more like angels than fairies. We're cute angels in the house of God serving our congregation lattes and chocolate brownies with a smile on our faces," joked Willow.

"Blimey, Willow, you're in a poetic mood today. That'll soon disappear when you start mopping the floor."

"No, I'll keep smiling regardless, no matter what cruddy jobs you give me. I'll be angelic all day. I've decided to enjoy the moment and not let things get to me."

"Good for you, Angel Willow First Class. Now go and get that mop and bucket. And don't get your wings wet!" said Susan in mock annoyance.

At lunchtime Willow unwisely decided to stay in the café and chat to Patti. Patti had been having troubles with her boyfriend and she wanted to go into all of the sordid details with someone. Willow was her captive audience. At the end of the twenty-minute conversation it was clear that Patti's boyfriend was not to be trusted and that Patti, herself, was no angel. Willow ended up blushing for the second time that day.

By the end of the day, Susan commented that Willow had earned her wings today for her help behind and in front of the counter and also for listening attentively to Patti while she described in detail her love and lust life.

Willow made a mental note not to get involved in matters of the heart with the opposite sex until she was at least an old-aged pensioner. Men were clearly a distraction and were, on the whole, assholes. Willow started smiling again and reflected on a good day at work as she said her goodbyes to her fairy godmother and the fallen angel.

As Willow walked through the library, a familiar dark shape took the shine off her day. At a table, studiously examining some papers, sat Daz, looking uncomfortable and totally out of place. He didn't see her as she headed for the exit of the library. The last thing she wanted was to get involved with him, again. Another asshole! She escaped into the fresh air and made her way towards home. She would make her mom and dad a meal tonight and be nice to them for a change.

Willow managed about fifty metres before she slowed down and stopped. She sat down on a vacant bench by the mobile fish and chip shop. She then spent the next three minutes or so arguing with herself in her head before the good angel prevailed and she walked back to the library and quietly sat opposite Daz.

"Hi, Daz."

He looked up, guilty and embarrassed. "Oh, hi, Willow. I...look, I...I wanted to say I was sorry about the way I was the other day at the Citizens' Advice Bureau."

"It seems as if that's all you do. Say Hi and then apologise later on. I thought you wanted my help, I thought you trusted me."

"I'm sorry...I mean, yes I do. I trust you and I need your help. I'm not good with people. I'm not good in certain situations. I lose it too quickly, too easily. I need someone who believes in me. Shaun believed in me."

"Look, I'm not Shaun. I'm a teenager with no experience of the armed forces. I haven't been in a war. I've never even held a gun, let alone fired one. I hate the idea of fighting. I'm not patriotic. I wouldn't fight for my country. I'm not brave. So, I'm nothing like you or Shaun."

"But you are brave. You stand your ground. You speak up. You don't give up."

"But I'm scared you might lose it with me."

"I would never do that, never. I would never hurt you."

"Thanks. However, I don't know what I can offer you. I'm barely out of school uniform. Half the time I'm still trying to work out who I am, let alone anyone else."

"But when you're around I don't feel so angry...most of the time," Daz smiled as he finished this sentence.

Willow smiled back. "Do you know what, Daz, today I've been likened to an angel and now you're describing me as a baby's pacifier...a dummy!"

"You're definitely nobody's dummy, Willow."

"Thanks, again, but I feel like one most of the time." Willow paused and then looked down at the papers spread across the library table. "What's all this?"

"They're bits of research I've been doing on a guy called Andrew Russell. There's a letter here I'd like you to read and I've printed off some stuff involving this guy. He clearly knew Shaun and I think he's linked to his death."

"Whoa, back up, soldier. You're going too fast. I'm a dummy, remember," Willow said, and for the next ten minutes Daz told Willow about the letter, the missing spread sheets that were still with Sameena, the manor house in Normandy, the accountancy firm Surety, Andrew Russell's interesting career and the partnership between Russell and Shaun that set up Home and Heart.

It was the longest monologue that Willow had witnessed from Daz. Occasionally, excitement got the better of him and she made him retrace his steps in the story. Willow looked at the documents and purposely pondered on everything in an attempt to slow Daz's imagination and suspicions from running away from him. By the time she had a clear-ish picture of what Daz had discovered Willow wasn't convinced that anything that he'd said would answer the question about Shaun's death, but Daz was sure that more questions needed to be asked.

"Who's going to ask these questions, Daz?"

"I am," replied Daz.

"You don't think this is a matter for the police?"

"Nah. They won't do anything."

"What's your plan, then?"

"Go to this posh house in Solihull and front up to him."

"Look Daz. This Andrew Russell isn't going to just talk to you. Why should he? He'll just shut his door in your face. Worse still you'll get in a fight with him. Then you'll end up behind bars...again!"

"But if you came with me …"

"No way, mister. I'm not getting between you guys. I only weigh about forty kilos."

"But if you were just there with me …"

Willow sighed. "Alright, I can't believe I'm saying this, but I'll come."

"Deal...dummy," said Daz, shaking Willow's hand.

"And don't call me that ever again, alright? I'm your guardian angel from now on and I have the wings to prove it!"

CHAPTER ELEVEN

Sam – Wednesday/Thursday

Sameena felt sick. She felt sick and fat. She couldn't wait to get out of her work clothes and put on her elasticated pyjamas.

Sameena had arrived home fairly late from work, only to be greeted by her mother complaining about her time-keeping and then immediately serving her up a large plate full of chicken biryani with a pile of chapatis and dahl at the table. There was no time to change out of her work clothes. She sat down and started eating, even though she wasn't that hungry. Regardless of how slowly Sameena ate her mother's cooking and no matter if she left a bit of food on the side and claimed she was full, her mother would be waiting, poised, ready to add more of her daily creation to her plate. If Sameena didn't praise her mother's cooking, or if she refused seconds, then her mother would be devastated. It wasn't as if Sameena's mother was a bad cook. On the contrary, her meals were restaurant quality, but she needed to hear this every time she served food to her or Sameena's brother and his family.

After the usual two large servings, Sameena forced herself to move to the settee and slumped in front of the TV for an hour or so while her mother quizzed her about her work day. Sameena was not able to give specifics, but she fed her mother with enough information for her to conclude that 'the world was going to the dogs.' This was one of her mother's favourite sayings since her husband hadn't returned from Hajj. Sameena had recently wondered whether her mother might enjoy the company of a dog during the day to keep her company. It struck Sameena that a ravenous dog would be a useful companion to at her meal times - when her mother wasn't looking.

Sometime before the ten o'clock news Sameena kissed her mother goodnight and with her briefcase in hand negotiated the stairs to her bedroom. It was an effort to climb the stairs carrying the weight of her briefcase and her mother's cooking.

Once inside her room, Sameena would change into her PJs and set up her laptop on her dressing table.

Tonight, there was at least an hour's worth of work to go through which entailed writing up reports from today's meetings with clients, researching the law and prepping for tomorrow's meetings. She sat upright, tried not to look at herself for too long in the mirror and focused on her screen.

Ninety minutes later, Sameena had ticked off almost everything from her work to-do list. She would normally find this activity satisfying, but tonight she was feeling uneasy.

First of all, when she looked down, she was sure that she could see a slight bulge appearing over the top of the elasticated waistband on her pyjama bottoms. This eating routine could not continue. She looked at herself in the mirror and decided to give herself a stern talking to.

The heated conversation with herself lasted ten minutes or so and covered gym membership, Slimming World, a very big hungry and homeless dog and the limitations of finding a really good job and a really good-looking partner for life if she was going to continue travelling down this route towards middle-age obesity. Sameena jotted down the following items for her personal to-do list to tackle at the weekend.

1. *LOCAL GYM – research prices*
2. *SLIMMING WORLD in Lichfield – contact*
3. *GET A DOG – broach the subject with Mom*
4. *NO MORE DESSERTS – tell Mom*
5. *BUY SOME SMALLER PLATES – Lichfield Market*
6. *BUY A CORSET AND SOME BIG PANTS – Amazon*

Sameena was also uneasy about the one item from her work list that was still to be ticked off. She had to attempt this now before she crawled under the duvet and turned the light out. In her briefcase were the few sheets of paper that Darren Mitchell had left at the CAB office the other day. He had stormed out and then Willow had left before Sameena had noticed the papers lying on her desk. Sameena had put them in her briefcase for safekeeping and they had remained there since. She felt duty bound to give the documents one last look before trying to track down the madman or the nice girl in order to return them.

Sameena took the papers out of a side pocket in her briefcase, plumped up her pillows and lay at a comfortable angle to study the figures. The more she read and re-read, the more she felt uncomfortable. The accounts literally didn't add up. There was something wrong. Either some pages were missing, the pages were only drafts, or someone had used a faulty calculator or had a very creative mind. Another hour or so later Sameena was still looking at the figures, but her eyes were telling her to get some sleep. She convinced herself that she needed a second opinion on these documents. It was the least she could do for Willow and her so-called friend.

Before she turned her bedside light off, she added one more thing to her to-do list for tomorrow.

7. PHONE BASH

But when she looked at her alarm clock, she realised that the phone call would be later this morning.

After a few hours' sleep and a busy start to her working day at Allcocks Solicitors, Sameena was beginning to flag. She had two difficult appointments with clients and was grabbing a quick tea break before her final meeting of the morning. She had already ticked off several items from today's list and thought that she could manage the phone call to her old friend before the end of her break.

"Bashir Hussain here, Netherstowe Accountants, how may I help you?"

"Hi, Bash, it's me, Sameena Akhtar, here."

"Hi, Sam. That was very formal!"

"Sorry, Bash. It was a bit. I was on automatic pilot. Anyway, are you OK?"

"Yeah, fine thanks. We were talking about you the other night. Are you avoiding us?"

"No, not at all. It's just that it's difficult leaving my mom for too long in the evenings."

"Well, why don't Faz and I come over to your place one night. I'm sure your mom would love to cook for us and we love eating her food."

"That would be great. Is Faz alright? How long has she got left?"

"About ten weeks. Although you wouldn't think it. She's hardly showing."

'Lucky woman!' thought Sameena. "Well, my mom's cooking will fatten her up, even if a baby isn't!"

"That's true. Sam, I've got a conference call in ten minutes, but I can phone you back later, if that's convenient for you."

"Actually, this will only take a second. It's nothing to do with our good friend Mary at Abbeyfields. It's something I got involved with a Citizens' Advice."

"OK. How can I help?"

"Some clients have left me have possession of some financial spreadsheets for an organisation and they don't seem to add up. I wondered...if I scanned them and sent them over to you, could you just give me your opinion? I don't want a report or anything, just your thoughts – between the two of us – you understand."

"Yeah, no problem. I'm free from about 4 o'clock this afternoon, so I can cast my eye over those accounts then."

"That's great. I'll speak to you later."

By 5.40 pm Sameena had given up on Bash. He was clearly tied up with his own stuff at the accountancy firm. She decided that she would leave in the next twenty minutes. She'd brought her trainers with her today so that she could have a gentle walk around Stowe Pool, thus beginning a gradual introduction to her new fitness regime. Sameena was just taking off her high heels when her office phone rang.

"Sameena Akhtar."

"Hi Sam, it's Bash. I've given these documents a good going over and I have to say that something's not right. There are some discrepancies with the figures. It may or may not be anything untoward, because we and your clients might not have the complete picture but, in my opinion, and it is only my opinion as an accountant, I think it warrants further investigation."

"Bash, thank you so much for that."

"Sam, may I ask how you or your clients got hold of these documents?"

"To be honest, Bash, I'm not really sure how they got hold of them or if they were given permission to have copies of them. I can ask them, but I'm not their solicitor; I met them only briefly in my capacity as an adviser. What do you think my advice should be to them?"

"Well, if they found these documents lying about somewhere, I would advise them to do the same, just dump them somewhere and forget about it. But if they have some sort of vested interest in the issue then they should see a solicitor or report it to the police," said Bash.

"It's that serious then?"

"There's a lot of money being siphoned off here. Yeah, it could be."

"Thanks, Bash. I'll try to contact them and discuss it further with them. By the way, are we meeting up with Mary again soon about the Lasting Power of Attorney issue?"

"Good old Mary - Allahumma Barik Laha. Yes, I thought we ought to have another go with her next week. What d'you think?"

"That's fine with me. I'll drop you a text with some of the times I'm free to drop by the care home and meet up with Mary. When we get together, I'll let you know what my mom says about cooking for the three of us. I'm sure she'd love to see you and Faz again."

"OK. Hopefully see you next week. And Sam, keep your distance from this situation. It may be above your pay grade and area of expertise. This could be quite serious."

"Thanks, Bash. I appreciate your concern. Regards to Faz."

Sameena put the phone down and stared at the opposite wall of her office. She had some thinking to do. She had some questions to ask herself and others. She was worried – particularly about Willow. The teenage girl could be getting involved in something that could cause her problems or even worse, put her in danger. Sameena needed to contact Willow and talk to her about her involvement with this Mitchell guy and those documents. But she didn't have any way of contacting her. Her brain started aching.

Sameena put her heels back on. The fitness regime would have to start tomorrow. Right now, all Sameena wanted was comfort food, large quantities of it - and she knew just the woman to provide it.

CHAPTER TWELVE

Daz, Willow - Saturday

Lichfield Station to New Street. A five-minute walk from the flashy new Grand Central to Moor Street Station and then ten minutes to Solihull. Willow wouldn't let him buy her ticket, so he bought two coffees from the stall at Moor Street while they waited for the train.

"Makes a change," he said as they hunched on the bench. "Me bringing you coffee."

Willow took a slurp. "What is this?"

"A hazelnut latte. They said it was very nice."

Willow nodded. "It is. What are you having?"

"Coffee."

The train came and they got on. "Thanks for coming," Daz said.

"I've got your back."

A couple of weeks ago, Daz might have bristled. Today he smiled, although it wasn't the warmest of smiles. He ducked his head to hide inside his hood. By half past ten they were standing outside the red brick station.

"Where to now?"

Daz pulled a crumpled piece of paper out of his pocket and showed her.

"And how do we get there?"

He shrugged. "Ask someone?"

She tutted and brought Google Maps up on her phone. "Look – it's only a twenty-minute walk from here." Holding her phone in front of her, she turned right and led the way down the road.

They soon turned left after the railway bridge, off the busy road of low modern flats, and the hedges and walls got higher and the detached houses bigger and further back from the road. Nobody walked here. The cars were sleek and expensive – BMW, Mercedes, Lexus and Jaguar. Daz thought they stuck out like a couple of dog turds on a wedding cake. He could feel eyes watching him – behind curtains, through windscreens and cameras. He imagined anxious fingers calling the police to come and clean up their streets. With every step he walked more slowly and hunched deeper into his hoodie. "I don't think this is a good idea," he muttered to Willow's back

"Don't be silly," she said without looking up from her phone. "We're nearly there." She threw her shoulders back and lifted her chin higher. This was her world and she didn't feel people looking at you like you were something they'd stepped in. She belonged to the people who did the looking. What was she doing, slumming it with him, and making herself feel better by giving him coffee that didn't cost her anything and stale cake?

He fell further back and was just about to hurry back to the station, when she called out breezily, "Here it is!" and turned around. "What are you doing back there? Come on!"

Because he didn't have the heart to hurt her – 'It would be like kicking Bambi,' he thought – he trudged reluctantly up to where she was peering excitedly through high wrought-iron gates at a house that was supposed to look old, but had probably been built ten years ago. It had bricks, timber and bay windows on the front, trees in pots on either side of a door big enough to drive a car through and a garage big enough to hold three more. A silver BMW Series 7 G12 stood outside. The number plate was RU55 TOP.

Willow rattled the gate. "How do we get in?"

"It's an electronic lock. They have to buzz us in." He looked around and pointed. Set into the wall was a metal grill with a button and a camera. "You have to press that and talk."

"Go on then."

He sighed and thumbed the button. Nothing happened. He shrugged. "Well, that's that," he said. "No one's home. Let's go."

But she stood in his way, reached across him and pressed the button again and again. There was a rattle from the speaker. "Yes?" said a metallic voice.

Willow pushed him and mouthed "Go on" at him. He leaned close to the grill. "Uh, yes, hi – my name is – my name's Daz – Darren Mitchell. It's about Shaun Wilde."

There was a long pause. "What about him?"

Daz didn't really know. He hadn't thought further than getting to this house. In his mind, he burst in like Rambo and choked a confession out of Russell with his hands around his throat. He hadn't considered talking. "He was my, uh – my friend. I want to talk to Anthony Russell about him."

The pause was shorter this time. "Look, I'm sorry for your loss, but I don't have time to talk."

"I saw him just before he died. He said he had to talk to someone – I think it was you."

"It wasn't. If that's all - "

Daz had run out of things to say. He wasn't good with words at the best of times, and this was worse. He looked at Willow helplessly, and she urged him on, giving him two thumbs up and mouthing words of encouragement. He turned back to the grill.

"He knew you were fiddling the accounts," he said.

There was a long silence, and Daz thought Russell had hung up. Then there was a buzz and the gates swung open smoothly and silently. Willow clenched her fist and punched the air in victory. She led the way up the block-paved drive, past the neatly cut laurel hedges to the front door. It opened before they got there.

Daz recognised Russell from his photo with Shaun, only now he wasn't smiling, as he peered round the half-open door. His hair was still black, probably dyed, but expensively cut, his face tanned, evenly from a lamp, and his body looked fit even if he was behind a desk now instead of out on building sites. He was wearing a Dolce and Gabbana polo shirt, Versace jogging bottoms and trainers with a logo that Daz didn't recognise. He had a chunky gold chain round his neck, winking under the towel draped round his shoulders, and there was another just as thick on his wrist. He had gold rings the size of knuckle dusters on his fingers.

He sized them up and seemed to relax. He even smiled, although it didn't touch his eyes.

"You'd better come in," he said. He had a local accent, and not Solihull local. He threw the door wide. "I'm just training. You don't mind talking while I carry on?"

The hall was bigger than Daz's flat, all white walls, tiled floors and chrome. A staircase with a chalk blue carpet swept up to a landing with half a dozen doors opening from it. They were all closed.

He led them through a living room with a TV the size of a cinema screen over a long low fire into a games room with chairs that looked as if they had come from luxury sports cars grouped around another huge black screen. He knew he was gaping like a kid in a toy shop, and he knew that Russell was doing this on purpose, but he couldn't help himself.

And he thought that this wasn't Willow's world either. He pictured her in a house with rooms lined with books, old furniture that smelled of polish and comfy chairs and a TV tucked away quietly in a corner. He supposed her father read newspapers at the table and her mother baked in the kitchen in a frilly apron.

They trailed Russell into the games room with a pool table, a full-size snooker table, air hockey, table football and a pinball machine. Finally, they got to the gym. It was better equipped than the gym Daz used to go to to back when he could afford it. Russell went to the running machine, beeped a few buttons on the panel and set off at a slow jog.

"You don't mind, do you?" he said in a voice that meant he didn't care whether they minded or not. "Now, how can I help you?"

Daz had to raise his voice over the whirr of the machine and the thump of Russell's feet.

"My friend Shaun," he began. Russell tapped the screen on the machine and it bleeped again and the machine got louder as it went faster.

Daz stopped talking. The pounding feet, the drone and bleeping of the machine. He forgot where he was and remembered where he wasn't. He could smell gun oil and diesel fumes, electronic voices crackled distorted in his ears, the roar of the engine drowning out anything that made sense, faces opposite him, framed by the Mk7 helmets, pale underneath their tan, smiling nervously and making jokes he couldn't hear, the tank tracks under his feet making everything shake –

Willow could see him going, like he had that time in the square. He was looking at something, but it wasn't Russell pounding along on his NordicTrack. There were beads of sweat standing out on his forehead. She edged closer to him. "Daz," she whispered in his ear. "It's me – Willow."

She didn't want to touch him – last time she'd done that, he had almost hit her, but she had to bring him back from wherever it was he'd gone to. "I've – I've got your coffee."

Somehow, the words seemed to reach him. His shoulders relaxed and his fists unclenched. He looked round and his eyes came into focus and he saw her. She watched a real spark of affection kindle there. "Thanks," he said.

Then Russell's voice, raised above the rumble of the running machine and the thump of his feet, brought him back completely to the present. "What about Shaun? I really am pressed for time today."

Looks like it, thought Daz. He studied the flickering numbers on the screen, counting kilometres and calories, spotted the Off switch and jabbed it. The machine slowed down with a whine and Russell stumbled and grabbed at the support bar.

"Hey!"

"Sorry, mate, but I need to talk to you about Shaun."

Russell rubbed his towel over his face. "Oh, yeah?" he said. "Well, I think I need to call the police." He slipped his Apple Pro Max from the little Velcro pocket on his arm. Daz had time to think that men who had never been in the army loved gadgets and lots of pockets to put them in.

"And I think I need to show you this."

He put his bag down and took out the Charity Commission letter. He handed it to Russell. He watched Russell closely as he read it and saw his knuckles whiten. "It's just a copy," he warned him. "You can keep it."

Willow didn't recognise the Daz who was in front of her now. He was cold and hard and completely in command of himself and Russell.

Russell shrugged. "This doesn't prove anything," he said.

"It proves you were using Shaun's charity as your own private piggy bank."

"Everything I did was completely above board."

"But it wasn't right. You know it, and Shaun knew it. He was going to speak to you the day he died."

Russell laughed. "Is that what this is about? You think I killed your friend? I'd have had a job – I was out of the country at the time. In the manor house in Normandy that the charity owns, funnily enough. So I couldn't have killed him. Anyway - " he waved the letter. " – this was all just a misunderstanding. We'd already arranged a meeting to sort things out when I got back – you can check with my secretary if you want. I'll give you her number."

Daz looked round. "Do you know how much it costs to kill a man? Twenty thousand pounds. You're rich enough to afford that. You wouldn't even have to get your hands dirty."

Russell's face grew hard. "You'd better have a good lawyer if you say something like that in public," he said frostily, then he took a breath and gathered himself in. "Look, I know you're upset about your friend, but the police have already seen me and they're satisfied Shaun killed himself. They don't know why and neither do I. Perhaps he had troubles in his private life. Who knows? Now I think you'd better leave."

He put a hand on Daz's elbow to guide him to the door. Willow tried to stop him, to push his arm away, cried a warning, "Don't touch him!" but it was too late. Daz grabbed Russell's wrist and twisted his arm up behind his back. He wrapped his arm round Russell's throat and squeezed.

"Daz!" Willow screamed.

Russell, gasping for breath, hooked his hand over Daz's arm and tried to tug it free, each jerk weaker than the last. The two men shuffled round, grunting. Willow started hitting Daz hopelessly on his back, shouting his name over and over again.

And as suddenly as it started, it stopped. It seemed to Willow that it had gone on forever, but Russell was still alive, slumped on the floor, wheezing hoarsely, so it could only have been seconds, and Daz stood over him, dazed, with his arms hanging like a puppet with the strings cut

Painfully, Russell hauled himself to his feet on the weights machine, and slumped onto the bench. He massaged his throat.

"Get him out of here," he choked out, "before I call the cops."

Willow treated Daz like a stray dog that had been kicked too much. She whispered his name gently, and, without touching him or making eye contact, she said, "Come on, come with me," and slowly started backing out of the gym. He followed her like a robot. She wasn't sure he even knew where he was.

The distance from the gym to the front door seemed like miles, and as they shut it on the white tiles and shiny chrome, she expected to hear police sirens screaming down the road. She found the button for the gate, it hummed open and clicked shut behind them. Daz looked round, puzzled.

"What happened?" he asked.

"You nearly killed a man, that's what," she snapped.

CHAPTER THIRTEEN

Willow, Daz - Saturday

"What the hell's wrong with you? You promised me that you would play it cool!" Willow had stopped, hands on her hips.

Daz looked at Willow, but it was a vacant stare.

"This isn't working. I've had enough!" Willow was just about to storm back to the train station when Daz beat her to it and marched off leaving her on her own outside Andrew Russell's gates.

"Daz, wait!" she shouted in vain. When he didn't stop, she started to follow. It didn't escape Willow's notice that this was the second time in just a few days that she was chasing after Daz, while he just ignored her.

Daz's march was quicker than Willow's run. But even if Willow could catch up with him, what would she say to Daz while he was in this sort of mood?

"You're behaving like a lunatic!" or "No more. I can't do this anymore. Forget it." Or "Planet Earth to Daz, are you receiving me?" or "You're on your own now. Over and out!"

Willow accepted that none of these remarks would help Daz as he needed to calm himself down, in his own time. So, Willow slowed down and followed him back to the station at a safe distance.

She remembered an occasion a couple of years ago when her parents followed her for half an hour around the streets of Lichfield. She had been invited to a party of a classmate, a rare event, which meant that she had to go and she had to impress. She'd spent ages in her bedroom getting glammed up, but when she came downstairs she had been bombarded with negative observations from her parents, particularly her dad.

"You're not going out dressed like that!"

"That skirt is too short!"

"Too much make-up!"

If that hadn't been bad enough, there followed a heated discussion on whether she could stay over-night, then what time her dad would pick her up, how many boys were attending the party and what Willow was and was not allowed to consume during the evening.

Willow remembered shouting in tears: "I hate you" and "I'm not going to the party. You've ruined it for me now!" to both of them and storming out of the house.

Her parents followed her. They didn't shout or scream at her, they just followed her. Once Willow's tears had subsided and she had gathered her composure, she slowed down and after twenty minutes or so, she walked back to the house.

There was no dressing down by her parents, no inquest or post mortem. They waited for their daughter to decide what she wanted to say and do next.

When Willow announced that she was going to her bedroom and she would see them in the morning, her mother calmly said, "No you're not, you've got a party to go to. Get changed, I'll drive you there and I'll pick you...no later than 12.30."

Willow smiled when she remembered that night. The party had been terrible, just a few girls moaning about their teachers and arguing about good or bad-looking boys. She rang her mother up at about 11.00 pm and told her she was ready to be picked up.

The next morning, the previous evening's trauma had been wiped from everybody's memory - until now – when a more mature Willow was silently following a childish no-brained hot-head.

Willow continued to walk at a brisk pace some ten metres behind Daz. She had to fight the urge not to shout at the top of her voice "Who's the fucking adult here?" but she contained herself and followed the silent strategy of her mom and dad.

Willow assumed that Daz was heading to the train station. She hadn't paid too much attention to the route on the way to Russell's mansion as Willow had spent most of the journey looking at Google Maps on her phone and listening to Daz moaning and cursing about how privileged some people were, and that even if the cards were stacked against him, he would get justice for Shaun.

Willow accepted that Shaun's death was a serious and sinister matter for Daz and she really did sympathise with him. However, (and Willow would never admit this to Daz) once or twice when he said the name Shaun, Willow's playful mind would transport her back to when she would watch the animated series *Shaun the Sheep* on TV. It took all of her willpower, or her 'willowpower' as her mom named it, to stop herself from smiling about those daft escapades involving Shaun and his woolly mates on Mossy Bottom Farm.

Daz had been pretty worked up even before they had arrived at Russell's house. Looking back on the meeting with Andrew Russell, it was destined to fail. Willow had warned Daz on the journey to stay calm and in control of the situation, but her advice had fallen on deaf ears. As much as she wanted to help Daz, Willow could not save him from himself. He was a ticking time bomb primed to explode at any time. What should she do? Tell him that he would have to carry on fighting for justice without her?

Willow could remember having this very same talk with herself in her bedroom a few days ago. Was this going to be a recurring conversation? No, it had to stop. This partnership had to stop. She would tell him on the train, if he wanted her to sit by him.

They stood on the platform at Solihull Station side-by-side at arms' length. Each stared straight in front of them. To any other prospective passengers on the 3.53 to Moor Street, Willow and Daz looked like two total strangers waiting for the next train.

"I'm sorry," said Daz, still not looking at Willow.

"Did you say something? I couldn't quite hear you," said Willow, turning her head slightly towards Daz.

"I said I'm sorry. I overreacted. I should have taken your advice. Sometimes there's just a red mist …"

"Let's talk about it properly and quietly when we're on the train. OK?"

"OK."

Daz edged a little bit closer to Willow and they exchanged a brief glance and waited for the train. They sat next to each other in a half-empty carriage. Willow waited for Daz to open the discussion. It took him a little while before he turned to Willow.

"I've got issues with my temper. That's one of the reasons I'm divorced …"

"Oh?" said Willow, warily.

"I react too quickly without thinking things through. That's what my wife used to say."

"But if you want my help, here's the deal. First, you need to see someone about that temper of yours and secondly, from now on, you're going to be really nice to me...even if you don't agree with me ... is that clear? If that's a problem for you, when we get back to Lichfield I'll avoid seeing you and there'll be no more free coffee and biscuits from the cafe. Is that understood?" whispered Willow in an authoritative way.

"Yeah. OK," replied Daz sheepishly before continuing, "And you think I'm scary! How old are you, Willow?"

"Just seventeen. My mom thinks that I act like I'm twice that age at times and my dad treats me like I'm seven, most of the time."

"Who do you take after?"

"I'm more like my mother, but I've a stubborn streak like my father. I get on really well with my mom, and my dad's OK, I suppose."

"Are you an only child?"

"Yeah. They're very...protective."

"Because they love you. That's what good parents do. I wish …" Daz paused.

"You wish what?"

"Oh...never mind. Let's just leave the past in the past," said Daz ruefully.

"But we can't do that if we're going to find out about Shaun's death. We may have to do some more digging into the past."

"So does that mean you're still going to help me?"

"Yeah, as long as you don't go mental on me again. No more fisticuffs like at Andrew Russell's house!" replied Willow with a semi-serious expression on her face.

"I'll try not to," mumbled Daz, adopting the role of a naughty school boy having been caught out by a disappointed teacher.

"So, what did you make of our friend Andrew Russell?" asked Willow, changing the topic and the atmosphere.

"He's not someone I would want as a friend!"

"To be honest Daz, he'd probably say the same thing about you!" said Willow, smirking.

"Yeah, I don't see many similarities between us, do you?"

"Not unless you have about a zillion pounds hidden in a bank somewhere. You don't, do you?"

"No, sorry to disappoint. I do have a bank account, but it's empty, not like Russell's."

"A bank account could be the only thing you two have in common. He's clearly in a different league to us. I wonder when Russell last travelled on a train in the cheap seats? The guy is mega-rich...I wonder how much of his wealth is dodgy?"

"Yeah, some of that money is bound to be dirty, but he's also a dirty liar. I didn't believe a word he said about the accounts. I don't trust him, but I'm not sure if he killed Shaun."

"What makes you say that?"

"Just a gut instinct. One minute he was gonna call the police and the next he lets us in and he kinda hints that there may've been a problem. He backed down too quickly," replied Daz.

"That doesn't mean to say that he wasn't somehow involved in Shaun's death."

"No, I suppose you're right."

"Sorry, what did you say?"

"I said you were...could be...right."

Willow cupped her ear towards Daz. "Did you just say I was right about something?"

"Very funny! Russell said something about there being a mix up with the accounts and he needed to sort it out. He could have been on the fiddle. That's how rich people get rich, they take from the poor. Maybe Shaun was going to confront him about the accounts."

"But it could have been a genuine mistake," suggested Willow. "Perhaps Andrew and Shaun were just about to sort it out before accountants or the tax office or...someone else started to examine the figures too closely."

"Yeah. You could be right."

"But to be honest, Daz, neither of us know the first thing about finances. You sell *The Big Issue* and I earn a few quid a week in a café and sponge off my parents. We're not the right people to judge. We need help from someone who knows what they're talking about."

"Who do you suggest...your dad?"

"No way...I'm not involving my folks in this. They would freak out if they knew what I was doing. They think I'm weird anyway, but if I told them that I was helping a middle-aged, ex-serviceman who has issues with his temper and was recently in trouble with the police, they'd probably send me to a nunnery!"

"God help the nuns! They'd all have dyed hair within a week!" Daz smiled at Willow. "So, what do we do? Who can help us?"

"How about going back to Sameena at the CAB?"

"Oh God! No! I'm not sure I could face her again. The last meeting wasn't good."

"And why was that I wonder?"

"OK, OK. I might have lost my rag."

"What do you mean 'might'? You stormed out. Sameena was perfectly OK with me. She's nice. She may know someone who could take a look at the accounts. That's if we're both pleasant with her and behave ourselves."

"God. You're a real pain in the arse, you know that, right?" observed Daz with a glint in his eye.

"I do. But just now, I'm the only person who's queuing up to help you. So, what do you say, play nice or not at all? That's the deal!"

"OK. You win. Deal. I'll be the perfect gentleman."

"I doubt that very much. According to my mom, there's no such thing as perfect men - just perfect women."

CHAPTER FOURTEEN

Sam, Willow, Daz - Monday

'That was excruciating, embarrassing and humiliating. I'm not doing that again, even if it only took twenty minutes!' Sameena thought, as she adjusted her clothing and left the Guild Hall in Lichfield.

She kept her eyes on the pavement directly in front of her to hide her shame as she walked briskly towards the CAB offices. She just hoped that no-one else had seen her at the Slimming World Monday lunch-time session. As if it wasn't bad enough standing on the scales in front of everyone else, stripped down to her tee-shirt and leggings, but then to be told that she had put on two pounds since last week was too much, literally. What was worse still, last week was her first week as a member at Slimming World and she had put on weight in those first seven days! Then, to top it all, the woman behind her in the queue was one of her clients and heard every word of Sameena's weighty news.

Sameena decided that she would have to speak to her mother tonight. No more seconds from her mom and she would have to serve herself half the quantity of her firsts. She would go jogging each night to avoid sitting on the settee and eating sweet stuff with her mother. Maybe she could buy an exercise bike and install it in her bedroom. It would be a great way to escape from her mother and her tempting food. She was not going to join a gym though, that would be another embarrassment. Her body bits bouncing up and down on the gym equipment wearing next to nothing. No way. Gymnasiums were for fit, thin posers who looked good already and didn't really need to exercise. She was not joining any more clubs. Going to Monday lunchtime Fat Club was bad enough.

'Was this how it was going to be from now on? A constant battle with her weight? A continuous struggle to look and feel good about herself? It was time to take action, she thought to herself.

Sameena's first action, as she walked along the street, was to fish in her briefcase for her post-weigh-in treat. Ironically, she found the chocolate bar caught up in between the pages of her Slimming World Members' book. Sameena took it out of her briefcase and as she passed a street-musician giving a terrible rendition of an Ed Sheeran song, she threw it in his flat cap that was positioned in front of him on the pavement.

'Step one,' she thought as she made her way to the offices, already feeling regretful and hungry.

"Hello, Thomas," she said as she opened the main door into the small foyer and waiting room in the Citizens' Advice offices.

"Oh, hi Sam, good to see you. You're in room 4 today. I'll let you settle in and then I'll sort you out a mug of tea and a couple of your favourite biscuits."

"Thanks, Thomas, that's kind of you. I'd love a drink...and some biscuits."

Sameena made her way to room 4 and took out her laptop and her notepad. She pretended that she had not seen the Slimming World book staring up at her from her briefcase. She logged on to the CAB Advisors' site and looked at her list of appointments for the afternoon.

Thomas knocked and walked in carrying a mug of tea and a plate of four Bourbons.

"Wow, thanks, Thomas. That will keep me going. Great."

"No problem, Sam. Your first appointment is here. Are you ready or do you need a couple of minutes?" asked Thomas.

"Yes, just two minutes, please, then I'll be ready."

"OK. Have a good afternoon."

"Thanks," replied Sameena as Thomas closed the door behind him.

Sameena scanned the list of appointments and noticed a familiar name at the end of the list. *Willow Cartwright (requested a follow-up with Sameena Akhtar).* Sameena was intrigued. It had been a week since she had seen or heard from Willow, but now she wanted to see her again. That was good, because Sameena also wanted to see Willow. She could hear Thomas talking to someone as he neared her office door and she realised that her busy afternoon schedule was about to begin. She took a last swig of tea and realised there was only one Bourbon left on the plate. She grabbed it and shoved it in her pocket for later. The diet would have to start tomorrow.

By 4.30, Sameena had seen four very different people with four very different issues. Each appointment was satisfyingly constructive where she could offer sound, practical advice. She had enjoyed the afternoon...so far, but now it was time for Willow. Would she be on her own this time?

There was a knock on the door.

"Sam, your 4.30 appointment is here. Ms Cartwright," Thomas said and then lowered his voice: "She's brought that bloke with her who got a bit weird last time, do you want me to hang about, just in case?"

"Thanks, Thomas, I think I'll be OK. Show them in."

"Hi," said Willow, she smiled at Sameena and inched herself into the room while gently pulling Daz with her. They both looked awkward as they took their seats on the opposite side of the desk to Sameena.

"It's good to see you both again. What can I help you with today, Ms. Cartwright...is it about the same issue that you talked about last time?"

"Yes, it is, but please, call me Willow, and you remember Daz...Darren Mitchell?"

"I do. We didn't have long together last time, but you made quite an impression."

"Yeah, Sorry about that, Miss Akhtar...I was out of order...shouldn't have walked out..." Daz looked at Sameena and then at Willow.

Willow gave a faint smile and nod towards Daz. For a brief moment she felt like a parent who had won a small battle with a bad-mannered child.

"Why don't you both call me Sam? Now, what's happened since the last time I saw you?"

Willow, with occasional snippets of commentary from Daz, proceeded to tell Sam about their own on-going investigations and adventures involving Andrew Russell.

Sameena sat and listened to this unlikely pair's story about taking on this powerful, clearly rich, possibly dodgy, character. Sameena didn't know what to make of it all. There were times when she wanted to swear out loud and other times when she wanted to laugh. Was this just a tale from a drama princess and her henchman? Was this merely the daft misadventures of a couple of cartoon characters? Perhaps if they had brought a large shaggy dog into the office with them today, Sameena would have thought she had been magically transported into an old episode of *Scooby-Doo.* But Willow and Daz seemed deadly serious, so Sameena sat there, listened and made a few notes.

When the story was told, Sameena felt the need to say something supportive and wise...but she was struggling. This was not what she was used to dealing with. Family issues...that was her specialist subject...not the dirty dealings of the underworld.

"Look, before I give you some ad...observations and thoughts...can I just say this," said Sameena alternating her gaze between the two of them. "I know you think that Mr Russell is probably not directly responsible for the death of Shaun Wilde, but he's not completely in the clear. When you came to the CAB offices last time you left some documents on my desk. I hope you don't mind...but I had a friend of mine, who has experience in finance, take a careful look at them. They do show some irregularities - serious irregularities. The sort that could end up with someone going to jail. Russell is a powerful guy. It's possible he has connections to some dubious people. This is not something that you two should get involved with. Please...for your own safety, drop this now."

"I can't! Shaun was my friend. One of my only friends. I can't just drop this. I need justice for him."

"Then at least distance yourself from Willow. It's not fair to drag a teenage girl into this...mess. Surely you can see that? You are older, service-trained. Willow is..."

"Hold on, Sam. Don't treat me like I'm a kid. Yeah, I'm not eighteen, but that doesn't mean that I haven't got a say in what I do and what I don't do. I've decided to help Daz. That's my own free will. You don't need to be an adult to have freedom of choice. I'm not walking away from this, yet. Maybe if it gets really heavy or scary, I might, but so far I'm OK and that's that!" Willow said.

"You know, you're really scary at times," said Daz to Willow with a smile on his face.

Willow and Sameena both tried to suppress slight smiles.

There was a knock and Thomas popped his head round the door, "Everything OK? Just to let you know that we're closing the offices in five minutes."

"Thanks, Thomas. We're almost finished."

"Sam, I'm sorry, I shouldn't have raised my voice. I'm not usually the one with the temper, it's normally Daz that blows his top."

"Harsh, but fair," admitted Daz.

"It's just that I hate people treating me like a kid and I hate injustice and I want to see this through. So, what do we do now, Sam?"

"You have to take this to the police. There is nothing else you can do. You have to let them deal with it."

"But they won't listen to me or Daz."

Thomas knocked the door and explained that they would have to end the session and, if necessary, a follow-up appointment would have to be made.

"I'll walk out with you," Sameena said to Willow and Daz.

Outside the offices, Willow and Daz looked despondent.

"Have either of you got anywhere to go right now?" asked Sameena.

Both Willow and Daz shook their heads.

"Let's walk into Lichfield, go to a café and talk some more? Is that OK with you two?" asked Sameena.

"I'll just text my mom and tell her I'm seeing a friend. She'll be cool with that."

"Do you know what," admitted Sameena, "I'll phone my mom and say the same thing. I hope she'll be cool with that!"

The three of them laughed and made their way to *the Faro Lounge.*

"Just to be clear, I'm paying. As long as you don't order five courses each," said Sameena.

"Suits me fine. Thanks," said Daz, who was gradually warming to Sameena.

"I don't think I could eat five courses," said Willow.

"You're really thin, Willow. I wish I had a figure like yours," said Sameena.

"My mom thinks I don't eat enough."

"Yeah, I've got an eating issue as well," admitted Daz, "I can't afford to eat!"

They laughed again.

"Well, I ought to own up to my problem with food, I can't stop eating," admitted a smiling Sameena.

After Sameena returned from the counter having ordered and paid for the food and drink, Willow revisited the conversation they were having before they left the CAB offices.

"Daz and I were just chatting about going to the police. We'd just get fobbed off. They won't take us seriously."

"Yeah, I agree. I've got a bit of previous at the station. There's a couple of plain-clothed detectives that rubbed me up the wrong way. And they won't listen to Willow. Which is a pity, as she talks more sense than most adults I know."

Willow blushed slightly and basked in the compliment for a second.

Sameena paused for thought. Then she looked directly at Daz. "If you're determined to continue with this then you will have to both go to the police station. But you'll have to take the lead and stay calm, keep your emotions in check."

"We tried that at Andrew Russell's place and it lasted about thirty seconds," replied Willow.

"Yeah...gone in thirty seconds," muttered Daz.

"This is no joking matter, Daz," said Willow. "We won't get anywhere if you can't control your temper. You need to play the game, their game. These people won't listen to you if you just shout or threaten them."

"But they press my buttons. It's difficult …" said Daz.

"So, you need to avoid this happening again. Daz, would you be up for some help? I might know someone who can give you some tips and tricks on how to control your temper. It could help if you are going to see this through. And it may benefit you in the long term. What do you think?" asked Sameena.

"It's not a shrink, is it?" said Daz, trying to stay calm.

"No, it's not a shrink. I assure you."

"Well...I suppose it can't hurt, can it?"

"But even if Daz can keep it together, they still won't listen to us. We don't know enough about finances. They won't take us seriously," interjected Willow.

"But they'll listen to me as your legal aid. You two can just prompt me with some of the details."

"That would be brilliant, but we don't have any money to pay you as a solicitor. I bet you charge a fortune," said Willow.

"And I don't have any money for a shrink," added Daz.

"She's not a shrink, and her help would be free. As for the rest...well...let me worry about that," replied Sameena.

CHAPTER FIFTEEN

Daz, Willow, Sam, Krys - Wednesday

Back in the same room, across the same table from the same faces, but at least the woman – Detective Sergeant Ken-something – had bothered to get changed. She was dressed in monochrome, black jacket and trousers with a belt with a gunmetal buckle and a charcoal t-shirt with a high neck. It made her face look paler than Daz remembered.

The DI, Tony Potter, didn't look that good. His skin looked grey, the bags under his eyes darker and his eyes redder. The beard wasn't neat now and the hair wasn't artfully ruffled, it was just a mess. The jacket was creased, the neck of his shirt was dirty and the tie askew. Daz recognised the signs of a man who had slept on a sofa. He slapped the same buff folder down on the cheap table again, but Daz was ready for it this time, and didn't flinch. He noticed, impressed, that Sam didn't either. Willow jumped back in her chair. Well done, Daz thought grimly, you can scare a seventeen-year-old girl.

"You again," snarled Potter. He glanced at the two women. "And this time you've brought reinforcements. What's the matter? Didn't think you could beat a police officer up on your own?"

Sameena took out a pad of her own and flipped it open with a snap. She could play that game too. She poised her Mont Blanc PIX ballpoint over the first blank page. It wasn't the most expensive Mont Blanc pen, but it was enough to intimidate, especially when combined with her Bottega business suit. It had been a bit of a squeeze getting into something she'd bought on a whim two years ago when her Dad was still alive and she thought she was going to be a high-flying lawyer, but Daz had filled her in on DI Tony Potter. She knew the type.

"For the record, I am Sameena Akhtar, representing my client, Mr. Mitchell. And you are?"

Potter sat back in his chair taken by surprise. He tugged at his tie and smoothed his hair. Daz could have cheered as he gave his name, but then he recovered himself and nodded at Willow. "And who's this then? His business manager?"

"This is my associate, Willow Cartwright."

"Willow?" sneered Potter.

"Yes. My father is John Cartwright of Cartwright, Bishop and Smith, the solicitors on Dam Street."

That rocked Potter back again, and Daz caught the Detective Sergeant hiding a smile. "Perhaps if we can get on?" she said. "I am Detective Sergeant Kendrick. How can we help you?"

"My client came to you - " Sameena flicked through her notes. " – a week ago and told you that he believed Mr. Shaun Wilde, the director of a local charity , had not committed suicide, but had, in fact, been murdered."

"Oh, yeah, that was when Mr. Mitchell assaulted a police officer," said Potter.

"And when he was held overnight in the cells, and interviewed under caution as a vulnerable person without an appropriate adult being present and released without charge. But that's not why we are here."

"Vulnerable person? Do me a favour." Potter's face was fixed in a permanent sneer.

"Mr. Mitchell is registered homeless and as a PTSD sufferer is protected under the 2010 Equality Act. I'm sure that your actions were an oversight rather than a deliberate attempt to exploit my client in a vulnerable condition, having just learned that his close friend had been killed. Now - " she folded her hands in front of her. " – do you want to proceed or shall we discuss Mr. Mitchell's detention?"

Potter sat back in his chair and folded his arms and crossed his legs. Daz noticed his smart brown brogues were now scuffed and dull. Potter saw him looking, angrily flicked an imaginary speck of dust from his trousers and glared. "Sergeant Kendrick?" he grunted.

Krystyna slid the buff folder in front of her. She glanced over her notes and then looked Daz in the eye. "At our last meeting you told me Mr. Wilde seemed 'sad' and he said 'comrades are supposed to help each other.' Is that right?" Daz nodded. "Anything you want to add to your previous statement."

Sameena opened her briefcase. "Since that interview, my client has come into possession of certain documents which throw Mr. Wilde's death into a different light." She placed the Charity Commission letter and the accounts in a neat pile in front of her.

Potter sat forward. "What documents?"

Sameena pushed them across the table. "We have had them analysed and there appear to be discrepancies which warrant further investigation."

"What discrepancies?" While Potter raised his voice and asked questions, Krystyna slid the documents in front of her and started to read.

"Where did you get them?" By now, Potter was half out of his chair and shouting. "If you've interfered in a police investigation - "

Daz could feel the anger boiling up inside him, and he shifted in his chair, ready to get to his feet and shout back, or worse. Sameena's cool voice cut through the roaring in his ears. "Detective Inspector, it was made clear to my client at the time of his release that there was no investigation. We are simply providing you with evidence that further investigation may be needed. And this time, it is more than Mr. Wilde appearing to be 'sad'." The last word dripped with sarcasm.

Krystyna leaned over and whispered in Potter's ear. He pulled a face and nodded. "As it happens, Ms. Akhtar, we have been contacted by the Charity Commission, in connection with Mr. Wilde's death. We will be pursuing further investigations, and these documents which you have been so good as to provide us with will be passed on to a forensic accountant." She glanced at Potter, but he was sitting back in his chair, sulking. "I understand Mr. Mitchell's concerns about the death of his friend, and I want to assure him that we are doing everything we can to get to the bottom of what happened."

She looked directly at Daz and smiled. The smile caught him off-guard. "Thanks," he mumbled. "That's all I want."

Willow patted him reassuringly on the arm. "Well done," she whispered.

Daz felt his neck flush red and looked at his feet.

Potter's lip curled and he stood up with a jerk, the chair screeching backwards. He gathered up the buff file from in front of Krys. "Well, this has all been lovely," he muttered, "but I think we're done here." He stood by the door. "Sergeant," he said pointedly.

Krys got to her feet with a sigh and exchanged a glance with Sam that spoke volumes. Potter waited for her to open the door and then barged out in front of her.

"What an arsehole," said Daz, as the door clicked shut.

Sam gathered her papers together and stood up. "Don't worry about her," she said. "I think she can handle him alright."

Potter shoved Krys into the nearest empty interview room. "Do you mind telling me what the fuck you were doing in there?" he snarled.

Krys met his eye. "Saving us from a lawsuit, sir," she said coolly. "That solicitor could have made things very difficult for us."

"We're the police, Kendrick. We don't get pushed around by some homeless guy who's lawyered up."

"But that homeless guy was right, sir – from the beginning. He said there was something wrong with Wilde's death, and instead of listening to him, we locked him up."

"If we listened to every druggie who walked into the station claiming he'd seen a murder we'd never get any work done. But that's not the point – we stick together, right? We never take sides against our own!"

"I wasn't taking sides, sir - "

Potter cut her off angrily. "'I understand Mr. Mitchell's concerns'," he mimicked in a mincing voice. "'I assure you we are doing everything we can.' You implied to that solicitor that I hadn't done anything."

"But we hadn't," Kendrick insisted. "Until we got the call from the Charity Commission, we had this down as a suicide. We didn't even log what that Mitchell said."

"Because it was the ramblings of a dosser, who I might remind you, had just attacked one of our own." He took a step closer to her, a step too close, and she could smell the staleness of him covered with too much deodorant and the stink of old tobacco smoke and the tang of alcohol on his breath. She could see the broken veins on his cheek and his nose, the yellowing of his eyeballs. She held her breath and held her gaze steady.

"I didn't want you here, Kendrick, I didn't want you on my team, but I was told I had to – it's all about the quotas, Krystyna, and the most important quota is our clear-up rate. Got it? We do what we have to do to satisfy the Charity Commission and that Paki lawyer and we put this case to bed. Is that clear?"

He carried on standing too close for a bit too much longer, breathing heavily in her face, his skin flushed with anger, and then spun on his heel, but only got as far as the door before he turned and came back. This time he got even closer. Parts of him were touching parts of her. It took every ounce of her self-control not to step back or break eye contact. She wanted to slap him, and scream, and knee him in the balls, and run, and cry and call him every name she could think of in English and Polish.

"You know what will happen if you don't get with the programme, Kendricks? One day you'll call for help, you'll press the emergency button on your radio, and nobody's going to turn up and you're going to get your head kicked in in the street. Got it?"

He stayed where he was and she thought for a moment he was going to lay a hand on her. She shifted her stance so she could get a good swing in, but then he suddenly seemed to deflate and when he left the room he looked pathetic, shoulders slumped and his head dropped. He didn't look back.

Krystyna breathed out and sat down. When her hands had stopped shaking, she reached into the pocket of her jacket and took out her mobile phone. She laid it on the table in front of her, pressed the red stop icon on the voice recorder and slid her finger over the screen to rewind. Potter's voice sounded tinny coming out of the phone's little speaker.

"...want you here, Kendrick, I didn't want you on my team, but I was told I had to – it's all about the quotas, Krystyna...have to do to satisfy the Charity Commission and that Paki lawyer...you'll call for help, you'll press the emergency button on your radio, and nobody's going to turn up and you're going to get your head kicked in in the street."

She backed the whole recording up to the Cloud and when she got up, her legs were steady and her hands weren't shaking. She checked herself in the one-way mirror. She looked pale, but she always did – thanks to her Polish heritage, along with those piercing pale blue eyes, the high, sharp cheekbones. She didn't look like she'd just been harassed and sexually assaulted by a racist senior officer, and no one needed to know – until the time was right.

In the meantime, there was a job to do, a suspicious death to investigate, not just another case to close.

She tugged her jacket straight and stepped out into the corridor and the busy hum of the police station.

Outside, on the pavement, Daz was almost dancing. "Did you see the look on his face? He looked like someone had pissed in his glass and told him it was lemonade!" He caught Willow and Sam looking at him, and the little old lady walking by. "Sorry," he muttered, "but you got to admit," he lowered his voice and glanced around, "it was fucking great!"

Sameena pulled a face. "He needed taking down a peg or two, but I don't think we've made the Detective Sergeant's job any easier."

"But they're going to reopen the investigation, right?" said Willow.

"They never closed it. They just didn't do anything about it. Because of the papers we've given them, and because the Charity Commission is asking around, they'll have to do something. Whether it's enough to satisfy you..." She shrugged.

Daz came down from his high like a shot. He'd felt like this before, only it had been drugs back then. One moment you're up, the next you're crashing and the real world comes rushing back in. "Wait a minute – you mean they still might not investigate Shaun's murder?"

"I know this is hard, Mr. Mitchell – Daz, but there is still no proof that he was murdered. Yes, we've shown that Andrew Russell was exploiting the charity, but that just goes to show Mr. Wilde's state of mind. He saw his life's work ruined and killed himself."

"No!" Daz shouted. "He was murdered! I know it."

"Daz..." pleaded Willow.

Sameena pressed her lips together. "Look, I need something sweet to eat. I'm going back to *the Faro*. If you want to come with me, and you promise to control yourself, you can, but I'll pay and I'll explain it to you."

She deliberately turned on her back and marched back towards the centre of town and after a moment they trailed along meekly behind her.

CHAPTER SIXTEEN

Daz - Thursday

Daz was up and raring to go before seven o'clock. He had some breakfast – courtesy of Sameena. She'd seen him in *the Faro Lounge*, getting the drinks – hunting through his pockets for enough money to buy two cokes and a small black coffee. It cost a lot more than McDonalds or Greggs, but he was too proud to show it. He'd just scraped up enough money by finding a pound coin in the lining of his jacket.

When they left, she said she just had to pop next door to B & M to get something. Five minutes later she came out with a plastic bag and handed it to Daz. You can't be *Magnum PI* without breakfast, she told him. She had been clever – there was just a loaf of bread and a litre of milk in the bag. If it had been bacon and eggs, tea and sugar, he would have said no. As it was, he took it and mumbled thanks without meeting her eyes.

There was marge and mixed fruit jam in the fridge and teabags in the cupboard, so he set off with a warm, full stomach. But before he got to play at being *Magnum*, he had to earn a living, so he needed to go and pick up some copies of the latest edition of *The Big Issue* from the local co-ordinator. She wouldn't be suspicious he had missed a couple of days – after all, homeless drug addicts were notoriously unreliable. Just so long as word hadn't got back to her that he'd been in and out of the police station.

He was locking his door when he heard one of the others on his landing open. He knew his next-door neighbour was an old man in his eighties with no family because he sometimes took his rubbish down for him, but this was at the far end. He turned and saw an olive-skinned man dressed in shabby clothes that had been in fashion two years ago. With a start, Daz realised that when the man looked at him, he could have thought the same thing.

Over the man's shoulder, in the narrow hall, Daz thought he saw someone else, but the door was quickly shut. The man watched Daz with the same kind of eyes that a stray dog has, ready to run from a kick or sniff cautiously at an offered hand.

Daz nodded and smiled. "Alright?" he said, and the man nodded back. Daz pointed at himself. "Daz."

Understanding lit the man's eyes. "Amir," he said.

"Haven't seen you before," said Daz. "Been here long?"

Amir nodded again and said yes, but he clearly didn't understand the question.

"Where you from?"

"Iraq," muttered Amir and he flicked his hood up over his head and scuttled down the stairs.

Daz knew the flat had been empty a fortnight ago, because he and the old man had talked about how terrible it was that a place to live should be empty when so many people were homeless, so he must have moved in since Shaun died.

Daz followed him down the stairwell that smelled of disinfectant and piss and arrived at the bottom in time to see a battered white Transit van pull up. The back doors banged open and it barely stopped long enough for Amir to scramble inside. Daz could see other men huddled on wooden benches pulling Amir in and shutting the doors. The van rattled off in a belch of diesel and the fart of a leaky exhaust. Something made Daz hurry to the curb and try to read the number plate before in turned the corner. Was it VF04 FXP? He repeated it to himself until he had got his phone out and clicked it in.

As he headed to the coordinator's he caught himself smiling. Perhaps Sameena was right – he was beginning to see things that were a bit sus everywhere.

By 8.15 he was at his usual spot. A man in a rumpled suit who went into the nearby solicitors – Cartwright, Thomson and Gray – gave him a hard stare, but his usual customers were pleased to see him and asked him where he'd been. He didn't want to tell them the whole, complicated story so he just said he'd been sick and to his embarrassment, most of them gave him some extra money. "Keep the change," they said, and he felt awful, mumbling thanks.

He sold out of his supply early and bought himself a coffee before Willow came out with a free one for him. He didn't want to see her today, didn't want any advice or kindness today. He wanted to take the day by the scruff of the neck and give it a good shaking. With the spare change he had, he bought himself a large cappuccino and headed for the cathedral.

This was the direction that Shaun had been heading when Daz had seen him last – marching like a soldier with his back straight, shoulders back, swinging his arms and marching towards his death.

He hadn't been in a church since his army days, compulsory attendance for Queen and Country, and this one wasn't an army chapel. Two sharp spires stabbed up at the sky, the soft brown stone turning black against the clouds, and in little carved niches all over the front stood statues, angels with wings and saints and prophets holding books and scrolls and kings looking noble, all staring at him from under heavy brows, daring him to enter. There was a great, dark double door in the middle and two smaller ones at the side. The one on the left stood open and one or two people were drifting in and out.

Self-consciously he slid his hood off his head and slipped inside. Straightaway a white-haired lady in a lavender two-piece stepped up to him, holding a leaflet. "Have you been here before?" she asked.

He shook his head and said, "No."

She pressed the leaflet into his hand. "There's lots of information in here, and there are volunteers who will answer any questions. We all wear one of these." She waved her lanyard proudly.

"Thanks," he mumbled, and pressed on.

He didn't know where he was going, but he soon found out. There was an area in the nave where the chairs had been pushed back and it was shut off by yellow tape. Inside the floor was cleaner, getting almost white the closer it got to the middle. Someone had scrubbed really hard here. This was the place then. This was where Shaun had died.

Daz sat down, bowed his head and closed his eyes. He didn't believe in God, and he wasn't praying, but he wanted to say something to someone. His lips moved as he tried to find the words, but they didn't come easily – grief and loss and anger and guilt were all mixed up together.

The chair next to him creaked and he came out from inside his head and looked round. A big man in a brown cardigan was sitting next to him. He had a blue lanyard around his neck like the woman at the door. He nodded his head at the clean patch beyond the tape.

"Terrible business," he said. "Did you know him?"

Daz shook his head and felt more guilty. "No – I – no, I read about it." He pulled himself together. What was he supposed to be doing today? Finding out about Shaun's last day, not feeling sorry for himself. "Were you here when it happened?"

The man puffed himself up. "No," he said, "but I heard all about it. Terrible carry-on, there's been. Nobody knows how he got up there." He looked up and Daz followed his eyes.

Underneath windows that were shaped like clover leaves there was a run of arches that reminded Daz of decorations on a wedding cake. "What is it?" he asked.

"That's the triforium," the man said, and his voice started to sound like a teacher explaining something to a bored and slow class of children. "It's just a decoration really – nobody knows what they're for. Some people think that in early Christian churches they were reserved for women. We just store rubbish up there, although the one on the north side now has thirteen stops from the new organ."

"Have you been up there? What's it like?"

The man patted his stomach, which pushed against the leather buttons of his cardigan. "Not recently," he chuckled. "You balance along planks and you've got to put on a harness and clip yourself onto a wire. One wrong step and you'd be over the edge - " His eyes came back down to the stone floor. " – like this poor chap."

"You think it was an accident, then?"

"Of course. If you were going to kill yourself, you'd take tablets, wouldn't you? There's a door over there - " This time he pointed with his head to a dark corner of the nave. " – that is supposed to be kept locked. I expect he thought he was going to climb up the tower, missed his step, and Bob's your uncle."

"Isn't there any CCTV?"

The man shook his head. "It would cost an arm and a leg to cover everywhere in here. Anyway, doesn't seem right, does it – spying in the Lord's house?"

"I suppose not," said Daz. One last try. "Was he alone? Did he talk to anyone?"

"You don't bring company if you're going to kill yourself, do you?" the man chuckled, and his cardigan shook, and then, abruptly, he stopped and he stared hard at Daz. "You're asking a lot of questions. Are you sure you didn't know him?"

Daz stood up and said that he was just interested and he thanked the man for his time. He walked around the whole cathedral before he was sure that he couldn't feel the man's eyes on him, and then he made his way to the little door the man had nodded at. He looked around, and tried the handle. It was locked. He drifted away to the shop and bought a postcard of the nave.

Outside, he sat on a bench and glowered at the cathedral as if it had killed Shaun.

Of course, the man was wrong – and right. Shaun wasn't trying to get up the tower because he wasn't interested in old churches. And he wasn't trying to kill himself. If you were going to jump, you'd go off something high, to make sure, not a short drop like the one from the 'trifor' thing, where you might just end up with a few broken bones or paralysed or brain damaged, if you were really unlucky. Or you'd jump in front of a train, or off a motorway bridge in front of a lorry. God knows, Daz had thought about doing it himself. It was the way a soldier would go, fast and certain and looking death in the eye, not quietly falling asleep with pills and booze.

Shaun wasn't like that. He was a fighter, not a quitter. Daz beat his thighs, got to his feet and howled, a wordless cry of anger and pain. A woman going past with a little girl wrapped her arm around the child and scurried on, casting a worried glance over her shoulder. An elderly couple going into the cathedral stared over at him, drew closer together and ducked inside. A moment later the woman with the blue lanyard thing came out of the door of the cathedral and watched him with her walkie talkie in her hand.

Daz didn't know what to do next, but he knew didn't want to go back to Sameena with nothing. There had to be something – if only the cathedral had CCTV...

CCTV! Even if the cathedral didn't, there were plenty of shops and offices that did, and Shaun would have walked past them and if someone was with him, or following him, it would be recorded. Daz would retrace Shaun's last footsteps and see if he could spot any cameras.

There was a café in the grounds of the cathedral. Daz climbed the steps and went in. He ordered a cup of coffee and looked around. High up on the wall above the counter, he saw the red eye of a camera winking at him. In his darkest days, he hadn't been above a bit of shoplifting to support his habit, and he had developed a sixth sense for CCTV.

He finished his coffee and set off down Dam Street, turning his head as he went. Old houses converted into offices and shops, all wanting to protect what they had – cameras inside and out, warning stickers on the windows and signs on the walls. Each one had filmed Shaun taking his last walk to the cathedral, and anyone who was with him, or following him.

He got to the bank on the corner of the market square. They would have cameras. He looked back up Dam Street. And there was that snooty solicitors – Cartwright, Bishop and Smith – one of them always gave him a look before he went in. Bet they had cameras too.

Only question now was – how to get hold of the film?

CHAPTER SEVENTEEN

Sam, Mary - Thursday

All care institutions have a particular smell, Sameena thought, as she went through the automatic doors into Abbeyfield Residential and Care Home. Some of the bad ones she'd been in just stank of urine and faeces, overlaid with a whiff of boiled vegetables and stale frying. This place was expensive so instead of cooking smells, fragranced cleaning products hid the stink of bodily functions. They were still there though, just hidden by money.

She signed in and went to Mary's room. Bashir was already there.

Sam had known him since they were six at Leigh Road Infants School. They both had parents who expected them to achieve – ophthalmologist, dentist, pharmacist, lawyer, accountant. Sam and Bash had gone for the last two, and supported, and commiserated with each other as they were pushed on and on. For a while it looked as though they might become an item, but somehow it had never happened, and then Sam's father had gone missing and Bash's parents had found Farzana for him and they seemed very happy together. And now Faz was expecting, and Sam was living at home with her mother.

Bash was laughing at something Mary had said. She patted his arm. "It's true," she said.

"I'm sure it is, Mary."

"You don't believe me," she said, reprovingly, and then looked up and saw Sam at the door. "Ah, Sam! Come in. Bash has just called me a liar!"

Sameena squared her shoulders, pasted on a grin and went in.

Bashir threw his arms up. "Help me out here, Sam. Mary has just told me that she invented Super Mario!"

Mary tutted. "Don't you believe him, Sameena. I didn't say that at all. I simply said I was studying Zen Buddhism in a monastery in Japan in 1980 when I met a man who was trying to develop a computer game for the Americans, and I told him to make it a love story and make it funny, like *Popeye and Olive Oyl.* The Americans are suckers for funny love stories."

Sameena sat down and looked squarely at Mary. "Now look, Mary," she said seriously, "Bashir and I are here because you don't want your children to get control of your finances. You say you are of sound mind and body - "

"Not so much of the body," Mary cackled, "but what can you expect when you're ninety-five years old?" She tapped her liver-spotted forehead with a finger distorted by arthritis. "Nothing wrong up here though!"

" – but it doesn't help our case," Sam pressed on, "if we have to go before the Office of the Public Guardian and you are making fanciful claims."

"Very sorry." Mary folded her hands in her lap, lowered her eyes and looked contrite, but Sam knew it meant nothing at all. Next minute she'd probably be claiming she had been there when Nelson Mandela took his long walk to freedom. "What do you want me to do?"

"First of all, let's see where you stand financially. If we can prove that you have made sensible investments with your money and you're not vulnerable to exploitation, then we have quite a strong position."

The next hour was spent talking about money and disappointing children. Mary clearly had enough of one and too much of the other. Whether her money came from inventing the bar code as she claimed, or something else, didn't matter – she was clearly a very wealthy woman. So long as it was invested wisely and no-one unsavoury could get their hands on it, Sam and Bash, and hopefully the OPG, were satisfied.

There were interruptions for weak tea, which Sam didn't like, and sweet cake, which she did. By the time they'd finished, she was feeling guilty about the cake and bossing Mary about and possibly helping a crazy woman deny her children their heritage. She also felt she was enjoying the time she had spent with Bashir a little too much.

After they'd said goodbye to Mary with a promise that they'd be back soon, and the unfortunate "You're such a lovely couple" comment ringing in her ears, she just wanted to hurry back to her office and do a lot of boring paperwork, but Bash stopped her at the door.

"Can we talk?"

"What about?" Her unnecessary abruptness surprised her.

He took her by the arm and led her into the foyer where armchairs were laid out in groups for families to sit and gather strength before they visited an aged relative or to recover afterwards. On a counter was a coffee machine that could give any variety of coffees and hot chocolate, and, under a glass cover, a selection of cakes.

Sameena took a cake and sat down. She knew she shouldn't, but it gave her something to do with her hands, and as she thought that, it reminded her of friends at university who smoked. "Holding a cigarette gives me something to do with my hands," they said. At least they were thin, though.

"What do you want?"

Even though they were alone, Bash glanced over his shoulder, leaned closer to her – close enough that she could smell his aftershave, which was still Hugo Boss Bottled, the one she used to buy him before she settled for just buying him a card on his birthday – and said, "I'm worried about you, Sam."

His words broke the spell. "You don't need to be," she said, bridling.

"But I am." He paused, trying to think of a better way to say what he had to say, and then just came out with: "You're mixed up with that guy who killed himself at the cathedral, aren't you?"

"What do you mean?"

"He was something to do with that Home and Heart charity, wasn't he?"

"So?"

"His name was plastered across the top of every page of those accounts you sent me – a week after he committed suicide."

Suddenly, all her tangled emotions seemed silly, and she found her mind clear and icy cold. She was back in the real world, not some impossible what-if fantasy. She had just admitted what he said was true, but she wasn't going to give any ground.

"Well, you don't have to worry any more." Her tone was cold. "My clients did just what you said and put it all in the hands of the police. So if that's all - " She started to rise, but he put a hand on her arm to stop her. She pulled back as if she had an electric shock and sat down again.

"I did a bit of digging around. The whole thing stinks. Home and Heart has - had - three trustees. The man who killed himself, a chancer called Andrew Russell and a man called Devereux, who is a director of the company that did the charity's accounts, and he just happens to be Russell's brother-in-law."

"You're not telling me anything new, Bash. Now if that's all, I've got to go."

She collected her things and stood up. The idea had struck her that Bashir was spinning this meeting out, that he'd got some silly idea in his head of rekindling something, and she didn't want to find out that she was wrong, or worse, that she was right.

He stood up with her. "But here's the thing. The guy who killed himself only took a salary from the charity, nothing else. All those perks – the manor house in Normandy, and the massive payments for ridiculous services, they all went to the other trustee, Russell and his wife."

"Well, it's all over now." What did she mean by that? She headed for the door so that she didn't have to think about it, but Bashir followed her and kept on talking.

"I mean, technically what they're doing isn't against the law, and the most they'll get from the Charity Commission is a rap on the knuckles. Maybe they'll have to step down, but when the public find out, the money's going to dry up anyway and they will just move on. That sort always do...they're like vampires. No wonder the poor guy topped himself when he found out what was going on. They'd destroyed his life's work right under his nose."

She stopped at her car.

"Still driving this old thing?"

"Things got a bit tight after Abba disappeared," she said, on the defensive again. She looked round and saw a large, dark blue BMW saloon in the car park. "That yours?" Bash had always liked his cars. She remembered his first one was a souped-up Ford Sierra that they used to go out in. Stop it!

"I'll be trading it in for an X5 when the baby's born."

"Family man now, Bash."

He smiled ruefully. "My parents are pleased. First grandchild."

She was going to say something about how they'd come a long way from Leigh Road Infants, but she pressed her lips together instead. Time to draw a line under a few things – Bash, Daz's murder investigation – and press the start button on her life. Move out from Mum's, lose weight, buy a new car!

"I wish you all the best," she said, and got in her car.

When she drove off, she could see Bash still standing in the car park looking after her.

Back at the office, she wrote up her notes about Mary's case, and cleared her desk of a lot of other stuff that had been piling up. When she glanced at the clock, she was surprised to see it was nearly half past three and she'd missed lunch completely, hadn't even noticed.

This goes to show what you can do when you're focussed, she thought. Somehow, after her dad disappeared, she'd lost that drive, and felt like she was muddling through. Even taking the job with CAB had just been a way of distracting herself – just like Daz and Willow. They were distractions. So was Bashir. She hadn't thought about him like that in years.

She sat up straight. Time to be moving on, and up. She scanned her desk. What else could she clear up before five?

There was a tap at her door and Mr. Allcock poked his head round. He was the senior partner, and even though she was working, she started guiltily.

"Have you got five minutes?" he asked. As if you could say no.

"Of course, Mr. Allcock." She followed him to his office.

His office was bigger and everything in it was better than hers. It breathed money and quiet power.

"Now then, Miss Akhtar, err, um, Sam," he began. Sam was wary. She knew behind all that minor private school umming and erring there was a sharp legal mind. "You know we're very happy with you here?"

She didn't know how to respond, but she was afraid this was leading somewhere bad, so she kept her face blank and waited.

"Your work is exemplary and you've brought in several new clients, who wouldn't normally come to us." Oh very good – quite racist, but prove it. And here comes the 'but.' "But there is one little issue I need to take up with you."

One of her university lecturers had told her that the best way to get a client talking was by saying nothing, so she folded her hands in her lap and studied the wisps of hair that floated around Mr. Allcock's head.

After a pause, he continued, "We applaud your social conscience, working at the Citizen's Advice Bureau and we wouldn't wish to stop you. However, we've been informed that you have been taking an excessive interest in a case involving a homeless man and the death in the cathedral."

Sam sat back. So that was it. Someone from the police in the Funny Handshake Brigade had had a quiet word with Allcock at the Lodge. Probably that bastard Potter. She almost laughed, but by pressing her lips together she controlled it into a tight smile.

"Just preventing the police from committing a miscarriage of justice. I think they quite appreciated it."

"Ah, good, so I assume it's all over now?"

Sam thought. Was it all over? Based on what Bashir had told her, it probably was. No murder, just the sad end to a good man who had had his life's work ruined. And the people who had driven him to it, they'd all get away scot-free. There was nothing else to be done, but find a way to tell Daz and Willow.

"Yes," she said. "It's all over. Will that be all?"

He was polite, smiling and nodding, so she stood up and headed back to her office, a box with utility desk and two metal filing cabinets. She sat down, admired her tidy desk and thought about tidying up her life.

Yes, it was all over.

CHAPTER EIGHTEEN

Sam, Willow, Daz – Friday

Sameena woke up suddenly when she heard a man in her bedroom. It took her a second or two to recognise the voice. It was a presenter from *Today* on Radio 4. It was her radio alarm. She was safe. No need to be alarmed. But the more she listened to the World News at 6.30am, the more it dawned on her that even though she was safe in her bedroom in Lichfield, the world around her was falling apart. Tragedies, disease, cruelty, murder, unfairness and hatred. She switched off the alarm and pulled the duvet up to her chin. She'd give herself five more minutes in peace and warmth before she jumped into the shower.

Sameena hadn't slept well last night. She had felt uncomfortable when she got into bed but she knew the reason why. She had eaten too many cakes during the day and then to top it all, when she got in from work, she'd felt obliged to eat all the food her mother put in front of her. In her wakefulness, Sameena had mithered about most of the people who had featured in her life over the last few days. Mr Allcock, Daz, Willow and her own mother. Then there were her 'normal' clients that needed her full attention as well as her 'abnormal' clients like Mary from Abbeyfield Care Home. Then there was Bash. He'd also taken a starring role in her fitful dreams and waking thoughts last night.

She really ought to get up now, but she was so cosy under her duvet in her pyjamas. They were no ordinary PJs, they were her favourite satin elasticated ones. These were not just any pyjamas; they were *M&S* pyjamas. The Dream Satin pyjama set in blue with white stripes cost more than she would normally pay for night wear but she liked the feel of them on her skin. She gently moved her hands up and down the satin as Bash re-appeared on Sameena's screen saver in her mind.

"Sameena, are you up? You'll be late. You need a good breakfast before you go," her mother shouted from the bottom of the stairs.

"Coming. Give me ten minutes. I'll just have a quick shower," replied a frustrated Sameena as she eased herself out of bed.

After a coolish shower, Sameena sat at her dressing table. She talked at herself in the mirror while applying a little make-up around her eyes to disguise her sleep-starved night. 'No more cakes. Less food generally. Look at flats/apartments with one bedroom. No more thinking about what might have been with Bash. Focus on real work by ending the wild goose chase with Daz and Willow today.'

There was a knock on her bedroom door. Willow's mother opened her daughter's door and headed to the bedside table with a mug of tea.

"Good morning, sweetie. How are you? Did you sleep OK?"

"Morning. Fine," uttered Willow through a dry mouth.

"Last night you said you were on an early shift at the cafe today so I brought you some tea before your dad and I leave for work in a few minutes," said her mother, gently stroking her long tangled pink hair.

"Thanks."

"Can I make you something to eat before I go?"

"I'll be fine. Honestly. I'll get something at work. I promise," Willow said to placate her caring mother.

"I love you, Willow Pillow."

"Love you too. See you tonight."

After her mother left her room Willow sat up in bed to drink her tea. She looked at her mobile, but there was nothing of importance to look at. Once she drank her tea, she would have a shower.

Her mom and dad shouted "Bye" up the stairs as they left for their respective jobs. Willow echoed the shout.

Once out of her own en-suite, Willow wrapped a towel around her and dried herself off on the bed, listening to some music. She then threw some working clothes on and sat at her dressing table to dry her hair. Even with a good hairdryer the process of getting it orderly and dry took about fifteen minutes. Willow pondered if it was time for a change. A new colour? A new style? Shorter? Maybe? Maybe not.

Maybe it wasn't her hair that needed to change. Perhaps it was time to make some big changes. She loved working at the café, but she knew she would grow to hate it if she stayed there for more than a year. In September she needed to go into further education or start a proper training course. She couldn't work in a shop forever. She knew she wanted to work with people, vulnerable people or children, but doing what? Definitely not teaching. No chance. The thought of being stuck in a classroom with thirty kids of any age was the stuff of nightmares. One-to-one would suit her better. Social worker? Psychologist? Counsellor? Yeah. As long as her studies would be at an FE college. She was not going to wear a daft school uniform ever again. But what A levels would she need to take? She decided to have a chat with her folks tonight.

It was time. Time to head off to work at the café. But it was also time to change direction and get serious about her future. No more serving coffee or wiping down tables. No more playing a part in an imaginary murder mystery novel. No more playing, full stop.

She gathered up her coat and small bag and was just about to leave when she noticed a text on her phone from Sameena.

Are you free for fifteen minutes later on today?

Somebody whispered, "Wake up."

Then again, this time followed by a nudge on the arm.

Daz woke with a start and opened his eyes. He was in the Old Methodist Church on Wade Street. He was sitting in a circle with a bunch of other addicts, all strangers to him apart from Eugene who was trying to revive him. Someone on the other side of the circle was speaking to the group.

"Sorry to nudge you, but you were beginning to snore," whispered Eugene. "I know you don't like shocks like that, but I had to do something."

"Thanks," replied Daz, sitting up straight in his chair.

Daz sat there pretending to listen to this guy droning on. How long had he drifted off for? Seconds? Minutes? Days? Just for a moment he considered the possibility that the events at the cathedral, with the police, at CAB and at Andrew Russell's house in Solihull were just part of a brief, dream-like nightmare. He wondered if Shaun was still alive. Was Sameena an imaginary person? Was everything OK? Normal? Normal, apart from the fact he was right now in a Narcotics Anonymous meeting, he sold *The Big Issue* to make ends meet and had no contact with his daughter!

There was a gentle round of applause and encouragement as the guy finally finished telling the group the latest chapter of his 'Journey to Sobriety.' Eugene thanked him for speaking and for his honesty and wound down the meeting with a prayer and the offer of a hot drink and biscuits.

As the circle disintegrated, Eugene spoke to Daz without the need to whisper. "Are you OK?"

"Yeah. Sorry about falling asleep …"

"Are you sleeping?"

"Clearly too much," replied Daz with a slight smile on his worn-out face. "I know this sounds crazy, but have I told you about Shaun's death, and Willow and this other woman helping me and trying to get answers?"

"Yes, you told me at the last meeting."

"Oh good...I mean...it's not good...but I thought it might not...never mind."

"So, what's the latest? Have you got anywhere in finding out what happened to Shaun?" asked Eugene.

"No, not really. A few dead ends...shit, I didn't mean it like that."

"Perhaps you ought to stop selling *The Big Issue* and become a stand-up comedian. The Guild Hall could do with a new act. Ladies and Gentlemen, we are lucky to have with us tonight an ex-soldier, drug addict and seller of the magazine that no-one wants to buy, but some people do out of guilt or pity...Darren 'Daz' Mitchell."

"Yeah, very funny. You should be the comedian. Ladies and Gentlemen...may I introduce the only black man who happily lives and works in Lichfield and is twenty years' clean...Eugene Tyler."

"Perhaps we could be a double act?"

"Or perhaps we have enough to do already. You lead these NA groups and have your hands full being my sponsor and I spend every waking moment trying not to relapse or think about the family I foolishly lost."

"C'mon, mate. You're doing really well. Just keep faith with the programme and life will get better. I'm not saying that you can change what happened in the past, but there is a brighter future for you. I know it. Look, I've gotta go and talk to a few others and make sure they're not pocketing the biscuits or my jar of coffee. I'll see you next time, but contact me if you need to talk."

"Yeah, will do. I ought to get back to my day job, if that's what you call it!"

Sameena walked into the library café and saw Willow chatting and serving a customer. Sameena couldn't stop smiling as she walked up to the counter. This teenager with long pink hair looked so confident and full of life. Everything that Sameena wasn't at her age.

"Hi, Willow. You said you could take a break at about this time."

"Yep. No problem. I'll just tell Susan that I'm having my lunch now."

"I'll see you outside."

Sameena left the library café and stood just outside in the fairly quiet market square. Wednesday was not a market day, so the temporary stalls were missing. The only businesses trading today were two vans parked up by the hideous statue, one selling fish and chips and the other offering ice creams.

"Hi, Sam, you wanted a chat?" said Willow as she came up behind Sameena and almost made her jump.

"Yes, shall we go somewhere for a coffee or something?"

"Sure. Oh look, there's Daz setting up. I went out earlier to give him a coffee, but he wasn't in his usual spot."

"I might see if he can join us. I'm sure I can persuade him with a free cake."

Ten minutes later the three of them were sitting at a table in their usual café with drinks and snacks courtesy of Sameena. It was only right and proper that she paid for their lunch as she had called the 'meeting.' It might well be their last after what she was going to say to Daz and Willow.

They listened to Sameena explain how she had enlisted the help of a friend called Bash and it was his view that the accounts and practices of Home and Heart were shady. Sameena emphasised that Shaun may not have been a main player in the scam, it was more likely to be Devereux and Russell, but that Shaun could well have killed himself after he discovered that he was implicated in the fraud.

"Are you certain?" asked Daz.

"No, I can't be certain. But it really looks that way to Bash...and me."

"I still think it's out of character."

"I know. I understand that you don't want to accept it. But maybe the way you ought to look at it is that Shaun was an honourable man. Suicide was not a cowardly act, but when he discovered that the charity was cheating people then he couldn't live with himself. He wasn't a crook or a cheat. Shaun was a good guy, trying to do good things for people."

"So, is that it, then?" asked Willow.

"How do you mean?" replied Sameena, knowing full well what Willow was really hinting at.

"Are you saying that we should stop looking into Shaun's death. Leave it all up to the police from now on?" said Willow, looking slightly defeated.

"I suppose I am. There is nothing else we can do," admitted Sameena.

There was a pause in the conversation. Each participant stared at their cup or plate.

Sameena had tried to let them down gently, but she still felt terrible for not being honest and owning up to Willow and Daz that she had to back away from this situation because her boss was pressurising her and she needed the job for the sake of her career. It was the right thing to do. She needed the security of her job so that she could save up for her own place to live and a better car to drive. Tomorrow would be a new day.

CHAPTER NINETEEN

Krys - Friday

Her full name was Krystyna Andzelika Wozniak-Kendrick. Back when she started as a police constable she was PC 26659 Wozniak and she had put up with all the racism and sexism that went with being Polish and a woman. Now she was a detective sergeant and married, she didn't have to put up with any of that. Apart from the remarks from her friends about racism and sexism in the police. And because she was tired of excusing the police to them, she had slowly stopped seeing them, and because she was tired of the casual sexism and racism with off-duty police, she didn't have any friends there either.

It was quite a lonely life, apart from her husband, Dan, a car salesman, but he really didn't understand why she wasn't ready to start a family – he was making good money now, and after all, she wasn't getting any younger. In fact, if you sat back and looked at it, a lonely life was a very apt description.

Looking back, she wondered how she had ever embarked on this course, starting with a degree in Psychology as her parents scrimped and saved to get her through university. Almost without thinking she had done two years as a CSPO and then drifted into the fast-track programme for potential detectives. She had a suspicion that her psychology degree, her sex and her ethnicity all helped, because for two years now she had been a DS at Lichfield Station.

These days, the only time she was happy was when she was doing her job, and the phone call that had just come through certainly made her happy. Potter was not at his desk – when was he ever? He disappeared so often his nickname was *Harry* Potter – and the call had been put through to her.

"Is that Inspector Potter?" It was a woman's voice, frightened. whispering

"No, he's...ah, unavailable. This is Detective Sergeant Kendrick. Can I help?"

"This is Emma at *Home and Heart.* A man's just come in, he looks very scary and he's told me not to move. He's going through Mr. Wilde's office, I can hear him breaking things - "

By the time Krys registered all she was hearing was the dial tone, she was out of her chair and yelling for a car and a driver. They raced through Lichfield on a Code 3, with lights and sirens and cars and pedestrians scattered in their wake. They were in Whittington eight minutes after Krys had taken the call and pulled up into the car park in a slew of gravel.

She was out of the car before it stopped, and the young constable driving tumbled out after her. They burst through the door and found the girl sitting sobbing at the big desk that looked like the top of a packing case to Krys. She saw the door of the inner office standing open and she gestured to the police constable to go in. As she turned her attention to the girl, out the corner of her eye, she saw him sidle up to the door and go in.

"I'm Detective Sergeant Kendrick," she said firmly, standing in the middle of the room and reassuring the girl she was in charge. "What's happened here, Emma?"

The girl mumbled into the tissue she had balled up in her hand. There was a jug of water and a glass on the desk. Krys poured her some and told her to drink. Drinking the water didn't actually help, but it made the girl concentrate on swallowing instead of crying.

"Now," she said, kindly, "tell me what happened."

"A man – like the other one – came in a black Range Rover. Told me not to move or he'd hurt me and he went in – in there." She nodded at the inner office. "I could hear him throwing things about. Then we heard your siren and he came running out and drove off."

"Sarge." The young constable's voice behind her.

She turned and as he opened his mouth to speak, she asked curtly, "Did we pass a black Range Rover going the other way?"

"Don't think so, Sarge."

"Which way is that?" She pointed down the road.

"Country roads mostly. It heads towards the M42."

"Put out an alert for a black Range Rover heading that way." She turned back to the girl. "Was there another man in the car?"

"I – I don't know," the girl sniffled.

"Possibly two men, should be considered dangerous," she told the constable. Back to the girl. "Now, Emma, can you describe the man?"

The girl shook her head. "They were wearing balaclavas."

"Alright. Was he taller than the constable?" The constable straightened up from talking into the Motorola strapped to his vest. The girl nodded. "Fatter or thinner?" The constable sucked his stomach in. Krys went on to ask her a series of careful questions that a defence lawyer couldn't tear to pieces, and then said, "PC Bartram is going to stay with you now, and I'll take a look in the office."

With his back to the girl, Bartram whispered, "It's a mess, Sarge. No wonder the girl was scared." Then, louder and cheery, "Now – Emma, is it? How about a cup of coffee?"

Stepping through the door, Krys told herself to remember that not all policemen were assholes.

Bartram was right. The office had been turned over. The photographs that were still on the wall were hanging lopsided and one empty frame lay smashed on the floor. The filing cabinets were yawning open and had vomited their papers everywhere. The desk was like the secretary's, but bigger, with retro metal drawers fitted. They had been yanked open and their contents spilled. The computer had been pushed aside to spread papers over the desk, but it hadn't been turned on.

If the office was being searched, whatever was being looked for wasn't on the hard drive. But only three quarters of it had been turned over. One tranquil corner was untouched. Either he'd found what he was looking for, or their arrival had disturbed him. She walked over to the two ridiculously low leather sofas grouped around a glass-topped coffee table made out of a tree root, sat down and surveyed the room.

This wasn't the action of a bent accountant or a crooked trustee. This was violent, but organised, without any waste of time. The bottom drawers of the filing cabinets were pulled out furthest and going up the others were less open, like a crazy staircase. This office had been searched by a man who knew what he was doing. Which meant there was something criminal going on with *Home and Heart.* Which meant that Daz might be right after all. Maybe Wilde had been killed.

She was lost in thought when she heard a foot scrunch on a piece of broken glass in the doorway.

"D'you mind telling me what's going on, Sergeant?"

It was Potter, looking a little less messed up than the office he was standing in. He sounded like the worst teacher in school, catching kids behind the bike sheds and trying to behave like he was in charge.

She stood up. "A call came through and I couldn't find you, sir. Looks like it might be connected with the cathedral death – I've put out an alert on a black Range Rover."

"I know. I've cancelled it."

"Sir?"

"I've spoken to the PC. What's happened here is that some chancer read about the suicide and thought the offices would be an easy target. Happens all the time."

Krys gestured around. "What were they looking for?"

Potter shrugged. "Money. Charities always have cash kicking about." He turned away. "Come on, let's go."

She gasped in frustration and sat back down heavily on the sofa. What was the point? This morning she'd even thought she was happy in her job, and then Potter turned up and tore that to bits too. Maybe it was time to give up and start a family. Her parents would be pleased – with grandkids and her not being in the police. They'd grown up in Soviet Czechoslovakia, they'd seen Russian tanks in Wenceslas Square and neighbours vanish in the night. They didn't trust the police.

'So that's it,' she thought. 'I'll hand my resignation in when I get back to the station.' She felt exhausted and heavy and at the same time light and empty, like all her troubles had been lifted off her shoulders. At least it didn't matter what Potter said or did now.

She levered herself to her feet and her hand slid down the side cushion of the sofa and she touched – what? She groped around and tugged out a bulky A4 envelope. She turned it over in her hands and felt it. There was something inside, some things inside, thin and roughly double the size of her notebook. She opened her mouth to call Potter back, and then pressed her lips together in a thin line and slit the envelope open with her nail.

She shook the contents onto the coffee table. Four dark blue passports with a bird – an eagle? – etched in gold on the cover and Arabic writing. She took a pen and a tissue from her bag and carefully opened one. Lemon yellow pages, more Arabic writing and a photograph of an unshaven man with haunted eyes. His name was Zaki el-Khalili, born in Iraq in 1980.

The three others: Rajab al-Mannan, 1984; Hussain al-Mohammadi, 1978; Sad al-Haider, 1993.

She flicked backwards and forwards, but she couldn't see a visa in any of them, or an exit stamp from Iraq. If these were the passports of Iraqis in this country, they were illegal immigrants. What were four Iraqi passports doing, hidden in a sofa in Wilde's office? Was this what the man was looking for? It felt like Daz's good friend Shaun had a dark side after all.

The weight that Krys had felt lift settled onto her shoulders once more, but this time it didn't seem to be weighing her down. This was evidence, and Potter couldn't ignore it – not when she presented it to him in front of a witness and a police constable. She slid the passports back into the envelope, and went into the outer office.

Potter was flirting with the secretary, who was uncomfortable, and the constable was standing awkwardly nearby.

"Sir?" He didn't turn round, although she could tell by the set of his shoulders that he had heard, so she said it again, louder. "Sir."

"What is it now, Kendrick?" he said irritably, over his shoulder.

She got herself between him and Emma, and said, "I found something in the office, sir, that I think you ought to take a look at."

And she upended the envelope onto Emma's desk.

"What the hell are these?"

The constable edged forward, curious.

"They're Iraqi passports, sir. They're all current, and they don't have visas or any of the relevant exit or entry stamps."

"Which means..."

"...which means that if these men are living in this country then they are illegal immigrants. I think this is what the man was searching for." She paused for a beat. "I think you should reinstate the alert for the black Range Rover...sir."

The constable looked even more awkward now. Potter glared at the passports, and then glared at the constable. "You heard her. Get on to the station. Tell them...in the light of new information, I am putting out an alert on a black Range Rover believed to be heading..."

"Towards the M42, sir."

"Got that, constable? Well, get on with it!" Potter barked, and the young man hurried outside.

Potter pulled a blue latex glove from his pocket and looked pointedly at Krys. "You haven't touched them, have you? You've probably contaminated this crime scene enough already." He shovelled the passports back into the envelope with it.

"No, sir," said Krys. And then, lowering her voice, "I think we need to take Emma back to the station. If this is to do with people smuggling, then she's seen one of them. She could be in danger if we leave her here."

An unpleasant gleam came into Potter's eye. "Good idea, sergeant. I'll take her back, see if we can get a photofit. You finish up here." He turned to Emma. "Come on, miss, it's your lucky day. You're coming with me."

With a little bit too much contact, he helped her to her feet and for a moment Krys thought he was going to say, "Get your coat – you've pulled." But he picked up her bag and guided her to the door. "My coat," she mumbled, and he draped it over her shoulders.

Krys followed them out, and as Potter shepherded the girl into the back seat of his car, she said to the constable, "Go with them. I'll finish up here and drive myself back."

They exchanged a knowing glance and the constable got quickly into the car alongside Potter. Potter looked puzzled for second, and then looked out of the window at Krys. She waved her fingers at him. He glared and roared off in a spit of gravel.

Back at the office, she gave a cursory look around, but in one respect, Potter was right. This was a crime scene now. She'd better leave it for SOCO – there'd be fingerprints to be taken, and documents for the forensic accountants to go through. She went to the car and radioed it in. Potter wouldn't be happy, but now one thing was for sure.

The homeless guy and the girl with pink hair were onto something.

PART TWO

CHAPTER TWENTY

Daz, Willow – Monday, Tuesday

Daz got up and had some breakfast. The usual – Honey Nut Flakes, toast and jam and strong tea with two sugars. It was time to get things squared away. Pick up some Big Issues and start selling again. Go to meetings. Get on with his life. While the kettle was boiling he went downstairs to check the shared mailbox. Maybe there was something in there that would get him moving on, something more than pizza menus or garish flyers for discount supermarkets.

There was. It was a long white envelope with a window that his name and address showed through. He studied it carefully. In his old life, letters like this had usually been bad news:

Dear Mr. Mitchell

This letter is to inform you that according to the restraining order application, a complaint is received against you, charging you for committing crimes and harassment on the applicant …

or

Unless you vacate the property within 7 days of the date of this notice, we will seek, without further notice, to evict you …

or

… you have again failed to comply and this means you are in breach of your Order and will be returned to court.

And then for a few years there hadn't been any letters at all because he didn't have an address, let alone a letterbox.

He tapped it on his hand. Probably better to open it in the privacy of his flat in case it was bad news and he broke down or got mad. He trudged back up the stairs more slowly than he had come down, and nearly bumped into Amir, who was wearing the same clothes as the last time that Daz had seen him, just a bit dirtier.

"Jeez! Sorry, mate," said Daz, looking up and taking an awkward step back. "I was miles away."

And then over his shoulder he saw another man like Amir, olive-skinned and black hair with watchful eyes.

He could have dragged himself back to his flat with his letter and they would have been three sad men just passing on the stairs, but something made him stop. He waved the letter at them. "Probably bad news," he said, more cheerfully than he felt. "Usually is, isn't it? You're Amir, right?" He stuck his hand out to the man behind. "Daz."

The man looked at it uneasily and then at Amir who nodded. He shook Daz's hand. "Faisal."

They tried to brush past, but Daz stood his ground.

"Off to work?"

They nodded and their eyes grew more wary.

"So what do you do?"

Amir and Faisal looked at each other. "Car wash," Amir muttered, and this time they managed to shoulder their way past him.

He watched them thoughtfully all the way down the stairs, and then headed back up, the letter in his hand getting heavier with every step. In his flat he dropped it on the counter and made a cup of tea. From his kitchen window he could see the road, and Amir and Faisal standing by the kerb, one with his hood up and the other with his collar lifted. They looked cold and miserable and nervous as they took glances up and down the road.

There was something a bit dodgy about that. And then the battered old white Transit van came rattling up the road. Once again the doors flew open and hands thrust out to drag the two men in. The doors banged shut and the van roared off in a cloud of diesel smoke.

Daz was fairly sure they were illegal immigrants. But how had they got a council flat? Hadn't Amir said he was from Iraq? Hadn't Shaun served in Iraq and hadn't Shaun got him this council flat?

He sipped his tea and shrugged. Not my problem. His problem was right there on the counter. He took a deep breath, picked the letter up and ripped it open.

Dear Mr. Mitchell,

This is to inform you that an appointment has been made for you with Ms. Pauline Linden of the Staffordshire Counselling Service –

He could hear his heart thudding in his ears and he realised he had been holding his breath. It was the counselling thing that Sam had set up. There was an address on Bore Street and a date. This Thursday!

Maybe things weren't so bad.

"Sometimes I just don't understand you," said Willow getting increasingly frustrated.

"Well, Willow, it's just the way I am. I'm too old to change now. I've voted Tory all of my life and I'm not going to change now!" explained her father across the dinner table.

"But didn't you used to support Birmingham City some time ago? You were a season ticket holder while they were a half-decent team. Then, when they got relegated you stopped going to the matches."

"Yes, that's true, but it wasn't just that. It wasn't fair on your mom to just go off every other Saturday to watch a game of football and leave you two on your own."

"Hey! Leave me out of this discussion. I was quite glad to get rid of you for a while," said Willow's mother, who was semi-smiling as she looked at her husband and her daughter.

"But don't you see," said Willow looking at her father, "the Tories are rubbish, they don't deserve your support. If you stopped being a member of the Conservative Party then you would show them that they're hopeless."

"And are the Labour party any better?"

"Maybe not. They're probably the same – a bunch of lying, cheating hypocrites - who knows, but if you don't show your disapproval or disgust, then nothing will ever change. C'mon, dad, I know you feel strongly about some of the things that the government are doing wrong. I hear you moaning all of the time. So, do something about it. Make a stand."

"And how do you think I should make a stand? By just cancelling my membership. What else can I do?" asked her dad.

"Well, how about joining me on the protest against continuing to construct HS2? You've said yourself that the money could be better spent. And look at all the countryside that's being obliterated around Lichfield. All the trees being chopped down. It's a criminal waste of money when times are really hard for so many people. And what's it all for? So a few people can travel by train a little faster to London. Has no-one realised that people don't need to travel for work as much anymore? It's expensive and pointless when you can meet up with people virtually so much faster than using trains, cars or planes. By the time it's all built, sometime in the future, it will be a thing of the past!"

"I agree with you. But I'm not going to chain myself to a tree or glue my hands to the tarmac on the A38. I'm too old. It's your generation that needs to take action."

"So, are you saying I can do those things?" asked Willow with a twinkle in her eye.

"No, your dad was not saying that," said Willow's mother quickly. "But if you feel strongly about certain issues, by all means support a cause as long as you don't put yourself in danger or others for that matter. As your parents our job is, first and foremost, to make sure you're safe. However, we both admire the fact that you know your own mind and get passionate about things. We love it that you want to help people and that you care about the environment. But Willow, we love you and we don't want you getting yourself into any sort of trouble. So keep letting us know what you're planning to do. Is that a deal?"

For the first time in the last five minutes Willow could not look directly at her mother or father. She stared at her plate in front of her and said quietly, "OK."

Willow's father used the relative silence to interject, "And also, we've been meaning to ask you about what you're thinking of doing next year. You're not going to carry on working in the library café are you?"

"No, I'm not, but I'll carry on there until September and then I'll start studying again. Probably at Lichfield Further Education College. I haven't decided what I want to study yet. I've got some ideas but I need to look at what they're offering."

"What do you fancy doing, sweetheart?" asked her mother.

"I know what I don't want to do. Nothing about money or sitting at a computer looking at spreadsheets. I want to work with people and for people. Improve people's lives. Perhaps courses like Social Care or Politics or Law and Order. I dunno. Maybe 'A' levels in Sociology and Psychology. I'll give it some thought and do some research on the college's website. Perhaps I'll go and do that now."

It was the perfect opportunity for Willow to leave the table and go up to her bedroom. She flicked open her laptop and stared at the screen, but her thoughts were not on the next academic year. Her thoughts were based around the last couple of weeks. The people she'd met and the situations she'd got herself into. For some reason she missed the excitement, but she also felt guilty that she'd not told her parents anything about her unwise and, at times, unsafe exploits.

The next day, Daz got moving. He wanted to shift some Big Issues and go to an NA meeting. He had a lot he wanted to talk over with Eugene. He shifted his pitch so that he wouldn't have to deal with Willow. He wasn't sure what he had in common with her now that they weren't hunting a murderer.

Anyway, she should be getting on with her life, going to college or something instead of working in that café, just like him. Getting counselling, getting a proper job, getting access to his daughter. That was how he was going to get on with his life.

He arrived early to the meeting and he surprised Eugene by standing up to speak.

"Hi, my name's Daz – Darren and I'm a drug addict. I was in Afghanistan and I didn't cope well when I came back. My wife threw me out. I can't say I blame her – I wasn't easy to live with when I got to drinking. After that I started sleeping on friends' sofas, but when I started taking drugs I ended up on the street. I had to do a lot I'm not proud of to survive, but to be honest with you, losing my family was harder than being homeless. You don't live for a roof over your head or your next meal, you live for the people you love. I haven't seen my daughter in four years.

"I had a good friend who got me off the streets. I thought he was like a saint or something, and then he died. For a little while I went crazy and I started thinking he'd been murdered and I started running around trying to prove it, but now I think he was just like the rest of us – some bits good and some bits bad. I guess he didn't have anything to live for, not like I do.

"This week I'm seeing a counsellor, and then I'm going to apply to see my daughter."

The words that had poured out of somewhere deep inside him dried up and he was left standing awkwardly in the circle. Eugene jumped to his feet and led the applause, thanking Daz for sharing. Afterwards he made him a cup of coffee.

"What brought that on, Daz? I didn't know you had that many words in you."

Daz shrugged. "I dunno. It just feels like there's something I've been putting off for two years now and I guess trying to prove Shaun didn't kill himself was just me trying to put it off again."

"Mm-huh. And what is it you've been putting off?"

"Step Nine. Make amends to persons we've harmed."

"And that would be...?"

"My wife and my daughter."

"That's what the counsellor is all about?"

"My wife has a restraining order against me. It was all my fault, but I've got to prove I'm a different person now. That solicitor who helped me when I got pulled in by the police has got me a counsellor to work on my – " He made quotes with his fingers. " – anger management issues. I start this Thursday."

"That's good, Daz," said Eugene, but then he frowned. "Remember this though. It's good that you want to make amends, that you want to be a father to your daughter, but that doesn't mean it will happen. Just because you get counselling, it doesn't mean the restraining order will be lifted straight away – or ever. I don't want you crashing and burning if it doesn't work out."

Daz managed to grin in the face of Eugene's cold water. "I know. One day at a time, right?"

As he walked down Wade Street, he thought he was almost happy. The sun was shining so he hadn't got cold and miserable selling *The Big Issue*, and he had sold all of them so he had some money for food and some for the rent and some left over to save. And he'd finally spoken at a meeting and it hadn't been as bad as he thought.

Today hadn't been a bad day.

CHAPTER TWENTY-ONE

Krys, Sam – Wednesday

Krystyna met Sameena at *the Faro Lounge*. She wasn't sure how welcome the police were at Citizen's Advice, and she didn't want to make it difficult for her by turning up at her place of work.

"Thanks for meeting me," said Krys after the drinks and cake had been set before them.

"Mmm-huh," said Sameena, through a mouthful of chocolate fudge cake. Krys wasn't sure if she was just enjoying the cake or speaking with her mouth full.

Sameena swallowed. "Are you sure you don't want anything? My treat."

It was about the cake. "No thanks, I'm fine," said Krys, sipping her black coffee.

"I wish I had your self-control," said Sameena wistfully.

"What do you mean?" Krys was puzzled.

Sameena laughed and pushed her half-eaten cake away. "So what do you want from me?"

Krys leaned forward. "This is just between us?"

Sameena laughed again, leaned forward as well and pantomimed a glance over both shoulders. "Of course."

Krys looked around suspiciously. "Why did you do that?"

Either she's got no sense of humour or no friends, thought Sameena. And then she thought: And what about you? What have you got? Ummi and an ex-boyfriend with a pregnant wife. She sat up straight and said, "It doesn't matter. What can I do for you?"

"When you first came into the station with the accounts from the *Home and Heart* charity and that man Mitchell, he was convinced Shaun Wilde had been murdered. Do you remember?"

"He thought it was the accountant."

"And he tried to beat him up."

"Allegedly."

"Well, although we found that the accountant was using the charity for his own benefit, Wilde himself was only taking a modest salary. The Charity Commission might give the accountant a slap on the wrist for what he was doing, but it wasn't against the law, and we thought that Wilde found out and that's why he killed himself."

Sameena could feel a 'but' coming and she felt she ought to help the policewoman along, but her professional experience wasn't to aid the police, so she said, "Well it all seems wrapped up, but somehow this doesn't feel like a social call."

Krys licked her lips. She was finding it difficult to come out and say what she wanted, because once she did, she was crossing a line, going outside the police force and there was no turning back. Sameena was used to clients who struggled to find the words, so she sat back and waited.

And then Krys let it out. She told Sameena all about the raid on the *Home and Heart* office and the Iraqi passports she'd found. "The black Range Rover was found burnt out on an industrial estate in Bromsgrove," she added.

"OK," said Sameena brusquely. "Now we know where we are. Why do you need my help?"

"Do you still have a copy of those accounts you gave us?"

Sameena nodded guardedly.

"I'd like your accountant to have another look at them, but this time, it's more than the charity being ripped off. I want to see if there are unexplained cash payments going in and out."

"Wouldn't the Charity Commission or your forensic accountant already have spotted that?"

"If they were looking for it. Anyway, there's always cash coming into charities – they don't have card readers when they're out on the streets rattling a tin."

"OK – but why do you want my fr – contact to do it, instead of going back to your boss?" Krys's face hardened and Sameena was fairly sure she knew the answer. "This is about the DI, isn't it? Potter? I didn't like him when I met him – he's the kind of racist, sexist, homophobic bully who gives the police a bad name and doesn't think twice about bending the law. But, hey, at least he keeps me in work."

If the policewoman agreed with her now she would have a layer of protection for Bash.

Krys knew what Sameena was doing. That moment in the interview room when she had shut Potter down had been a pleasure, even if what followed hadn't been, but she was still a policewoman and solicitors were the enemy. She had put one foot across the line already, but this was jumping with both feet. Did she have a choice? She took a breath. "DI Potter has tried to shut this investigation down three times now. I want to be sure I've got something solid to go to him with, to force him to carry on – "

"Even if it costs your career?" Sameena found her advocate skills kicking in against her will.

"Even if it costs my career." She had made her choice.

"Then you'd better tell me what you suspect, so that my contact knows what to look for."

"Alright." Krys ticked off her suspicions on her fingers. "One: I think the charity might be a front for people trafficking. Two: if it is, then money will need to be laundered, and I want to know if the charity was being used for that. Three: I'd like to know who and where the money is coming from. And four: for your client Mitchell, I'd like to know if Shaun Wilde was directly involved."

Sameena sat back and dragged the plate in front of her. "Not much then?"

"But if I'm right," Krys said with a warning note in her voice, "your fr…contact needs to be very careful, because these are very dangerous men."

She does have a sense of humour, thought Sameena. "And maybe Mitchell was closer to the truth about Wilde's death than he thought."

"Alright," said Sameena, "I'll speak to my friend, but I'll leave it up to him. I can't make any promises."

Krys nodded. "That's all I'm asking," she said. She stood up and drained her cup. "I'll be in touch."

She marched out and Sameena watched her go. If you didn't know she was in the police, you'd have guessed the army, she thought.

Only last week she'd told Daz and Willow to leave it to the police. She thought she was walking away from all that nonsense, and getting on with life, and now she was right back in. What was the line from that mafia film? "Just when I thought I was out, they pull me back in." This was going to take some thinking over. She ordered another slice of chocolate fudge cake.

"Bash?"

"Sam! Twice in a week! What have I done to deserve this?"

She cut straight to the chase. There was no point getting personal because there was nothing to be personal about.

"You remember those accounts I sent you last week?"

"You mean the *Home and Heart* ones?"

"Yes. And you said there was money being siphoned off."

"I said that two of the trustees were using the charity like a private bank account and that the guy who topped himself was probably straight."

"Would you look at them again?"

"Why? I thought you told me your clients had put this in the hands of the police."

Ah! And here was the problem. This time she had to tell him even less and ask him to do even more. "I did. They have," she said hurriedly.

"Then the police could do this a lot better than me. They've got forensic accountants who specialise in this sort of thing."

While she was thinking about what to say and how to say it, Bash broke the silence, and she could hear the concern in his voice. "I'm still worried about you, Sam. You've got involved in something, haven't you?"

At least he had given her a way in. Be a bit honest. "I might have. But it's OK, I'm not in danger. I'm just trying to get some information for someone." True, almost true, and true again. "A different someone."

There was another silence, and this time it was Bash who was thinking. She knew he was thinking about all the things she had been thinking about when they had stood in the care home's car park a week ago. She heard him sigh, and knew that he had reached the same conclusion.

"Alright, Sam," he said. "What do you want me to do?"

She gave him the detective sergeant's list. He laughed humourlessly. "Nothing dangerous then. Just people trafficking and money laundering. And possible proof of a murder."

She laughed as well, but not so seriously. "OK," she said. "Maybe it's a little bit dangerous. You can always say no if you want to." Which was a mean thing to say, but that would teach him to get married and have a family.

"No, no, it's alright," he said quickly. "I've still got the PDFs so I'll take a look at them, and if I find anything I'll let you know. It might take a few days – I do have an actual job, you know, so I'll have to do it in the evenings."

"Faz won't mind?" Oh, God, how old was she? Fifteen? This was the sharp legal mind that Mr. Allcock was praising a week ago. Turned to a pool of hormones because she couldn't forget that the life Farzana was having should have been hers.

"Why should she?"

"I don't know...I just thought..." And that sentence just died a natural death.

"She knows all about you, Sam – I told everything about the things we got up to as kids." She thought he was going to start with "Do you remember the time we – " and she really hoped he wouldn't because she didn't know how she'd stop him and then she'd start crying.

"OK," she said.

And then there was another pause. This was the moment Sameena should have said "Well, thanks, let me know if you find something" and hung up, but she didn't and the silence stretched.

"Anything else?" Bash asked, and it sounded like he wanted there to be.

"No – I...no, that's it," mumbled Sameena. There was a long moment before Bash's phone clicked and she was sure she heard him breathing.

She banged her phone on her forehead. "Idiot! Idiot! Idiot!"

CHAPTER TWENTY-TWO

Daz – Thursday

Today had been a good day. Daz was standing at the sink, washing up after his tea. He looked around his kitchen at everything shipshape and squared away, the counter clear apart from the kettle, and cooker wiped down and clean, the refrigerator with the letter from his counsellor neatly held in the middle of the door by a *I heart Lichfield magnet.* The army might have made a mess of his life, but it had taught him how to be tidy. Maybe the counsellor could teach him how not to make a mess of his relationships.

Looking out of the window he saw the white van pull up and the two Iraqi men – Amir and Fai-something – tumble out of the back. They looked dirty and dog-tired like they'd just come back from a war zone as they dragged themselves to the flats.

He turned away. Not my problem. What was it the counsellor had said? Why are you worrying about things that don't matter to you? She said, "Tell yourself 'Thinking about this is of no use to me now. Let it go.'"

So he did.

It had been a good day because he'd sold all of his Big Issues on his new patch. It wasn't close to the bank where people bought it because they felt guilty when they got money from the cashpoint, but people coming out of the restaurants and cafés near him full of food they didn't need felt guilty too. And sometimes they brought him sandwiches and drinks as well. It was better than his old patch!

He took his bagful of sandwiches and cans of pop he didn't need to Wade Street and shared them at the meeting. He hoped that the offering might make the counselling session go well. At two-thirty he took a deep breath and headed for Bore Street. It was literally three minutes away. He felt nervous.

"You've been in a war zone and on the streets. How bad do you think it will be?"

"She's going to ask me to talk about my feelings."

"Not talking about them is what got you into this mess in the first place, isn't it?" That had been good advice from Eugene.

The room needed a coat of paint and had a sash window that overlooked a dark paved and walled yard with a few sad plants in large pots. Squashed into it was a shabby couch and two worn armchairs and a low table between them. There was an open box of tissues on the table, with one tissue poking up like a little white tongue.

Ms. Pauline Linden stood up to meet him. She wasn't what he'd expected. She wore her hair like a golden helmet, bright red lipstick and twinkling green eyes under dark eyebrows. A black and red blouse that matched her lipstick, a black pencil skirt with a wide black belt and boots. She looked like she should be on the telly. But then, he hadn't known what to expect.

"Mr. Mitchell?" She stuck her hand out like a man. He took it. "Take a seat."

"Should I lie down?" he said, sitting on the couch.

She laughed like a man too. "I think the chair will do."

He perched on the edge.

"So, Sameena tells me you're trying to see your daughter."

"Sameena? Oh, Sam! How do you know her?"

"We were at school together. Now, back to you. Tell me about your daughter."

He had been worried that the hour would be full of awkward silence, but he never had a problem talking about his daughter. "Her name's Amy. We called her that because me and the wife loved Amy Winehouse when we were getting together, and our Amy seemed just the same from the moment she was born, you know, proper little ball of fire, wouldn't take anything from anyone..." He tailed off. "Anyways, my wife's got a restraining order against me – after I...you know." She didn't know, but she could guess. "I want to show her that I've changed."

"I don't think you can say that you've changed. No one can. But you can say that you're trying to change. So, do you want to start?" Darren nodded. "Well then, tell me how you ended up here."

And he did. He was surprised how clearly he saw the trajectory of his life. It had always seemed such a mess before, and he realised what a skilful interrogator this woman was. She would have done well with the prisoners in Afghanistan. Afterwards he felt clear and light.

"Now what do you think you need to do next?"

"I need to contact my wife, I suppose."

"And how will you do that?"

Then they were off again. Anything he said, she responded with a question which made him think and plan more carefully, taking control, instead of letting situations and his emotions bounce him around. She never let him blame himself, someone else or something that had happened.

It was just like talking really. Something he'd never done before. Well, of course he'd talked before – to his parents, mates, squaddies, soldiers – but all you ever talked about was school or telly or football or orders or the enemy. Nobody talked about how they felt, because then they might start crying and everyone would see and everyone would laugh. The last time he'd talked like this, it had been to his doctor, and he'd prescribed medication and then a stronger one, the long slow slide to drug addiction and the streets.

He liked it. So he talked some more, and it got off topic. He stopped talking about planning for the future, and he talked about the past – the sad things and the funny things. Family, school, the army, the war – he called it 'war' even if the politicians called it 'an armed conflict' – and how he'd ended up on the streets. The times when people walked past him blank-faced and hard-eyed and how he'd wished he was dead and the times when some act of kindness like someone bringing him a meal deal out of Sainsbury's made the world seem a better place.

"You don't want to beg outside Waitrose," he explained. "People who shop there will walk right past you. Sainsbury people have got money, but they don't try and hang on to all of it."

"What about Tesco shoppers?"

"They don't have any spare change."

She shared the joke with him and they both laughed. Then she said, "But that's all in the past. There's nothing you can do about that. What about now?"

And that brought him back to Shaun and the present.

"It sounds like he's a good friend to you," she said.

"He is – was. He's dead and they say he committed suicide."

"That's sad. Why do they say it was suicide?"

And that opened up a whole new can of worms. She let him talk and he talked – about Shaun's death which couldn't possibly have been suicide and the police trying to write it off, and Willow and Sameena, and the papers he had found at the *Home and Heart* offices and Andrew Russell and his crooked accountant brother-in-law.

When he ran out of breath, and fell silent, she left a pause and then said, "And how much of that can you do anything about."

"I can prove he was murdered," Daz said fiercely.

"And will that put you in harm's way?"

Daz shrugged. "Might," he muttered. "It's not the first time I've been in danger."

"And how did that work out for you?"

The pause was much longer this time. "I'm not saying you're wrong, Darren, but I want you think about why you do the things you do when so many of them are self-destructive. Could it be that you do them because you know they give you something to blame and reason not to change?"

An even longer pause, and then he asked her what she meant, and she gave him examples of how he'd sabotaged his life, and he justified himself, and she asked questions and the next thing he knew, she was glancing at her watch on a stainless-steel bracelet studded with zircons and said, "Well, Mr. Mitchell, that's it for now. Same time next week?"

It was like magic, time had flown - and he hadn't even cried.

CHAPTER TWENTY-THREE

Willow, Daz – Friday

"Do you want your break now, Willow?" asked Susan.

"Yeah. OK. Thanks," replied Willow as she was wiping down a recently vacated table at the Library Café.

"Are you going to take a coffee and a cake out to Big Daz?"

"I would, but he doesn't seem to be selling *The Big Issue* in his usual place. Perhaps he's left Lichfield for one reason or another. I haven't seen him for three days.

"I wouldn't worry about it, Willow. That sort of person often gets restless and has to move on. They can't seem to settle to anything. That's why they're on the streets," said Susan.

"I suppose so...it's just strange that he should just disappear like that. He's sold *The Big Issue* in pretty much the same spot since I started working here. I'm surprised he didn't tell me he was going. Anyway, I won't be long. I'll just get some fresh air and be back in fifteen minutes or so."

"OK. See you then."

Willow grabbed her coat and made her way outside. Friday was market day. She recognised most of the stall holders and smiled at a few friendly faces – the fruit and vegetable guy who shouted out how much a punnet of strawberries was every two minutes, the nice aging hippy who framed pictures and the woman who sold leather handbags and other accessories. They were regulars. Every Tuesday, Friday and Saturday – come rain or shine. As regular as Daz, but as she wondered across the market, Willow could see that he was still not there in his usual spot. Surely, he hadn't left Lichfield just like that, as Susan suggested. Maybe he was just ill or perhaps he'd decided to stop selling *The Big Issue*. Or could it be that he was just fed up that no-one seemed to want to listen to him or believe him that his friend had been murdered.

She looked along Dam Street as far as the cathedral but there was no sign of Daz. There was nothing she could do. She didn't know where he lived. She had no contact details for him at all. That's probably how he wanted it and liked it. No-one to answer to. A free agent.

Willow walked back towards the café. For some reason she looked up the High Street towards *the Faro Lounge.* She thought back to the times she had spent in there with Sameena and Daz. Willow smiled to herself as she remembered some of their conversations and banter. There was Sameena trying to talk herself out of buying a cake before claiming that her diet would start tomorrow. Daz, the tough, bitter army man, who seemed out of his depth, but was slowly revealing a better side of his nature.

Willow ambled past the market towards *the Faro Lounge* in a world of her own only to be awoken from her memories by the shouting of two words.

"Get lost!"

A few heads of shoppers walking towards Willow briefly turned around, assessed the situation and then carried on with their own business and busy lives.

"Just leave me alone."

"Or what? You old tramp!"

"Yeah, who'd buy that crap anyway? Not after you've been touching it."

Willow continued to walk towards the noisy confrontation. She could make out three teenage boys, not much older than her, facing up to...Daz.

"Look, you've had your fun. You're very funny. Now fuck off!" shouted Daz.

"Call that work? Begging for money… you tramp...Get a proper job, you arse wipe!" the teenagers fired a volley of insults at Daz.

"Hey! What the hell d'you think you're doing?" shouted Willow at the three lads as she positioned herself in front of Daz.

"Mind it, little girl. This has nothin' to do with you!"

"Yeah, leave it, Willow," whispered Daz as he put his hand on Willow's shoulder.

"No, I'm not leaving it! What's going on?" demanded Willow.

One teenager, who had slightly distanced himself from his two mates, tried to justify their actions "We're just having some fun. Just messin' with him."

By now a few passers-by had stopped passing and were creating a small crowd around *The Big Issue* seller, the petite teenaged girl with weird hair and the three taller youths who were acting tough.

"You mean you were harassing him. There are witnesses here who will supply evidence to the police when I call them on my phone, once I've taken photos of you all." Willow reached into her back pocket and produced her mobile. By the time she held up her mobile to her face and pointed it vaguely in the direction of the young tough men, they had been reduced to naughty boys, quickly leaving the scene, swearing and gesticulating at Willow and *The Big Issue* seller as they scurried off.

"Well done," said an older member of the small crowd.

"Good on you," a young mother pushing a pram agreed.

Within seconds the crowd had dispersed and Willow turned round to face Daz. Daz was looking at the ground.

"Excuse me," said Willow in a posh voice, "may I trouble you for a copy of this publication you're selling? I hear it's rather good."

Daz looked up. "Not everyone likes it," said Daz looking at Willow, his embarrassment and shame slightly melting from his face.

"So I gather," said Willow as the colour returned to her cheeks and her heart rate normalised. "Can we sit down for a minute? I have a few questions."

"Yeah, sure," said Daz pointing at a vacant bench outside B&M.

"First, what are you doing here? You don't usually stand here."

"No...I just thought I could try up here instead...see if it's any better."

"I've been looking out for you this week...to see if you wanted a coffee and stuff, but you were gone."

"Sorry about that...missing in action. Didn't mean to worry you. Just fancied a change."

"Right. And you didn't think to tell me that you changed your pitch," said Willow with slight annoyance in her delivery. "I thought you might have been ill or decided to move to another town. I had no way of contacting you...I suppose I just wanted to know that you were OK."

"But I thought that we'd decided to move on with our lives. There was nothing else to investigate...it was just a dead end."

"Yeah. I know. There was nothing else we could do. The police weren't that interested."

"No help at all. I'm just gonna have to accept that I'll never get to the truth."

"Anyway, my second question is, what the fork was going on just now? What did you do or say to those twonks?"

"Nothin'...really...they just like mouthing off. They think they're big and clever. Every so often they stand in front of me and just say things. I just stand there and take it. I can't really do anything about it. If I raised my hands to them, they'd go running off to their mommies and daddies. After a while they get bored and bugger off."

"I bet you want to use your army combat skills on them, don't you?" asked Willow.

"Yeah, but what good would that do? Eugene says we give other people control over our lives when we say that they 'make us' angry. He says it's usually what we say or do that brings conflict in our lives. He says we must take responsibility for what we do, and practice forgiveness."

Daz sounded like he was parroting something. "He says a lot, doesn't he?" she said, pulling a face. "Who is this Eugene?"

"He's my sponsor in NA. Anyway, if I did anything I'd be the one in trouble with the police. I'm trying to keep my nose clean at the moment. It's important that I don't get into any trouble. There's stuff that I'm trying to sort out in my life," admitted Daz.

Willow stopped herself from asking Daz to explain and gently enquired, "Doesn't anyone come to help you when morons like that are horrible to you?"

"Sometimes, but not often. Most people just walk on by. There aren't many super heroes in Lichfield. The only one I know is this mouthy purple-haired Supergirl who appears out of the blue from time to time."

"Well, I was just passing, I'd just had my lunch of kryptonite and chips, before going back to my undercover job at the library café."

"Can you tell Supergirl, the next time you see her, that I don't need her help. I can look after myself and I don't want her to get involved. I'm OK. Seriously, Willow. Thanks, but I'm OK, really. I can deal with it myself."

CHAPTER TWENTY-FOUR

Sam, Willow – Monday

Willow was tired at the end of her shift at the café. For a Monday it had been unusually hectic. It was non-stop all day. She didn't even manage to have a lunch break. She would sleep well tonight, she hoped. But first, she had an appointment before she headed home.

Her weekend had also been busy. She had gone shopping with her mother on Saturday. They had taken the train into Birmingham and spent a lovely day together having 'girl time,' as they put it. They had browsed the shops in The Bull Ring, walked along the canal by the National Indoor Arena and had lunch sitting outside a restaurant in the sunshine, over-looking the canal. Willow's mom liked to spoil her daughter occasionally. She had bought Willow a couple of tops, a skirt and a pair of skinny jeans. Most importantly, her mom had funded a change of hair colour from pink to purple. This was Willow really wanted for some weird reason Willow had not wanted any new clothes but it was a good excuse for the two of them to have some time together without the whiff of testosterone in the air. Willow was grateful for that. And she was grateful to her mom. She loved her mother because she was kind, generous and understood her, unlike most people.

On Sunday, Willow spent the morning and some of the afternoon at the care home. There were a variety of smells and odours for Willow to contend with, but she was used to it. She had chatted to several of the residents who were not being visited by relatives. Some of them recognised Willow, others couldn't remember her, but were still happy to tell her about their memories from the last century. Willow had a light lunch in the café with Mary, followed by a game of Scrabble. Willow wasn't quite sure if some of the words Mary came up with were in the Oxford Dictionary or any dictionary, for that matter, but it wasn't worth arguing with Mary.

At about three o'clock Willow made her way home. As the weather was still pleasant, she decided to walk once around Stowe Pool. She needed to breathe fresh air and have some thinking time.

After the family sat down together for their Sunday evening meal, Willow went upstairs to her room and sent a text to Sameena.

Now, at 4.45 pm on Monday afternoon, Willow was walking slowly towards the Citizens' Advice offices. When Willow had contacted Sameena yesterday and asked to meet up, she hadn't expected Sam to agree to it the next day. She messaged Willow to meet her at the end of her shift at the CAB office.

When Willow arrived and opened the front door to the building, she recognised the guy who appeared to be the supervisor/receptionist.

"May I help you?" enquired Thomas.

"Oh, hi, I'm meeting Sam...Sameena."

"You don't have an appointment? I'm afraid we're closing in the next five minutes. Do you want to arrange a time for an appointment with her next Monday?"

"No, that's fine. I'm here to have a friendly chat with her. Not advice as such. We'll probably walk to a café and talk there."

"Oh, OK. Well, she'll be free after her last client leaves. I'll tell her that you're here."

"Thank you. I'm Willow, by the way."

"Yes. I recognise you from before."

Five minutes later Sameena arrived in the waiting room.

"Hi, Willow. Wow, new hair colour – I like it! Sorry, I'm running a bit late. Shall we head off into town for a drink?"

"That would be good. I didn't expect you to see me so soon. This isn't a problem for you, is it?"

"Don't be silly. I could do with some sensible conversation after a weekend with my mother," said a smiling Sam.

"Wow, I don't think anyone has ever called me sensible before. I'm not sure that I like it. It makes me feel mature and old."

"Sorry. Is the word 'sensible' quite insulting to a teenager? OK, let's go to a cafe and have an irresponsible conversation about stupid things."

"Now you're talking!" said Willow smiling back at Sameena.

Five minutes later they were sitting in *the Faro Lounge* with drinks and cakes in front of them. Sameena suggested a table in a dark corner of the cafe. This was not because they were discussing top secret information, but because Sameena was in danger of being recognised. There could be Slimming World spies in here or Faro staff who would think that she was a permanent fixture in the café.

"We ought to find a different place to meet occasionally. I'm beginning to be treated as a regular when I go to the counter to buy food and drinks," whispered Sam. "Anyway, what's up? Are you OK?"

"I'm good thanks. I just wanted to tell you that I saw Daz on Friday. Well, I sort of bumped into him. He was trying to sell *The Big Issue* in a different spot."

"What do you mean 'trying to sell *The Big Issue*'?" asked Sameena.

"Well, when I saw him, or should I say, heard him, he was having a slanging match with some idiots."

"That sounds like Daz!"

"No, I think he was the innocent party, this time. These lads were just picking on him. Daz said to me that it happens once in a while. But it was a bit weird. He just stood there and took it from these numbskulls."

"That's good, right? Maybe Daz is starting to understand the consequences of acting before thinking. I suppose doing what he does, he's always going to have to deal with some unpleasant characters."

"Perhaps, but later on he said that he couldn't afford to get into any more trouble. So, it seemed as if he was backing off from everything to do with his friend's death. I couldn't believe it. A few days ago he seemed so pumped up about getting to the bottom of what really happened to Shaun."

"It sounds as if he's accepting the fact that he may never know why Shaun fell to his death at the cathedral. He may have a few suspicions, but that's it. It feels as if he's drawn a line under the incident. It's probably best that he does, he's clearly struggling with things."

"So do you feel the same way? Just leave it. Forget all about it. Move on."

"I suppose I did, but I'm now beginning to think something is still not quite right. I've had a conversation with a of couple people regarding Shaun's financial links with *Home and Heart* since I last saw you. You remember Detective Sergeant Kendrick , DI Potter's second in command?"

"Yeah, what did she want ?"

"My help, in a nutshell. Reading between the lines, I don't think she trusts Potter or the system. Without going into the ins and outs, there appears to be unaccounted-for money coming in to the charity. She wanted my friend Bash to have another look at the accounts. It was clear that this wasn't part of the official investigation. So, Bash had another look."

"Did he find anything interesting?"

"He phoned me back last night. There was nothing funny about money going out, but he found some odd cash payments from a Rory Winters going in. He says there are always cash payments going into charities, but these seemed unusually large so he Googled him and found a rich ex-soldier who imports artefacts from the Middle East...who fought in Iraq in the same unit, at the same time as Shaun."

"Now that is a bit weird," said Willow thoughtfully. "Shaun and this guy Winters were in Iraq and when I spoke to Daz on Friday he mentioned a couple of guys living in his block of flats who he said were immigrants. Said they were working in a car wash. They didn't want to talk and they left him in a hurry, got in the back of a van and were gone. Just like that."

"You're joking...I need to contact Daz. Do you know where he lives?" asked Sameena.

"No, but I managed to get a mobile number off him the other day. I'm not sure if it'll work, but it's worth a try?"

“Thanks, said Sam as she added Daz’s number to her phone. “Look, Willow, I’ve got to go. I’ll contact you tomorrow and keep you updated.”

“Alright, as long as you do. I don’t want to be kept out of the loop. I want to be part of this.”

“I promise...it’s just that you’re...”

“If you’re going to say ‘too young to be involved’ I’m gonna scream like a baby. Treat me like an irresponsible teenager who thinks they’re immortal, OK?”

“I’ll try. I’ll be in touch with you tomorrow.”

CHAPTER TWENTY-FIVE

Daz, Sam -Tuesday

They were sitting in Sameena's Ford Focus.

"I told Mr. Allcock I was working from home this morning and I followed the van. I know where the car wash is."

"Sam, this is crazy. This isn't Grand Theft Auto. It's a couple of illegals doing the only job they can get for cash. That's what I was doing this morning until you dragged me off my patch. I'm not going to make trouble for them."

"It could be bigger than that, Daz. It could be people trafficking, and human slavery and it could be connected with Shaun's death."

Daz sighed and slumped back in the passenger seat. "My counsellor told me I should learn to step away from situations that could trigger my anger."

"Pauline?" said Sameena. "She's very good, isn't she?"

He was surprised. "You've seen her?" Sameena nodded. "What for?"

"She helped me with my eating disorder. Open the glove compartment, would you? There's a tin of boiled sweets."

He handed them over, and noticed it was more than just one bag – Bassetts All-Sorts, Haribo, Maynard's Jelly Babies, and Rowntree's Fruit Pastilles. It was a sweet shop in there. She caught him looking. "I know, it didn't work for me – but you seem to be doing very well," she added hurriedly.

"I was," he said grimly.

She scrabbled through the tin, found a purple one and popped it into her mouth. She wiped the icing sugar that dusted her fingers off on her skirt, tossed the tin into his lap and grated the car into gear.

He looked at her. "What?" She looked back. "I'm keeping my sugar levels up."

They drove north into one of the poorer areas of Lichfield. You never saw car washes in nice areas on the south side, Daz thought. But who would want a car wash on their doorstep? The thumping generators driving the power hoses, radios playing loud music and the workers shouting to each other in foreign languages. And the cars. Residents would be straight up the council.

"There it is," whispered Sameena.

He hadn't noticed she'd pulled up. Across the road was an old petrol station, but now it was "Mr. Miyagi's Wax On Wax Off Car Wash." Everything Daz had thought about was going on, plus a queue of cars with their engines running and soapy water flowing into the street. He'd forgotten about that. People living on the Darwin Park estate would hate that.

He looked hard to see if he could spot Amir or Faisal, but he couldn't see them. Maybe she'd got the wrong place. "You sure?" he asked.

"Of course. Now this is the plan. I'm going to drive round the block, drop you off at the corner and get my car washed."

"That's not much of a plan."

"And we'll look for evidence of slavery, like – " She started ticking off on her fingers. " – cash only paid to the manager and no receipt, it's too cheap, the workers aren't wearing protective clothing like goggles, gloves and boots."

"And what do I do?"

"This." She reached behind for the bag on the seat behind her and took out a camera. "I want you to take photographs. The other sign of slavery is long hours. If we take some date-stamped photos now and come back ten hours later and the same workers are still there, it's more evidence."

Daz was dubious. "It looks complicated. And new," he added.

"I bought it yesterday. It's really easy. It has auto-focus and everything. You push this to zoom and this to take the pictures."

"I'll look a bit obvious standing on the pavement taking photos."

"You don't have to. If you stand on the corner, you're hidden by the pillar box. You can rest the camera on the top and it'll look like you're just standing there!" Sameena was excited, and it made Daz wary.

"You know this isn't a game, right? This is dangerous. I've met people on the streets who've escaped from stuff like this and their slave masters are pure evil. They don't think about human life any more than you do about stepping on an ant."

"And that's why we have to stop them. If you don't want to do it, give me the camera. You can get out and go home. I'll do it myself!"

Daz was surprised at Sameena's ferocity – and so was Sameena. She thought her social conscience went as far as one day a week at Citizens Advice, and here she was prepared to charge into the jaws of...something. Or maybe nothing.

"Alright," Daz growled, opening the car, "I'll do it. But listen to me. Drive in, get your car washed and get out again. Don't do anything stupid."

He got out and banged the car door and she eased the car slowly away.

That was the trouble with Willow and Sam – Sameena, the counsellor had called her Sameena. They were nice people and they'd helped him through a rough patch – Sam had kept him out of jail – but they had no idea. They were nice people with nice little lives. They had no idea how easily the bottom could drop out of a safe life and leave you somewhere dark and dangerous.

With the camera hidden in the pocket of his hoodie he slouched to the corner and took up his post leaning against the pillar box. He fumbled with the camera until he saw a picture of his foot appear on the screen and then he casually rested it on top of the box. Trying to look as if he was waiting for someone, he zoomed in on the car wash. He felt like he was back in a patrol base in Helmand, as exposed as a fly on a Christmas cake.

He started snapping. He wasn't sure what he was taking pictures of, or even if he was taking pictures at all, because he was trying to look in the opposite direction. In the end he decided to hide the camera in his hand and do a recce. He walked down the street past the car wash, the camera in his hand against his leg. He clicked away again, looking straight in front of him. When he got to the junction he looked back and decided to try again. He couldn't check the camera now, but some more pictures taken even closer might be better.

He crossed the road and walked back up, the soapy water from the car wash gurgling in the gutter next to him. He got his phone out and pretended to talk to the first person who came into his head. It was Amy. It was always Amy.

When he got to the car wash, he stopped. He could see a lot of men wading around in running water in just their trainers and grimy tracksuits, plunging their bare hands into buckets of soapy water. He started talking too loudly and waving his arms about too much and thumbing the shutter button, raising his voice every time the camera whirred. And he started getting into the conversation with his daughter.

"No, I'm telling you, it went really well...she says if I keep going to the sessions then she'll speak to this solicitor she knows...yeah, the visits would have to be supervised to start with, but later maybe we could go to McDonalds or the cinema...we could even go away on holiday."

And down the empty line he could hear Amy getting more and more excited. He was in a bright world where everything that had gone wrong in his life was put right, and he didn't hear the raised voices in the car wash.

"Why can't you give me a receipt? I want to see the manager. Get your hands off me!"

Slowly Amy's voice and Sam's voice blended into one and confused Daz. He looked round and realised where he was, standing on a dusty rundown street, with the sound of a thumping generator, hissing water and tinny radio music behind him. He spun round.

Sameena was outside her car, her arm being held by a stocky, swarthy man in a boiler suit and wellington boots. She was holding onto the open door of her car and trying to pull free. She looked angry and scared.

"Oh for fuck's sake!" Daz stuffed his phone and the camera in his pocket and sprinted onto the forecourt, his feet splashing in the soapy water. "Hey! What do you think you're doing?" He used his best top-of-his-lungs soldier voice. "Get your hands off her!"

Everything got very quiet and, like looking down the sight of a gun, the colours got brighter and sharper, where everything else was dull and blurred. The only things that stayed clear were Sameena and the man. He hadn't felt like this for a long time, not since he was far away in the heat and dust of Helmand.

He laid a heavy hand on the man's arm and the man tried to jerk away, but then he turned and he must have seen something in Daz's face that frightened him because he let his hand fall. "She just a silly bitch makin' trouble," he stammered.

"Doesn't matter, mate – you don't lay hands on a woman." Daz didn't recognise his voice.

He glanced at Sameena and saw that she was scared too – but not scared of the man. She was scared of him!

"Get in the car, lady," he grated.

Like a sleepwalker, Sameena did as she was told.

"Now drive away." She crunched the car into gear, and with a last frightened glance at him, she sped away in a spray of foam and water.

Daz glanced around, suddenly aware that everyone in the car wash was looking at him. There were a lot of frightened white faces behind their windscreens and a lot of brown faces watching him with no expression at all. He recognised that look – they were trying to become invisible. He'd seen it in Afghanistan on the faces of men, women and children when the army or the Taliban passed by.

And he recognised two of the faces too. Amir and Faisal. Although their faces were blank, their eyes sparked as they caught sight of him.

The man noticed them too. "What you lookin' at? Get back to work, you lazy bastids."

One by one they dropped their eyes and moved away. Now with a space between him and Daz he turned back. "What about my money?" he demanded. "She owes me five pounds."

"You should have thought of that before you started threatening her."

Daz backed away with his eyes on the man, and when he felt there was enough distance between them, he turned and hurried off.

His back felt as wide as a bus and he expected to hear feet pounding on the pavement behind him at any minute, but he made it to the corner untouched. He turned it and leant weakly against a wall.

His hands were shaking. He recognised the signs. He had often felt like that coming back off patrol. He usually needed to unwind with a drink, or some weed. Now he couldn't. He looked up at the sky and took a deep breath and closed his eyes. He tried to feel the mellow sun on his face, not the dry heat of Afghanistan, and to smell the car fumes, and the fish and chip shop and the curry house, and not the stink of diesel in the camp.

He heard the car pull up in front of him and he looked down sharply, ready to fight. It was Sameena in her little Ford Focus. She wound the window down.

"Daz! Get in!"

He didn't want to, but he didn't want to walk back to his flat either. He lowered himself in and banged the door shut. She managed to drive off without grinding the gears. There was an awkward silence, and then she said, "Daz, I can't thank you enough."

Daz clenched his hands in the pockets of his hoodie because he was worried what he would do with them. "What the fuck were you thinking? What did I tell you to do? Drive in, get your car washed and get out."

He was angry now – not angry because she had put herself in danger, but she'd put him in danger – in danger of getting into something with the man at the car wash and in danger of getting arrested – again. Just when he was straightening his life out. She could have cost him everything. With their cosy little lives, Sameena and Willow had no idea.

"You don't understand," protested Sameena. "I was just trying to get more evidence."

Daz thumped his fist on the dashboard and she flinched. "No, you don't understand. Those two men at my flat, Amir and Faisal. They recognised me. They pretended they didn't, but I could tell. You put yourself in danger and then you did the same to me. You just don't do that in combat."

"But that's great," said Sameena excitedly, without even thinking of saying sorry. "That's more evidence. I only asked if he took card and asked for a receipt. I was trying to get more proof and it looks like we've got it. Plus what Bash told me about the accounts and I think we've got enough to take to DS Kendrick."

Daz dragged the camera out of his pocket and tossed it in her lap. "You'd better have that then. I bet you can find some more proof for her there."

"Thanks, Daz – with this, plus what Bash told me about the accounts is going to be more than enough for her. Now she can force Potter to keep the investigation open."

Daz grunted. "You can drop me off here." He reached onto the back seat and got his bag. "I've got the rest of my *Big Issues* to sell."

She pulled up, he got out and banged the door. She was so full of adrenaline, so pleased with herself, that she didn't notice the slump in Daz's shoulders as he walked away.

CHAPTER TWENTY-SIX

Krys, Sam - Wednesday

Detective Sergeant Kendrick strode purposely along the footpath towards her scheduled rendezvous. She was late! Late for the meeting and late for her husband. She had promised to make an effort and get home earlier just once this week. No doubt he would start cooking their evening meal and make a big fuss about it when she arrived home late...again.

Krystyna started to slow down when she saw Sameena sitting on a park bench by the miniature golf course in Beacon Park.

"Hi, Sameena. I don't want to sound rude, but I've got a million things on my mind and I told my husband that I would cook tonight. I'm a bit pushed for time. So what can I do for you? And why couldn't you have just phoned or come to the station?"

"I'm sorry but I needed to speak to you in person and you didn't seem comfortable in *the Faro Lounge* the other day. I also didn't want it to be official by coming to the police station or bump into your boss," said Sameena while staring at a handful of parents and their young children having fun in the adventure playground.

"Are you OK?"

"Yes...sorry...you must be really busy with all of the cases you have to deal with."

"It is busy, but I love my job...most of the time. Some days I don't want to go home. Anyway, what can I do for you?"

"Look, I don't want to keep you. It's just that I spoke to my friend about the accounts following our meeting at *the Faro Lounge*. But there's been some other developments regarding the Cathedral death."

"What do you mean 'developments'? That's the sort of thing I would say as a police officer talking to a member of the public. Don't tell me that you, Daz and Willow are still playing at being amateur detectives?" said Krystyna raising her voice slightly with a piercing look in her eyes.

"Well, no, not intentionally. We just stumbled on some things we thought you might be interested in. And anyway, you asked for my help, remember. Very top secret. 'This is just between us' you said and then listed your concerns about Potter and the charity money. So, don't criticise me if I got involved because you asked me to get involved." Krystyna was not the only one to raise her voice.

A silence fell between them that felt like ten minutes before Krystyna spoke.

"I shouldn't have asked you to speak to your friend about the charity's accounts. I'm sorry. It wasn't right. I don't want you being involved with anything risky or dangerous."

'Too late for that!' thought Sam. "Well, I ought to tell you briefly what we found out. Perhaps after that you can thank me and go ballistic at me at the same time. But just hear me out first. Promise?"

Krystyna agreed.

Sameena explained that Bash had looked at the accounts again and could trace some payments that were not documented properly. Laundered money almost certainly. Possibly false names. His recommendation was that the accounts needed serious forensic analysis to get to the truth about where this money was going from and to.

Sameena then told Krystyna that Willow had found out that some men living in Daz's flat did not appear to be ex-services and were working in a local car wash. She described the events from yesterday, without it sounding like she and Daz were Starsky and Hutch conducting an undercover operation. In a calm, matter-of-fact way she explained to Krystyna what she saw and described the reaction of the boss at the car wash to her when she tried to pay by credit card. She added that they had taken photographs.

Krystyna waited patiently until Sam had finished – then she went ballistic."You three just can't stop yourselves, can you? You should know better than getting involved in this. Willow is a teenager and Daz, well, he's unstable to say the least, but you're supposed to be a law-abiding, respectable, role model. You shouldn't have followed the van or taken photographs without permission. No good will come of this. It won't do any of you any good. Let us do our job from now on.

I'll pass this information on to Potter on the understanding that you let us handle the case. No more amateur detective work, is that clear?"

Sameena felt like a primary school pupil being told off by her teacher but she curbed her instinctive urge to say sorry, deciding instead to fight back. "So, don't I get a thank you for giving you all of this info? Without us you'd have nothing to go on. At least we're doing something...unlike some of the real police!"

"But we are working on Shaun's death, I assure you. It's just things take time and we have to keep our cards close to our chests. Unlike you three!"

"So is that a 'thank you' then?"

"Yes," replied Krystyna, grudgingly starting to smile.

There was another silence.

"This feels like one of those old movies where one spy secretly meets another one on a park bench and passes over a document hidden in a folded newspaper," said Sameena trying to lighten the mood.

"I'm afraid those days are long gone. Spies don't swap briefcases or take a newspaper from a supposed stranger any more. They just use their phones and the internet. No-one needs to go to the park or meet at a particular time. Useful intelligence is passed on any time of day or night, which may seem convenient, but most of my info hits my mobile in the evenings or wakes me up when I'm asleep . As you can imagine, that doesn't go down well with Dan, my husband."

"Been married long?"

"Feels like it. But some days it feels as if we don't know each other at all. What about you? Anyone special?"

"No. I decided a while back to focus on my career goals. Relationships can get in the way, if you're not careful."

"Mmm. I know what you mean . Anyway, I must go. I've a meal and an argument waiting for me when I get home. Take care...and...thank you."

Krystyna headed back to her car in the pay and display at the edge of Beacon Park. She texted Dan that she was running late and would be leaving the station soon. If she was going to be late, did it matter by how much?

Sameena did not have to hurry home either. Her meal would be waiting for her whenever she arrived at her mother's house. Just now she preferred to carry on sitting on the park bench watching the children and adults playing happy families on the swings, slides and roundabouts.

CHAPTER TWENTY-SEVEN

Krys - Thursday

Sameena had taken the hint and emailed her the photos and Bash's comments on the accounts. Krystyna had them in a buff folder on her desk. Now she was just waiting for Potter to get in so she could put it on his desk.

He was late – again. His clothes were rumpled, a three-day old shirt and one or two shaving nicks. His bald spot was showing through without his hair gelled in place. His eyes were bloodshot. In the office, the gossip was that his wife had thrown him out and he was sofa-surfing. Not that she should be pointing fingers at anyone having relationship problems.

But they both had a job to do. She followed him into his office with the dossier in her hand.

Potter sat down with a groan and dry-washed his face with his hands. Through his fingers he saw Krystyna and groaned again. "What now, Kendrick? I'm not in the mood today."

She dropped the folder on his desk.

"What's this?"

"Evidence that there may be more to Shaun Wilde's death than we suspected." She said *we* to soften the blow, but it was all him.

"Not this again," he growled. I told you – it's been put to bed. Wilde killed himself, the accounts are the Charity Commission's problem, and the raid on the office was a robbery by some out-of-town chancers. We have targets to meet. This isn't one of them."

He swept his arm across his desk and the folder and a framed photograph and the telephone tumbled onto the floor or into the standard-issue metal wastepaper bin. The crash made everyone outside turn round or peer over their computer screens.

Krystyna took a beat. She could feel all the eyes burning into her back and she imagined the comments.

"She's poking the bear again."

"You'd think she'd be tired of Potter ripping her a new one by now."

"She'll be clearing her desk by the end of the month."

She knew because she'd heard them. Sometimes when she came into the room and the conversation stopped in an awkward silence, or because they were said to her face. She wasn't going to last; Potter would still be here, so they sided with him.

She waited until she thought the hubbub in the office had died down, and then she said with no tone in her voice, "I've another copy, sir, and if you don't want to look at it, I'll take it to the Detective Chief Superintendent and the Chief Constable if I have to."

Potter sat back heavily in his chair. It squeaked under him and rolled away from his desk. "What is it you want, Kendrick? My job?"

She held his eyes. She was thinking, 'No, sir, I just want you to do your damn job,' but all she said, as gently as possible, was, "Just look at the folder, sir. It shows links between Wilde's charity, and money laundering, and people trafficking and slavery."

"And where did this information come from?" he sneered. "Your homeless friend, the hippy girl with the pink hair, and the Paki solicitor?"

She bent down and picked up the file so she wouldn't have to speak and assembled the papers and photographs in order. She set it gently in front of him. "Just take a look at it, sir. It's good intel."

He sighed, slid his chair up to his desk and flicked it open. This was the time to be quiet. Potter had been a good copper once. She had to wait and see if he still was. Her husband Danny loved to fish. He said, "Fishing is patience and faith awaiting a nibble." She was sure he had thought of it himself, but that's what this felt like now. Would Potter take the bait?

He spread out the photos, flicked the accounts back and forwards and glanced at the notes she'd made, based on what Sameena had told her. Outside, the usual office chatter had started up again, but here in Potter's office, there was just the rustle of paper and Potter's raspy breathing.

At last he pushed his chair back and looked up.

"Alright," he said. "There might be something here. What do you suggest?"

In her head she was punching the air and shouting "Yes!" but she kept the smile off her face and said, "There seems to be a link between the charity and the car wash. I think we should conduct a raid. And then there are those unexplained payments linked to Rory Winters – I think he needs looking into."

"Right." He levered himself to his feet. "I'll speak to the Chief and set up the raid. You did some work with Serious Crime and the Fraud Squad when you were training, didn't you? Look into this Winters bloke."

And he strode out of the office, calling "You and you, with me" to a sergeant and a constable who were trying to keep their heads down over their desks and hurried out, leaving them trailing in his wake, grabbing their coats off the backs of their chairs.

Krystyna went slowly back to her desk. She didn't know whether to laugh or cry. She'd got Potter to reopen the investigation and he'd cut her out of it. If she was honest, had she expected anything else? With a sigh, she sat down in front of her computer and started calling up info on Rory Winters.

He had, as Sameena had said, been in the Staffordshire Regiment in Iraq in 2005 and 2006 so he must have known Shaun Wilde, but while he left the army and set up his charity with Russell, Winters had stayed on as part of the Iraqi Training and Advisory Mission. After the allied withdrawal in 2011 and the ensuing chaos, he disappeared from the radar, reappearing in 2015 trading in Middle Eastern antiques.

She found a website called "The Silk Road" which listed a Rory Winters as director alongside a picture of a man who had the look of a soldier about him. His hair was fashionably floppy now, but the set of the mouth and the level look in the grey eyes made her think of someone who had been tested under pressure. She browsed through a selection of Quran stands and Kilim rugs and brass trays and ewers. Nothing that she wouldn't expect to find selling in Little Beirut on the Edgware Road. She put a call through to a friend in the Fraud Squad who gave her the number of someone in Serious Crimes who specialised in online crime and he gave her the email address of an expert in conflict antiquities, and she fired an email off to him about Winters.

Maybe Potter had been right to give her this job after all. She was certainly better at it than anyone else here, but she knew if she turned up anything of value, Potter would find some way of claiming it as his own.

Potter got the raid set up for tomorrow and spent the rest of the day staying out of the office. First of all, he could avoid that bitch Kendrick in case she came up with any more work or threats, and he needed to sort his life out. He couldn't sleep in his brother's spare room indefinitely, living out of a suitcase. And he needed a drink. He phoned in to say he was following up some leads.

The Lichfield Masonic Lodge was in Tamworth. Potter drove over. He could get a taxi back and send a constable to pick up his car in the morning. He had a curry at the Royal Bengal to line his stomach and then settled in a corner of the Lodge's licensed bar for an evening of steady drinking. It was a place where a policeman could get quietly drunk without a finger being pointed at him.

Alcoholism had crept up on him quietly. Sometimes at parties, and then at weekends and evenings as well when he got promoted and the job got more stressful. He hadn't even noticed that things were going wrong until Ellie, his wife, told him he needed help and by then it was too late. He just knew that it started with needing a drink to unwind at the end of the day and get to sleep, and then being unable to sleep unless he'd had a drink.

He didn't think he was an alcoholic, he just used alcohol to take the rough edges off the day – like when he woke up in his brother's house because his wife wouldn't have him back until he sorted himself out, or when some jumped up little DS threatened to go over his head, or a smart-mouth Paki tried to make him look stupid.

He said hello to a few people he knew and ordered a double scotch – a nice single malt Laphroaig. There was cheaper stuff behind the bar, but he wasn't a falling-down drunk. He could sip perhaps three of these drinks over the evening and then drive home. Perhaps he'd only have two and call in on Ellie, persuade her to change her mind and take him back.

He glanced down and the glass was empty. He looked at the clock over the bar – it was half past eight. He'd only been here five minutes. How had that happened? He noticed a couple of men standing at the bar watching him and quickly looking away when he caught their eye.

He ordered the same again and went back to his table. He stared at the clock. He was going to make this one last an hour and then leave. He'd show them. He watched the minute hand jerkily tick off two minutes and lifted his glass for just one sip. Nothing touched his lips. He held the glass up in front of his face. Empty.

How had – ? He levered himself to his feet and bumped his table as he made his way back to the bar. He made the same again gesture.

When the bartender set the double in front of him he said quietly, "You're not driving home, are you, sir? I can call you a taxi. Wouldn't want one of our own boys in blue getting done for drunk-driving."

Potter drew himself up. "Oh, yeah? When I want your advice I'll rattle your cage."

One of the men standing at the bar turned to him. "Steady on, old man. No need for that."

Potter squared up to him. One minute he'd been talking about torts and abatements and now he thought he was Billy Big Bollocks? "Oh yeah? And what are you going to do about it?"

He felt a heavy hand on his shoulder and spun round. The man he was staring at had steady grey eyes that didn't look away when Potter got right in his face breathing whisky fumes and it made Potter step back and bump into the man behind him. He stumbled and the strong arm on his shoulder shifted to his armpit and stopped him falling over.

"Why don't we sit down and I'll buy us both a drink." He made a *One more round for everyone* gesture with his finger, cupped Potter's elbow and guided him back to the table in the corner.

Embarrassed at being held up and by the reasonable tone, Potter allowed the man to lead him.

"So you're with the police?"

Potter nodded. "Tony Potter, Detective Inspector, Lichfield Police."

The man stuck his hand out. "Winston," he said. "Roy Winston." They shook hands. Whiskies appeared in front of them, Winston raised his glass to Potter and took a sip. Potter tilted his and took a gulp.

"Haven't seen you here before."

"I'm up on business. I run a company down south."

"What do you do?"

Winston grinned. "Bit of this, bit of that. Whatever it takes to make a buck. Quite boring really. Not like you. Must be really interesting." He took Potter's empty glass. "Let me get you another one."

Blurrily, Potter watched him go up to the bar and exchange a few words and a laugh with the men standing there. Probably laughing at him. So what? They wouldn't be laughing when they came to him and asked him to fix their wives' parking tickets.

Another full glass appeared in front of him and he wrapped his hands around it but fought to keep it on the table. "So you were telling me about your work, Tony," said Winston.

Potter shrugged. "It's mostly routine – burglaries, car theft, assault, that sort of thing, but once in a while something comes along. We're investigating a murder at the moment." The glass was at his lips and he drank half of it and set it down. He misjudged the distance and it hit the table hard. Some of the liquid slopped over his fingers and he had to fight not to lick it off. He wiped it on his jacket.

"Go on," said Winston. Potter looked up, confused. The spilled drink had distracted him. "You were telling me about this murder you're investigating."

And Potter opened the floodgates.

The suicide that wasn't, the charity and its dodgy accounts, the passports and the allegations of human trafficking and slavery, and the bitch DS, the bitch lawyer, the silly bitch with punk hair and the homeless druggie. It was all bullshit of course, but with the amount of noise the bitch was making ("Which one?" "All of them.") now he had to raid a damned carwash. And the mastermind was supposed to be a fucking antiques dealer!

"A raid? That sounds exciting."

"Not really. Just a lot of cars and people running around shouting. And if they're illegals there'll be a lot of tears and then Immigration Enforcement and Serious Crimes get involved and we end up with all the paperwork, and there'll be leftie protesters outside the station shouting at us. Honestly, it's all more trouble than it's worth and I'd rather have a £5 full valet."

Winston laughed and agreed with him. "Can I get you another?"

Potter tried to focus on his watch. Was it ten to nine or ten? Was it that late? How had that happened? He lurched to his feet. "Better not. I've got to be up bright and early tomorrow."

"The raid?"

"The raid."

Winston got up with him. "Look," he said, "tell me if I'm out of line, but why don't you let me drive you home. I'm staying at a hotel in Lichfield anyway."

Potter put a hand on Winston's shoulder – partly to steady himself, but also because he was getting sentimental. "That's very kind. And I'll tell you what, I'll show you the carwash we're going to raid tomorrow. Give you a bit of a thrill."

Winston put and arm round his shoulder and guided him to the door.

"That's very kind of you," he said.

CHAPTER TWENTY-EIGHT

Krys – Friday

The alarm went off early. Krystyna automatically swung her arm out of bed and hit the STOP button.

Danny made a series of muffled noises and protests interspersed with the odd muttering that Krystyna could identify from the other side of the bed. "Ugh...middle of the night...bloody job...normal people...can't go on like this...ugh." Krystyna's husband pulled the quilt over his head.

"Sorry, go back to sleep. I'll re-set the alarm for 7.30," said Krystyna as she gathered her clothes for the day and headed for the bathroom.

While she was under the shower Krystyna wondered if she should have stayed in the spare bedroom last night so as not to disturb her husband this morning. These days, she admitted to herself, there was little point sharing a bed anyway. But when she thought about it, he was being the unreasonable partner. Often, at the weekend, he would get up early to go fishing with his mates at Chasewater. Some Saturdays and Sundays when she was not at work and could enjoy a lie-in, he would be the one to set the alarm early and make a noise sorting out his fishing clobber. Was Danny a good catch? Recently she had her doubts. Maybe, just maybe, she should throw him back in the pool and go fishing herself.

Once dressed Krystyna hurried downstairs and downed a black coffee and a bowl of cereal as quickly as possible. She wanted to be parked up just round the corner from the car wash well before it was due to open at 8.00 am. She guessed that Potter had arranged the raid by the Serious Crimes Unit for about 8.15-30. It was usual police practice to hit potential criminals early in the morning, but not too early. They needed to see unlawful practice in action, but before the perps had their wits about them.

She sat in her car watching the odd individual walking along the pavement. To pass the time she played *What's My Line?* It was easy to spot the kids dawdling to school, but the adults, young and old, were more difficult to pigeonhole. Those walking dogs were either retired, unemployed, had a day off work or were working from home. Those looking smart and walking purposely were clearly off to work. Perhaps heading for the bus stop or the train station. She refined her game with this next group of pedestrians. What did they do for a living? She literally had a split second to make an assessment on them as they passed her. She based her judgement on their clothes, hair style, age, and any other tells that stood out. Krystyna punctuated the silence with the odd word or phrase –*Twenty-something IT whizz kid, Receptionist, Estate Agent, looking forward to retirement, Hairdresser, Office worker apologising to his partner on the phone, Ageing hippy social worker who thinks he looks good with a bald head and a pony tail, Expectant mom counting off the days before she can put her feet up and then give birth.*

Krystyna realised that she had arrived at her blind observation spot far too early, but in some ways playing this silly game was more fun than having breakfast with her husband – her first unreasonable partner.

What of her second unreasonable partner – Detective Inspector Tony Potter? There had been no contact from him this morning. Was he still pissed off with her after yesterday's encounter? Was he keeping her in the dark on purpose or was he just being his normal incompetent self? Krystyna wondered what he was like at home. She knew he was married, but she had never met Mrs Potter. Poor woman. Being married to that asshole. Or perhaps he was a different person at home. Perhaps he was kind, considerate and compassionate. Or maybe he was just a c –

Her mobile lying on the passenger seat lit up and buzzed. Speak of the devil.

"Kendrick!"

"Sir."

"Where are you?"

"I'm positioned just around the corner from the car wash. I was waiting for Crimes and Immigration to initiate the takedown. I was going to give it until 8.15."

"Get round here now!"

"But…"

"Now!"

It took Krystyna less than 30 seconds to drive into the car wash entrance. In front of her she could see Potter talking to a group of uniforms and a couple of 'high ups' from Serious Crimes.

Behind the group of men was an empty car wash. No cars, no car washers, nothing.

Potter turned to look at Krystyna as she turned off the ignition. Through the windscreen she could see Potter saying something to the group and they all laughed. He then marched towards her as she got out of her car.

"A word, Kendrick. Over here. I don't think you want others to hear what I have to say to you."

"What's going on?"

"That's what I'd like to know. As you can see there's no-one here. I've had to send Immigration officers back to HQ. They weren't pleased to say the least. Neither are Serious Crimes. I mobilised them for this morning at short notice only to discover the place is deserted. There's not even a bucket of soapy water to arrest! What the hell were you playing at, Kendrick?"

"It was solid intel, sir."

"Yeah. Solid intel from that bunch of amateur misfits. Well, maybe I'm wrong; after all I've only been doing this job for over thirty years, but I think they're just some weird saddos who think that everything is a conspiracy. They're probably all users or boozers. Even if there were some dodgy things going on here yesterday, they probably got spooked and cleared off. This has been a costly waste of time, Kendrick. It makes me look bad and you should have learnt by now that I don't appreciate that, particularly from someone who's been doing the job for only five minutes. Since you were assigned to me I've been really patient with you. I've supported you. But you were clearly promoted too quickly – a young foreign woman who ticks all the boxes – but in my book you need to do the time to be a good detective, not just a pretty face."

"Pardon me!?"

"You heard. I'm taking this further, Kendrick. I can assure you that you will be walking the beat before this month is out. There's no way I'd ever recommend you for a Detective Inspector job. You need to have a real good think about your future in the police force. You will drop this case right now. I don't want you anywhere near it. In fact, piss off home and get out of my sight for the rest of the day!"

DI Krystyna Kendrick held it together while she got back in her car. She tried to avoid the stares from Potter's cronies as he re-joined them on the empty forecourt. Krystyna drove off and kept driving along the A38 for a few miles with angry and frustrated tears in her eyes. She turned into the entrance to Branston Water Park and parked her car in a secluded area of the car park away from passing dog walkers or fishermen. She was no longer in the mood to play *What's My Line?* or be reminded of her husband's hobby. She wanted to sit in her car and sob.

The tears came flooding down her cheeks. No matter how many tissues she used she could not stem the flow for ten minutes or so. During that time, she attempted to make sense of the recent events and Potter's reaction. She knew what her reaction was; it was anger and frustration. She was angry that the characters who ran the car wash had somehow known in advance about the police raid. She was angry that so many busy officers had wasted their time on what appeared to be a false lead. But above all she was angry about what Potter had said to her. She had worked hard to be in the position she was. She was a damn good police officer and now a bloody good detective. And along the way she had not received any favouritism in her training. In fact, Krystyna had experienced the opposite in the training college and in her first few years on the beat. She had put up with a few men who took great delight in demonstrating their antiquated views on females. Over that time, she developed coping strategies that ranged from challenging what they said or did, laughing it off, laughing at them or letting the bullets bounce off her armoured vest. Occasionally, in a private moment at home, she would get tearful, but nothing as bad as today.

Why was she so angry and frustrated today? She supposed that it was Potter's horrible comments coming out of the blue. Yes, he was known as *Potter the Tosser* by many in the station, but he was not often that personal and nasty to his colleagues. It had caught her off guard when he said those things to her on the forecourt. She was gobsmacked and then so frustrated that she did not defend herself or even go on the attack. She had rolled over submissively in front of him and she hated herself for it.

Even though Krystyna hated herself today she was not going to be beaten by the tosser. She would be back at her desk tomorrow with a bullet proof vest under her blouse.

She glanced around her. On the passenger seat were a pile of wet tissues. From the side windows of her car, she could see that the world was still turning – the trees were swaying in the breeze and people were peacefully enjoying the day. And that's why Krystyna joined the force – to ensure that most people could enjoy each day without fear. That's what she needed to hold on to.

She promised herself she would hold on...somehow. Potter wouldn't be her boss forever.

So why had she driven to Branston Park rather than go home? Yes, Danny would be at work, but why not go back to her place of safety and comfort? That was another question that would have to be answered at some point.

But more immediate questions kept re-surfacing from Krystyna's lake of tears. What spooked those guys running the car wash to disappear overnight? Were they tipped off about the proposed raid? Did Sameena say something or do something to create suspicion when she visited the car wash? Did she go too far? Whatever she did, it clearly created panic. Perhaps Potter was right. Were Sameena and Daz playing the parts of amateur detectives who were completely out of their depth? She would have to have a quiet word with Sameena in the next week or so...preferably before she was demoted!

Krystyna's mind kept asking questions – if it wasn't the actions of Sameena and Daz, then what could have caused the car wash to disappear overnight? Was there a tip off from within the force? If that was the case it meant that someone at the station or beyond had a vested interest in people trafficking. That would spark an internal investigation and that was serious. Very serious.

Krystyna continued to sit in her car pondering all of this. It was too early to make these claims to anyone else...until she had some proof.

Potter, particularly, would not welcome this line of enquiry. He wanted the whole thing to go away and he'd told her to drop it right now. Today.

Krystyna sat there motionless for a couple of minutes, but the cogs in her head kept turning.

Suddenly she broke the silence.

"Oh no. Not Potter. It can't be?"

CHAPTER TWENTY-NINE

Willow, Daz, Mary – Saturday

Saturday morning in the Cartwright household. Things had quietened down a bit since Willow had agreed to go back to college. No more pointed "Can't lie in bed all day if you haven't got an education. Got to get up and find some work!" comments.

But today she was up before anyone. With nothing else going on, she was taking Daz to meet Mary. It would do them both good. Mary didn't know and Daz hadn't sounded keen when she phoned him.

"But I hardly ever see you anymore. This will be something else we can do together, and you'll love Mary. She's a bit crazy, but she's full of stories and you never know which ones are true. She claims she invented Super Mario and knows the Dalai Lama."

"I dunno. I might have something on," the voice mumbled down the line.

"Oh, come on, it'll be fun. And anyway, if you say no, you know I'll just keep going on at you until you give in."

In the end, he did give in and she arranged to meet him by Stowe Pool on Saturday morning at ten, which was why she was gulping down her breakfast at half past nine.

"You're in a big hurry," said her mother, still in her dressing gown. "Where are you off to?"

"I'm going to see Mary, and I'm taking Daz! Gotta dash!"

With half of her mother's sentence "Are you sure that's wi – " floating in the air behind her, she grabbed her big hippy sling bag and flew out of the house, banging the door behind her.

Daz was waiting for her by the Pool. He was shaved, wearing a shirt under a Harrington jacket that had seen better days, but was clean, light brown chinos and a parade ground shine on his shoes.

Willow stood back with her hands on her hips.

"Look at you, Mr. Mitchell. You scrub up well."

Daz shrugged awkwardly. "Can't go and see an old granny in street clothes," he mumbled.

"She's called Mary and you're gonna love her. Come on."

She looped her arm through Daz's and half-led, half dragged him to Abbeyfield Residential Home and said nothing as Daz looked around.

Armchairs with cushions and low coffee tables with views out through bi-fold doors onto a patio with rattan furniture in a fashionable grey and then onto raised beds filled with flowers and herbs. Small trees stood around in pots and clematis were trailing over an arbor. Inside there was a smell of coffee – good coffee, not instant.

Growing old wasn't so bad – if you had money. And then the thought came to him that he might not live to be old and even if he did, it wouldn't be in a place like this. It would be huddled in his flat, with barely enough to pay for food, let alone heat and light, or back on the street, and then he'd be lucky to be alive at fifty.

He shivered and drew his shoulders up against the thought.

"Why so glum, chum?"

Daz shrugged. "This all a bit depressing, that's all."

Willow wrapped an arm around him and tried to give him a hug, but he leaned away from it. "Come on, Daz, we've got loads of reasons to be cheerful – I'm going back to college and my parents are off my back. And you're going to see your daughter."

"One day at a time, right? It's what we say at our meetings, and you said almost the same thing to me on the day I nearly knocked your head off."

There was a long awkward pause.

Willow was the first person to shake herself out of it. "Come on, let's go and see Mary. She's ninety-seven, but she still manages to have fun."

They squeezed into the lift and rode up to the second floor.

It didn't smell of coffee up here. It was the same smell Daz had got used to in hospital when he came back from Afghanistan. It was the smell of the last meal that had been served – he got a strong whiff of bacon – and antiseptic. And shit. With a strong scent of old lady perfume on top.

There was the blare of a television from a room filled with armchairs, but only a couple of residents sunk into them. The rest were in their rooms and Daz caught glimpses of frail bodies sunk into hospital-style beds while televisions on the walls flickered colours soundlessly over them. A face with sunken cheeks and the mouth hanging open. He'd seen dead Afghans looking like that in Gereshk. An old man with rheumy eyes without a spark of life in them looked up at them as they passed by.

"Come on!" Willow dragged him on into a room at the end of the corridor. Before they got inside they heard the music.

"That's 'Where's Your Head At'," said Daz, standing dumbstruck.

"I told you Mary was fun," said Willow. "Come and meet her."

They went into a small room dominated by another hospital bed, but this room smelled of life. There was a definite whiff of patchouli and joss sticks. The beige colour scheme was broken up by bright posters advertising Pink Floyd and the Who – Daz had heard of them – and the Yardbirds. He'd never heard of them. Willow hadn't heard of any of them.

On the big screen TV on the wall grey-faced men in white coats and monkeys with human faces belted out the classic nineties house track. A woman dressed like a nurse but not behaving like one was pleading with the white-haired old lady in the wheelchair to blow out the joss sticks and turn down the music.

"We've got the Yesterday channel on in the lounge!" she was shouting.

"But I like this," the old lady insisted in a voice that wasn't old or quavering. "Don't let the walls cave in on you!" she sang and tried to twirl her wheelchair.

Willow stepped into the room. "Don't worry," she said firmly. "We'll take over."

The old lady spun round. "Willow!" she cried. "They're trying to stop me having fun!"

The carer was glad to leave, and Willow quickly turned off the television. "Mary," she said, "we've come to take you out."

Mary's beady eyes quickly shot over Willow's shoulder to take in Daz. "And who's this fine figure of a man?"

"This is my friend, Daz. He was in the army, like you."

"I wasn't in the army, bless you, my dear, I was one of 'Dilly's Fillies.'" She studied Daz hard. "You look like a man who's seen combat. I should know – I've seen a few. Where were you stationed?"

"Afghanistan, Mrs...Miss...ma-am," mumbled Daz.

"Call me Mary, dear. Everybody does. Afghanistan, eh? I was there in 1963, I think...on my way to Kathmandu. Money went a long way back then, and we stayed for weeks. We went to the giant Buddhas carved out of a hillside in Bamiyan, I remember."

"The Taliban blew them up," said Daz, and Willow threw him a warning glance.

"Oh, what a shame. Still silly mistake – it was only a statue. As the old Buddhist monk said, 'If you see the Buddha on the road, kill him.'"

This time Daz looked at Willow and she shrugged. Mary laughed. "Oh, don't mind me, dears – just my old hippie ways coming out. So where are you taking me?"

"I thought we could go to the café?" said Willow.

"I'm in more of a pink gin mood today. Let's go to the pub. Come on, Daz, you look like a big strong lad – let's get rolling!"

Mary navigated them to the oldest pub in Lichfield. "Look at this," said Mary, waving her arm to take in the oak beams, benches and oak timber floor. "It's older than America!"

They settled into the inglenook with their drinks in front of them, Willow settling for a half of fruit-flavoured cider, Daz with a glass of lemonade and Mary got her pink gin. Mary insisted on paying. "I'm very rich, you know," she said in a loud whisper to Daz. "I invented the bar code."

Willow was pleased to hear Daz just say, "Really?" raising his eyebrows.

"Well, of course, you should know all about that. It's Morse Code really."

"Sorry, I don't know it," said Daz.

"But you're a soldier. How did you communicate in the field?"

"We used radio and mobile phones. It's all satellites these days."

"Look, it's easy," said Mary, ferreting around in her handbag for a pen and dragging a napkin over. She drew a dot and dash. "This is A." More dots and dashes followed. Soon she had the whole alphabet spread out in front of her and she started teaching Daz like a school mistress. "No, like this."

She banged on the table with the flat of her hand. "Da di di – " One long slap followed by two short. "Di da – " One short, one long. "Da da di di." She sat back. "That spells Daz. Now you try."

Avoiding the eyes of the other people in the bar, aware of the hot flush on his neck, Daz tapped lightly on the table. "Da di di..." She prompted him and he meekly finished his lesson.

"Well done. Of course, the trick is to be able to understand it in your head quickly. When I was young I could do forty-five words per minute. I don't suppose I could do that now, but I bet I could get above thirty. Come on, Daz, test me."

Daz looked imploringly at Willow.

"I'll do it, Mary." Willow took over, wrote out a sentence and converted it into Morse Code while Daz sat back and sipped his drink. He really didn't like being in the pub at all, it was full of temptation. He liked the warm smell of beer all around him, and he could remember clearly that first sip. There was nothing like it, and every swallow after was just trying to recapture that moment of bitter happiness on your tongue. But Eugene had warned him about trading one type of addiction for another and since he had started recovery he had avoided alcohol. This was the first pub he had been into in over two years.

He looked down and noticed his glass was empty. He hadn't been aware of drinking it. He sat on his hands and tried to take his mind off of thinking about it. He concentrated on Mary's lesson, while Willow was droning out di's and da's, he stared at the dots and dashes that scrawled across the napkin. It reminded him of something, but he couldn't remember what.

He kept turning it over in his mind and was surprised to hear Willow speak his name. "Daz? We should be getting Mary back."

They pushed her back taking in Stowe Pool and Mary showed him Willow's house. He was surprised to see how big and modern it was. He glanced at Willow and saw a tiny crease frown between her eyebrows. She doesn't want me to know where she lives, he thought.

They dropped Mary off and she tried to delay them as long as possible with stories and "little jobs" she needed doing, but when they finally got out Daz stuck his thumb out in the opposite direction from the way Willow was going.

"I'm heading this way."

"Oh, I thought we could walk back together." Willow looked disappointed and he nearly changed his mind, but then he remembered that puckered brow and he stood firm and silent. "OK then, see you next week."

He turned and walked away. His phone buzzed in his pocket. He got it out. It was Sameena.

"Hello?"

"I'm afraid I've got some bad news about the car wash, Daz..."

CHAPTER THIRTY

Daz – Sunday

Krystyna had told Sameena and Sameena had told Daz and Daz had no one to tell. He was raging and all of the advice that Eugene and Pauline the counsellor had given him counted for nothing. He couldn't stop thinking about it, and he wanted to do something about it. Anything.

He pounded on Amir's door. Until his hand hurt and the old man at the far end came out.

"They've gone, Darren. Did a moonlight. Got up for a pee in the middle of the night and I heard them going. Saw them from my window get in the back of a Transit with a suitcase."

Daz thanked him, offered to run any errands he needed and thought Amir and Faisal couldn't have vanished without trace. He had to get into the flat, and if there was nothing there, he could go back to the car wash.

He waited impatiently until he knew the afternoon quizzes were on and the old man would be asleep in front of the telly and he went back to the empty flat with a kitchen knife. You don't spend two years on the streets without learning how to open a locked door without a key.

He slid the thin blade in the gap between the door and the doorjamb. He wiggled it at the striker plate until he caught the latch bolt and popped the door open. A waft of damp emptiness and stale air floated out. He slid in and pushed the door closed behind him.

The flat was laid out like his, but the other way round. His smelled of burnt toast and fry-ups. This one smelled of tobacco smoke and curry. He went quickly to the window and drew the curtains.

He checked the kitchen and living room first. There was a mug on the coffee table half-filled with cold milky tea. He sniffed at it – it had a spicy smell that was familiar. Some of the soldiers he fought with got into chai tea, but he preferred to stick to good old builder's brew with three sugars. Next to it was a saucer overflowing with cigarette butts. They didn't smell English either.

A foreign newspaper written in funny squiggles had been left open on the sofa. A small TV sat on top of a DVD player on the floor. Open DVD cases with colourful covers and more of the squiggly writing were scattered about. On the wall above the TV was a picture that he recognised from his time in Afghanistan as a piece of Islamic script.

There was still food in the cupboards in the kitchen – not much, just cornflakes, bread and jam, tea and instant coffee. The only thing that made it any different from his kitchen were the small jars of pungent spices. There were unwashed dishes in the sink.

The bedroom had the same feel of people who had left in a hurry. It smelled stale, the bed was rumpled, the wardrobe door hung open and there was still a blue shirt hanging on a wire coat hanger. Some unwashed socks and underwear had been thrown onto the bed. He had walked through houses like this on patrol in the army, civilians running for their lives and leaving everything that wasn't needed.

Finally he looked in the bathroom. There was a bucket and a plastic jug by the toilet and on the shelf under the mirror there were some chewed sticks. He'd seen the Afghans using them as toothbrushes.

There was nothing else to see here. He slipped out and closed the door behind him. But there might be something to see at the car wash. He didn't imagine Potter would have conducted a very careful search.

He had to wait until it got dark, but he couldn't settle to anything. He turned the TV on, flicked through the channels – news, comedies, quizzes and people with too-white teeth shouting at one another. He tried to play one of his games, but he kept on crashing, dying or losing.

When it was barely dusk he pulled his warm peacoat on over his hoodie and set off. It had only been five minutes away in Sameena's car, but it was a half hour walk in the dark and the cold. He sniffed the air. It felt like there might be rain. Life on the streets made you very aware of the weather. You had to do everything you could to stop your stuff getting wet. It never dried out and that damp sank right inside you. But now, rain would be good – it would keep prying eyes inside.

When he got to the car wash he did what he'd done before – he walked past slowly so he could take a recce. Then he turned round and went back and stood in the shadows to make sure there was no one there. Police...or anyone else!

It all looked pretty dead. People didn't walk out much at night in this area. They gathered by the brightly-lit takeaways, off-license and late-night supermarket down the road, eating and drinking in the road because they had nowhere else to go, or they didn't want to go home or perhaps they just wanted the company – or a fight.

Daz dodged across the road and onto the forecourt. Surprising how quickly it had dried out. Out of the range of the street lights, it was dark and he flicked his torch on, swept it round and turned it off again. No point drawing attention to himself. He didn't see anything lying around – the place had been stripped clean. He'd had COs like that who had insisted on leaving no trace when they struck camp.

Come to think of it, the whole disappearing act had the feel of a military operation about it. They must have got wind of the raid sometime after Sameena had handed their info over to the DS and by the next day they were in the wind.

At the back of the forecourt was a rusty old half-container they had been using as an office. Perhaps he'd find something in there. Shading his torch with his hand he tried the handle. It opened with a clang. He snapped the light off and froze. He counted sixty Mississippis and then another sixty before he moved again. Nothing. He slipped inside, pulled the door to and shone his torch around.

It smelled cold and damp in here. There was an old office desk pushed up against the back wall. He went through the drawers, but there was nothing there. He hadn't thought there would be. The police should have swept the area carefully, even if their target had fled. There were some sticky tape marks on the wall where things had been sellotaped up, but they were all gone too. There was nothing on the floor either when he swept his torch across it.

So that was it. Every time it looked like he might be getting close to the truth behind Shaun's death he hit another dead end. First the accountant and now this.

He should have listened to Eugene and Pauline the counsellor. He'd always been like this. Once he got his teeth into something he couldn't let go. It had got him into trouble at school and in the army. When he was discharged the doctor had told him he had an obsessive-addictive personality. And then they booted him out. He just knew he always felt a terrible anger on the inside and he was terrified of someone getting hurt if it was ever unleashed.

He eased the door open and stole a look. All clear. The last thing he needed was to get arrested for B and E now. He'd got a counsellor, a solicitor and a chance to see Amy. Maybe even a ghost of a chance to put things right with his wife. Cheryl - dammit her name was Cheryl. When they split he'd tried to stop thinking of her as person with a name because it was too painful. He'd turned her into a thing – "the wife."

Eugene was full of mystical quotes. When he said, "There's a saying by an Islamic sage that goes 'You have to keep breaking your heart until it opens'," Daz had sneered and said he'd had quite enough of Muslims in Afghanistan to last a lifetime thank you very much.

Was Sameena a Muslim?

He slipped out and pushed the door shut. It had started raining. There was a fine drizzle blowing across the forecourt. Daz turned his face to the wind and the rain and let it wash over him. These days he could go home and take a hot shower, change his clothes and dry out. Pauline had advised him to keep a gratitude journal. She said he'd feel better and look forward to things which would help him set goals.

He hadn't started yet, but he did feel grateful.

And he made the one mistake a soldier on patrol should never make – he was so wrapped up inside his head he forgot that everyone was trying to kill him. He heard the whistle of something flying through the air behind him, he saw stars explode across the blackness and he felt no pain –

He was dragging bodies out of the back of a Snatch Land Rover that had been blown apart by an IED. 'Mobile coffins,' the soldiers called them. They were passing them up into the IVF Warrior. Some of the bodies were screaming and thrashing about, some were as dead weight as sacks of potatoes. They dripped blood on him, smeared blood on him, grabbed at him, eyes staring at him out of blackened faces, pleading, crying for their mummies. Beneath the screams was the booming of the cannon on the Warrior and red flashes lighting up the night sky. Red flashes –

He opened his eyes and couldn't make out what he was looking at. There was a black wall he was leaning against. There were a pair of shoes on the wall. Scuffed and brown, dirt caught in the little holes that decorated them. How were they standing on the wall?

The world tilted. He was lying on the ground. The back of his head felt wet and warm. He blinked slowly. The shoes were still there. One of them moved, scraped along the ground, vanished from his sight.

Pain exploded in his stomach with a thump. His body leaped backwards to get away from the hurt at the same time as he curled around it. Again and again. The world turned into red. Even the pounding into his flesh stopped, the agony continued. It throbbed through every part of his body.

He opened his eyes. The shoes were right in front of him. One swung back. It was going to smash into his face. He watched it, unable to move. What a stupid way to die. Not a soldier killed fighting in Afghanistan. A *Big Issue* seller beaten to death in a car wash. Cheryl, Amy. He shut his eyes and waited.

Nothing happened.

He could hear his heart, his breath rasping in his throat. The grit of shoes walking away. He opened his eyes. He was leaning on the wall again, the shoes were on the wall again, vanishing into the distance. They shrank to a pinprick, and then the world slid sideways and went black again.

CHAPTER THIRTY-ONE

Daz, Willow, Sam, Krys - Monday

"I know he's your father but you can't stay too long."

"I just want to make sure he's alright."

"Darren...Darren...your daughter's here to see you...is that OK?"

"Ugh...wha...what are you doing here?"

"Hi, Dad. I know it's been a while, but I just wanted to see you. You gave Mom and I quite a shock when we found out that you were in hospital. You got attacked, is that right?"

"I don't understand..."

"We'll be OK now. Thank you, nurse. I promise I won't be long."

"Well, if you're sure, but don't tire him out. He took quite a beating by the looks of it."

"Twenty minutes...tops."

The nurse walked off and left father and daughter staring at each other.

"How did you know I was here? What the fuck is going on?"

"Hey, that's no way to talk to your daughter!"

"But you're not my daughter!"

"No. I know that. But I wasn't sure that the nursing staff would let me see you if I wasn't a relative," whispered Willow as she sat in the chair at the side of his bed. "Oh, I almost forgot, I got you something to make you feel better. I didn't think you'd like flowers, so I got you this." Willow took a chocolate bar from her jean jacket and placed it on his bed.

"A Mars Bar. Just what I need at the moment. It will help me rest even if I can't work or play."

"What are talking about? Did you get kicked in the head or something."

"No, I don't think so, but pretty much everywhere else. How did you know I was in hospital, anyway?"

"I'm your forking daughter. I just sense these things," said Willow with a smile on her face.

"No, seriously, Willow. How did you find out?"

"Well, believe it or not, one or two people in Lichfield actually care about you. DS Kendrick phoned up Sameena late last night and Sam messaged me this morning. I told my boss at the café that I needed the day off and she was OK about it . I jumped on the train to Burton and here I am. Anyway, enough about me. What happened and how bad is it? And no 'it's just a scratch' bullshirt."

Daz relayed the events of yesterday at the car wash, as far as he could remember. But his story came to a full stop when he got to the part when something struck him on the back of the head and he hit the ground.

"Once I was down, I think I got a kicking in the chest and stomach mainly. Apparently, I have a bloody big cut across the back of my head, a couple of broken ribs, more bruising across my front, a sprained wrist, some cuts and scrapes on my face and this very attractive shiner."

"So, not a scratch then?"

"No."

"And no idea who did this?"

"None."

Daz strained his eyes trying to remember anything about the attack, but nothing appeared in his mind.

"Are you OK? Shall I get the nurse?"

"No, I'm fine. I was just trying to remember something...but I can't."

"Do you want me to go? Do you need to sleep or rest or something?"

"No, I'd like you to stay, if you don't mind."

"I don't mind, but the nurse might want me to go."

"Leave her to me. She's not going to stop me seeing my daughter after all of this time. By the way, your name is Amy Mitchell and you live in Birmingham."

"Good to know."

"Why do you say 'fork' and 'shirt' instead of swearing like normal teenagers do?"

"Have you never seen 'The Good Place' on Netflix?"

"Do I look the sort of person who has Netflix?"

"Fair point. Well, it's a comedy series about a group of four weirdos who die and think they've gone to heaven, but it ends up being hell. The woman in it likes swearing, but when a swear word comes out of her mouth it comes out differently. I just started saying it and it's become a habit."

"Yeah...well...I know all about weirdos with habits...first hand. Perhaps I died and I'm in hell and no-one's told me yet?"

"Hey, don't get morbid on me. It's just a comedy show."

"Sorry, Willow."

"Excuse me. Who's Willow?"

"Sorry, Amy."

In an hour or so, Daz couldn't sweet talk the nurse anymore and his 'daughter' had to leave so that the staff could serve the patients their lunch. Daz was left alone. He rested and slept fitfully during the afternoon trying to remember the key events at the car wash, but nothing came to the front of his mind. Instead he pictured Amy, the real Amy. It had been a couple of years since he'd seen her face-to-face but somehow it felt like a life time. He couldn't blame Amy for giving up on him or his ex-wife for not encouraging her daughter to keep in touch. Not after he self-destructed. It was all his fault and now he had to put it right. He wanted his daughter to love him, respect him, trust him and enjoy a few conversations, even if they were teasing one another. Daz's mind wandered back towards Willow. His new friend. Probably, one of his only friends. Willow was a century apart from Daz and their life experiences were so very different, but he enjoyed her company, even if she was a pain in the neck at times. He wanted that with his daughter, Amy. Over the last few hours, it dawned on him that re-connecting with his daughter had become much more important than finding out what actually happened to Shaun.

Daz was woken up by a different nurse later in the day. He took Daz's temperature and blood pressure and gave him some pain killers. Daz managed to look as if he had swallowed them until the nurse left. He spat them out and hid them inside the empty Mars Bar wrapper and threw the litter in the bin by his bedside.

He was then served his evening meal by a large, friendly woman with a blue plastic apron that was stretched to breaking point. While the other patients on the ward could be heard complaining about the food to each other, Daz enjoyed every mouthful. When the big blue apron returned to take his empty plate, he made a point of telling her that the food was great. She returned some minutes later with a dish of cake with custard that looked twice as big as anyone else's portion. He smiled to himself as he concluded that he always liked a woman with big portions. As he chuckled to himself he felt his sore ribs protesting and objecting to his politically incorrect observation.

Sometime later Daz decided to stretch his legs and visit the toilet rather than use his pee pot. He was quite pleased that he could walk OK and it was just sudden turns of his body that were painful. He made a decision as he climbed back onto his bed that this would be the last night he would spend at Burton Hospital. He could cope OK at home in his flat. It may mean that he would have to stay indoors for a couple of days before he could sell *the Big Issue* again, but although he could not fault the NHS staff, he didn't like being fussed over.

It must have been about 7.00 pm when Daz had more visitors and more fuss. Sameena and the policewoman arrived.

"Hi Daz, so sorry to hear about...yesterday...how are you feeling now?" asked Sameena touching Daz's arm.

"OK, thanks. You should see the other bloke."

"Did you see the other bloke?" said DS Kendrick, staring at Daz with a serious tone.

Sameena glared at Krys and tried to re-set the conversation by lowering her voice. Sameena quietly emphasised that primarily they both wanted to know that Daz was OK as they had both been worried about him. But then Sameena explained that DS Kendrick would need to ask him some questions as a matter of urgency and that Sam was there to represent him or counsel him, if he wanted.

With that, DS Kendrick started asking Daz a series of questions that centred around why he was at the car wash site yesterday. What did he hope to achieve by going back there when he knew it was deserted, and did he realise how much police and medical time he was taking up by playing at being a detective? As Krystyna became more frustrated by Daz's dismissive responses, Sameena had to intervene again as other patients were paying more and more attention to the heated discussion. Krystyna composed herself again and tried to calmly ask Daz about his attacker or attackers. Could he remember anything about the assault? For the second time today Daz described his attack; initially from behind and then being kicked in the front when he was lying on the forecourt. He then displayed a few of the resulting injuries as if to prove that he was telling the truth.

"That's all I forking remember, OK?" Daz exclaimed, thinking of Willow as he said it - she would have smiled - if she was here.

Sameena again stepped in and announced, "OK, so we've established that Daz just went back to the car wash to see if there was any evidence that had been overlooked. He was not trespassing as there were no signs indicating that he couldn't walk around the site. While legally walking around the site, he was attacked without provocation. Fortunately, a passer-by saw him lying on the ground and called for an ambulance. Therefore, I would strongly suggest that Daz has done nothing wrong here. He is the victim and should not be treated as an offender. He should have our support over this incident."

"That may be the case, but Daz should not have been there in the first place. And if you recall, only a few days ago you were both at the car wash interfering with police business," retorted Krystyna, not prepared to back down, completely.

The male nurse was attracted by the raised voices and came over to Daz's bed.

"I'm afraid you'll have to leave. Right now!" said the nurse, looking at the Solicitor and the Cop, pointing to the door of the ward. In his world, while a doctor was not present, his word was final, and he was happy to show these two comparatively highly-paid professionals the exit door.

As Sameena turned towards the door she mouthed at Daz "Sorry" and "I'll see you tomorrow."

Krystyna walked briskly away and probably couldn't hear Daz say quietly "Fork Off!"

As Daz drifted off to sleep, his mind was made up. He was out of here tomorrow, no matter what the doctors said.

He woke up once during the night when a thought struck him. But it wasn't a thought, it was a brown leather shoe. The shoe that had hit him in the face while he was on the ground at the car wash.

CHAPTER THIRTY-TWO

Daz, Willow, Sam – Tuesday

Daz discharged himself. He was tired of being asked the same questions over and over. And he'd been hiding the painkillers they kept trying to give him. You can't give a recovering drug addict drugs, everyone knew that. But he'd seen the canula in the back of his hand and he'd felt good the first time he came round after the kicking. Like he was wrapped up in cotton wool.

He thought it was morphine. He'd taken most things. He'd got the glow and he was fairly sure if he said the pain was worse they'd give him a higher dose. A higher dose to get high.

That's why he had to get out of there. Against doctor's advice. He had to sign a waiver.

Once he was standing outside, he had no idea how he was going to get home. He hadn't gone out with any money, and Lichfield seemed like a hundred miles away. But he had his phone, and he had Eugene's number, so he made the call.

He had to hang about for three hours with no money and nowhere to go. He stayed in A & E until he couldn't stand the bleak misery any longer and then he stood outside, but the wailing of the ambulances brought back too many bad memories, so he walked aimlessly, a thing he had done many times when he had nowhere to go.

When his phone rang and Eugene told him he had arrived, Daz had no idea where he was. He was standing by a canal, brown water flowing slowly by him. It took another half hour for Eugene to find him.

He was very quiet as they headed back down the A38 in the warmth of Eugene's car. In the end, it was Eugene who spoke. "What were you thinking, Darren? You could have broken your sobriety."

"Nothing about the broken ribs and the concussion?"

"I don't care about those. I just want to make sure you don't end up out of your head and back on the streets."

"Won't happen. I hid the painkillers they gave me and took the drip out as soon as I realised what was going on."

"You were lucky. If you stuck to selling *Big Issues* it wouldn't have happened. What on earth were you doing poking around a deserted car wash? It had something to do with Shaun Wilde's death, I'm guessing."

Daz shrugged and then winced as pain stabbed through his body. He'd have to come up with another way of being sulky and saying nothing for a while.

"You've got to understand, Darren – you're an addict, and you always will be. And this obsession with Shaun's death is just another addictive behaviour."

"Isn't that just what NA is all about?" Daz was surprised to hear the sneer in his voice. "Swapping bad addictions for good ones? Following the Twelve Steps – going to meetings, making reparations and all that?"

"Yes, but they won't get you killed. And you won't fall off the wagon. If you keep on trying to prove Shaun was murdered, both of those could happen."

The rest of the journey passed in awkward silence. At least, Daz felt awkward, but Eugene seemed to be at peace, driving at a steady 56 mph, handling the slow lorries and the fast cars with equanimity. When they pulled up outside Dimbles Court he didn't offer to help Daz back to his flat. "See you at the meeting tomorrow?" he said.

"If I can make it," grunted Daz, trying to get out without groaning. He knew Eugene was watching him as he walked up the path, and he thought of the last time he had seen Shaun, walking off to his death with his shoulders back and his chest out, and he tried to do the same. When he got to the stairwell and out of sight, he leaned against the wall. He was damp with sweat.

It took him ten minutes to climb the first set of stairs and then he had to rest before he could carry on up to his flat. Once he got inside, he struggled to the kitchen, gulped down a glass of water and almost crawled to his bedroom.

He collapsed on the bed and fell so deeply asleep he didn't feel any pain.

Something was buzzing. In his dream he was in a garden with flowers bobbing in a gentle breeze and a lawn of bright green grass and the sun shining, but somewhere there was a bee. A big bee and it was going to sting him. Spinning round he couldn't see it, but it was always behind him, getting louder, closer.

The sting woke him, and he felt his phone vibrating in his pocket. He struggled to get it out, wincing.

"Daz?"

"Who is it?" he groaned.

"It's your daughter – "

"Amy?" He sat up in bed and for a moment he felt no pain. The rush of blood to his head almost made him faint.

"No, silly, your daughter – Willow." He heard a giggle and he slumped back on the bed.

"What do you want?" he muttered. He did well not to curse her out and hang up.

"What do you think? I rang the hospital this morning to see how my Dad was and they told me he'd discharged himself. So I've come round to see how you're doing. I'm outside your front door."

He took a breath, controlled himself and said, "I'm fine. You can go away."

"I'm going to stay here banging on your door until open you it – and if you don't I'm going to call the police and tell them I think you've collapsed and they'll come and break it down." She lowered her voice. "There's already an old man out here watching me and he might call the police anyway."

He hung up and, groaning, rolled off the bed and tottered through the living room, leaning on the sofa on the way. When he got to the door he squared himself up and opened it.

Willow was outside, smiling brightly. She held up a Sainsbury's bag. "I bring gifts," she said.

"What?" He was too surprised to be angry.

"Food. We need to build you up. Go and sit down and I'll cook you breakfast and get the rest of this stuff into the fridge."

She squeezed past him carefully and marched into the kitchen, leaving him to push the door shut with a sigh. He trailed after her. "Why are you doing this?"

"I told you," she said, without turning round, busying herself at the cooker. "You need looking after. Oh, and there's one other thing"

She hunted around in her big shoulder bag that looked like it had been made out of two bits of carpet sewn together. She came out with a photo in a frame and held it out to him.

"What is it?"

She just pushed it forward with a big grin on her face. It was the photo he had taken in Shaun's office a month ago – it seemed like a year ago now. The four faded faces stared at him out of a cheap black plastic frame.

"I got it done at Boots," she said. "Something to remember your friend by. Now, sit down; food'll be ready in five minutes."

He would have argued with her then, but he smelled the frying bacon so he sat and stared at the picture, trying to see something in it that would explain everything that had happened since it was taken, but it was just a picture of four young men at the beginning of their lives with no idea of what was coming next.

Willow clattered and banged around with the pots and pans. The flat had been furnished and equipped second-hand by *Home and Heart* when Daz moved in and he'd sat on the sofa, watched the television and played games on the old X-Box and slept in the bed, but in the kitchen he only used the kettle the toaster and a pan to heat things out of cans. He'd never been much of a cook, his mom had done it, the army had done it, and Cheryl had done it.

Five minutes later Willow put a full English breakfast down in front of him. "I hope you appreciate it," she said. "I had to touch bacon for you."

"You're not a vegetarian, are you?" he asked with his mouth full of bacon, egg, beans and fried bread.

"Vegan," she said. "I had to cook eggs for you too, but it's margarine on your toast."

"Tastes good," he said, stuffing some into his mouth. "Where did you learn to cook like this?"

"It's easy. Watching mom, TV and reading. How do you not know how to do a fry-up?"

The banter passed back and forth as it used to before Shaun's death and all that had followed in its wake. It was easy and pleasant and made Daz think that maybe Eugene had been right – he was risking everything. He had to focus on what was important – family and friends. Staying sober.

"I'll be back tomorrow to check on you. You're not well enough to go out for food so I'll bring some."

And as she was heading out of the door, she said over her shoulder, "And Sameena's coming round later on this evening."

Daz was dreaming again. He was back in Afghanistan. His dreams and nightmares often took him there. He was watching a trail of ragged and barefoot refugees with sunken, hopeless eyes stagger past him with all their worldly belongings on their backs. Men, women, children, rangy dogs and skin-and-bone donkeys. He turned his head to see where they were going. The never-ending line snaked its way up a road to a deserted car wash. He looked back, he looked down. They were all wearing shabby brown shoes, rhythmically stamping along. Those feet stamped down, the dust rose up. Thump, thump, THUMP!

It was the front door again. He guessed it was Sameena, and he'd guessed she'd be just as awkward as Willow if he didn't answer.

He set his teeth and levered himself up from his chair. If he was going to stop groaning and wincing, he might as well start now.

He walked slowly, bent over and pressing his arm across his ribs, but as he opened the door he straightened up and smiled.

"Sameena."

"Oh, Darren – Daz, I'm so sorry."

"Nothing to be sorry about. You didn't make me go back. Come in." He stood back and made a welcoming swing of his arm, which hurt, but he hid it behind his smile.

Just like a copy of Willow, Sameena held up two plastic bags. "I've got some of my mother's cooking. Hope you like samosa, pakora, chicken tikka, chana dahl and kofta."

"That's everything I order at the Star of India," he said, and then, aghast, added, "That's not racist, it?"

Sameena laughed. "This is better than anything you'll get from a takeaway. And for dessert there's kheer and ras mali, with jalebi, gulab and barfi to fill up the empty corners afterwards."

"Did your mom make all of that?"

"Well, not the sweets. We get those from a shop in Birmingham. But everything else."

Once again the kitchen was full of the sounds of plates and pans rattling and once again Daz eased himself onto the sofa. The flat was soon filled with the delicious smells of hot spices. Quite different from the ones he had experienced in Afghanistan and those he had smelled in Amir's flat. No different than the smells of French, German and English cooking, he supposed, although the only French cooking he could think of was snails and frogs' legs, and the Germans ate a lot of sausages. In England there was fish and chips and a full English breakfast and a Sunday roast. He would love to sit down around a table on a Sunday with a family again.

Sameena clattered a full plate down in front of him. "I hope this is enough?"

"This is great."

She sat down beside him with a plate as loaded as his. He picked up a fork and she tore off a piece of naan and scooped some curry into her mouth. He watched her. "How do you do that? It always falls off when I try."

She gave him a lesson. "If it's meat or potatoes, pinch it. Otherwise, make it into a little spoon and scoop. Make the rice into a ball with your fingers. Your fingers are going to get messy anyway."

After that, things got quiet while they shovelled food in. Halfway through, Daz got up and said, "Want a cold drink?"

Sameena looked up. "Anything but beer. I'm Muslim."

"That's OK," said Daz. "I'm a recovering addict. It'll be lemonade."

Sameena was flustered and blushed. "I'm sorry. I – I didn't know."

"That's why I discharged myself. They gave me morphine while I was out. My sobriety's back to day one." He set down two glasses of lemonade.

"Oh, Daz, I'm sorry. It's all my fault." She looked so downcast he patted her on the shoulder.

"It's alright. Really. I've been beaten up before, I've fallen off the wagon before. And at least this time it wasn't my fault." Sameena opened her mouth and he hurried on, "And it wasn't your fault either. It was the fault of who tipped off the car wash about the police raid."

Sameena sat back. "So who do we think it was?"

"Someone in the police. I've met plenty of cops who sell information – to the papers and the villains. There are some bigger crooks in the police than outside."

"But we can't prove it. So what do we do next? Give up? I don't think the Detective Sergeant will help us again."

Daz took a deep breath. "It goes against everything I believe in – but I think we should stop. It's not doing me any good, and it's not helping you either."

"I just wanted to see justice done. Otherwise, what's the point of the law?"

"I know, and I wanted to know who killed Shaun and why he died. But I guess we don't always get what we want."

"True." Sameena gathered up the plates and took them to the sink, returned with the jalebi, gulab and barfi. "If we're lucky we get what we need."

"I really need to see my daughter," said Daz, picking up the biggest, stickiest sweet he could find. "What do you need, Sam?" he asked before he crammed it all into his mouth.

"I really need to stop eating so many sweets," she said, and they both laughed.

CHAPTER THIRTY-THREE

Willow, Sam – Tuesday

Willow sat there in body but not in spirit. She had perfected an engaged look on her face even though there should be a Vacant sign hanging from her neck. Most evenings the Cartwright family sat around the dining table, in the same chairs eating their different meals. Vegan, vegetarian and meat. It was a nightly ritual that could not be broken, no matter how hard Willow tried. And every time Willow sat down she asked the same question to herself, 'Why can't we be like normal families and sit in the living room eating our food off trays while watching the telly?' But there was no point asking the question out loud anymore as it was always met with the same responses from her dad and mom.

"No, this is family time."

"It's the only time of the day that we spend quality time together."

"There's only rubbish on the TV at this time."

"We all need to catch up with each other, hear about our own days, the good and the bad."

"I can't eat off a tray anyway. The settees are too low. I'd drop most of my food down my shirt. I'd need to wear a bib."

"You spend a lot of each evening in your bedroom, Willow. It's the only chance we get to talk to you."

"Willow!"

"Sorry, what?"

"I said, do you want to come to the Food Festival in town this weekend?" asked Mrs Cartwright.

"I can't on Saturday. Sue's asked me if I can do a full shift that day as Lichfield will be packed with punters."

"Surely the visitors won't eat in the café that day. Not with all of that street food on offer."

"You'd be surprised. People still like to sit down and eat and drink not just walk about the stalls."

"I know what you mean," interjected her father, "I hate eating on the run. You can't beat sitting at a proper table and enjoying your food." As Willow's old man spoke he spread his arms out signifying the long wooden dining table in front of him that was at a perfect height for him.

Willow refrained from rolling her eyes at him but instead playfully pointed two fingers at him under the table, out of sight of her dad.

"The library's closed on Sunday. We could have a look around then, if you'd like," Willow said to her mom.

"That would be nice. We could eat meat-free stuff while we're walking round, without your dad moaning and groaning."

"Even if we leave dad at home, we'd still hear him moaning at the market."

"Hey, you two. Are you ganging up on me again?"

"It's no more than you deserve. You're like that old guy from that comedy show from a hundred years ago."

"Victor Meldrew!" shouted his wife pointing at her husband with one finger above the top of the table.

"Yeah, that's right. Moany Meldrew," agreed Willow, smiling.

"I do not moan...that often. Do I?"

"Yes!" came the female chorus. They all laughed and then started talking about their favourite comedy shows. Quite naturally, there was little consensus on the type of comedies they all watched and enjoyed. Willow mostly streamed her shows and watched them on her laptop at night in her room. Her mom and dad enthusiastically spent the next five minutes recounting their favourites from the good old days when "TV comedies were actually funny!"

It was during these times when her mom and dad were chatting together about their past shared experiences that Willow wished that she had a brother or sister to talk to. It would even up the odds. A sibling would distract some of the attention that always seemed to be focussed on her. At the dining table, in particular, the spotlight was forever pointing at her. Some days she just wanted to melt into the shadows, instead of being centre stage.

Suddenly Willow was brought back to Earth by another question.

"Willow, have you thought anymore about joining that youth drama group that you mentioned a few weeks ago?" asked her mother.

"Um...I haven't given it any more thought. I've been kinda busy recently with the job, and the care home...and other stuff...I s'pose I could pop into the Garrick Theatre one lunch time and find out more."

"It would be good to have something to do in the evenings. You don't see many of your friends at the moment."

"I agree with your mom, Willow. Don't you get bored stuck in your room in the evenings?"

"No, dad, I'm actually fine. I socialise enough during the day. In the evenings I just want to chill. I get peopled out."

"We're not criticising, love," Willow's mom jumped in, "it's great that you want to be home with us. Some teenagers your age are never in. Their parents haven't got a clue where they are or what they're doing. I'm happy that you're not like that. You don't mix with the wrong people. You don't take stupid risks. It's just..."

"What, mom?"

"It's just that you don't seem to have much of a social life since you left school. Are you OK? Are you happy?"

"Yeah. I'm fine. I'm happy on my own without those bitchy girls from my old school or an immature boyfriend who I can't trust or talk to sensibly. And anyway, once I go to college in September, I'll meet new people and I'll be having all-night parties here every weekend. Will that satisfy you both? "

Willow's mom and dad glanced at each other. "As long as all of your friends eat and drink at the table!" quipped Willow's dad, trying to change the mood.

"I'll make sure to tell them to put all of the booze and drugs on the table as they arrive," said Willow and her serious expression turned into a smile aimed at her dad.

"Sorry, love, were we moaning at you again?" asked Willow's mom.

"Yes you were. I'm used to dad having a go, but not you mom...Mrs Meldrew."

Willow's mom smiled and said, " Guilty as charged...Mrs Moany Meldrew."

"Yeah...married to Mr Moany Mason Meldrew."

"Hey, watch it. I know you like to take the micky about me being in the Masons but it's my group of friends and we do some good in the community. It's not a weird cult or anything like that. Most of the time we just have a chat about everyday things. It's a form of escape. Like this drama club would be for you."

"But it's a posh men's club with secret handshakes and stuff. It's not exactly modern and inclusive, is it?"

"Not necessarily, but we don't do any harm. We try to be a force for good. We have some strict standards."

"And no-one ever breaks the rules?" enquired Willow.

"Well...hardly ever. Funnily enough we did have to escort someone out of the Lodge meeting room just the other night. He'd been drinking far too much and started getting loose-lipped about his job."

"Is it a rule that you can't talk about your job?"

"No, but he was telling some of us about things that clearly shouldn't have left his place of work. Confidential details. He shouldn't have told us and we really didn't want to hear about it," admitted Willow's dad.

"So what was this bloke's job and what was it all about?" asked an interested Willow.

"Well, if I told you then I would be behaving like him, wouldn't I?"

"But I'm not a Mason and never can be, so who's to know if you give me a few vegan tit-bits."

"No names, no pack-drill, but I can tell you that he's a police officer and went on and on about a colleague who was getting on his nerves. It follows on from that suicide in the cathedral a couple of weeks ago. Apparently, there's some locals that believe it was a murder not suicide. There's a guy who's leading this conspiracy theory and getting a bit of support, which is making this police officer look incompetent..."

"I'm sure Willow doesn't want to hear all about this..."

"No...it's OK, mom. Carry on...please...I'm quite interested..." said Willow, trying to sound disinterested.

"OK. Well, that bit of what this chap was saying was just about OK, but then he started to talk about an operation that was planned that would bring this matter to a close."

"So what was the operation? Did he give any details?"

"Yes, he did. Particularly to this one member of the Lodge who seemed interested. But because he was getting louder and louder there were quite a few of us listening in on his rant about his colleague and this raid that was about to take place on a local car wash. It sounded ridiculous to me and some of the other members. We weren't sure to begin with if he was just making all of this up as he'd drunk far too much. But he continued to divulge information of a .... how can I put it...a sensitive nature...so we had no alternative but to tell him to leave. His membership at our Lodge is probably in doubt now."

"Do you know this police officer well?"

"No, not really. He's not a close friend or anything. To be honest, from the brief conversations I've had with him in the past, he's not my sort of person. Anyway, enough about that. I'll clear the table. It's my turn."

"I think I'll go and do some research on that drama club at the Garrick. Is that OK, if I go upstairs for a bit. I'll come down later and you can inflict a terrible comedy show on me."

"We'll hold you to that," replied Willow's mom.

Once upstairs, Willow closed her bedroom door shut. Researching the drama group at the Garrick Theatre was the last thing on her mind. She lay on her bed and instead of busying herself on her laptop, she reached into her jeans' pocket for her mobile. She scrolled down her list of contacts.

"Hi, Willow. Are you OK?" asked Sameena.

"Yeah. Have I caught you in the middle of anything important?"

"No. I'm just in my bedroom changing into my comfortable elastic PJs before I try to eat some of the food my mother has cooked for me. I've eaten far too much already today. I took some food round to Daz's flat and ended up eating half of it. Anyway, what can I do for you?"

Willow then conveyed to Sameena what she had just found out from her father about the incident at the Lodge and they agreed that there was no doubt that Potter was the main player in the drama. He was in the centre of the spotlight. And Willow and Sameena needed to act. Tomorrow.

CHAPTER THIRTY-FOUR

Willow, Sam, Krys – Wednesday

They met Krys in the park again and sat on the same bench. Willow felt like a secret agent.

"This had better be good," said Krys grimly. "Last time we met, it nearly cost me my job."

"I think this will do more than keep you your job," said Sameena smugly. She nudged Willow. "Tell her."

Willow took a deep breath and told the hard-faced detective sergeant everything her father had said about the drunken policeman and afterwards an awkward silence settled over the three of them. Krys stared at the ground in front of her, Sameena stared at Krystyna and Willow stared at both of them. Finally Sameena spoke. "Well?" she said. "What do you think? It's Potter, isn't it?"

"So?" Krys did not look up.

"He got drunk, he blabbed about the car wash, anyone in the lodge could have heard him, and they cleared the place out before the raid. We were right!" Sameena was getting excited.

"So what if he did?" Krys was still glum, uninfected by Sameena's mood.

Willow had promised to tell the policewoman what she knew and then say nothing – leave it all up to Sameena: "I'm a solicitor – I know how to handle the police." But she was clearly getting nowhere. So Willow butted in.

"Oh, come on – the least you can do is come and talk to my dad."

The silence dragged on a bit longer and Willow started to feel very uncomfortable and then the policewoman looked up. Her face was stony, her eyes were cold.

"Why should I? Every time I get involved with you lot, my life gets fucked up."

"Sergeant!" Sameena was shocked, mostly on Willow's behalf, but a little for herself.

"It's alright, Sam," said Willow. "I've heard much worse. Like – " She started listing all the rude words she could think of and even made some up, sure that these X-ers wouldn't know the difference.

A little old lady was walking by with her dog. She tutted with disgust before scuttling on.

"Willow!" Sameena was shocked for the little old lady now.

"Come on!" said Willow, exasperated. "We all know there was something wrong with Shaun and his charity, and the car wash was proof until Potter f – forked it up. Who was this man he told at Dad's lodge? I bet he's got something to do with it. If he does, you get to find out what's going on. If he doesn't, Potter will never find out anyway!"

Both of the women stared at Willow. Who was this girl with the purple hair who was talking so much sense? Sameena thought she'd like to have her beside her in court, handing her papers and whispering advice and Krys thought she'd like her beside her in the interrogation room.

Krys set her jaw. "Alright," she said, standing up. "We'll forking do it!"

Willow leaped to her feet with a "Yes!" and a punch in the air.

"One more thing," said Sameena. "What does sudsing and toff mean?"

Willow burst out laughing.

Mr. Cartwright was not best pleased when his daughter turned up at his offices with the police in tow. His secretary said, "Your daughter is here, Mr. Cartwright," and his heart lifted with surprise and sank with worry at the same time. When she added, "With a policewoman," his heart went through the floor.

He hurried to the door, flung it open and ushered them both in, avoiding the secretary's eye, and knowing that this was going to be reported straight back to the senior partners.

"What's all this about, Willow?" he asked, putting himself between her and the policewoman. "What have you done?"

"Oh, Dad," Willow said, exasperated, "I haven't done anything. This is Detective Sergeant Kendricks...and she wants to speak to you."

"Me?" He sat down hard in his chair. "What have I done?"

"You haven't done anything either! It's about what you told me yesterday." He looked blank. "You know – about the drunken policeman at the Lodge."

A light dawned in Mr. Cartwright's eye and his face darkened. "That was told to you in confidence," he said grimly, glancing at the DS.

"Oh, come on, Dad. What you heard has got something to do with the man who died in the cathedral and Daz the homeless guy who got beaten up at the car wash looking for clues – "

Krys thought it was time she took charge and she put on her best police voice. "Mr. Cartwright," she interrupted. "We believe you may have some information that is vital to an ongoing investigation. Now you can answer my questions here informally or we can question you at the station, formally under caution."

She didn't know whether any of that was true and she'd never pulled the tough cop routine on a solicitor so she had no idea if it would work. If it didn't, she hadn't a clue what to do next. She watched Mr. Cartwright closely, using the old insect-under-a-microscope stare – she might as well use every weapon at her disposal. If that failed she could always offer to sleep with him.

And Mr. Cartwright collapsed back in his chair. "Alright," he said, blowing out a breath. "What do you need to know?"

"May I?" She sat down before he nodded his permission and took out her notebook. "You were at the Masonic Lodge in Tamworth when a policeman, Detective Inspector Potter, got drunk and started talking loudly about a raid on a car wash. Is that correct?"

Cartwright nodded again.

"What exactly did he say?"

Cartwright pressed his lips together and thought. He was thinking how much to tell this hard-faced policewoman with the high cheekbones and how much he could hold back to protect his fellow Masons without ending up in an interrogation room at the station.

In the end he told her almost all of it, and when she started questioning him the rest came out.

"So who was there?" Her pen was poised.

"Well, there was myself, obviously and Potter and the bartender."

"Is that all?"

"Well, a couple of other members."

"Names?"

He gave them, reluctantly, firing an angry look at Willow. One was a doctor and the other an accountant, the Senior Warden and Treasurer of the Lodge. "You won't question them, will you?"

"Not unless I have to. Anyone else?"

"There was the man who Potter was talking to. He kept buying him drinks."

She looked up. "Do you know who he was?"

Cartwright shook his head. "He was a visiting member."

"Could you find out?"

"He'll have signed the visitors' book." She carried on staring at him. "Oh, you mean now? But the Lodge is closed now. I'd have to contact the Senior Warden to get the key." And still she stared. Willow was embarrassed for her Dad, seeing him crumble before her eyes. No one should see their father humiliated and she hated Detective Sergeant Kendricks for doing it in front of her. He sighed and picked up the phone.

Willow was sent home with the words "I'll talk to you later!" ringing in her ears and Kendricks and her Dad went to the Lodge. When they got there the Senior Warden was waiting for them. He was a retired head teacher and Captain at the local golf club – the one Cartwright was trying to get into. He didn't look happy.

"What's all this about, Cartwright?" he said, as if he were talking to a naughty schoolboy.

Krys pushed in front of Cartwright and said, "Mr. Cartwright is helping us with a police investigation. We believe one of your members may have been involved in criminal activity and I need to see your guest book."

The Senior Warden peered at her over his glasses. "You know that the Chief Constable is a member here? Perhaps I need to speak to him first?"

"Please do – tell him that one of your members compromised a police operation," said Krys, more confidently than she felt.

"Hmm." The man tapped his key in his hand. She wondered how long he had been playing at being headmaster and why the members put up with it. At last he opened the door and led the way in. "Normally we only have women here on ladies' night."

"How very 1970s of you." She felt Cartwright wince behind her. "Where's the visitors' book?"

It was lying on the bar, sapphire blue and leatherbound with gold gilded pages. The name of the lodge was gilt-embossed in a discreet font on the front in the bottom right corner and the most recent page was kept with a blue and gold silk marker.

The Senior Warden flipped it open and regarded it like late homework with pursed lips like. Krys stepped in front of him and shouldered him aside. She ran her finger down the column and stopped by the date for a week ago. She tapped on the name.

"Who's this?" she said. "Rory Winters."

Chapter Thirty-Five

Krys – Thursday/Friday

Krystyna looked at her watch as she opened the front door – 9.32 pm. She could hear a gun shot and some expletives. She was too tired to react as a police officer. She knew it was only her stupid husband playing on one of his stupid shoot-em-up games. She walked into the living room. There he was sitting on the settee with his hands clutching the games controller staring at the TV screen. There were three empty take-away containers and a dirty plate lying on the coffee table in front of him.

"Hi, hon. I got fed up waiting for you. I got myself a take-away. I assumed you ate something at work," he said without taking his eyes off the screen.

"No, I was actually too busy to eat. It's been crazy at the station today..."

"Good...that's good..."

"So shall I just get something from the kitchen myself then?"

"Great. I'm just half way through this level..."

Krystyna shook her head and surveyed the room. It looked and felt like a scene from one of her husband's games – Zombieland.

"I've got an early start in the morning. I'll sleep in the spare room. Good night."

"OK, hon."

After half an hour of making and eating some toast and drinking two mugs of decaf coffee, Krys was snuggled up in the spare bed. It was no longer spare. It was essential to their living arrangements. Once upon a time she had thought of this room as the nursery/first child's room. But those thoughts had faded with time. Not that she didn't want kids. She did. But not with the moron downstairs who sold cars for a living and watched re-runs of *Top Gear* and played violent video games to relax. It was like being married to a brain-dead Jeremy Clarkson or maybe just Jeremy Clarkson.

Krystyna lay in bed thinking about the day's events. To say it was eventful was an understatement. She would have welcomed the chance to unload and go through it all with someone who would listen and cared, but there was no such creature here in Zombieland.

The day had started early as usual. She'd gone into work that morning with a sinking feeling. How was she going to report Potter and who to? She had various reports to write up at her desk that kept her mind off that problem. But while she had been typing her mind had wandered back to her conversations she had had the day before with Sameena, Willow and her father and another problem. Things had moved forward but Krys had felt sorry for Willow and worried about how the father and daughter meeting would go when Mr Cartwright said to Willow "I'll talk to you later." Krys made a mental note to contact Willow on Friday to see if she was OK.

Back to today. By eleven-ish Potter had not graced her or the team with his presence. There had been no contact with the front desk. Krys assumed he was still in bed after another bender.

It was only when she was summoned to attend a private Zoom meeting in a vacant office along the corridor that she was aware of the reason for Potter's absence. Clearly the Senior Warden at the Tamworth Lodge had made good his threat to complain to the Chief Constable...it just hadn't worked out quite the way he expected.

The Superintendent for South Staffordshire was on the other end of the meeting. SP Houghton spent five minutes of his busy schedule with Krys briefing her on matters that had come to his attention. The upshot was that DI Potter had been placed on sick leave for an indefinite period due to stress and that she would be promoted to acting Detective Inspector with immediate effect. Krystyna, after a brief period of shock, verbally accepted the promotion and then tried to find out more about Potter's 'stress.' All that Houghton would say was that Potter's 'stress' had led to excessive drinking, inappropriate behaviour and breaches of confidentiality. He closed down the conversation then, congratulated her on the temporary promotion and wished her well.

She walked back along the corridor to her desk and sat down gazing at her computer screen. As the Americans say 'she needed a minute' because in a matter of minutes she had gone from Potter's lackey and whipping girl to the head of Lichfield's detective squad. Her mind was racing. The questions piled up in her head. Was she the reason for Potter's stress? Had she let him down? Had she not supported him properly? Was this all about the Shaun Wilde investigation or was it bigger and wider than that? Would Potter ever come back from this or take early retirement? Would she get the job permanently if that happened? Would she be able to lead the team? Would the team be OK with her in charge? How much more money would she be on?

With none of those questions immediately answerable she set about the task in hand. She scribbled a brief plan of action in her notepad.

1) Get team together in briefing room in 30 minutes.
2) Inform team about Potter's sick leave and my acting DI position.
3) Update team on car wash incidents and possible people trafficking.
4) Team to investigate a Rory Winters – the name on register at Masonic Lodge.
5) Question/possible arrest of Winters on involvement in people trafficking at car wash.
6) Is there a connection to Shaun Wilde death?

Krys thought about the three hours that had followed her promotion, listing the order of events as they happened and her thoughts.

Two of 'her' team were in Burntwood investigating a domestic incident, but managed to get back in time for her briefing. The other two were in the office already.

No real response or surprise when she announced that Potter was on 'sick leave.' The team seemed relieved when she told them that she was taking over as acting DI. She got a thumbs up from two of the team and there were smiles and a 'yeah' from the others. Was that because they liked her, respect her or did they think that she would be a soft touch after Potter?

The briefing went well. She was clear and thorough. She asked the team for their thoughts and comments. She praised them for their input. It felt very different to when Potter was leading a briefing.

She then divided up the team in order to get a full picture on Winters. The background check and contact details delivered:

- *Soldier in Iraq*
- *Stayed in Iraq to work for an oil company*
- *Moved back to London area*
- *Antiques dealer now based mainly in Cambridge*
- *Travels around England on business a great deal*
- *Contact made on his mobile*

Winters agreed to meet her the next day at Cambridge Police Station to answer questions with his lawyer present. She and a trusted colleague spent the rest of the day until 5.00 pm prepping for the meeting with Rory Winters.

Although she was shattered and craved sleep, Krystyna could not now stop herself reflecting on the day up to that point, evaluating how it had all gone under her fledgling leadership. She smiled to herself. She was quite pleased with her planning and organisation.

Friday was a wasted day. She enjoyed the new experience of being driven down to Cambridge and being called "guv" ("Don't call me 'ma'am'," she had said. "Makes me sound like the Queen."), but interviewing Winters had quickly taken the shine off the day.

The man didn't look like an ex-soldier. His hair was suitably modern and he wore the same sort of clothes as Potter, only on him they looked good. He gave the appearance of a successful businessman – only the eyes were watchful, but was that his military training or just good business?

Before he answered any of their questions he looked at his solicitor and if the man nodded, Winters spoke. But whenever Krys or her colleague asked him about human slavery, he had an answer for it. He brazenly denied his involvement in anything concerning a car wash. The day they were asking about he was visiting an old army buddy, Major Ballinger at Whittington Barracks, and he was sure the Major would provide him with an alibi if they asked.

He challenged Krys and her colleague to find any evidence at all that would prove that he was involved in people trafficking. He repeated on several occasions that he was now a successful businessman, having served his country in Iraq and that it was outrageous that a man with an outstanding reputation should be treated in this way.

Acting DI Krystyna Kendrick then changed her tack and asked about the day of Shaun Wilde's death.

This seemed to catch Rory Winters off guard. It felt as if he was not expecting this line of questioning. Mr Winters, through a series of probing questions, admitted that he'd heard about the suicide at Lichfield Cathedral. He knew Shaun, they'd been in the Staffies together, but he wasn't a close friend any more – they'd lost touch with each other when they left the army. When asked about the day of the suicide, Rory Winters informed Krys that he wasn't in Lichfield on that day.

Krystyna was duty-bound at that point to pursue Winters' claims. More work needed to be done to corroborate this information, one way or another. Reluctantly, she let Winters leave, pending further investigation. She would have to talk to this Major Ballinger. She was not prepared to let this all go. Not yet. That still didn't sit well with Krystyna.

Nor did the text she'd got from her husband when she checked her phone:

Home late tonight. Don't wait up x

She put it to the back of her mind and got one of the team to go to the Barracks and check on Winters' alibi. By the time they were skirting Birmingham on the M6 Toll, she got the call back that the alibi checked out. By the time they got back to the station she was angry at everything – Winters, her husband, Potter, Sameena Akhtar and Willow Cartwright and her father and the bloody Masons and Darren bloody Mitchell.

She wrote up her report and went home to a cold, dark house. She finally texted Dan:

What time will you be back?

She made herself some toast while she waited for a reply. It came.

Late. We're stocktaking. Don't wait up x

He was a used car salesman, for God's sake. How hard was it to stocktake – all the cars were sitting on the forecourt. He was either out drinking or having an affair. She was surprised to find that she didn't really care, apart from the fact he was treating her like she was stupid.

Bloody men!

She watched TV until ten without seeing it and went to bed. She lay there without sleeping, trying to find the words in her tired mind to describe Winters:

Arrogant, Confident, Entitled, Condescending, Unflappable, Nasty, Tosser.

If Krys hadn't been so tired she might have been amused by the two word acronym that her list gave her.

When she heard the front door open and close quietly she checked her phone. It was eleven-thirty. She listened to her husband creep up the stairs and get ready to go to bed. The bed creaked as he slipped in beside her. She forced herself not to breathe deeply to see if she could smell booze or perfume. She closed her eyes and feigned sleep, just in case. She didn't lie well either.

CHAPTER THIRTY-SIX

Daz – Monday

"The case against him is tenuous," Sameena had said. "He wasn't in Lichfield the day Shaun died and he has an alibi for the assault on you," she said.

And that was supposed to be it – again. Everything stopped – again.

Story of my life, Daz thought. Eugene would have told him to focus on what was important – getting his daughter back. Pauline the counsellor would have told him to focus on what he could control – getting his daughter back. And of course they were right...but he just couldn't let it go.

There was something...it ran like a thread through all of this, and back through his own life too. The Army. It had saved him and then broken him, and when he was on the streets it had saved him again when Shaun the ex-soldier reached out to him. And now the ex-soldier Winters had an alibi from another soldier – Major Ballinger at Whittington Barracks where they had all started – Daz, Shaun, Winters and Ballinger.

Daz had to speak to Ballinger, to hear from his own mouth that Winters was sound, that he wasn't involved in people trafficking or Shaun's death. Just one more time, and then he would stop, and focus on what was important.

He jammed his hands in the pockets of his hoodie and flicked the hood up and walked along the main road to Tamworth. The countryside was the same, ploughed fields, trees, hedges and birds, he even saw a rabbit hopping about, but the sky was grey and heavy with the promise of rain. It suited his mood and he didn't feel lifted this time.

Soon enough he was walking with thundering traffic on one side and grey palisade fencing on the other. Inside he glimpsed the red brick buildings he remembered so well. Not a lot had changed in there in twenty years – only on the outside. He got to the gates and stopped, read the sign:

Army Training Regiment
Lichfield
INITIAL TRAINING GROUP

He didn't know how long he stood there staring, but it must have been long enough to set off alarm bells somewhere because suddenly he heard a firm voice behind him say "Can I help you, sir?" He recognised the tone – he'd had enough run-ins with the Military Police. He took his hands out of his pockets and turned round slowly.

He hadn't noticed the white 4x4 pulling up behind him. It had Day-Glo flashes and the words *Camp Security* on the side and two blank-eyed soldiers inside, both staring at him through the open window. He met their gaze and said, "I trained here."

"I understand that, sir, but you can't stand here – it's a security risk."

You don't understand anything at all, thought Daz. "I was in the Staffies, too," he said. "Look." And slowly and carefully he pushed his sleeve up to show them the tattoo of the knot topped with three feathers. "Stand Firm, Strike Hard," he said.

The two MPs leaned forward to see the tattoo. "Thank you for your service, sir – but I'm going to have to ask you to move along." There was a little more iron in the tone now. A "Don't make me tell you three times" feel, but Daz stood his ground. "I'm here to see someone," he said.

"Who?"

For a panicked second he couldn't remember the name Sameena had given him. "Major – Ballinger."

"And you are?"

"Mitchell, Daz – Darren. Private. 25432307."

The MPs looked at one another, then one of them unhooked the microphone from the dash. He spoke quietly, and the other one kept a steely watch on Daz. He knew the man's hand was resting on the butt of his Glock 17.

The MP stopped talking and his head swivelled like a robot. "No one knows you," he said, and the other one started to open the door. Daz was suddenly aware of the traffic slowing down as it went by, heads craning to see what was going on.

"No, wait," he said hurriedly. "It's important. Tell him it's about Shaun Wilde and Rory Winters."

The Major's office was warm after the cold drizzle outside, even though it was a typical army office. Standard desk, standard bookcase and filing cabinet. On the wall the standard portrait of the Queen. Only the chair looked expensive – like something from a sci-fi movie. Major Ballinger was standing behind it.

He looked like every major Daz had ever met. Back straight, every crease sharp. You never noticed if they were tall or short or if they had a moustache. All you saw was the uniform. But this time Daz noticed the eyes – they reminded him of someone.

And then he realised it was like ooking in the mirror. That same haunted look. The Major smiled and stuck out a hand, but the welcome didn't stretch to his eyes. "So you knew Shaun?"

Daz shook the hand and then sat in the chair it gestured to. It felt awkward, sitting down in front of a major. He'd never done it before. He dragged his beanie hat off his head.

"Yeah – he, uh, he helped me get back on my feet."

The Major sat as well. "He was a good man. He'll be missed. You were in Afghanistan?"

"Helmand, sir."

The Major looked down and fiddled with a pen on his desk. "You had it worse than us, I think," he said.

"Where were you, sir?"

"Iraq – with Shaun and Rory."

He got up and the chair rolled away smoothly behind him. He led Daz to a framed photograph on the wall. It was black and white and looked faded next to the Queen sparkling in her diamonds and blue sash. Daz had seen it before. Four young squaddies, smart in their fatigues, their right sleeves pushed up displaying their tattoos and staring hard at the camera. It was the one Shaun had had framed on the wall in his office - the one Daz had photographed.

"That's me," said the Major, tapping one of the fresh faces. "And there's Shaun – and that's Chris." A shadow fell across Ballinger's face. "He died in Basra. Laid down his life rescuing a wounded comrade on patrol." He stiffened up, and pointed to the last face. "And that's Rory Winters who Chris is looking at. He really looked up to him. How did you say you knew him?"

Daz kept his eyes firmly fixed on the photograph. "I, uh, here's the thing – I, uh, don't actually know him."

He felt the atmosphere in the room grow frosty and he didn't want to look the Major in the face. He knew what he would see there. Cold, hard eyes weighing him up – was he friend or foe – should I let him live or kill him? He'd seen that look in the mirror too.

"And yet you mentioned his name to security," the Major said. His tone was grim.

Daz took one last look at the innocent young men unaware of everything that was in front of them, their smart uniforms and the tattoos and he turned back to face the real world. He met Ballinger's gaze. "I don't think Shaun killed himself," he said more confidently than he felt. "I'm trying to find out who might have wanted him dead. Rory Winters' name came up."

"This again? I've had the police up here asking the same questions, and out of respect for the fact you served your country, I'm going to tell you the same thing I told them. He's an old friend who's been visiting me – he stayed at the base on Thursday night and went home on Friday. End of story. Is there anything else?"

Daz held Ballinger's eyes. "Do you know where he was when Shaun was killed?"

The Major's mouth set into a thin line. "I think it's time for you to leave," he said. He stepped behind his desk. Daz didn't see him touch anything, but the door behind him opened and when he looked round two burly, grim-looking soldiers were standing there.

"This gentleman is just leaving. Kindly escort him off the base."

Daz had been walked between a guard before and he knew what to do – and what not to do. He locked eyes with Ballinger until the Major sat down and picked up a paper on his desk and pretended to read it. He felt an arm on his elbow and knew better than to shake it off.

He was marched out of the camp and found himself back on the Tamworth Road. The Camp Security vehicle was sitting in the lay-by and the two soldiers inside watched him as he put his hand to his head. It felt cold and he realised he no longer had his beanie. It was somewhere in the camp. Force of habit had made him take it off in the presence of a senior officer and he had put it down somewhere. Well, nothing to be done about it – they wouldn't let him back on the base now. He'd have to find a new one in a charity shop. He flicked his hood back up, thrust his hands into the pockets of his hoodie and headed back to Lichfield.

CHAPTER THIRTY-SEVEN

Daz, Willow, Krys, Sam – Tuesday

Daz knew how the army worked. "We can neither confirm nor deny." It meant "We're as guilty as sin, but you can't prove a thing." The more it looked like Shaun had killed himself, the more people told him Shaun had killed himself, the more Daz was convinced that someone had killed him.

Eugene would have something to say about it and so would his counsellor. Not dealing with the real problem by obsessing about something else. Eugene would tell him it was a substitute for drugs – and maybe he was right. Pauline would tell him he was scared of renewing his relationship with his daughter.

And they were both right.

But he was right too. Something just didn't sit well with him about Shaun's death. He'd been the last man to see him alive, and he hadn't behaved like someone on their way to kill themselves. He'd behaved like someone on their way to sort something out.

So he wasn't the last man to see Shaun alive, was he? That was the person who killed him.

And with everyone else giving up, what else could he do for the man who had saved his life? Not give up, start feeling sorry for himself, drink, take drugs and let his life fall apart for a start.

First things first. What had saved him in the Army was routine. Especially after the ADHD diagnosis at school. So breakfast as usual, and then off to pick up more *Big Issues* from his co-ordinator and out onto his patch selling them. Once he'd got enough money he could go shopping and restock his cupboards.

Funny how at school the routine had made him worse, but once he started his military training everything had been better. He'd met other soldiers who'd struggled once they left the Army, not just because of the things they'd seen and done, but because they missed always knowing what they had to do, and their lives had fallen apart just like his had.

Which was why he owed Shaun – he had shown him how to make your own routines and stick to them.

There was still police tape across the Iraqis' flat on his landing and the old man at the end muttered darkly about "Bleedin' foreigners making trouble." A week ago Daz might have agreed with him, but when he thought about how he had spoken to Sameena now his face grew hot.

Maybe he should go and see her. He'd ask Willow today if she came out with a coffee, but he was a bit worried that that part of his life was over too.

Never mind. He squared his shoulders. Routine – that was the thing.

He didn't see Willow, but he sold all his *Big Issues*, and he had enough money after he had done his shopping to buy a coffee for himself. It felt good to sit in a café like a normal person. When he was young he had thought life was boring – that's why he joined the army. He'd wanted to see far away countries and meet exciting people...and he'd ended up killing them. Now he knew how precious boring was.

What he wanted now was a boring nine to five job and a boring life that he could invite his daughter into.

Willow wanted excitement. It's why she had left school – not just because of the bitches she was at school with. Every day she thought, is this all there is? But when she looked at her parents that didn't look any better. And working in the coffee shop...well, Susan the manager was nice, but once you'd exhausted last night's TV and gossiping about the customers, they didn't have much to talk about.

"Well, what do you want?" her father had asked her once, exasperated.

"I don't know," was the miserable answer. And then a list of what she didn't want.

So applying for college had to be done carefully. She didn't want to narrow her options.

She sighed. When had things got this difficult? She remembered going to dancing on a Saturday morning and wanting to be a ballet dancer. She couldn't wait for a tutu, and then to go up on her points. That tutu and those ballet shoes were gathering dust on the top of her wardrobe now. And the piano lessons – they'd never taken. She just didn't practice, and now she wished she had. To sit down at the keys and make music. If only her parents had made her do it.

She sat up and squared her shoulders. What was it Daz had told her his counsellor had told him? We can't control situations, but we can control our reactions to them. Alright then, stop regretting the past and worrying about the future. As Dad said, "What do I want?"

An hour and a half later she was done. She still wasn't sure what she wanted, but she'd narrowed it down a bit and her choice of subjects gave her a few options she was interested in: mathematics, biology, English language and literature meant she could go to uni and study to be a sociologist, or a psychologist or a counsellor. Or even a criminologist, and then, if she wanted, she could get fast-tracked as a policewoman!

Although why she was thinking about joining the police she had no idea. She'd always seen herself in the caring professions. That's why she went to visit Mary – but over the last few weeks she felt like she'd grown up a lot. The anti-establishment girl who had left school at sixteen because she didn't like the rules, the religion and the conformity, wanted to make a difference helping other people who were struggling too.

Maybe Daz had influenced that decision. Sameena too – a solicitor who worked for more than just money. And Krystyna, the policewoman who seemed to be on the side of what was right instead of on the side of the rules.

Feeling at least ten years older, she went downstairs and her Mum asked her if she wanted a cup of hot chocolate with marshmallows in it.

"Yes, please."

"You go and turn the TV on and I'll bring it through."

And just like that she was eleven years old again, coming home from school to watch *Home and Away* with Mum. Do we ever grow up? she wondered. Dad seemed like he had, when he was in his office, or laying down the law at home, but he'd behaved like a small boy in the head's office when Krystyna challenged him. And Daz behaved just like a spoiled little brat a lot of the time.

Maybe only women grow up, she thought, sipping her hot chocolate, licking marshmallow off her lip and watching *Loose Women*.

Krystyna couldn't decide if being Acting Detective Inspector was a blessing or a curse. Her new job was putting a great deal of pressure on her and taking up all of her time. She wanted to do a good job, no, more than that, she wanted to do, in PEEL speak, an Outstanding job. She had to convince her masters, (and they were masters - every one of them was a man!) that she could step into Potter's boots and not just substitute for him, but improve the Lichfield team. In her mind, not that she would share this with anyone, just from Potter being on sick leave automatically improved the day-to-day running of the unit. Being without him was a bonus, but there was still a huge workload to get through. Her Acting DS was inexperienced and it took up at least an hour every shift training him up. Then she had to look at all of Potter's active cases and decide what, if any, could be put on the back burner. Then she had to re-assess her caseload and respond to any new incidents that were directed towards her. She also, had to keep her team sweet and make sure her immediate line manager was kept fully informed of any serious developments on any on-going cases.

Within a few busy days and restless nights Krys had come to the conclusion that the unfortunate events at Lichfield Cathedral could and should be now classified as suicide – unless any other information came to light. This wouldn't please Daz, or Willow for that matter, but what could she do? She realised that she had become too invested in Daz's version of events. A sad and troubled guy who had not just lost the plot, but had lost his only real friend. But, in the end, there hadn't been any solid or concrete evidence of murder. The only material that was solid and concrete were the floors of both the cathedral and the car wash.

Krystyna felt guilty for shelving the case, but it had to be done. She comforted herself knowing that the local community would accept that Shaun Wilde could not cope with his dodgy dealings inside the charity and consequently took his own life. Her bosses would be delighted that there was no longer a murder to investigate and that they could re-position their limited resources on other crimes. She would tell her superiors that the case was at an end unless new information came to light. She secretly hoped that there would be no new light at the end of this particular dark tunnel.

Would this make Krys sleep better? She doubted it. Her workload would still be crazy without this murder/suicide investigation. But she couldn't complain. It was her choice to step up into Potter's role and now she knew that those above her with bigger and shinier badges would be looking down on her and making judgements. She was a youngish woman with a bit of an accent. She had to succeed and prove herself in this role, no matter how long Potter was off work for. She also had to be seen as being competent and worthy by the other non-males on the police force.

One male that would not be awarding her any medals at the moment was her husband. When they did cross paths at night or in the morning they were both cross with each other. Her husband was angry at her because his needs were not being met by her – she spent too long at work; she didn't cook anymore, she didn't clean the house anymore, she was too tired for sex and often slept in the spare bedroom. Krystyna was angry at her husband because he was a selfish and thoughtless arsehole. If the Jeremy Kyle Show was still being aired, they would have been the perfect couple to feature. But this was not a TV show, it was real life. And there was only so much anger and frustration that could be vented.

So the happy couple continued to wear brave faces, existing in parallel, next to one another. The animosity simmered while they both privately came to the same conclusion - that things had changed irrevocably. The opportunities to talk things through and compromise had been missed and the marriage was now heading into the dark tunnel, neither of them able to find the emergency brake.

There were three partners at Allcocks Solicitors. Mr and Mrs Allcock were in their fifties, both very intelligent, smartly dressed and personable. Then there was Mr Hawley. He was an odd bod and had an odd body to match. There was something or perhaps many things that made Sameena feel uncomfortable when she was in his presence.

One of his most annoying habits was to tap on Sameena's office door and make casual conversation which felt like he was checking up on her. Ever since he spoke to her about her involvement in the suicide case, Hawley had had his eyes even closer on her and he had made it clear that her work at the Citizens Advice office should not interfere with or detract from her work at Allcocks. He had asked for her assurance that the excessive interest in the death at the cathedral was over now and she had said yes. That was it. Sam could not involve herself anymore with Daz's obsession to get justice for Shaun Wilde.

Sam sat at her desk at Allcocks and felt deflated. For all sorts of reasons she had enjoyed her time with Willow, Krys and even Daz. It was different to the mundanity of the usual work at Allcocks and the CAB. It was also a slight escape from the tedium of living with her mother.

Sameena felt guilty for feeling this way. She enjoyed her work, most of the time, although it wasn't a thrill-a-minute. She loved her mom, even though she got on her nerves. Sam felt so sorry for her. She had lost her husband without any certainty about what had happened to him.

Sam wondered if the disappearance of her father was why she had taken such an interest in Daz's plight. Daz was just looking for answers as to why his friend had died just as Sam was trying to make sense of her dad's vanishing act. Is this why Daz's case had struck a chord with Sameena? She didn't know. But what she did know was that the questions about Shaun Wilde's death had not been fully answered. And she was torn between pursuing her interest or avoiding the risk of being disciplined by the partners at Allcocks.

She was conflicted. Was she confused about more than just the death at the cathedral? She wasn't even sure if she was or not! Was she just dissatisfied with her life? Was she unhappy with other things? Her appearance? Her feelings towards Bash? Questions. Questions. But no answers.

For now, at least, Sameena promised herself that she would keep her head down and work hard. She would also save hard so that one day she could live independently and distance herself from her mother. Perhaps she would move away from Lichfield but, for now, Sameena would bide her time. Something had to change. She hoped.

CHAPTER THIRTY-EIGHT

Sam – Tuesday afternoon/evening

Sameena picked at her plastic salad box with her plastic fork. She sat at her untidy, busy desk. In front of her was her laptop, the phone, her diary, her notepad, her mobile phone, several pens and highlighters, several opened folders and two reference books on the law. But in the middle of all of this mayhem was the unappetising sight of lettuce leaves, slices of cucumber, onions and tomatoes and three short sticks of celery. This was her lunch. No additions or extras. No cheese, no boiled eggs, no bread or salad cream. This was definitely not a meal or, come to think of it, even a snack. A snack, in Sameena's mind, consisted of something sinful such as chocolate or biscuits or, better still, chocolate biscuits.

Sameena hated this current diet plan. She felt really uncomfortable eating primarily food that was grown in a field and did not see the inside of an oven. She needed proper comfort food. Food that made her feel happy and fulfilled. What would make her feel happy now was a cake from *the Faro Lounge* or a cheese and pickle sandwich from *The Tasty Cafe* or …

"How are we today, Miss Akhtar?"

Sameena jumped and a slice of tomato dropped from her fork onto her notepad.

"Oh, hello, Mr Allcock, I didn't see you there. In fact I haven't seen you all morning."

"No, I've had one appointment after another. I just wanted to check that you are OK and keeping yourself busy."

"Well, as you can see from my desk, I'm busy. Thank you. Is there anything you actually want?" Sameena asked trying to hide her contempt for this obnoxious man.

"Not particularly. I'm just doing the rounds. Making myself visible to the team." And with that Allcock disappeared. Sameena looked back at her laptop and returned to her work.

At close to five o'clock Sameena heard a ping on her mobile. It was Bash.

Are you free to talk?

Can I ring you tonight instead?

Sure. 9 ish?

OK x

X

"Hi, ummi," Sameena shouted as she opened the front door.

"Oh, there you are. I was starting to get worried. Are you OK, babbu? You look tired."

"Yes, ummi. I'm just tired. A day of paperwork. I've got a blinding headache."

"They work you too hard at that place. Come and sit down and I'll get you some tablets and a glass of water. I should think you're hungry after a long day, aren't you?"

"To be honest, I'm starving. This new diet isn't working. I'm hungry all of the time!" Sam smiled at her mother, but ummi just shook her head.

"I'm glad I made plenty for tonight's meal then."

After Sameena swigged down the painkillers, she took off her heels and lay along the settee. She would just close her eyes for five minutes until her meal was ready.

"Sameena, sweetie, your meal's ready," Sam's mother whispered in her ear.

"Thanks, ummi. How long have I been asleep?"

"An hour or so. You looked so peaceful. I didn't want to disturb you. But you ought to eat something. Has your headache passed?"

"Yes, thank you. Something smells nice. There's nothing like home-cooked food! Don't let me have a second helping though. I'm dieting...or trying to."

"You need to keep your strength up though...and I've made some warm kheer for later...one of your favourite desserts."

"Ummi! You know I'm trying to lose some weight. That's really naughty of you...but also really nice," replied Sameena, blowing her mother an exaggerated kiss.

By the time Sameena staggered up the stairs to her bedroom it was just after 9.00 pm. She stripped down to her underwear and lay on the bed. It was time to ring Bash.

"Hi, Bash. Sorry I couldn't take a call earlier, but I've been extra busy in the office."

"That's OK. Is everything alright?" replied Bash.

"Yeah...yeah ...it's just that Allcock keeps checking up on me...finding reasons to visit me in my office..."

"Is he harassing you? Is he making you feel uncomfortable...you know what I'm saying?"

"No, no – it's not like that. He's not a pervert, he's OK really, but he likes to make it known that he's my boss and he's keeping an eye on me."

"Remember Sam, not all men are perfect like me. Anyway, how's your mother?"

"Fine She's downstairs watching *Doc Martin* or *Chicago Med* or another one of those medical dramas. She loves those shows like *Casualty* and *Holby City*."

"I remember. We used to spend many an evening sitting on the settee watching them while your mother would try to diagnose the patients out loud before the so-called doctors did."

"Yeah. She still does."

"I really do like your mother, Sam."

"She really likes you too. Perhaps more than me."

"Pardon? Do you mean that your mom likes me more than you do?"

"Oh God, sorry Bash, that came out all wrong. That's not what I meant at all. You know I lo – like you. You're my best friend...always...anyway, why did you ring me? Was it just to tease and embarrass me?"

"No, that's just an added extra. My main reason for calling you was about the accounts you asked me to look at. You know, the Rory Winters and Shaun Wilde stuff."

Sameena closed her eyes and cursed silently. Just when she was trying to distance herself from the Cathedral death and focus on her real job, something or someone dragged her back in again. Sameena took the bait.

"What is it, Bash?"

"Well, I did some more digging. Don't ask me to explain how I managed to get this information, but let's just say that someone, who's name I've conveniently forgotten, helped me, very discreetly, to look into Winters' payments over the last eighteen months or so. Most of the payments are credited with real names to legitimate organisations, but there is a pattern of payments that didn't make sense. That is until we cross-referenced those payments with the *Home and Heart* accounts. Sam, there's definitely a link between Winters and Shaun Wilde. There are regular payments going from Winters to Wilde."

Sameena didn't know if she was pleased to have this information or not. She believed and trusted that what Bash and his 'friend' had found out was right. He was a numbers guy after all. Sameena was not a numbers person, but she could add up 2 plus 2. The trouble was right now she was not sure if the answer was 4 or 5.

"Sam, are you still there?"

"Yes, sorry, Bash, I was just trying to make sense of this in my head. This stuff that you and your friend have done in order to get this information...is it criminal?"

"Let's just say that the information I've given you is easy enough for others to find out if they were pointed in the right direction...but not by me or my friend. We would have to deny our involvement in this for the sake of our jobs."

And for the sake of your lives, thought Sameena trying not to be over-dramatic. Sam's mind was racing now, but she didn't want Bash to be further involved in this murky situation.

"Bash, thank you so much for this information. I'll somehow find a way to convey this to the police without implicating you guys in any of this. I'll speak to you soon. Goodnight, Bash. You're a star."

"Goodnight, Sam. Sweet dreams."

Sameena lay there on her bed feeling cold. Partly because she was only wearing her underwear and partly because she was beginning to realise that Shaun Wilde was not the charitable man that Daz thought he was. It wasn't certain by any means, but Sam couldn't help joining the dots and coming to the conclusion that Wilde was involved in people trafficking. To what degree he was guilty was debatable, but he was part of a serious criminal offence. This was organised crime and any organisation has more than one person involved. Shaun Wilde was part of this revolting group of individuals who valued money more than life. And if that was the case then Wilde's death might well have been at the hands of others in this army of criminals.

Sameena shivered. She quickly put her pyjamas on and took shelter under her duvet. This was not the day she wanted. Perhaps she would feel better in the morning. That's if she could sleep! And if she could sleep, there would be no sweet dreams.

CHAPTER THIRTY-NINE

Daz – Wednesday

Another day and everything the same. It was what he wanted. Well, not quite the same. He hadn't seen Willow in nearly a week and he had been getting his morning coffee at Maccy D's, but today bang on eleven o'clock, here she was coming across the market square with a cup of coffee in one hand and a cake wrapped in a napkin in the other.

He wasn't quite sure what to say, so he said nothing, and she filled the awkward space with a waterfall of words.

"I'm really sorry I haven't been out to see you, but I've been so busy!"

"It's OK," he mumbled, but she gushed on.

"Finally agreed with Dad what I'll study at college. I might become a policewoman! Can you imagine that?"

"Not really," he said. "Anway, you should be getting on with your life, going to college and meeting people your own age, not hanging out with me."

Willow looked aghast. "That's not it at all," she burst out. "You – "

"No, really," he pressed on. "It's true. Look at me – I'm getting on with my life. The local co-ordinator has said she might be able to get me a job at a builders' yard. With a job and a counsellor and Sameena, I might be able to get to see my daughter at last."

Willow flung her arms around his neck. It was a bit embarrassing, being hugged like this in full view of everyone. He kept his arms by his sides so no one got the wrong idea about *The Big Issue* seller and the young girl.

"Daz, that's wonderful!" she cried. "I knew you could do it!" She stepped back, regarded him thoughtfully, catching her lip with her teeth, her head on one side. "Look, I don't want us to drift apart, just because we're doing different things. Do you want to come to see Mary with me again tomorrow?"

"I don't know," said Daz, doubtfully. "I've got to see about this job, and..." He tailed off lamely.

"Oh, come on," Willow pleaded. "Mary really enjoyed it last time, talking to you all about that code stuff – "

"Morse."

"Yeah, that. And Afghanistan and everything. Oh, come on, puh-leeze!"

Daz shrugged. "OK," he muttered, and stepped back when she tried to hug him again.

"I'll meet you here at eleven o'clock tomorrow."

And with that she was off, flying back to the café and her new life. Daz didn't know whether he was happy or sad. Your choice, he thought. Be happy. But he felt some kind of sadness for something lost coil around his heart as he set out for the NA meeting at the church.

"What's the matter with you?" said Eugene, handing him a bad cup of coffee.

"I don't know," said Daz. "I should be happy." And he told him about the job, and the counsellor and Sameena and the chance to see his daughter.

Eugene punched him lightly on the arm. "That's great, man. I knew you could do it."

Daz shrugged. "I know. It's just that something doesn't feel quite right."

"That you don't deserve it? Everyone else deserves to be happy and you don't?"

"Something like that."

Eugene took him to a chair and sat him down. "Listen," he said. "You're not the only person who feels like that. Everyone in this room probably feels the same, they're all living with guilt over mistakes they made in the past and the pain they caused to others, and they all acted selfishly and destructively, but look at them – " He took them all in with a sweep of his arm. " – they're all basically good and worthy. They're not the same people they were – and neither are you."

"If you say so, Eugene."

"I do say so, Darren. And I say that if you don't let go of your guilt you're going to end up like that guy they found in Stowe Pool."

"What guy?"

"It was years ago," said Eugene. "Years before I came to Lichfield. It was a big story at the time apparently. A homeless man who'd been a bit of a fixture begging outside pubs on Bore Street - one day he was gone. They fished him out of Stowe Pool a few days later. There was some talk at the time about whether it was suicide or murder, but the coroner returned a verdict of death by misadventure. No one was sure, but someone thought he'd been in the army and the locals had clubbed together to pay for his funeral and scattered his ashes in St Chad's at the far end of Stowe Pool among the war graves. He could have fallen in drunk, but he could have chucked himself in. You're not going to do that, are you?"

Daz thought long and hard. There had been times in his darkest days and after Shaun had died he could have gone off the rails, but he'd made it through. He was going to be alright. "No, I'm OK," he said.

"Good to hear," said Eugene. "So what are you going to do now?"

"I've got to go to the library and do some research."

"Sounds interesting. What on?"

"Morse Code."

At least Eugene knew what Morse Code was, so he didn't feel as old as he had when Willow looked at him like he was talking a foreign language.

Back at the library, back at a computer, he fired up Google.

There was a lot of boring stuff about some guy called Samuel and American railroads, but that wasn't what he needed for tomorrow when Mary started going "Di dah di dah" at him again. He scrolled down a bit further, and there it was – a pageful of lines and dots, each one with a letter by the side.

Again he had that prickle in the back of his mind that he'd seen those patterns somewhere before, but it stayed there. He focused back on the screen.

The length of a dot is one unit (he read). A dash is three units. The space between parts of the same letter is one unit. The space between letters is three units. The space between words is seven units. Whatever the hell that meant. He read on and found what he wanted – one dot and one dash was A and one dash followed by three dots was B. It went down through the alphabet and numbers 1 to 9 and then 0.

He realised that he'd been concentrating so hard that his face was all screwed up, and his jaw ached from clenching his teeth. It was like being back at school. He dry-washed his face with his hands and stretched to take the knots out of the muscles in his back. He printed it all off to study later at home. And since he had nothing else to do, he typed *homeless man drowned Stowe Pool* into Google.

The name came up straight away in an online copy of the *Lichfield Mercury* from 2001 – Brian Spencer.

"Emergency services were called to Stowe Pool on early Sunday morning after reports that a body had been seen floating. They later confirmed a body had been recovered and was pronounced dead at the scene. He was later identified as Brian Spencer, a homeless man who was well-known locally and was frequently to be seen on Bore Street. An inquest is expected to take place."

Daz scrolled down a bit more. A few months later (no hurry, he thought grimly, for the homeless man), he found a report of the inquest. It wasn't a long report.

"An inquest into the death of Brian Spencer, the homeless man found drowned in Stowe Pool in March has returned a verdict of accidental death. Mr. Spencer was found to have had over 200 milligrams of alcohol per 100 millilitres in his bloodstream and the coroner said that possible visual impairment due to the high level of alcohol may have led to him falling into Stowe Pool and drowning. Other cuts and abrasions on his body were consistent with a fall."

Daz had seen similar cold-blooded accounts about the deaths of men he had fought alongside. *Killed in action. Died as a result of wounds or injuries sustained* – cold words for the death of friends with families who loved them. He wondered who had loved Brian Spencer and he moved the mouse once more.

Apparently a lot of people. No family, but a lot of friends. Eugene was right. There had been a collection at the pubs and cafés on Bore Street which had raised enough to cover the funeral costs and because he had turned out to be an ex-soldier his ashes had been scattered amongst the Commonwealth graves in St. Chad's. The Staffordshire Regiment had even been asked for, and provided an honour guard of six soldiers to bear the coffin.

There was a more detailed report, but Daz's eyes and back couldn't take any more. Neither could his emotions.

So that was that. Armoured with his Morse code research and the knowledge that Eugene was right, people were mostly good and worthy or trying to be, Daz left the library. He thought he might go and lay some flowers in the churchyard and tomorrow he would try and be kind to Mary and maybe if there was a God He would notice and perhaps He would help him to see Amy.

CHAPTER FORTY

Daz, Willow, Mary – Thursday

"Alright, Bob!"

Daz swivelled round to see Willow standing in front of him.

"Willow, don't creep up on me like that. I almost shh...pissed myself," replied Daz.

"So you made it then. Looking sharp, if I may say so, even for a grumpy old git," said Willow, giving him the once-over.

"Yes, I said I'd come with you? I can't tell you how much I'm looking forward to spending a couple of hours with that mad old woman."

"Do I detect a bit of sarcasm?" asked Willow.

"Well spotted. You may well have a career in the police, if they allow weirdos with bright-coloured hair into their ranks!" said Daz smiling.

"It might make a colourful change to have some different-looking officers patrolling the streets."

"Perhaps. But don't join the police force just to make a point. It's a tough, dangerous job. It's one thing trying to make a difference but you need to enjoy the job you do and be safe at the same time."

"Wow!" said Willow. "That was a sensitive thing to say...for a grumpy old git!"

"Will you stop calling me that or I won't come with you to see Mary."

"OK. Sorry. I suppose you're not that old...compared to Mary. So, are you ready to go, Bob?"

"Yes, but why are you calling me Bob?"

"*Bob the Builder*...isn't that what you're going to be soon?"

"Yeah...but I might change my mind and be a policeman instead. After all I'm kind, empathetic and non-judgemental. What d'you think?"

"God help us all! Come on, Bob the Plod or we'll be late."

By 11.30 Willow, followed by Daz had signed in at Abbeyfield Residential Home. They collected Mary from her room and wheeled her onto the patio. Daz was amazed at the beauty of this small but well-kept private garden for the residents to use. They sat around a circular table with a huge parasol shading them from the sun, drinking tea that was brought out to them by one of the carers.

"Are you both OK sitting here? I thought it might be a little hot lugging me down to town today. If you stay for a while I'll talk one of the nurses into getting you some food for your lunch. They do some nice meals and it won't cost you anything. Are you both hungry?" asked Mary.

"Yes, that would be great," said Daz before Willow could reply. He knew how little his young friend ate. Daz was not going to miss out on the chance of free food.

"That's very kind of you," said Willow reaching over to Mary's wheelchair and gently squeezing her hand.

"You two look as if you could do with a decent meal inside you. Eat while you can, that's my motto. You get to an age when you lose your appetite for various things and then life isn't as much fun from then on."

"Were you a big eater then Mary...back in the day?" asked Willow.

"I ate when I could. We were rationed in the war and later when I traipsed across Europe and Asia there were days when we ate next to nothing. We would spend our money on booze and smoking various things," said Mary, winking at Daz and Willow.

"So, this is when you were a young hippie?" asked Willow.

"No, I thought I told last time I saw you, I was in my forties. The hippy trail wasn't just for youngsters like you. There were people of all ages from Europe and even the States who wanted some adventure and to experience a different way of living."

"How did you travel?" asked Daz.

"I hitchhiked for some of the time...jumped on communal buses and trains sometimes. Whatever was cheap and available."

"Who did you go with?" asked Willow.

"Just my friend – the back pack. But you were never on your own. There were always people to talk to. I made some great friendships along the way."

"I bet you have some good memories," stated Daz.

"Those were some of my happiest times. After my divorce, footloose and fancy free. Seeing some of the world. I did the trail a couple of times and visited some wonderful places."

"What were some of your favourites?" asked Daz.

"Let me...think.Tehran...Herat...Kandahar...Kabul...Peshawar...Lahore. I particularly loved Afghanistan. The people were so kind and friendly. The country was picturesque. It was like a lost paradise."

Daz's expression changed. He wasn't expecting to hear that from Mary.

"What's wrong, young man?" asked Mary.

"Nothing. I just have a different view of Afghanistan. I don't have any fond memories of the place," replied Daz.

"I saw Afghanistan at its best. Before the Soviet-Afghan war in the 1980s and followed by the US and the UK at the beginning of this century. Sadly, the place became a broken mess. Just corpses and rubble. I'm afraid, young man, you saw Afghanistan at its worst..."

"Yeah. We thought we were doing some good. But we weren't," said Daz sadly.

"You were just doing your duty...following orders," said Willow sympathetically.

"We were, but Mary's right," said Daz sullenly. "Best intentions and all that but nothing got any better. Too many people suffered and lost their lives."

"Actually, I'm feeling quite hungry now," said Willow, trying to change the mood and the topic. "How about you two?"

"Yes, I could eat something," said Daz.

"OK. Let's have some lunch. Can you push me into the dining room?" said Mary.

Within ten minutes they were each making in-roads into hot meals. The conversation on the futility of war was confined to recent history as Mary changed the topic and told Willow and Daz stories about her various romantic and not-so-romantic assignations before and after she was married. Mary went into graphic detail describing some of the private moments of her love life. Mary's lack of shame and her inability to turn down her own volume control meant that the other residents and canteen staff in the dining room were served up with X-rated anecdotes and images. Fortunately, some of the residents in the dining room were oblivious to her stories as they were no longer blessed with a good sense of hearing or were in a world of their own. Even so, by the time they had finished their desserts, Willow's cheeks were burning with embarrassment and Daz too was feeling a little uncomfortable.

Mary then returned to one of her favourite topics – Morse code. She was keen to show her embarrassed friends some more rudiments of the language.

"Willow, I'm going to give you the first names of three of my boyfriends. Write them down on this serviette with a gap between each one."

Willow complied.

"George...Victor...Stan."

Willow wrote them down.

"Now I want you to write their names down underneath in code. Ready?"

"Yes, Miss," said Willow with a smile on her face.

"Now G is dash, dash, dot. E is dot, O is dash, dash, dash. R is dot, dash, dot, another G dash, dash and dot and then another E. What was the E, Willow?"

"Dot," said Willow.

"That's right. Well done. You're on the way to learning Morse code."

It was then Daz's turn. He reluctantly had to spell Victor and then Stan in code.

By the end of this mini-lesson the serviette was covered in dashes and dots. Daz stared at the serviette for a few seconds while Mary explained to Willow what the next lesson on Morse Code would involve when she visited her next.

Daz shut out Mary's voice and focussed. There was something about these seemingly random marks on the tissue that was stirring something in the back of his mind, but he couldn't join up the dots and dashes. Where had he seen these markings before? He folded up the serviette and put it in his pocket.

Daz and Willow wheeled Mary back to her room. They said their goodbyes and then signed out of Abbeyfield Residential Home.

Daz and Willow made their way back to the centre of Lichfield. As they walked, they laughed and joked about Mary's unfiltered stories. Although it was not admitted out loud, Daz and Willow had enjoyed both Mary's company and that of each other.

CHAPTER FORTY-ONE

Daz, Krys – Friday

Another good day. Daz was beginning to wonder what he had done to deserve it.

The session with Pauline was even better than the first one – maybe because he knew what to expect so he didn't put up so many walls. "It always happens," she told him, "when people realise I'm not the enemy. And neither is anyone else," she added.

"And how have things been since last week?" she asked.

Well, he'd uncovered a human trafficking ring, got beaten up and sent to hospital and got a dirty cop busted. A pretty ordinary week in the life of a recovering alcoholic getting himself back together. He shrugged. "Same old same old," he said.

"That's not what Sameena told me," she said with a smile.

Bollocks! He'd forgotten that Pauline knew Sam. "Yeah, well," he said sheepishly, hanging his head and looking at his hands between his knees. "One or two things happened."

"You were very brave. You might have saved some lives. You certainly saved Sameena from a difficult situation. Why wouldn't you want that to be recognised?"

He mumbled something about anyone could have done it and she said, "But they didn't – you did. You did a good thing. Can't you acknowledge that?"

"I've done a lot of bad things too."

"Haven't we all?" she said. "One doesn't rule out the other. Sameena feels very guilty, by the way about getting you beaten up."

Daz looked up in surprise. "She didn't get me beat up. That was all my own stupid fault."

"Well, there you are then. Sometimes we feel guilty about things that aren't even our fault."

He looked at her closely. He wasn't sure whether he'd just walked straight into her trap or the conversation had just gone that way. Either way, he didn't have an answer, but he was surprised to find he was feeling better when he walked out of the quiet shabby office on to the bustle of Bore Street as people headed for pubs and restaurants.

He headed for his spot and sold his last few *Big Issues* to the lunchtime crowd, and turned for home. The walk was always nice, whatever the weather, past the cathedral and round Stowe Pool, although this time he got a chill thinking about the homeless guy, Brian Spencer, who'd drowned there all those years ago.

Life turns on a sixpence he thought. Barely two weeks ago that might have been how he would have ended up, just a forgotten nobody who died somewhere, cold and alone. Now the sun was shining and the birds were singing. Even the walk through the rougher parts of The Dimbles wasn't so bad.

He started saying "Hello" to people he passed on the street. Some smiled and said "Hello" back, some ducked their heads and scuttled passed, but it didn't matter. By the time he got to the flats, he was whistling. It was tuneless, it might have been "Rehab" or "What Katie Did" – he wasn't sure and it didn't matter anyway. He was happy.

He pounded up the steps to his flat. He got to his landing and saw that the door to Amir's old flat was open and the police tape was hanging limply from the splintered door jamb.

He stopped, looked around and listened. Everyone knew it was empty. Maybe someone homeless had broken in. Or a druggie looking for a place to crash. He'd done both himself in the bad old days.

He knocked on the door of the old man's flat. If anyone had seen or heard anything, he would have.

"Who is it?" An angry, suspicious voice on the other side of the door.

Daz stepped back so that he would show up clearly in the spyhole.

"It's me, Mr. – " He realised he didn't know the old man's name, so he mumbled something. "Daz Mitchell from across the way."

"What do you want?"

"Someone's broken into the empty flat. I wondered if you'd heard anything?"

"No." It was a flat end-it-all word, and then he heard slippers shuffling away and the television being turned up.

Daz gently pushed open the door of Amir's flat. "Hello?" he called, but only silence hissed back at him and the smells of foreign cooking and foreign cigarettes.

He eased his way in. Everything was the same as the last time he had been in except that the newspaper and DVDs were now scattered all over the floor, and the picture with the Islamic writing had been taken down and removed from its frame. The cushions on the sofa were upended and the coffee table turned over. And in the middle of it all lay a dead man.

Daz had seen enough dead men to know without feeling for a pulse. There was something about a body when life had gone. It looked deader than something that had never been alive.

He crept forward and felt the body. It was stone-cold. Face down, there was nothing about it he could recognise, but he was fairly sure he didn't know him. The clothes were good and clean, the haircut was fresh and from what he could see of the face, neatly shaved. There was a strong whiff of some expensive cologne – definitely not Lynx.

He backed slowly out of the flat, reaching for his phone in his back pocket. It was like a sign – but he didn't know if it was a good one or a bad one.

It was a bad one. Krys stepped out of the flat and pushed back the hood of her bunny suit – what she called the white jumpsuit you had to wear at a crime scene – and slipped off the blue latex gloves and booties. "It's him," she said to her sergeant. "It's Rory Winters. "Who found the body?"

The sergeant jerked with a thumb behind him at Daz, who was standing with his hands thrust into the pockets of his hoodie, looking hangdog. Krys sighed. "You're a real bad penny, you know, Mr. Mitchell," she said over the sergeant's shoulder.

"Not my fault," Daz said. "I saw the door was open, went in to check and as soon as I saw the body I came out. I didn't touch anything."

"I'm sure you didn't. We've got your fingerprints on file from last time anyway."

"Do you know who he is?"

"We do. Do you?"

"Why should I?"

Krys held up her fingers and started ticking off points. "Because he was found in the flat next door to you. The flat that you said housed trafficked workers, who worked at the carwash that you staked out and got beaten up at – is that enough?"

Daz flared up. "Well, I don't. I only saw the back of his head. I thought he was a drug addict or someone homeless or something. It's always the same with you lot. You try and help and next thing you know, you're being accused of something. I should have kept my mouth shut."

"We'd still have been knocking on your door, Mr. Mitchell. You've got to admit it's quite a coincidence."

"So?"

"You keep turning up in all the wrong places." She glared angrily at him and felt she had to add, "You should be grateful it's me here and not DI Potter. He'd have you in a cell by now."

And Daz felt he had to shove his wrists out and say, "Go on then."

Just before things got out of hand one of the SOCO team came out and whispered in Krys's ear. She glanced at Daz, and ducked back inside the flat. He hung about, unsure whether to go or not. The other detective sergeant fixed him with a slide-under-the-microscope stare, but Daz had had enough of those to last a lifetime. He stared right back.

Then Krys came out again. "Mr. Mitchell?"

"Yeah?"

"Just to be clear – you came home, saw the flat had been broken into, went in, found the body and phoned the police. Is that correct?"

"Yeah."

And didn't touch anything in the flat?"

He looked away, looked back. "No."

"Then would you care to explain this?" From behind her back she brought out an evidence bag, and inside it Daz could see a beanie hat. It looked a lot like his beanie hat...the one he had lost.

"It's a hat," he said with a lift of his chin.

"A hat we found under the body, Mr. Mitchell."

Daz felt the pit of his stomach rise up into his throat and he swallowed it down again. "A lot of people wear hats like that," he said.

"So they do. People like you. Perhaps you'd be good enough to go and get your hat – so we can rule it out of our investigation." Even as she spoke the words, Krys could feel a smile hovering on her lips, they sounded so ridiculous. But they were deadly serious. Her sergeant detected the change in the atmosphere and shifted himself to block the stairway in case Daz made a run for it.

"I...I lost it."

"Mmm." Krys glanced at her sergeant now, and then put his feeling into words. "Darren Mitchell, I am placing you under arrest on suspicion of murder. You do not have to say anything, but it may harm your defence if you do not mention when questioned something which you later rely on in court. Anything you do say may be given in evidence."

CHAPTER FORTY-TWO

Daz, Krys, Sam – Friday afternoon

Sameena sat next to Daz in the interview room. She had received a garbled message on her phone from Daz an hour ago just as she was clearing her desk. She was looking forward to a weekend of over-eating and slobbing mostly in her pyjamas. She had given up on her latest diet for the time being, but she would wear her track suit during some parts of the day, just in case she felt the need to exercise or walk to Hindley's, her favourite cake shop in Lichfield.

But for now she was in the police station with Daz and a plastic cup of water for company. He had phoned Sam, his one phone call, from the corridor outside his holding cell, explaining that he had just been arrested for the murder of a guy in his block of flats.

Sameena knew from that moment that her weekend plans would be changing. She would not be changing into her PJs for a while. Sam had agreed to be Daz's advocate for his first interview having explained that she wasn't a criminal lawyer. He'd insisted that he wanted her by his side to begin with. Sam grabbed her briefcase and made her way quickly to the police station.

At the reception counter Sameena showed her ID to the police officer on the desk and explained who she was and her reason for being there.

A few minutes later Acting Detective Inspector Krystyna Kendrick appeared in the foyer. Krys and Sam nodded at each other in acknowledgement, but their respective jobs and the roles they were about to play, did not allow for any warm pleasantries, only cold professionalism. Erased from their memories, just now, were the casual chats they'd shared over cake in a local café and their discreet liaison on a park bench in Beacon Park.

"Ms. Akhtar. Thank you for getting here so quickly. I believe Mr Mitchell has asked you to sit in on our first interview. I expect you would like a little time with him before we begin the process," said DI Kendrick.

"Yes. Thirty minutes will suffice. Now, if you show me where you are holding him, the sooner we can 'begin the process' and then we can 'all' go home for the weekend," replied Sam in her best facetious voice.

"Well, we'll see...if you would like to follow me and I'll take you to see Mr Mitchell. Thirty minutes...no more...Ms. Akhtar."

Fifty-five minutes later Sameena and Daz were waiting for Krystyna to arrive. Sameena had purposely not kept to the thirty minute slot that she was told to keep to and now Krystyna was playing mind games by keeping them waiting.

In the fifty or so minutes Sam was in the room with Daz, she had first managed to diffuse Daz's anger and hatred of the police. This used up ten minutes before she got him to recount the events of the morning when he returned home from the counselling session with Pauline. Sameena went through the events with him three times, satisfying herself that there were no discrepancies or inconsistencies in the narrative. In the last ten minutes or so they had together, Sam had gone through her do's and don'ts of how a person should conduct themselves in a formal police interview. She stressed how important It was for Daz to keep calm and not fly off the handle. In the back of her mind Sameena could still remember her first encounter with Daz at Citizens Advice some weeks ago. He could not afford to be aggressive or lose his cool with the police today. The finger was pointing at him for murder and he was already skating on thin blue ice. Even after her pep talk, Sam was not convinced that Daz would be able to stay calm. She was the one that was more stressed about this interview and she feared for Daz's future.

When Sam, reluctantly, informed the police officer stationed outside the door that she and her client were ready for the interview, they were led down a corridor to Interview Room 2.

Daz and Sam sat in silence in the interview room for what seemed like a lifetime before DI Kendrick and a colleague walked in and sat down opposite them. Kendrick switched on the tape at the end of the table and for the benefit of the recording she gave the interview a context, explaining the date and time of the interview and the people present.

"Can I start, Mr Mitchell, by asking you what you were doing entering a flat that was taped off to the general public. An act, may I remind you, that is against the law," said Kendrick, staring into Daz's bloodshot eyes.

"I live on the same floor. I was going back home and was about to go into my flat when I saw the door to the empty flat had been forced open."

"So, why didn't you phone the police?"

"I did...later...after I went inside and saw the dead guy on the floor. Look, I've told you this already...a few hours ago...have you lot got bloody bad memories or are you all just thick or something?" replied Daz.

Sameena coughed. As Daz turned to face her, Sam gave him a piercing stare.

"I am trying to clarify the events of this morning, Mr Mitchell. You just need to answer my questions for now. You know how this works, Mr Mitchell. It's not as if it's your first time in a police station, is it?"

"No."

"Have you ever been in that flat before?"

"Yeah."

"When exactly?"

"I dunno exactly. A while back. I've told you before that there were some odd things going on. Some foreign guys lived there for a while. They worked at that car wash and then one day they just disappeared. I had a look around. Can't remember when. Before you lot came in and searched it."

"So you haven't been in the flat since the police searched it?"

"No...I told you …no...the door was locked and taped off. I couldn't get in even if I wanted to."

"And did you want to, Mr Mitchell?"

"No! How many more times have I got to tell you all this?"

Sameena coughed again and stared at Daz, again.

"So, just to clarify, today was the first time you have entered the flat since it was searched by the police. And you were not wearing this hat today." DI Kendrick slowly slid a sealed evidence bag across the table towards Daz. It contained the beanie hat that he was shown at the flats earlier.

"No, I wasn't."

"But this hat, or one very similar, belonging to you, has been lost recently...by you."

"Yeah...seems like it."

"And this is the hat that was discovered by us under the body, the dead body, that you found when you entered the flat without police permission, earlier today."

"Yeah."

"And you are saying that you didn't go near the body and you don't know the name of the dead person."

"I couldn't get a good look."

"Did you want to get a good look?"

"Well, no, not really . I just knew that he was dead. I've seen more than a few dead guys in my time in the army. As soon as I realised he was gone, I rang the police. You're not telling me I did the wrong thing. Should I have just left him and gone back to my flat, made myself a cup of tea and listened to the radio and pretended I didn't see what I saw?" asked an exasperated Daz.

"No. I'm not saying that. I am just trying to piece together your movements and actions earlier today and what part you played in the death of Mr… this person," said Kendrick, keeping her powder dry as to who the victim was.

"Well, you can check on my movements quite easily, if you want. You can ask me and ask the people I had contact with."

"We will. So tell me what you did and who you saw earlier today?"

"I got up. Had breakfast. Left the flat at about 9.00. The door to the next-door flat was secure and the tape was in place. I've been checking every day, wondering how long this flat is going to be out of commission. An empty flat going to waste. It's criminal. Then I sold some *Big Issues* in the middle of Lichfield. Then I went to a counselling session in Bore Street…"

"Who was that with?"

"Her name's Pauline...something."

Sameena spoke for the first time.

"It's Pauline Linden. 19 Bore Street. She has an office there, if you need to check."

"Thank you Ms Akhtar. We will. Carry on, Mr Mitchell."

"Then I sold the remainder of my batch of *Issues* and then I made my way back to the flat at about two o'clock. That's when I saw the flat door next to mine had been forced. So from about nine to two o'clock I was out of my flat. I spoke to quite a few people during that time. Pauline for one and loads of folks who bought *The Big Issue* from me. Ask them. They'll tell you I was out and about all morning."

"Don't you worry, Mr Mitchell, we will."

"So, can I go now?"

"Not yet, Mr Mitchell. We will need to confirm your alibis and we are waiting for the pathologist's report. You will be staying here tonight, at least, and then hopefully we'll get a clearer picture of the events by sometime tomorrow. I'll keep you both posted. My colleague will escort you back to your holding cell, Mr Mitchell."

Daz quietly swore, but remained relatively calm as he received this information from DI Kendrick. As he got up he nodded at Sameena and gave her a stoical smile. Sam, in turn, squeezed his arm and told Daz that she would be back in the morning.

Sam was left in the room with Krys. "Well?" asked Sam.

"Look, I can't say too much. I'll hurry the pathologist along and speak to this Pauline person. It's going to be tough to get any conclusive witness statements from people who may have seen Mitchell selling *The Big Issue.* But we'll try. I'll keep you informed. It may be that Mr Mitchell may need a criminal lawyer to represent him. I don't know yet."

"Have you considered that this may be a set-up? Perhaps the body and the hat were placed at the flat next to Daz's to incriminate him?"

"OK, Miss Marple. Leave the police work to us. But, yes, that is a line of enquiry I'll be pursuing. I'll show you out."

Sam left the police station. She worried about the next twenty-four hours. Would Daz's story hold up? She wanted Daz's account to be true. She wanted him to be innocent. But would the police be as confident about Daz's innocence? She was not so sure. She was feeling so stressed. She just wanted to go to her bedroom and sleep. She didn't want to talk to anyone else today or eat anything.

But Sam had a phone call to make. She phoned her mother and spun her a story that she had been out for something to eat with some of her colleagues and wouldn't need a meal tonight.

If Sam had had the energy to think, she would have realised that for the first time in weeks, she was not hungry at all.

CHAPTER FORTY-THREE

Willow – Saturday/Sunday

Willow's phone rang. Being deliberately against everything, she had left it as the very boring factory-setting *Marimba*. No ironic old-style phone bells or Ed-bloody-Sheeran. She looked at the screen. It was Sam.

"Hello?" It was ten o'clock, but her voice was still croaky from sleep and Sameena didn't recognise it.

"Willow?"

"Um, yap?" She tousled her hair and checked the time on her phone. It was still early. "Whassup?"

"It's Daz. He's been arrested – again."

Willow sat bolt upright in bed. "Oh, for fuck's sake!"

Sameena was shocked by the obscenity. Willow was only seventeen – when she had been seventeen she hadn't even known that word. Willow was talking again. She'd missed it. "What?"

"I said, 'What's he done this time'?"

"Oh." Sameena gathered her thoughts. "Probably nothing, but he's been arrested for murder."

"Murder!"

"Calm down. A dead body turned up in the flat next door to his, and the police found his hat underneath it – "

"Did he do it?" Willow burst in. "Who was it?"

"The police won't say, but they know. I think it's got something to do with the car wash – "

"But did he do it?" The trouble was, at the same time as she was absolutely sure he couldn't have done it, there was a little worm of doubt burrowing away at the back of her mind. She wanted Sam to say, "Of course not." But she didn't.

"I don't think so," she said slowly. "He found the body and reported it to the police. He's got a pretty solid alibi. But you know what his temper is like...and they found his hat underneath the body."

"What?" Willow was shouting down the phone again, and now she was out of bed and striding about her room because she had no idea what to do next.

"They're waiting on forensics, but I think they'll release him today under investigation because they don't have sufficient grounds to charge him. Daz says it's a fit-up. He thinks it's something to do with that friend of his who committed suicide."

"But who would do it? And why?"

"And that, Willow, is the fifty-four-thousand-dollar question."

They talked for a few minutes more, round in circles, going nowhere, both of them trying to convince themselves that the man they'd grown to like wasn't a murderer. The conversation petered out into long awkward pauses and in the end Sam said, "I'll phone you as soon as I hear anything."

The phone went dead and Willow threw it onto the bed. She screamed and stamped her feet in frustration and didn't hear the door open behind her.

"Everything alright, love?"

Willow turned round, fell into her mother's arms and sobbed her heart out.

Five minutes later they were all seated around the table in the kitchen. Her parents were just relieved she wasn't pregnant. She'd been moody and secretive enough these last few weeks.

"So you're saying this homeless guy – "

"Darren."

"Whatever his name is – you're saying he's been arrested for murder."

"Not arrested – he's being released under – "

" – under investigation. Yes, I know. Funny that, considering I'm a solicitor – "

"John." Her mother's tone was warning. "I know you've been trying to help him, Willow. But this seems like a time to stand back, until...well, until things are sorted out."

"No, it isn't," Willow protested. "Don't you see, he was right all along, about everything. He was right about that man Russell using the charity like a private bank, he was right about it being used for people trafficking. He was even right about the slavery at the car wash! You helped bring that down, Dad! Why shouldn't he have been right about his friend being murdered in the first place, and this all just trying to shut him up?"

John Cartwright sighed. "Even if that's true, I can't have you consorting with a murderer."

And Willow sighed as well, but louder. "Dad, I'm not consorting and he's not a murderer. He's a hero – he fought in Afghanistan, he's had PTSD, he's been homeless and a drug addict, but he's getting his life back together. He's going to counselling and NA, he's getting a job – he doesn't deserve this!"

Cartwright was going to say nobody got what they deserved, but he saw the tears welling up in his daughter's eyes and he just couldn't. "Alright," he said. "But what can we do to help? It sounds like he's already got a solicitor."

"He has – Sameena Akhtar. She works at Allcocks."

He nodded seriously. "Then he's in good hands."

"But it's not going to go away, is it? So long as he keeps going on about his friend being murdered, he's never going to be safe from them, is he?"

"Them?" repeated her father. "Who's them?"

"Oh, I don't know," cried Willow, exasperated, "but it's never going to go away, is it? He's been beaten up and hospitalised and now he's been framed. They're never going to stop."

Cartwright stopped being a father and slipped back into his solicitor voice. "Given everything you say, what do you think you could do that would a) help Mr. Mitchell, and, more importantly, b) keep you safe?" Or perhaps he was being more of a father now than he had for a long time.

"It's easy. Daz has even thought about it already. The day his friend died he said he was meeting someone and he walked off in the direction of the cathedral. That's where he ended up dead an hour later."

"Oh yes, I remember that," said Willow's mother. "It was on the news about a month ago. The poor fellow fell from the gallery or something, didn't he?"

"Daz doesn't think he did, and after all that's happened to him, I think he's right."

"But what proof do you have?" The solicitor again.

"It's not what proof I have, Dad – it's what proof you have," said Willow gleefully.

"I beg your pardon?"

"Look," said Willow, leaning forward and drawing imaginary streets with her finger on the marble top of the island they were all sitting around. "This is your office, right?" Her father nodded. "And this is Daz's patch, right outside."

"Don't I know it," he grunted. "All our clients have to go past him. We tried to get him moved on, but – "

"Really, Dad? You did that?"

"Willow?" Her mother laid a warning hand on her arm.

It could have gone either way. She could have screamed at him , stormed out and moved out and not gone to college and they could have lost touch with one another, and never seen their grandchildren so she only heard about her father's death months later - or she could take a deep breath and focus on what was important – saving Daz.

She tapped on the counter top. "That's where Daz met his friend," she said calmly. "What if, after he left him, he met someone or someone followed him and it was caught on camera? Like the CCTV at your offices, Dad?"

An hour later, and against his professional judgement, father and daughter were letting themselves into the offices of Cartwright, Thomson and Gray. The alarm buzzed in the hallway until John Cartwright punched in the code, and then everything became quiet except for the ringing in their ears. The building was nearly two hundred years old, the walls and doors were thick and the bustle of a Saturday on Dam Street was left far behind.

John went to the receptionist's office and opened the computer. He typed in a password, and moved the mouse around. He settled the cursor on an icon that looked like a magnifying glass and clicked the mouse. Black and white images of people seen through a fish-eye lens walking up and down Dam Street appeared on the screen.

"Alright," he said. "What date? If it's more than two months ago it may have been wiped."

"It was a Monday. Just a minute." Willow got her phone out and started scrolling. "Here it is." She showed him the date and he moved the slider at the bottom of the screen backwards. People moved jerkily into the past, the screen went dark and then things happened with an odd glow – people walking dogs with eyes like saucers, phones that lit up like light sabres – back and back through six packed weeks of Willow's life. She saw her Dad coming in to work every day at nine o'clock and leaving at five, all in reverse. And most days the still figure of Daz with his bundle of *Big Issues*. There were even occasional glimpses of her tearing past. And then …

"Here it is. What time?"

"Well, let's see...Daz gets here about eight-fifteen to get the morning rush hour, and then he stays until about ten-thirty. That's when I usually bring him a coffee – "

"You do what?" The father who would cut his right arm off to spare his daughter a single second of unhappiness warred with the parent who would do anything to protect her.

"It's just a coffee, Dad. A freebie from the café."

He washed his face with his hand. "Alright," he said patiently. "So let's say we're looking at a two-hour window from about eight-thirty."

Slowly he eased the slider back. "Look!" said Willow, pointing over his shoulder. "There's Daz!"

He was walking back to his spot. The time on the slider said ten-thirty and Willow remembered that was the day he had nearly hit her. Better not tell Dad about that.

"And look – that must be his friend! Ha! He just saluted him!"

John started easing time forward. The man walked away, Daz watched him go and then turned back to his customers, but Willow and John watched Wilde carry on down Dam Street, and a man stepped out from a doorway in front of him, his hand thrust out. Wilde hesitated and then took it. The man shook hands vigorously, Wilde reluctantly.

"Who's that?" shouted Willow in her father's ear. "What's going on?"

"Just wait," he said. "Watch."

Against his better judgement, he was getting caught up in the conspiracy theory of a homeless recovering ex-drug addict with PTSD and a teenage girl.

The two men on camera talked for a moment and then walked on side by side towards the cathedral.

"Run it again!"

He did and they watched it again, holding their breath, leaning closer to the screen. They ran it in slow motion and kept stopping it.

"Can you see who it is?"

"No, it's too far away – but I've an idea."

And at that moment, John Cartwright stepped across a line, and took his daughter to the tearoom on Cathedral Close and asked a friend – well, another member of the *Free and Fraternal Order of Accepted Masons* – who managed the place if they could look at his CCTV.

CHAPTER FORTY-FOUR

Krys, Willow - Early Monday

It was 7.13 am on Monday morning. For Krystyna Kendrick every day was now a work day and every time of day was a work time. The weekend had flown by without her having any 'me' or 'us' time with her husband. She had been at the police station for considerable chunks of time during Saturday and Sunday. She had over twenty active cases that needed her time and attention. When she wasn't staring into the eyes of suspects, witnesses or colleagues, she was staring at a screen researching all sorts of weird and worrying things or emailing fellow officers or writing reports. This was her life now.

Detective Inspector Kendrick's job had been really busy while Potter was around but now 'acting up' as a result of his temporary departure, her body was always on the move and her brain was perpetually falling asleep through tiredness. She couldn't remember the last time she sat in front of the TV and stayed awake for a whole hour of a thriller or crime show. She couldn't remember the last time she and her husband had a long meaningful conversation – or a quickie, come to think about it!

Krys sat at her desk in a comatose state staring at her monitor while her hands and mouse were doing all of the work. She half-remembered a time when she watched cop shows on the television and was amazed that the star of the detective series only seemed to have one case to deal with and would have another five or six minions to help out. That wasn't the real world of policing nowadays. Perhaps it never was, but the caseload of every real detective, even in a small city like Lichfield, was becoming unmanageable. Being a detective was no longer just about being a good cop with an inquisitive mind. Today, a detective needed additional superhero skills in time and sleep management, people management, diplomacy, politics, leadership, touch typing and juggling. Not that anyone thought they were superheroes anymore. The police seemed to be the villains of the piece.

Suddenly Krys was shaken from her slumbers by a sheepish police officer knocking on her door.

"Yeah, come in," called Krys through the half-glass door.

"Sorry to disturb you, ma'am" said the female officer, "but there's someone downstairs who said that he urgently needs to speak to you. He said it was concerning one of your ongoing cases, the suicide at the cathedral."

"Thanks, but it's probably just someone wanting to waste our time giving us a useless piece of information about the date when the cathedral was built or how many bibles have been nicked during the last year. Just take his contact details and a brief statement and then send him on his way."

"Ma'am, he said you might fob him off, but he was adamant that you would need to hear what he has to say and see what's on the memory stick that he and his daughter have brought with them."

"Well just take the thumb drive off him or make a copy and I'll have a look at it later."

"Ma'am. Mr Cartwright was insistent. So was his daughter. And she said...that you owe it to...Daz...to speak to them now."

"Was the man's daughter a teenager with weird hair?"

"Yes, ma'am."

Krys swore under her breath.

"OK. Bring them up here. I'll see them. And another thing...don't call me Ma'am or Guv...DI Kendrick will do...it's not as if we are acting in an old TV cop show." She said that with a faint smile on her lips.

A couple of minutes later John Cartwright and his daughter were shown into Krys Kendrick's office.

"Mr Cartwright...Willow...come and sit down. What can I do for you?" said Krys politely.

John and Willow Cartwright sat down next to each other across the desk from Krys.

"Well, first of all, can I say that I'm not impressed that you've allowed my daughter to get involved in a police investigation regarding the recent death at the cathedral. She's a minor and vulnerable," stated Cartwright assertively.

Willow bristled and whispered, "Dad" into his ear.

"Mr Cartwright," Kendrick interjected, "your daughter has not been directly involved in any cases run by the Lichfield police force. From what I can gather, Willow befriended a *Big Issue* seller, Darren Mitchell, before the incident at the cathedral took place. She has been helping and supporting Mr Mitchell over the last few weeks. You may or may not know that Mr Mitchell has some...issues...and your daughter seems to be the only person that can keep him relatively on the straight and narrow. I can assure you that these conversations and meetings between the two of them were independent from our investigation and have not been encouraged by me or my team."

"So are you saying that this is the first time that you have been in the company of my daughter?" asked Cartwright, sounding every bit a prosecuting lawyer.

"No. I'm not saying that. I've met Willow on several occasions, but these meetings have been low-key, social gatherings not formal conversations about police business."

"That's right, Dad. If anything, Krys has been the one to tell me if I was over-stepping the mark," said Willow, sounding every bit a defensive teenager.

"Krys?" asked Cartwright.

"Yes, Krys, that's her name. She's been looking out for me and over the last few weeks I've...come to respect her," said Willow blushing slightly.

"Well, anyway, we haven't come here specifically about my daughter's relationship with you. I was dragged into this over the weekend when I discovered that my daughter had been informed by a local solicitor that this Darren Mitchell fellow had been arrested on a murder charge and was in police custody. She was understandably very upset. I'll be having words with this solicitor later this morning. But for now I want a few answers as to why Willow, a minor in the eyes of the law, became involved and is receiving calls from a solicitor into an ongoing police investigation."

"Mr Cartwright, can I say again, that your daughter is not involved with the police investigation. I cannot speak on behalf of the solicitor, but I suspect she...or he...rang Willow out of courtesy and as a friend, rather than as a client."

"That's right, Dad. Sam was just letting me know what was happening to Daz. She knows I've been worried about him recently. She's just someone that I've got to know over the last few weeks. Through Daz."

"Be that as it may, DI Kendrick, I would appreciate it if the Lichfield police force respect my wishes to not involve my daughter in this investigation from now on. Do you have children, DI Kedrick?"

"No...I don't," replied Krys and supressed her conflicting emotions immediately.

"Well, my wife and I were only able to have Willow and she means the world to us. We love her and I don't want her to be put in any danger, do you understand?"

Willow cringed, blushed and touched her father's arm as Krys nodded.

"However, I, or should I say, we, have come here primarily on another matter. We want to supply you with some information that may or may not help your enquiry. It may help Mr Mitchell's assertion that the gentleman who fell to his death at the cathedral was murdered rather than committed suicide. And, also, it may or may not, give you some food for thought regarding the murder charge that Mr Mitchell is now facing," said Cartwright, producing a memory stick from his suit pocket.

"Before I consider this evidence, Mr Cartwright, and for the benefit of Willow, because I know she cares about Mr Mitchell, I can tell you that Darren Mitchell was released on Saturday evening."

"Yes!" Willow exclaimed and punched the air in front of her.

"Willow, just because he's been released doesn't necessarily mean that he's innocent of the murder of the man in the flat next door to his. He is still under investigation and we are waiting on some scientific reports to come back to us before we can move forward. Daz is not in the clear yet. Do you understand?"

"Yeah, OK, I get it," acknowledged Willow, "but you really need to look at this video footage that we uncovered. It's best if my dad explains it to you."

John Cartwright took five minutes detailing the amateur investigation that he and his daughter had undertaken over the weekend. He explained that on the memory stick were two videos from external cameras facing the street on the day of the death at the cathedral. The first footage was from his office where he worked and the second was from the tearoom on Cathedral Close.

Then Krystyna plugged the memory stick into her laptop. She played the recordings three times each without saying a word. Each time her eyes grew a little wider as she focused on the screen.

When Krys finally looked up from the screen she saw a satisfied smile on John and Willow Cartwright's faces.

DI Kendrick couldn't help herself and smiled back at them.

CHAPTER FORTY-FIVE

Daz, Sam – Monday

It was time for Sameena to have a serious word with Daz. Her number one job as his solicitor was to get him access to his daughter. How could she do that if he kept getting arrested? She wasn't a criminal lawyer. It wasn't something you could do over the phone, so she grabbed her handbag, made an excuse about "having to pop out" without stopping and jumped in her *Focus*.

She was used to The Dingles now. She parked her car where she could see it from Daz's window, took her handbag with her and locked everything else in the boot. She could hear him sneering at her. "Really? Who d'you think is going to steal that?" Bash would have said the same thing. Him and his BMW. She loved her little car. Or she told herself that because she couldn't afford a new one.

She clutched the handbag close to her chest as she scuffed up the gritty concrete steps and along the passageway to his door. The stairwell smelled of industrial-strength disinfectant and she expected a hoodie-wearing youth to leap out from somewhere, knock her to the floor and snatch her handbag. Probably call her "a Paki bitch!" too. It was a relief to get to Daz's door. She knocked, looking round.

A chain rattled behind the door and it opened a crack. She stepped forward, expecting it to swing wide, but it didn't move and she almost stumbled back. "Daz?" she said to the one eye that regarded her coldly through the slit.

"What do you want?"

"Can I come in?"

The door closed and she thought he was shutting it in her face, and then it opened just enough to let her in. She had to squeeze past him and she avoided the sullen look he gave her. She went into the living room and was shocked by what she saw.

The thin curtains were drawn and the dingy bare bulb hanging from the ceiling barely lit the blizzard of papers over the table, chairs and the floor. Mugs, empty or half-full with cold black coffee, a bowl with a few soggy cornflakes floating in some grey-looking milk, a plate with a half-eaten sandwich – limp, watery ham poking out between two slices of papery white bread – and a pizza carton with a couple of triangles of congealing meat feast.

The room smelled of unwashed clothes and food that was beginning to turn rotten.

Under the dim light Daz didn't look much better. He was unshaven and bleary-eyed, his hair sticking up and his clothes rumpled. She realised that he was smelling too. Was he back on drugs? She'd advised a few recovering drug addicts at the Citizens' Advice Bureau and she'd seen a few of them relapse. It looked a lot like this.

"Daz!" she said, shaken. "What's going on?"

"I'm never going to win, am I?" he said, collapsing onto the sofa. "Every time it looks like I'm going to get my life back together, someone smashes it to bits all over again."

She sat down next to him and resisted the urge to take his hand. Now wasn't the time to tell him to "straighten up and fly right" as her Dad used to say, so she changed the subject.

"What is all this?" she said, gesturing at the chaos of papers on the coffee table, the sofa and the floor.

"Research," he grunted.

She looked at the papers. There were some headed with the *Home and Heart* logo, and some print-offs of old newspapers and copies of the accounts she had given to Bash.

"Research into what?" She didn't want to sit down, so she stood in the middle of the room.

He shrugged. "Just stuff." He fixed her with a stare that went right through her. "What do you want?" It was the look of a man who had stared at another human being and then snuffed their life out. It scared her, but she had to say what she had to say.

"Look, Daz – I don't want to say this, but..."

"Just say it. You don't want to be my solicitor anymore."

She dumped her handbag on the table and some more of the papers slid onto the floor as she sat down beside him. "No, it's not that at all," she said hurriedly. "Of course, I want to help you. I'm not just your solicitor. I think we're friends, aren't we?"

"But?"

He wasn't making this easy. "But you've got to stop getting arrested, if we're going to get you access to your daughter."

"It's not my fault. I was just in the wrong place at the wrong time."

"You make a bit of a habit of it, don't you?"

"You mean like when I was beaten up at the carwash?"

There was an awkward silence, that stretched out uncomfortably and then it snapped as they both broke out laughing, Daz's a chesty wheeze and Sameena's a snort as she tried to stifle it. She wasn't sure if they were both laughing at the same thing, but it broke the tension anyway.

"So anyway," she said when the laugh had subsided to chuckles and sighs. "If we can keep you out of trouble for the next few weeks, you keep going to counselling and you get this job, then we might be able to overturn the restraining order against you and you might be able to see your daughter again."

Daz almost bounced up and down. "Great!"

"Slow down – I said might. And then we need to write a letter setting out your contact proposals. If it doesn't end amicably, we might have to go to court. Do you want that?"

"I can pay if that's what you mean." The bouncing stopped and the glower returned. Sameena knew he had PTSD, but the way he swung from high to low – could he be bi-polar?

"That's not what I meant at all," she said, more calmly than she felt, now that she thought she was in a room with someone who was mentally ill. "I mean it's not pleasant – is that how you want to re-establish relationships with your wife and daughter?"

"I just want to see Amy again...and maybe patch things up with Cheryl – show her I've changed."

"Then the way to go after I've established contact might be mediation. Could you do that?"

"I'll do whatever it takes." He sounded genuine and Sameena breathed a sigh of relief.

"OK then, I can make a start on that and you – you stay out of trouble. Perhaps you should just focus on your research." She moved her handbag and turned over some of the papers. It was an old newspaper article. "What's this? 'Emergency services,' she read, "'were called to Stowe Pool on early Sunday morning after – "' She read on silently, her lips moving. "Who's Bruce Spencer?"

Daz snatched the paper from her hand. "Nobody," he said. "Just someone Eugene told me about."

She should have known better, but she picked up another sheet covered with letters and dots and dashes. "Well, what about this?" Maybe she just didn't want to leave him on his own.

"Oh, that's just something that Willow got me mixed up in."

Sameena smiled. "She can do that, can't she? What is it?"

"She got me visiting some batty old woman who claims she invented the bar code. Says she's really rich – could be true. She's staying at some swanky, expensive care home – "

"Not Mary?"

"Dunno. Claims to have travelled all over the world. Says she was a code breaker in the war. Keeps trying to teach me this – wodjacallit...Morse Code stuff."

"That's her, alright, and she really is rich. Believe me, I should know, I'm her solicitor. What a small world. Anyway – "

She stood up, picked up her handbag and knocked over the framed photograph that was sitting in the blizzard of papers. "Sorry." She picked it up and looked at it. "Who's this?"

"That's a photo of my friend Shaun, the one who helped me when I was homeless and got me this flat."

"The one who – "

"Yeah." Sameena had been going to say "killed himself" and Daz was thinking "was killed" and the words hung between them, so Daz filled the space with a lot of chatter. "It's him and his mates from basic training back in the eighties – just up the road at Whittington."

"And who are the others?"

Daz pointed them out. "That's Shaun, that one's Rory Winters, that one died in Iraq, and that one's Major Ballinger. He's back at the barracks in charge of initial training."

"They don't look very happy. What are they doing?"

"Oh, they're just showing off their tattoos – like this one." He pushed his sleeve up, showed her his tattoo of a knot and three feathers. "It's the coat of arms of the Staffies." She looked at him blankly. "The Staffordshire Regiment. I was in it. So was Shaun."

"And what's that underneath their tattoos?"

"I dunno. Probably did it themselves with a biro and a pin and made a mess of it. Mine was done by a professional." He stared at it for a moment and then quickly rolled his sleeve down again. Too many memories.

"No, there's something different about theirs." She squinted, then got her mobile out and used the camera like a magnifying glass. She studied the photo closely. "It looks like some of Mary's Morse Code."

"What?" Daz sat bolt upright on the sofa. "Let me see."

She passed him the phone and the photo and he grabbed them out of her hand. He peered hard at it, and then rummaged around on the table through the papers. More of them showered on to the floor. "Where is it?"

Sameena picked one up off the floor and thrust it at him. "Looking for this?"

He snatched it from her, and then started looking between the two. He was muttering under his breath, "Da di di di. B. Di da di. N or R." Suddenly he started scrabbling around and patting his pockets. "Pen," he said to her.

"What?"

"Pen. Fucking pen. Quick!"

She dug around in her handbag and found an old ballpoint. He snatched that too and Sameena started getting worried about his mental state again. He started writing laboriously with his tongue between his teeth. There were crossings out and curses and then he sat back and threw the pen down. "Fuck," he breathed.

Sam leaned across. "What?" she asked. She could see he had spelled out B-R-I-A-N in capitals. "What does it mean?"

"It means I know who killed Shaun Wilde," he said grimly.

"What?" Honestly? Couldn't she say anything else? She was supposed to be a solicitor.

Daz sprang to his feet and started stuffing things – the picture, the Morse Code sheet, the copy of the old newspaper, and the sheet he had written on – into his backpack, all the papers getting scrunched up. "I've got to go."

"Wait!" At last, a new word! She laid a hand on his arm because she couldn't think of anything else to say. Things were moving too fast.

He shook her off and squared up to her. "I've got to go," he gritted out into her face.

"Where are you going? Daz – stop! You can't afford to get into trouble again now. Think about your daughter." Now she couldn't stop talking. All the words just came tumbling out, and it was too late.

"Sameena," he said slowly, "get out of my fucking way."

Clutching her bag to her chest, she stood to one side and he slammed out, leaving the door wide open.

"Shit. Shitshitshitshitshit!" She grabbed her phone from the table. Her hands were shaking so much she couldn't unlock it. "Fuckfuckfuckfuckfuck." At last, she managed to enter her code and hit speed dial and held it to her ear. It rang and rang. "Come on, come on, come on – " She was almost in tears and then Willow's cheery voice said, "Hello? Sam?"

"Willow. We've got a problem."

CHAPTER FORTY-SIX

Krys – Monday

There was yet another knock on Krys' office door. The same police officer who interrupted DI Kendrick much earlier on in the day, when the Cartwrights wanted to see Krys, sheepishly entered the room.

"Ma...DI Kendrick...sorry to disturb you, but there is a Major Stuart Ballinger downstairs. He told the front desk that you wanted to see him," announced the officer.

"Yes, I do. Thank you. Can you bring him up for me?"

"Of course."

Two minutes later the officer knocked on Krys' door again and held it open for Ballinger to stride in. He was an imposing figure, standing almost to attention but looking down at Krystyna Kendrick sitting behind her desk trying to make sense of the many documents in front of her.

"Major Ballinger, please take a seat and thank you for coming in at short notice."

"Detective Inspector Kendrick, isn't it?"

"Yes, that's correct."

"Although I am more than willing to assist another person who is serving Queen and country, I am not sure why you have invited me here. I can spare you a little time. But, as you can imagine, I am a very busy man," the Major replied, sitting opposite the Acting Detective Inspector.

"I appreciate you responding to the request and I hope this won't take up much of your time...Major," replied Krys trying to sound sincere. "Would you like a drink? Tea, coffee, water?"

"No, thank you. Can we just get on with this, for goodness sake."

"OK then," said Krys sitting up in her chair, placing a brown folder in front of her on the now tidy desk surface and staring straight into Ballinger's eyes.

In a matter of moments DI Kendrick had transformed herself from Detective Lieutenant Columbo to Detective Chief Inspector Jane Tennison.

"Shaun Wilde. How long have you known him?"

"Sorry, who?"

"Shaun Wilde. The name not ringing any bells, Major Ballinger?"

"Erm, yes, I'm just trying to re-collect..."

"Perhaps, you remember his name from the news recently. He died a few weeks back...in the cathedral.

"Yes, come to think about it, I remember the news coverage. Tragic."

"Very. Any other connection with Mr Wilde?"

"How do you mean?"

"It's a simple question, Major Ballinger. I would have thought a man in your line of work would prefer to deal in absolutes. I know I would. So, again, Major, did you have any other connection with Shaun Wilde?" said DI Kendrick, ramping up her questioning.

"Yes. I knew Shaun Wilde. But a long time ago. We served in Iraq together. We served in the same regiment for a while. He left the army and we lost touch. I believe he then became involved in charity work."

"If you lost touch, how were you aware of Wilde's involvement in a charity after he left the army?" Kendrick asked.

"The men at the barracks in their spare time often talk about past and present soldiers. They recount stories about their fellow soldiers. You have to appreciate, Detective Inspector, that the army is a family. We have each other's backs in combat and away from battle we de-stress by sharing personal stories about ourselves and others. I dare say someone knew about Shaun Wilde's life once he was out of the army and that info got passed up the line to me. It's nothing new for me to have some intel on my past colleagues."

"So, that is all you know about Shaun Wilde. Those snippets of information from talk at the barracks in Whittington?"

"Yes. I'm sorry but that is all I can tell you. Now if that is all, Detective Inspector..."

"Do you mean that that is all I can tell you or that that is all I'm willing to tell you?"

"I beg your pardon, DI Kendrick?"

"You see, Major, we know there is more than you have just told me. We have irrefutable evidence from several sources that you were in contact with Shaun Wilde recently in Lichfield. Major Ballinger, I can stop this interview now, if you like, while you arrange for a lawyer to represent you or you can just tell me informally about why you were speaking to Mr Wilde after all of this time. It's your choice. But the sooner you fill in the gaps in your story, the better for all of us."

Ballinger wriggled slightly on his chair and was silent for a few seconds before clearing his throat.

"May I have some water, Detective Inspector?"

"Of course."

Krystyna swivelled her chair to her mini-fridge and took out a small plastic bottle of chilled water and slid it across the desk towards the Major. He stared at the bottle and then took a sip. He couldn't remember the last time he had taken a drink from something that wasn't glass.

"I will not waste any more of my time or yours, Detective. I've had contact with Shaun Wilde. As you know, I have a little involvement with the *Home and Heart* charity. The charity tries to help out with some ex-soldiers who have fallen on hard times since leaving the armed forces..."

Ballinger paused realising what he had just said. "I apologise about that unfortunate use of words. The Major continued. "Shaun Wilde was an advocate for those ex-servicemen and he strenuously helped those men find homes, even if they were temporary dwellings. He also tried to organise paid work for them so that they could re-build their lives. I got involved in a supportive, but overseeing capacity, to help out *Home and Heart.* I wasn't particularly hands-on because of my full-time role at Whittington Barracks."

"So you met with Mr Wilde regularly or rarely over the last few years?" asked Krystyna.

"I would say that we had more contact over the last couple of years, particularly the last six months or so."

"Why was that?"

"There was a difference of opinion on...how can I put it...the aims and methodology of the charity. Wilde had a different view on the people that we should help. Some of the rest of the organisers of the charity felt that we should be broader in our reach."

"What do you mean?"

"We...the charity decided that we should help some civilians from war-torn countries to make a new life for themselves in this country. Mr Wilde did not agree. He just wanted to help our own *heroes*. On several occasions we had words about this."

"So, what was the outcome of these exchanges?"

"I'm not entirely sure because another member from the charity said he would liaise with Wilde and talk some sense and reason into him."

"And who might that be, Major Ballinger?"

"His name is Rory Winters."

Krystyna Kendrick looked up from the notes she was scribbling in her pad and looked at the Major. "Sorry, I didn't catch the name of your colleague. Can you repeat that name?"

"Yes, Mr Rory Winters."

Krystyna wrote the name in upper-case letters in her note pad and underlined the name.

"And this Rory Winters was tasked by you to persuade Mr Wilde to change his mind about the work that the charity was doing?"

"Well not entirely, the charity just wanted to become a little more inclusive, that's all."

"And what was Mr Wilde's objections to this inclusivity?"

"Wilde thought that the charity might be somehow breaking the law, but I was led to believe by Mr Winters that these civilians from other countries had all the proper documentation and were approved asylum seekers."

"Would you have the records of these *approved asylum seekers*?"

"No, I'm afraid not. You would have to ask Mr Winters about that. He was the one primarily that dealt with the personnel side of 'housing' people, particularly now that Mr Wilde is no longer with us..."

A knock on Krystyna's door made her glare at the window. It was that young policewoman...again. DI Kendrick gestured to the police officer to wait outside her door for one minute. At least, she hoped that would be the message that she was trying to convey to her young colleague.

Krystyna apologised to the Major for the interruption and walked to the door and opened it slightly. "Yes!" she snapped.

"Sorry, boss...I mean Detective Inspector. I was told to come to your office straight away and give you some information."

"Well...what is it?"

"There is a situation at the Staffordshire Barracks..." said the police officer.

The Major's head swivelled round. "What is it? What situation?" He then stood up and straightened his uniform. "What's going on?"

The police officer waited for a nod from Krystyna before explaining the situation.

"We have had a report that a man has found his way onto the barracks campus and then become aggressive. He is being held but apparently he insists on speaking to the Major."

"Would you like a couple of my officers to see to this?" Krystyna offered.

"No, it's fine. It's probably just the usual lefty pacifist protester that has nothing better to do with his time. I'll make a phone call back to base and find out more details and then, with your permission, I'll go and sort it out. Is that OK with you, DI Kendrick?"

"Yes. I'll be in touch later, Major Ballinger."

"Fine. You know where to find me," said Ballinger.

CHAPTER FORTY-SEVEN

Sam, Willow – Monday

Willow got an Uber. Her parents wouldn't have approved – "They don't drive safely, they drive too fast, they're always on their phones. They might be drunk or on drugs. What if they attack you?" – so she didn't tell them. She caught it round the corner where her nosey neighbours wouldn't report back.

She was at Daz's flat in ten minutes and she'd been on the phone the whole way, but it was still a shock when Sameena let her in.

"Jesus!" she said. "What a mess!"

"I think he took getting arrested again really hard. I thought he was on drugs when I came, but I think he's depressed."

"Do you know where he went?" Suddenly things were really urgent. Is this what happened to old soldiers when they couldn't cope anymore? "He's not going to kill himself, is he – like Shaun?"

"I don't think so. When he dashed out, he said he knew who had killed Shaun."

"Oh my God! So he's going to confront a murderer!"

"Or someone he thinks is a murderer – either way, this isn't going to end well."

"Right," said Willow, taking charge. She pulled back the curtains and let the daylight in. "What did he say before he left?"

"Well..." Sameena ran through everything that had happened up to the moment when he dashed out of the door.

"OK," said Willow when she had finished. "What have we got?" she started ticking the points off on her fingers. "It's something to do with Morse code, that picture and someone called Brian who Eugene knows about."

"Who's Eugene?"

"That's his sponsor in NA."

"Then that's who we need to see. Daz lost it completely after he spelled that name out. It must mean something."

"But how do we find him?" asked Willow.

"I guess we have to go to a meeting."

They both got their phones out and started scrolling. It didn't take long to find, and Willow thought briefly of Daz and his Nokia phone and his trips to the library, laboriously printing out his research.

"It's in the Methodist Chapel..."

"...it's on Wade Street..."

"...and there's a meeting today at twelve..."

"...it's twelve-forty already..."

"Come on!"

They grabbed up as much of Daz's research as they could cram into Willow's backpack and dashed out in Daz's footsteps, banging the door behind them. And on the landing they bumped into his next-door neighbour, the old man, struggling up the stairs with two heavy bags of groceries. Potatoes, bread, frozen vegetables and cheap meat went flying everywhere. The old man sat down heavily on his backside. Willow and Sameena pounced on the food scattered all over the floor and started stuffing it back into the limp carriers. Willow helped him to his feet and Sameena handed him his bags.

"We're really sorry," she said.

He gave her a hard stare, snatched the bags from her hand and muttered, "Paki bitch!" as he pushed past her.

Willow gasped. "Hey!" she shouted after him, but Sameena put a hand on her arm.

"It doesn't matter," she said.

"But he shouldn't – "

"But they do. I'm used to it – I just thought it was going to be a boy in a hoodie instead of an old man." She pulled Willow down the stairs. "Come on. We've got to save Daz!"

"From himself," added Willow.

"Again."

They piled panting into the car and Willow shouted directions as Sameena for the first time in her life broke the speed limit and flung them around in the car racing round corners in a squeal of tyres. Horns blared and fists were shaken at her through her rearview mirror. She parked on double yellow lines in Wade Street.

People were beginning to trail out of the arched double doors. They didn't look like drug addicts, thought Sameena – and then she thought, what does a drug addict look like? Just like everyone else.

They hurried inside to find a lone black man putting the chairs back in rows. He turned round as they skidded to a halt, bumping into one another.

"Can I help you?"

"Are you Eugene?" asked Willow.

"Ye-es."

"We're friends of Darren's."

He smiled. "Ah, you must be Willow. And you are?"

"Sameena Akhtar. I'm his solicitor."

"Does he need one?"

"He might. We're afraid he's going to do something foolish and we're trying to stop him."

"Something foolish?"

"He's going to confront a killer...or at least, someone he thinks is a killer."

Eugene dragged three chairs into a triangle and gestured for them to sit down. Sameena could see why Daz kept coming back to this man. He was the calm in the eye of the storm. They explained as best they could, interrupting each other, correcting each other while Eugene nodded, his eyes flicking between the two of them.

When they had finished, he sat still and silent. Willow wanted to get up and shake up. She bounced her knees nervously up and down.

"Brian," said Eugene at last. "I've no idea who that is. Daz said I'd mentioned him?"

"Right before he said he knew who had killed Shaun Wilde."

The last time I saw him we talked about how he felt he didn't deserve to be happy. I told him he needed to stop feeling guilty or he'd end up like the homeless guy who drowned in Stowe Pool."

"I've never heard of that," said Willow, but Sameena was already scrolling on her phone.

"It happened ages ago – "

"'Emergency services were called to Stowe Pool on early Sunday morning after reports that a body had been seen floating,'" read Sameena. "'They later confirmed a body had been recovered and was pronounced dead at the scene. He was later identified as Brian Spencer, a homeless man who was well-known locally and was frequently to be seen on Bore Street.'"

"That's got to be him!" Willow burst out. "But why does it mean Daz knows who killed Shaun?"

"Wait. I said the tattoos looked like Morse Code and he snatched the picture off me, and started writing things down. He was going 'dadeedadeeda.' I thought he'd gone mad."

"That's it then," cried Willow. "It's the picture."

She brought it up on her phone and they all leaned in to look at it. Sameena pointed. "He said that one was Shaun, this one was killed in Iraq and that's Rory. And he said this one is called Major Ballinger and he's something at the Whittington Barracks."

Willow zoomed in on the tattoos. "They look like Daz's," she said, "but those lines underneath – we need a pen! Quick!"

Not again, thought Sameena, digging another old ballpoint out of her handbag.

"Now get Morse Code up on your phone," Willow ordered. Sameena found a Wikipedia page and Willow started writing on her hand, her tongue stuck out of the corner of her mouth, her head swinging between her phone and Sameena's. Then she gasped and sat back. "Look!" she said, holding her hand up for both of them to see. "It says BRIAN!"

"But what does it mean?" asked Eugene.

"I don't know, but why would four squaddies at Whittington Barracks in the nineteen eighties have the name of a dead homeless man tattooed on their arms? And what does Daz think it means?"

"Well, two of the men in that picture are dead, so whatever it means, it's dangerous," said Sameena. "I think we should take this to Krys."

"Really?" said Willow. "Well, I can't do it. I've just left Krys and she as good as told me to keep my nose out of police business."

"And I saw her on Friday and she told me exactly the same thing."

There was a silence while they stared at each other. Eugene broke it.

"Perhaps I can," he said.

It took some working out. "We can say he came to you distressed..."

"...and he told you he knew who'd killed Shaun..."

"...and then he told me it was something to do with a homeless man called Brian Spencer who drowned in Stowe Pool nearly twenty years ago..."

"...and he showed you a picture on his phone of four soldiers..."

"...and he told you their tattoos spelled out Brian in Morse Code."

They sat back. "Well," said Sameena. "That seems to work. Are you sure you want to do it, Eugene?"

"I've been Darren's sponsor for nearly two years now. He comes to meetings, calls me when he's having trouble with his demons – I'm not about to give up on him now," said Eugene, standing up. It was a sign that the meeting had ended and Willow and Sameena stood up too.

"What if the police don't believe you?" asked Willow.

"I'm a black recovering drug addict living in Lichfield, "said Eugene. "I think I can handle the police."

CHAPTER FORTY-EIGHT

Krys, Eugene – Monday

Acting Detective Inspector Krystyna Kendrick didn't feel like acting anymore. She could hardly keep her eyes open, let alone speak the correct lines to the audience she was performing to. It was a mad, mad, mad world she was working in. One minute it was quizzing suspects, the next minute it was managing her team, the next she was reporting to her superiors and then there were always complaints by the general public to deal with. Unfortunately, very few plaudits and compliments were ever handed out.

Krystyna remembered a few months ago watching half an hour or so of the Oscars ceremony in America. The audience spent the whole time mesmerised by these self-important movie stars giving their 'thank you' speeches and explaining to the adoring fans just how demanding the life of an actor is and how difficult the role was to play. They somehow forget to tell the audience that they were being paid a million dollars a second to perform in front of the cameras and that the screenwriter and director were the ones telling the actors what and how to say their lines.

For Krystyna there was no script – it was a case of making it up as she went along, while trying to keep professional, sane and conscious. Was the extra responsibility and salary worth it? She didn't know for certain yet, but one thing she was sure about was that she couldn't keep this pace up for much longer. Perhaps she was just trying too hard to impress the powers that be, her team and herself.

She needed a break – not a breakdown, just a break for a few minutes where she could get out of her office. She had been cooped up for too long in her own prison cell dealing with new information on a few old cases and liaising with and delegating to others in the building. She wanted just a short distraction away from her desk.

Krystyna headed for the small kitchen-cum-canteen to stretch her legs and escape from her responsibilities. The room was empty. She grabbed a mug and was just about to make herself a coffee when a voice took her by surprise.

"Would you like me to make that for you...DI Kendrick?"

Krystyna turned around to find the young police officer right behind her.

"Oh hello again, no, it's fine, thank you. I'm perfectly capable of making...I'm sorry...I don't know your name..."

"It's PC Willets."

"No...what's your first name?"

"It's Jen...short for Jennifer."

"Well, Jen, let me make you a drink. What would you like?"

"Just a white coffee please, DI Kendrick. Thank you so much."

"No problem. And I think, as it's just the two of us in here, you can call me Krys...short for Krystyna."

"Thank you, but I'm going to find it difficult to call a superior officer by her first name."

"Who told you I was superior?" asked Krys with a smile on her face.

"No...I mean...a higher ranking person."

"Jen, let me tell you something. I maybe older than you and with a few more years of experience in the force than you but that doesn't make me superior. You may have to take orders from me, but you are every bit as important in this building as I am. And in our civvies we are just Jen and Krys. Now take a seat and I'll bring you over a coffee and you can tell me about what made you want to be a police officer."

Twenty minutes later, and feeling refreshed and human again, Krystyna returned to her electronic paperwork. Just when she was making a dent in today's to-do list, she received a call from the reception desk. Her eyes rolled as she grudgingly replied with a sigh "Can you escort him up to my office, please."

A minute later her door opened and a tall, well-built black man filled the space left by the door.

"Mr Lascelles? You asked to see me urgently. Please take a seat. How can I help you?"

"It's Eugene. I'm not one for formality. Please call me by my first name."

"OK...Eugene. I can spare you a few minutes. What is this about? And why do you need to specifically talk to me and not one of my colleagues?"

"Well, I gather you are leading on the Shaun Wilde case. And I have some information that might be pertinent to your investigation."

"And who told you that I was in charge of that case Mr...Eugene?"

"A guy who I work with."

"And who might that be, Eugene?"

"Darren Mitchell."

At the mention of Daz's name Krys found it difficult to stop her eyes rolling and her mouth tutting.

"Are you sure you work with Mr Mitchell? I thought he worked on his own selling *The Big Issue*?"

"Yes, he does, but I work with him in a different capacity. I'm his sponsor at Narcotics Anonymous in Lichfield. I shouldn't really have told you that, but I need you to believe me that what I have to say is important. It could stop another fatality in Lichfield."

"OK, Eugene. You have my attention. What have you got to tell me that's so important?" asked Krystyna, opening her notepad and taking the top off her pen.

"I've known Darren for two years. He's found life extremely difficult since leaving the army. He's estranged from his wife and daughter as a result of his addiction and his short temper. But in the time I've worked with him I've found him to be a nice guy inside. Admittedly, he has a rough exterior and he comes across badly at times..."

"Yes, yes, I know Darren Mitchell, only too well, I'm afraid. If you've just come here today to give me a character reference on behalf of Mr Mitchell, that's very kind of you and I'm sure he'll appreciate it. But I'm very busy...so if that is all...Mr Lascelles?"

"Eugene. And that's not why I came. If you could just spare another minute or so of your precious time, then I'll leave you to get on with your desk job!"

"Two minutes...Eugene...OK?" said Krystyna with a touch of anger in her voice.

"That's all I need," he replied and began to spin the yarn that he created alongside Willow and Sameena. "I stopped by Darren's flat earlier today to see how he was doing. When I got there he was looking through some documents and photos. He was quite agitated. He was rambling on about Shaun Wilde's killer and how he was going to get revenge for Shaun. He showed me a photograph of Shaun with some of his old army buddies. He said this was all the proof he needed. He went on to mention the tattoos on their arms. Each of them had the same markings which was in Morse Code. The code spelt out a name – Brian. I tried to get him to calm down, but while I was making him a coffee he stormed out of his flat."

"That seems to be in character for Mr Mitchell."

"Yes, as I said, Darren has a short fuse, but Detective Inspector, I haven't seen him like this before. I think he's going to do someone harm...or harm himself."

"Have you any idea where he could have gone after he left the flat?"

"No. I stayed in his flat for half an hour or so to see if he was coming back after cooling off, but he didn't. So I looked around the flat to see if there were any clues to where he would have gone. While I was looking I found two printouts that I thought you might find useful."

Eugene gave the two sheets of paper to Krystyna that Sameena had given him after printing them off in her office. One was a copy of the photograph of the four army buddies with their tattooed arms on show and the other one was a copy of the front page from The Lichfield News from twenty years ago reporting the tragic drowning of a homeless man called Brian Spencer in Stowe Pool. Eugene could feel his cheeks burning as he told this fictional account of what happened at Darren's flat, but Krystyna was too engrossed in the documents to notice.

"And you think these tattoos on their arms spell out the name Brian, the name of this drowned man?"

"I'm not an expert in Morse Code, but it would be worth getting your guys to check it out. Also, you might want to identify the guys in the photograph. It may have triggered Darren's outburst when he talked about revenge and then stormed out of his flat. But, Detective Inspector, it's not my job to tell you how to do your job. I'll leave it with you. I've had my two minutes and I know how busy you are," said Eugene, with a slight smirk on his face.

Krystyna did not respond to Eugene's barbed comment, instead she focussed her eyes forensically on the photograph in order to identify the men in the group shot. When she eventually put the photograph down, she looked at Eugene in a different way. She was also looking at Shaun Wilde's case differently.

"I'd like to keep hold of these documents, if I may?" said Krystyna sounding a good deal more conciliatory now. "Eugene, thank you for coming in and giving me this information. If you could give the person on the reception desk your contact details as you leave I'd be grateful. I can assure you that I'll pursue this swiftly through the correct police channels and we will endeavour to find Mr Mitchell before he gets himself into any more trouble." She stood up and shook Eugene's hand and immediately regretted it as his was twice the size and he clearly worked out. She quickly dismissed the unprofessional thoughts that were creeping into her head. "Thanks again, Eugene. I'm really grateful that you came in."

She watched him leave her office, expelled a deep breath, picked up her mobile and scrolled down to the number she needed.

"Good afternoon. Is that the Whittington Barracks? Good …This is Detective Inspector Krystyna Kendrick, I'd like to speak to Major Ballinger...I spoke to him earlier today at the police station, but he had to leave as there was a problem with an intruder...Yes, I'll wait…"

A minute later the voice at the barracks returned.

"No problem...He's not there? ... When did he leave? ... He didn't return after coming to the police station to see me? You had a message that he had an urgent appointment to attend...Did he say where? No...And what about the intruder? How was that resolved?

You just let him go on the Major's instructions...I see...Thanks...If the Major does show up at the barracks today, will you ask him to contact me as soon as possible...Thank you again."

Krystyna put down her mobile and picked up the landline phone in her office.

Within a couple of minutes she had approval from her boss to put out an APB on Major Ballinger from the Whittington Barracks.

CHAPTER FORTY-NINE

Daz, Willow – Monday

The cathedral didn't smell like the chapel. The chapel smelled like a place of work. This was more like a museum. Daz sat on a chair in the nave. It felt different from the last time he had been in here.

Then he had been trying to work out if Shaun had killed himself and why. Now he was here to meet Saun's murderer. And he knew why. He remembered the words of the Serenity Prayer they spoke at the NA meetings:

"God grant me the serenity to accept the things I cannot change, courage to change the things I can, and the wisdom to know the difference."

He prayed now for the courage to change what he could and get justice for Shaun.

The chair next to him creaked. Not a fat man in a cardigan this time. Without lifting his eyes, he glanced across. Black shoes polished to a spit shine, khaki trousers with a knife-sharp crease, Sam Browne belt over a khaki tunic with burnished brass buttons. On the lap, a peaked cap with the Staffordshire Regiment badge held by a pair of brown leather gloves.

Daz looked at the face. Major Ballinger was staring straight ahead at the altar.

"You won't get any help there, Major," Daz said quietly. "I know you killed Shaun Wilde, and I know why."

"Not here, Private," Ballinger hissed, standing up and setting his cap on his head. "Follow me."

He marched to a corner of the north transept and the soldier in Daz made him follow. They pushed past a "Temporarily Closed to Visitors" sign. "Don't worry," said Ballinger. "No one would think of stopping a soldier."

He stopped at a small arched door with black cast iron hinges.

Daz stepped back. "Going for a repeat performance, Major?" he said. "Push me over like you did Shaun? Ain't gonna happen – they keep that door locked now."

Ballinger took a large shiny steel key out of his pocket. "Not if you've got a spare. Our engineers can make anything if you give them the specifications." He turned it with a clunk and opened the door. "Coming? I'll tell you everything."

Daz stepped in reluctantly, and Ballinger closed and locked the door behind them. "Wouldn't want anyone disturbing us, would we?"

They squeezed up a dark and narrow winding staircase that smelled of dust. Daz could hear Ballinger's leather soles grating on the stone steps behind him. Dim light filtered in from above and the stone walls softened into brown as they reached the top. Daz moved back, poised on the balls of his toes as Ballinger appeared behind him.

"Welcome to the triforium," said Ballinger, waving his arm expansively. "We can talk safely here."

"Is that what Shaun thought too?" Daz's anger flared.

"Ah, that was unfortunate." Ballinger tapped his lips thoughtfully. "It's why I asked you to meet me here. To explain."

"Explain what? How four young squaddies killed a homeless guy, and Shaun couldn't live with the guilt anymore and wanted to go to the police?"

Ballinger took a glove off and used it to dust off a seat on a pew which had been moved up here from the nave. He sat down and said, "It's not that simple." He patted the bench beside him. "Sit down. I'll tell you everything."

Keeping his distance, watching Ballinger warily, every muscle in his body tense, Daz sat down. Ballinger dry washed his face with his hands and said, looking down at the dusty floor between his polished shoes, "It's a nightmare that began twenty years ago and it's never ended. Just when you think you're going to wake up, it starts all over again. Sometimes I think it's never going to end."

He glanced up at Daz. "Do you remember what it's like being a young squaddie going through basic training? Leaving home, thinking the world was going to open up for you, and instead it got smaller. Forty teenagers stuck together in a barracks, being shouted at every hour of the day and night, told what to think, what you can do and when you can do it. That's the time when you make friends that last the rest of your life." He paused and swallowed hard. "There was me, Shaun, Rory and Chris. When we were given leave we'd head into Lichfield and get drunk and try to forget about it all."

Against his will, Daz nodded. He remembered it only too well. "Lots of guys didn't make it," he said.

"Some just quit. But we didn't – and neither did you. We did what it takes." He seemed to go very far away. "We got drunk, we got into fights, and one night – " He dropped his head. "One stupid night...you remember the Earl of Lichfield?"

"I live in Lichfield. Of course I do."

"That's where we always used to go and drink. And there was this homeless guy always hanging about, asking for spare change and we thought it would be funny to get him drunk. We started on pints and switched to shorts...I can remember every detail as if it was yesterday." He pushed the centuries of dust around with the toe of his shoe. "We went to the off-license and got cheap cider and cans and headed to Stowe Pool. We sat on a bench in the dark and carried on drinking. The homeless guy, he couldn't get enough."

"He was called Brian. And a lot of people loved him," said Daz through gritted teeth.

"I know that now – we discovered it later, but at the time, he was just some dosser who didn't matter. Remember how basic training broke us down and taught us to see people as pieces of meat that we could kill if we had to."

Daz stood up angrily with balled fists he had to fight to keep by his sides. "Don't make excuses. Just admit what you did!"

Ballinger leaped to his feet and faced him, his face red and spittle in the corners of his mouth. For a second Daz thought he would have to fight, and he was ready. He'd fought in worse places than this, and the Major was looking a little soft. Too much time behind a desk, not enough on the streets. Ballinger must have realised it too, because he stepped back and turned away.

"It was a joke. We were just kids – stupid, drunken kids. Chris took the rest of the drink to the other side of the Pool and we told this Brian character that he could have it if he swam across. We couldn't stop him. He jumped straight in and we cheered him on. We could see him splashing around – he was doing really well. And then somewhere near the middle, the splashing stopped. He didn't shout for help or anything. One minute he was there and the next he was gone."

"You could have gone in after him," Daz said to his back. "No man left behind – that's what soldiers say, don't we?"

Ballinger turned around. "You don't understand. We were young and we were drunk. Chris and Shaun wanted to go to the police, but Rory and I persuaded them not to. We told them it wasn't our fault, that the way he lived, he would have died soon anyway – we just hurried the process along. We said it would ruin our careers – we weren't working class squaddies off some estate – "

'Like me,' thought Daz, anger flaring in his eyes and his fists clenched so tight they hurt.

"We were going to make something of ourselves. So we walked to the barracks, got put on Restriction of Privileges for being late back to camp and we read all about it in the local paper a week later."

He raised his chin defiantly. "You think the next twenty years were easy? We were never the same again." He held up four fingers and started counting them off. "Chris took it worse. We lost him in Basra. He died rescuing colleagues under heavy fire, and he was awarded the King's Gallantry Medal posthumously, but we knew he'd committed suicide. At least some good came out of his death.

"Then there was Shaun. He waited until we got back and he bought himself out. Set up that charity for homeless soldiers – of course, you know all about that. I helped where I could, but I kept my name out of it. After it happened, we weren't that close anymore.

"I decided I'd do my best to carry on and be the best soldier I could be. I was always fair, never asked my men to do anything I wouldn't do myself. You can ask any of the men who served under me – I did my best to put things right."

He realised he was running off at the mouth and the look in Daz's eye meant he didn't believe him, or care. He shrugged. "Finally, there was Rory. In some ways it was worse for him than anyone. It was as if Spencer's death flicked a switch inside him. He got a reputation for being a hard man – with his colleagues and the enemy. He left the army before he was dishonourably discharged. He stayed in Iraq – claimed to be involved in the antiques business, but what it really was, was people smuggling. He treated them worse than the antiques he did export. He treated everyone like they were things."

There was a long pause. Daz knew Ballinger was going to admit to something and after that he would either turn himself in, or try to kill Daz too.

"It's why I had to kill him. He knew the police were closing in on him and he tried to blackmail me to get him out of the country. I dumped his body in one of Shaun's flats that he used to house his slaves – "

Daz felt a jolt go through him. He grabbed hold of Ballinger's lapels with both hands. "Wait a minute! That was you? The body in the flat next to mine? The one I got arrested for?" And a light bulb went on in his head. "That was Winters? And my hat the police found under the body...I left it behind in your office. You set me up!"

Ballinger shook him off. "I just wanted to throw the police off the track. You were getting too close, asking too many questions. It was two birds with one stone."

Daz took a breath. "So you killed Winters, tried to frame me. But why did you kill Shaun?"

Ballinger shrugged. "He was like Chris. He couldn't let it go. He thought if he poured all his time and effort into his charity, he'd feel better about what we'd done, but he didn't. In the end, he told me he was going to the police to confess. I couldn't let that happen."

"That's what he meant about meeting someone and getting something off his chest. He met you here and you pushed him over."

"I couldn't let him destroy everything I'd worked for..." Ballinger sagged for a moment, and then straightened up as if he were on the playground. He looked at Daz like a soldier he was punishing for disobeying an order. "And I can't let you do that either."

Daz wasn't ready for the attack when it came. Ballinger launched himself at Daz and he found himself against the low stone balustrade, an arm like an iron bar pressed across his throat. Ballinger's eyes were blazing red and his teeth bared like an animal with spittle gathering at the corners of his mouth.

Everything beginning to swim, Daz lashed out as hard as he could and his fist caught Ballinger high on the temple. It hurt Daz more, but it knocked Ballinger back and gave Daz time to get his balance. He lunged forward as Ballinger swung at him, ducked under the arm and found himself behind the Major. Without thinking, his arms slipped round the man's neck in a choke hold.

Ballinger reached over his shoulders and clawed at Daz's face and drummed his hard leather heels on his shins, but Daz clung on grimly, and slowly Ballinger's attack grew weaker. Daz could feel his weight sagging in his arms, and he edged the limp body towards the balustrade.

He slackened the grip enough to let a little blood flow back to Ballinger's brain and he felt the man begin to stir. "Is this what you did?" he hissed in his ear. "Were you man enough to fight him, or did you push him when he wasn't looking? Was this the last thing he saw?"

Daz shoved the upper part of Ballinger's body over the balustrade. The Major was now desperately trying to cling to the dry sandstone lintel, but his fingernails just rasped over it.

One more little shove, and he would be gone. Shaun would finally be avenged.

"Daz!"

Willow's voice rang through the cathedral.

Looking down, over Ballinger's shoulder, over the balustrade, there on the stone floor below, a pale face with dark dots for eyes framed by bright purple hair.

"Don't do it!" She was screaming at him and other faces had turned and were looking up. There were shouts and gasps and screams and people were running away or towards him or just frozen still. "The police are on their way. They know all about Ballinger. They know he killed Shaun and Winters. He's going to go to prison. You don't have to do this!"

Daz thought about Brian Spencer, left for dead because it would have ruined a career. Shaun killed because he would have ruined his career. And himself, framed because he was going to ruin his career.

"No!" he shouted. "He deserves to die. His kind always get away with it. It's people like me and Brian Spencer who suffer! Not this time!"

He pushed harder and Ballinger scrabbled for a grip, his legs flailing. There was more noise from below – shouts and screams and gasps from people who didn't understand.

"Daz!" yelled Willow. "What about Amy? Does she want her dad to be a murderer?"

The words struck Daz through his red rage and he eased the pressure just enough that Ballinger's feet touched the floor and now Daz could hear the clatter of feet beneath him.

Police were pouring in, some of them in helmets and body armour with rifles in their hands. "Armed police! Everybody down!" somebody yelled in a battlefield voice. Daz's grip on Ballinger tightened and he swung him this way and that as red dots of light started to blossom on him. "Let him go and show me your hands!" All shouting the same thing over and over and on top of each other like angry echoes. He couldn't think.

"Darren!" Krys's voice behind him was clear above the chaos and everything fell silent. He swung round. She stood at the top of the stairs, her face was pinched with worry, but she spread her hands to show they were empty and spoke calmly. "We've video footage of Major Ballinger meeting Shaun Wilde. Your friend Willow brought it to us. We can place him here at the cathedral with your friend minutes before he died. Forensics will turn up the evidence we need now we know what to look for."

Daz shook Ballinger by the neck. "He killed Winters too – and tried to frame me."

In her earbud Krys heard a quiet, grim voice say, "I've got a clear shot. Am I good to go?"

Krys shook her head, the hairs on the back of her neck prickling as she realised she was being watched through a telescopic sight. "Then we can look into that too. You've got two good friends, Darren, and they've brought us enough evidence to clear Shaun – and you – and convict this man and finally give Brian Spencer justice. It's over, Darren. You can let him go."

A dam broke inside Daz and he let Ballinger go. The man stumbled away from him into the arms of two burly policemen bursting up the stairs. As they manhandled him and handcuffed his hands behind his back and read him his rights, Krys gently led Daz away.

In the nave, Willow burst through the police cordon and flung herself at him. "Daz!" she cried, making his neck wet with her tears. "I'm sorry. After I got your text about 'sorting it out at the cathedral' I told the police. I couldn't bear it if anything happened to you."

He hugged her tight. "Don't worry about me, Willow. I'm fine. Everything's gonna be alright now."

CHAPTER FIFTY

Daz, Potter – a month later

Daz was back on his beat and he found he was a minor celebrity. He'd been in the papers and even interviewed on the local news.

"Now tell me, Mr. Mitchell, when did you first suspect that Shaun Wilde hadn't committed suicide?"

He shrugged and tried not to look at the camera. "Shaun was a good guy. He cared about other people. He just wouldn't have done that."

"But you were beaten up and arrested and broke up a human-trafficking ring trying to prove he'd been murdered. Most people would have given up. Why didn't you?"

The microphone was thrust under his nose and he felt uncomfortable. He felt more uncomfortable still watching it back later on his television. "I owe Shaun everything. He got me off the streets and a job. He got my life back on track. I couldn't let him down."

"And it looks as though you've solved the twenty-year-old mystery of the death of the man called Brian Spencer in Stowe Pool."

"He was homeless like me," Daz muttered, looking down. "I'm glad we found out what happened. Perhaps he can rest in peace now."

The reporter made a cutting gesture with her hand and the cameraman lowered the camera. They'd been filming at his patch on Dam Street, him wearing the red jacket clutching a few *Big Issues* because she'd said it would look better. She thanked him and said they were just going to shoot a few reaction shots. As he walked away he saw her looking at the camera with a serious face and nodding. On the evening news, the shots of her face and him talking had been cut together and it looked as if they had been talking at the same time. Don't believe anything you see on the telly, he thought.

But walking home people stopped him and shook his hand and when he'd sold out of *Big Issues* they kept trying to press money in his hand. In the end he said, "Please give it to The British Legion. I don't need it." He'd have said *Home and Heart*, but the Charity Commission had removed its charitable status what with Rory Winters being dead and

Russell, his wife and her brother buggering off to France and it being used as a front for human slavery and all.

Now he was back on his patch for the last time where it had all started. Next week he started in the builder's yard. To start with he would be just carrying stuff around, loading and unloading the trucks, but who knew where it would lead? Maybe he'd be a brickie – or a plumber or a plasterer, that's where the real money was. Or he'd get his forklift licence. Or his HGV! 'Steady on, Daz,' he thought with a rueful grin. 'You haven't even started yet.'

Ten-thirty and all his magazines sold. No point waiting for Willow. In the last month he hadn't seen her as often. She was thinking about the future too. She was only doing two days a week at the café now, the other days taken up with working at her Dad's office and Krystyna had got her a one day a week placement at the station. Maybe he'd end up with two friends on the police force. And a solicitor! Funny how life turned out.

Well, he could afford a cup of coffee at Maccy D's...and maybe an apple pie with the radioactive-hot filling. He headed for the door and then froze mid-step. Perched on a high stool in the window, hunched over a cardboard cup and glowering at the world going by was Potter. Ex-Detective Inspector Potter.

He looked like hell. His clothes, the smart sports jacket and the skinny trousers, were rumpled, the shirt dingy and dirty at the collar and cuffs. His eyes were baggy and reddened, his face was puffy, nicked with shaving cuts: red cheeks, red nose – Daz recognised the signs of a man who's been on a bender. The neat goatee was now a straggly beard. The gelled hair was now just greasy and hanging lankly over his face. His shoes were beating out a nervous tattoo on the footrest.

His shoes! He'd seen those shoes before. He'd seen them clean and shiny, and he'd seen them scuffed and dirty standing on a wall.

Daz's first instinct was to run in, grab Potter by the scruff of the neck and drag him out and give him a good kicking. But somewhere in the last month a lot had changed. Somewhere in the dust and scattered furniture in the cathedral, he had lost his anger. Perhaps it had fallen to the stone flags and died there instead of Ballinger.

He straightened up, strode in, ordered two coffees at the counter and carried them carefully over to Potter.

"I thought you could do with a refill," he said. "I dunno how you take it so I got you white and – " He ferreted around in his pocket. " – here's some sugar."

Potter looked round blearily, first at the cup, then the hand and then his eyes travelled up Daz's arm to his face. He didn't recognise him at first, and for a second Daz experienced a weird feeling where the world had flipped over. There was Potter, run-down, battered and beaten and here he was – washed and shaved, new trainers and a touch of Lynx Africa. And in that moment, any anger Daz felt just seemed to wash away and all he saw was a man standing where he used to stand.

Recognition flared in Potter's eyes. "Get the fuck away from me," he growled. "You ruined my life."

"Listen, mate – I know something about ruining your life, and let me tell you, it's not other people who do it to you – you do it to yourself."

Angrily, Potter pushed his hand away and the coffee slopped on the Formica bar top and onto Daz's wrist. He jerked to his feet and the stool he was sitting on fell over with a clatter. As he stumbled over it and stormed out, people looked round.

"It's OK," said Daz. "He's feeling sick. Must have been something he ate," he added with a grin and followed Potter out.

He stalked him as Potter lurched up Conduit Street. He was heading for Wetherspoon's, thought Daz – somewhere you can get a cheap drink at ten o'clock in the morning. He was unsteady and people were giving him a wide berth, but they were noticing Daz too, their eyes widening in recognition, then leaning their heads together and whispering.

Daz couldn't shout after him now, and he couldn't run, so he did a sort of loping walk, trying to catch up with Potter. Potter glanced over his shoulder, saw Daz getting closer, and increased his speed to a shambling jog, bumping into pedestrians coming the other way, and stumbling into the road.

There's going to be an accident, thought Daz, and slowed down. He was fairly sure where Potter was going, and when he turned the corner he saw him heading into *The Acorn*. Daz wasn't keen on following him in, but he squared his shoulders. Nine hundred and thirty-two days clean, he thought. I can do this.

Inside it was dim and there was a foggy smell of beer. Potter was at the bar, ordering a Guinness. Daz went and stood next to him.

"It was you, wasn't it?" he said, without looking at him. "It was you who gave me the kicking at the car wash."

Potter put a handful of change on the bar and took his drink to a table. Daz watched him in the mirror and ordered a coffee. He carried his cup over and sat down.

"It was the shoes," he said. "I recognise the shoes. Why did you do it, man?"

Potter took a long pull at his drink. It left him with a frothy moustache that he didn't notice. He stared at Daz over the rim of his glass. "Do you really want to know?" His voice rasped, roughened with too many cigarettes.

"You put me in hospital, so yeah, I'd like to know."

"Alright then." He took another long pull and set the glass down, but he misjudged the distance and the glass hit the table with a bang and some of the drink slopped onto his hand. He wiped it on his coat.

"I think you might have had enough," said Daz.

Potter sneered. "You sound like my wife...my soon-to-be ex-wife."

"Yeah, wives are good at spotting things going wrong before we do. Trouble is, all they can do is tell us...we've got to sort it out ourselves."

Potter just stared at him with contempt. "Do you want to know why I gave you that kicking?" Daz nodded.

"I knew I'd said too much about the raid on the car wash to that guy Winters at the lodge. That's why they cleared out. I blamed Kendricks for it, but I knew it was down to me. I had to go and make sure there wasn't anything that pointed to me left lying around. I'd gone back to tidy up. And then you walked in."

"So that's it? I was just in the wrong place at the wrong time?"

Potter gave a harsh, humourless bark of laughter. "Well, you'd been making a lot of trouble for me, and somehow you'd got Kendricks convinced there was something wrong with that guy Wilde's death so I can't say it wasn't a pleasure." He grinned at Daz, and he got a whiff of bad breath – cigarettes and greasy food.

No big conspiracy, no secret plot to shut him up. Just a drunken policeman whose life was running away from him. Daz sat back and looked at Potter, taking another slurp of Guinness.

"Well, that wraps everything up," he said and started to stand up, but Potter laid a hand on his arm and pulled him back down.

"Don't you want to get your own back?" he breathed. "Wait 'til you can get me on my own and give me a good kicking."

"I've been where you are, Potter – and what I needed was a helping hand, and not the toe of someone's boot."

Potter dragged his hand away. "What d'you mean?"

"You're an addict. I've been where you are, man – I know."

"You don't know anything. You're just a dosser who got lucky." Potter waved him away. "Go on – clear off."

Daz stood up. "I was a dosser with a home and a job and a family until drink and drugs took it all away from me. But you're right. I got lucky. I've got a chance to get them back." He looked down at Potter hunched over his drink, both hands wrapped around his glass and he shrugged and turned away. He could walk out now, leave Potter to vanish down the rabbit hole – but he couldn't do it. He turned back, borrowed a pen at the bar and wrote his phone number on a beer mat. He dropped it on the table in front of Potter. "I'm starting a new job on Monday," he said, "so I won't be on my patch in the square anymore, but if you want some help with your problem – give me a call."

He left quickly after that. He didn't want to see what Potter did with the beer mat.

Outside it was bright and the street was full of people, smiling, talking, laughing, dawdling or hurrying with shopping. The smells were good too – coffee, fish and chips, curry – even the faint hint of diesel. It was all good.

Daz lifted his chin, squared his shoulders and straightened his back. "Stand Firm, Strike Hard," he said to himself as he marched down Conduit Street as if he was on parade.

EPILOGUE

Daz, Willow, Sameena, Krystyna - Four Months Later

Although the weather was surprisingly kind for an October morning, there were very few people at the funeral. St Chad's Church felt empty during the service. When most of the congregation gathered around *Bletchley Mary's* grave in the churchyard, there were less than twenty people watching the coffin lowered into the ground. There were a few distant family members of Mary, a few representatives from her care home and a small group of unlikely friends that had come to support each other and say their goodbyes.

The quartet stood to one side, side-by-side as everyone else left the churchyard. Leaves fell from the trees and there were tears in their eyes as they remembered and honoured Mary.

"I'm not sure green hair quite goes with your outfit," whispered Daz to the young woman standing next to him.

"Shut up old man, you're not my dad, you know," replied Willow in a hushed tone with a slight smile on her face.

"I'm just practising on you. At the moment my actual daughter's easier to handle than you!" said Daz and received a gentle thump on the arm from Willow.

"Hey you two. Break it up or I'll have to arrest one or both of you," said Krystyna.

"Sorry, Detective Inspector Kendrick. We were just play-acting. You remember what that's like to act, don't you? But now you're a real Detective Inspector, not an acting one, does it mean that you'll have to be serious all the time?" said Willow.

"Yeah, and now she's a proper copper we'll have to bribe her with coffee and cakes at *the Faro Lounge* every few weeks," added Daz.

"Please don't mention cakes," interjected Sameena," you don't know how hard it is to stay on this Slimming World diet."

"But it's paying off. I can already see the difference," Willow said. "Keep it up, Sam!"

"Thanks. It helps going to the gym once a week with Krys."

"And imagine how much less you'll eat when you move out of your mother's house and into your new flat next month," said Krys.

"Will your mum be alright without you?" asked Daz.

"I think so. I'm only three streets away. I've got a feeling I'll be getting quite a few visits and food parcels from her, even though I'm on this strict diet. Have you seen your ex-wife much since your daughter's been back in your life?" asked Sam.

"Yeah, a bit. We're OK, pleasant to each other, you know. Our daughter acts as a bit of a go-between."

"Someone else acting, then?" said Willow pulling a face at Krys.

"Watch it young lady. I've got a pair of handcuffs in my handbag and I'm not afraid to use them."

"Hey, that would be wrongful arrest. You do realise that one of the "A" levels I'm studying at college is Law."

"God help us!" exclaimed Daz," another woman who'll be telling me what's right from wrong!"

"Hey!" the three females objected a little too loudly and then they all started quietly laughing and feeling a little guilty as they were still in the graveyard.

"Sorry, Mary," said Willow looking at the grave. "It's just that this plonker thinks he's better than the rest of us because he's got a proper job now as a builder."

"It's in a builder's yard."

"And he's probably earning more money than I am as a solicitor," said Sam.

"It's in a builder's yard."

"Well, if you're making all this money, Daz, perhaps you can buy the drinks at the Faro in a couple of weeks' time," said Krys.

"Fair enough," conceded Daz.

"Anyway, I'd better get back to the station. Hopefully there haven't been any crimes or misdemeanours in Lichfield while I've been away from my desk this morning."

"Probably not, cos I've been watching Daz very closely all the time we've been in church," said Willow.

"Very funny...but seriously, there's been too much sadness and tragedy in Lichfield this year," Daz said.

"Yeah, I couldn't agree..." replied Willow, but before she could finish her sentence she started to cough.

Daz patted Willow gently on the back and as the four of them moved away from the graveyard he said, "I've got a feeling this is going to be a much better year."